Surrounded by Strangers

Hawley—

It's finally here!!

Thanks for your patience and support — it is much appreciated

Love,

3/03

Surrounded by
Strangers

by

JOSI KILPACK

BONNEVILLE BOOKS ™
Springville, Utah

ISBN: 1-55517-679-8
e.1
Published by Bonneville Books
an imprint of Cedar Fort, Inc.
www.cedarfort.com

Distributed by:

Cover design by Nicole Cunningham
Cover design © 2003 by Lyle Mortimer
Printed in the United States of America
10 9 8 7 6 5 4 3 2 1

Printed on acid-free paper

Library of Congress Cataloging-in-Publication Data

Kilpack, Josi S.
  Surrounded by strangers / Josi Kilpack.
    p. cm.
  ISBN 1-55517-679-8 (acid-free paper)
  1. Mother and child--Fiction. 2. Custody of children--Fiction. 3. Kidnapping, Parental--Fiction. 4. Sexually abused children--Fiction. I. Title.

PS3561.I412S87 2003
813'.6--dc21

                        2002155070

To my parents.
Walt and Marle Schofield,
For their love, patience and prayers—
I am one of the lucky ones

Acknowledgments

I'd like to take a few lines and acknowledge the people that made this book possible, although words are not enough.

First and foremost to my wonderful husband Lee, for your continued support of my writing. Without your patience and encouragement, I couldn't do it. I'm a very lucky woman and I thank God for you every day.

Thanks to my kids as well. Although you likely think all moms are as distracted as me, I can't fully express my gratitude for each of you. You are my continued source of joy and inspiration and my life would not be complete without your smiling faces.

Also, special thanks to Jason and Julie Peterson. Your tour of Harrison, Arkansas, as well as Branson, Missouri, gave me the details I'd have never gotten without you. I appreciate your willingness to arrange childcare, introduce us to Coco, float the river, and show us the sights; I hope we get to do it again.

To the rest of my family, friends and readers, thanks for believing in me; your enthusiasm is much appreciated.

And finally, to my Father in Heaven, for bringing all these gifts into my life and giving me the opportunity to give what I have and love what I do.

Prologue

November 13, 1999

"This is Gloria Stanton," she said into the phone as the wind blew against her back. There was a slight buzzing on the line and she plugged her other ear so as not to miss the instructions.

"You're in Colorado?"

"At a gas station outside of Boulder," Gloria confirmed as she looked toward the darkened gas station a few yards away. It was after midnight. Everything outside the city was closed.

"You're making good time," said the unidentified voice on the other end of the line. "Get back on I-25 and head north. You'll come to Fort Collins in about an hour. There's a Chili's restaurant on College Avenue. Wait in your car by the dumpster behind the building. At 2 a.m., a representative will meet you there. She'll flash her lights twice. If you don't follow her immediately, she'll leave. So pay attention. She'll lead you to your first shelter."

Gloria finished scribbling the instructions on the notebook she'd brought from the car. "How long will we be there?" she asked nervously. This was so unreal.

"Long enough to get your new identification," the voice said. "In the beginning we like to move you around so you'll be harder to track. In addition to the IDs, you'll get some training for you and your kids. We recommend you stay in shelters and safehouses for at least the first year. If you plan to go out on your own after that time, we'll need to teach you how to do it and not get caught. How much money do you have?"

"I have almost twelve thousand," Gloria answered nervously, thinking of the cash now hidden in her jockey box. Carrying that much money just added to this insanity. She thought back to the day almost three months ago when she'd found the anonymous note. It had been left under the wiper blade of her car at the courthouse. The note had simply said to call this number if the courts failed to protect her children. At the time she still believed everything would work out, but she'd hidden the note anyway, just in case. It was hard to believe that she now chose to trust people she'd never met, instead of the system she'd been raised to believe in.

"Excellent. What year is your car?"

"It was new last December."

"Any idea how much equity you've got in it?"

"My husband bought it," she said, looking back at the sleek lines of the Black Range Rover which David had brought home almost a year ago. "I don't know anything about the financing." She hadn't picked it out, not even the color. As with most things in her life at that time, David took care of it. He'd handed her the keys, patted her shoulder and said, "Are you the luckiest woman in the world or what?" The memory of how he'd said it, the way he cocked his head to the side and winked, caused her to clench her jaw. She felt as if she'd lived a lifetime since then.

"We'll probably have to ditch it someplace, or sell it for parts," the voice said as if that were no big deal. "We'll help you get something older and cheaper when you need it. You'll need the rest of your money to cover expenses for a long time, so don't be hasty in spending it." Gloria nodded, although no one but her children, watching from the car, could see her do so. She'd never worried about money. Not as the youngest child of an orthopedic surgeon or as the pampered wife of an attorney. *Things are going to change,* she thought as she looked down at the $120 boots she'd bought a few weeks ago. "And no matter what, don't contact *anyone,*" the voice continued. Gloria didn't respond right away. Her heart ached. This evening, she'd said good bye to her parents and promised to contact them as soon as she was settled. Even when she'd made the promise, she knew it was one she might not be able to keep, but the reminder of all she was leaving behind was a painful one

"Gloria," the voice said after waiting for her reply. "You cannot break that rule, no matter what. If you can't agree to it, then go back home before anyone knows you left. You'll put the entire organization in jeopardy if you tell anyone where you are. Do you understand?"

"Yes," Gloria said softly as the first tear slid down her cheek. This had gone beyond fantasy, beyond planning; it was real, and she was frightened. It was impossible to imagine a life without her family and friends. Especially after all the support they'd given her during the last few months. But she'd made her decision. Despite how painful it was, she knew she was doing the only thing she could do. "I won't call."

"Make sure that you don't," the voice said sternly. "You'd better get going."

The line went dead, but Gloria held the phone until the dial tone returned. Slowly, she replaced the phone and walked back to the car while her children watched her carefully. She had hoped they'd have fallen asleep by now, but even they seemed to sense the magnitude of what was happening. The wind whipped her auburn hair into a frenzied kind of dance, but she was too intent on her thoughts to notice. *We can still go back,* she told herself, *I can forget all about this.* But she wasn't turning back. Just hours ago, she had loaded the car with essentials, emptied all the accounts she had access to, and turned her back on her former life. Tomorrow night, when she didn't drop off the kids, David would be suspicious. By Saturday, there would be a warrant for her arrest. She was entering a whole new world for the sole purpose of saving her children from their father. *Please Lord,* she prayed silently as she pulled her jacket tightly around herself, *don't let me forget that I'm doing the right thing.*

Chapter One

April 2, 2001

Gloria Stanton no longer existed. She now went by the name Pamela Bennion, her children Kathryn and Nicholas were now Darla and Kenny. For all intents and purposes, Gloria and her children had completely disappeared. In the two and a half years since their disappearance, there had been warrants issued, flyers posted, and mailers mailed; all in hopes that someone somewhere would recognize their faces and tip off the FBI with their current whereabouts. It hadn't happened. Gloria had remained well hidden in a procession of shelters and safe houses across the nation for the first two years. Then, she and the children made the decision to move out on their own. With the help of the Safe Children Network she had found identification and housing. She had found a job and the children were enrolled in public school for the first time. They'd been on their own almost six months now and Pamela found the independence refreshing, if not a little scary sometimes.

Pamela pulled her car into the chewed up asphalt driveway and turned off the engine. The blue Toyota she'd driven for the last year was old and ugly, but it was unobtrusive, dependable transportation. She grabbed her purse off the passenger seat and stepped out of the car, trying to keep her feet from dragging as she walked up the cracked sidewalk that led to the front door.

Working night shift wasn't as bad as she'd thought it would be in the beginning. The kids slept while she worked, and she slept while they were at school. But when she returned home each morning, she was so tired she could barely stand.

The front door squeaked on its hinges and scraped across the warped floorboards of the small entryway when she pushed it open. Stepping over the threshold of her house, despite how dilapidated it might be, relaxed her. This was home, a small rental in Harrison, Arkansas, and she loved it here.

"No TV before school," she said with a *you-know-better* look at her children. Darla and Kenny moaned when she clicked off the television set, but they didn't argue. They knew the rules, even if they pushed the boundaries now and then. Pamela shrugged out of her light jacket and threw it over the back of the ratty old couch before entering the kitchen area.

The orange Formica countertops no longer assaulted her visual sensibilities at every glance, and the persistent mildew that formed around the base of the faucet no longer caused her continuous offense. She ignored the roach motels in the corners and had conditioned herself not to think of the rat traps in the cellar. Those things deserved very little of her thoughts. They were all part of the package—part of the changes she'd accepted in her life. She did, however, allow memories of the part-time housekeeper she'd had back in Salt Lake to filter into her mind now and then. Three times a week she'd had an angel from heaven come to keep her house in top condition. Karina had made trips to the gym and beauty salon possible. She'd done dishes, vacuumed, dusted and watched the children too. It had been wonderful. A sigh of longing escaped Pamela's lips, but she quickly snuffed out the memory. This was the life she lived now and she was determined to accept it with as little complaint as possible.

"How was work, Mom?" Darla asked as she rinsed out her cereal bowl and put it in the sink. Darla's long brown hair, so similar to her mother's current style, or lack there of, was pulled into a ponytail at the base of her neck. Her wide hazel eyes reflected maturity beyond her nine years and reminded Pamela of just how much growing up all three of them had done since leaving Salt Lake.

"It was all right," Pamela said, rubbing Darla's shoulder as she crossed the kitchen to the fridge. "I made thirty-three dollars in tips."

"Thirty-three?" Kenny repeated, with the awe possessed only by those who had little concept of what it cost to pay the basic expenses for three people. "Can I get a bike now?"

"We have to pay rent on Monday," Darla told him in her *all-knowing-big-sister* voice.

Kenny looked forlornly back into his cereal bowl and Pamela's heart ached just a little. The jewelry box in her closet still held almost four thousand dollars. It was their emergency fund and although she was tempted to dip into it, she knew she'd leave it alone. She only needed to remember the price of filling Darla's last two cavities, or Kenny's allergies, to be reminded why it was so important to keep her emotions separate from her finances. There was a jar in a cupboard that held the money they were saving for bikes. She added to it whenever possible, and expected that by May they'd be able to get bikes for both children.

She pulled one of the rickety kitchen chairs out from under the table and sat down next to her six-year-old son. "We'll get you that bike, kiddo," she said with a smile as she smoothed his hair. "I promise."

"When?" he whined, looking up at her with those big blue eyes that still reminded her of his father.

"Donny asked if I'd work Sunday night. Maybe I can—"

"On Sunday?" Kenny interrupted her, his eyes wide with surprise. "You can't work on Sunday."

Pamela looked from her son to her daughter. They both stared at her. "I know I don't usually do that, but it's an extra shift and we need the money." Darla pursed her lips and made herself look busy straightening up the counter. It was a reaction so typical of her own, that Pamela nearly smiled. Kenny continued to stare.

"But it's the Sabbath," he finally said. "You're not supposed to work on the Sabbath."

Pamela looked at him and marveled at his integrity. Her children hadn't been inside a church since they left Salt Lake. Part of her took pride in being able to instill values in the children by herself, but another part mourned that they didn't hear the gospel taught from more lips than her own. For a few moments she debated further explanation, but one more look at Darla's silent disappointment made up her mind. "You're right," she admitted. "It's a good thing you guys are here to keep me righteous."

Just then, a horn honked outside. Pamela rose to her feet. "There's the bus," she announced as she hurried to the hooks by the door that held the children's jackets and backpacks. Within seconds, both children were out the door. Pamela waved until the bus disappeared around the corner before going back inside. She passed Kenny's half-eaten bowl of cereal on the table and told herself she'd do dishes when she woke up, as she headed down the short hallway to her bedroom.

The top hinge of her bedroom door was loose, so the door didn't close without a fight. She left it open today, sank onto the mattress, and slipped off her shoes. She then removed the black cotton pants and and shirt that made up her waitress uniform. As she reached for her nightgown hanging on the back of the door, her eyes caught her own reflection in the floor-length mirror on the wall. Her temple garments were very ragged. She looked at them for a moment and shook her head. Three years ago, she would never have worn them in such a state. Now, she just hoped they could hang on a little longer. She didn't have a clue about where to buy new ones in Arkansas. And, thankfully, she knew the protection and promises they represented were still effective, despite their condition. She thought of the covenants they symbolized and couldn't help but think of the man she had made many of those covenants with, almost eleven years ago. A man who, she was sure, still wore his temple garments, too.

In retrospect, it seemed odd that when she married David Stanton she had truly believed it would last forever. He had just finished law school at BYU, and she was a freshman on campus who saw in him everything she wanted to see. They were introduced at church and began dating steadily within a few weeks. Her parents thought he was too old for her at first, but his charismatic personality won them over. Pamela's father even helped him find a job at the law offices of a friend. Throughout their courtship, he indulged her with gifts and continual flattery. He told her everything she wanted to hear, spared her from the things she didn't want to know, and promised to take very good care of her. And he fulfilled that promise, maybe even too well. Looking back she realized she'd had a very narrow view of the world.

It had been twelve years after her parents had decided their family was complete when Pamela had come along; Surprise! By the time she was nine years old, all her siblings were married and starting families of their own. She'd had a happy childhood and was basically raised as an only child. The effect of her birth order was that she had two parents and five siblings to make sure she was well cared for. There was always someone to help her when the trials of youth disrupted her perfect life. David had come into that life just as her first attempt at independence got underway. They had a whirlwind courtship and an extravagant wedding celebration. She was eighteen years old and felt she had the world by the tail. Many people thought it was too fast, too rushed; but she didn't.

David was beginning a promising career, so they bought a house within six months of their marriage. It was a proverbial Mormon fairy tale. The financial trials her college friends struggled with were no longer a worry and she settled into her wonderful life without regrets.

But now, ten years later, she had different challenges. There were many things about life she didn't understand back then, a lot of things about people and relationships that she never learned. Since leaving that life behind she'd had to learn everything she'd missed, and it hadn't been easy.

From the beginning of their lives together, David worked long hours in order to "give her the life she deserved." She whined about the time he spent away from home, but remembered her own father's hospital schedule and came to appreciate what she saw as a good work ethic. It wasn't *that* abnormal to have her husband, like her father, gone so much. Besides, she was busy with her schooling until Katie was born and even continued as a part-time student until she became pregnant the second time.

When Nicholas was born, however, the perfect life she planned to live was forever changed. A car accident when she was just weeks away from her due date had ended in a healthy infant, but a hysterectomy as well. She'd planned to have a houseful of kids, but there would be no more babies. It was perhaps the first time things hadn't worked out the way she expected, her first true dose of reality, and there was nothing she could do about the change. The loss overwhelmed her. David responded to her grief by hiring a nanny, a housekeeper and then working longer hours he said were necessary to pay for the added help. Her family comforted her, encouraged her; they did all the things, which she now realized, David should have done. But he wasn't an emotional man and she didn't have the energy to dwell on his lack of concern. Besides, he was disappointed too; his future was also changed forever.

Eventually, she was able to accept the hard reality and make the best of it. She'd been blessed with two healthy, happy children. From that time on they became her whole life. She hardly noticed how unfulfilling her marriage had become, or how distant from one another she and David became. Maybe as the children grew she would have craved a closer relationship with the man she had married, but at the time, things seemed all right.

David began taking Katie on outings about the same time she started kindergarten. He claimed that she was finally old enough to know how to behave. He'd never taken the children by himself before then. But soon, he was watching both kids so that Gloria could run errands or attend enrichment meetings in the evenings. She appreciated David's involvement and felt closer to him than ever before.

The bedwetting started shortly after Katie's sixth birthday. Then came her anxiety each time her mother left the house. She had always been such a mellow child that it was an odd change. So, Pamela consulted with the all-knowing *Parents* magazines she'd saved since Katie's birth and became convinced that it was just a childhood phase which would pass. But it didn't go away. It got worse. Before long, Katie was throwing full-blown tantrums when her mother would leave. She also began hitting other kids at school and cried about everything. David seemed concerned about the situation, too, but insisted that giving in to Katie's demands on her mother would be counterproductive. His attention to and affection for their daughter increased and Pamela expected that the extra parental attention would bring the phase to an end.

Then one weekend, David went out of town. Katie was more relaxed than she'd been for months and Pamela seized the opportunity. Mother and daughter drank hot chocolate and painted each other's toenails after Nicholas, then only three years old, went to bed. Pamela had no idea that their girl-talk would be so important. First, they talked about school, friends and church. Then Pamela explained that she was worried about her little girl. "If anything is wrong," she'd said lovingly, "you can tell me—no matter what it is." Katie looked at her mom for a few moments, a look of relief on her face that Pamela would never forget. In the moment it took for her daughter to blurt out what David had done to her, Pamela's whole life changed.

The disbelief had slowly turned to shock and she had asked her daughter to tell her exactly what happened. After hearing the childlike explanation of things she couldn't have known any other way, Pamela never doubted the truthfulness of Katie's accusations. She called a lawyer the next morning. When David returned home, his bags were packed and waiting on the front porch with a letter explaining he would never touch their daughter again. David immediately hired his own attorney and pulled out the big guns. The divorce was granted almost immediately. But because of the allegations, David's visitation rights were indefinitely suspended pending a criminal trial.

In hopes of privacy, Pamela refused to make any statements to the press. David, however, wasn't nearly as considerate. The papers reported that her accusations were false, the result of ongoing depression and a vindic-tive personality. Her every flaw became front page news, while David's campaign hailed him as the perfect father. No one wanted to believe that a successful, actively religious man like David Stanton would hurt his own daughter. It seemed to intrude on the base belief that this kind of thing didn't happen in apparently successful, religious families. But Pamela believed. Furthermore she vowed to do whatever it took to save her child from future abuse—no matter how high a price she had to pay.

The squeak of the bed as she sat on it brought Pamela back to reality. She pushed the thoughts away and refocused her attention. Even with deep cleansing breaths it took almost a minute to push the anger away. Despite everything, she was trying hard to forgive. She needed her energy to make a better life for her children. The first step had been to overcome her hatred toward the man she'd once loved, and she was still working on that first step.

She put on her nightgown, undid the braid in her hair and laid back on the pillows as exhaustion overwhelmed her. Just as she drifted off to sleep, she remembered that she needed to see how the things in Utah were going. Despite her promise not to call home, she'd had to make contact with someone. She was always very careful, and so far no one had suspected, but it had proved to be impossible for her to break all ties. The warrants for her arrest were awaiting her return, as was the court order demanding her children spend two weekends a month with their father. There was little hope that anything had changed, but she would check and see anyway. Even if there'd been no legal progress in getting another hearing for the charges against David, she was anxious to know how her parents were doing and to get word to them that their youngest daughter, despite the crazy circumstances of her life, was doing just fine.

Janice Fillmore shut the door to her daughter's room and headed toward the stairs. It was 8:30 P.M. The kids were in bed and she finally had some time to herself. She tripped lightly down the stairs, already thinking of how to spend the few precious hours left before her body gave into the fatigue of raising four children.

"Why don't we watch a movie," she called out as she turned the corner to enter the living room where her husband had been reading *The Ensign* in preparation for his home teaching appointments tomorrow night. She quickly stopped and her expression darkened. Ron Fillmore shot his wife a warning look and she forced a chilly smile. "David," she said evenly, trying to think of an appropriate greeting. 'Nice to see you' would be a terrible lie and 'It's been a long time' was much too warm. She finally settled for a dry, "Hello."

He smiled back at her, but they both knew he disliked her as much as she disliked him. She hadn't been particularly fond of him when he and Gloria had been married and her feelings certainly hadn't changed for the better since the divorce. Right after Gloria's disappearance he'd come over, demanding that Janice help him; but at that time Janice really didn't know where Gloria was and he'd never tried to contact her since then. She wondered why he was suddenly interested again after two and a half years. The silence was heavy until Ron broke it, "David wants to talk to you for a minute."

Janice took a deep breath. "I don't have anything to say to you."

"Look—it's been two and a half years," David said, his voice sounding almost sincere. "She has to have called someone. I'm checking with everyone who she might have possibly contacted. I just want to know how my children are. That's all."

Ron's eyes were telling her to play it cool, and in order to do so she had to wait several seconds before responding. "I don't know where she is."

"You're her best friend, Janice. I just want to know if you've heard from her and if they're all right." There was a pleading in his voice that made her even more suspicious. She didn't buy his *concerned father* act for a minute.

"I haven't heard from her,"—*lately*, she thought. "I'm sure if there were a problem I would have. Now, you'll have to excuse me, I have something I need to do upstairs." She quickly turned and went back upstairs to her room. Being anywhere near that man made her skin crawl.

A few minutes later, Ron opened the door to their darkened bedroom. Janice was silhouetted against the window where she looked out to the street below. Ron came up behind her and wrapped his arms around her waist. She leaned into him and watched David's Mercedes disappear down the street. "I hate that man," she whispered sadly. He'd forced her best friend away, but far more important than that—he'd ruined a part of his own daughter's life and it could never be restored. "So help me, Ron," her voice trembled. "I hate him."

Chapter Two

Sunday morning at ten o'clock the Bennion family sat around the kitchen table in their Sunday best, while Pamela taught them about Joseph Smith's first vision. They'd been "meeting together" like this since getting their own place six months ago and, although it seemed silly at times, Pamela knew it was important to teach them everything she could. Putting on their nicest clothes seemed to invite a better spirit. She tried to make the account interesting, but realized that she couldn't make a visit from God any more interesting than it naturally was. After the makeshift lesson, Pamela pulled out the green hymn book—one of her past-life treasures—and together they sang "Joseph's First Prayer." Then Darla said the closing prayer and Kenny hopped up from the table.

"Can we go for a drive now?" Kenny asked. Most Sundays included a drive after "church."

"You bet," she said as she stood. "Darla, plug in the crock pot while I get my shoes."

"Which way should we go?" Pamela asked some time later. They had driven through the local neighborhoods for a few minutes, looking at the dogwood trees getting ready to flower and watching squirrels bound across the sprawling lawns. In their six months of residency, they had still seen very little of the area. Now, they had to decide on a new area to explore for today. There were countless roads in every direction that weaved along the rolling hills referred to as the Ozark Mountains. They weren't really mountains, in Pamela's mind at least. They were nothing like the Rocky Mountains she'd grown up gazing at; but they were beautiful in a different way. The sign welcoming drivers to the City read "*Harrison, Ozarks all around you*" and it was a very good description. Harrison was built within the very heart of the Ozark forests, the clearings made specifically for man's growth. They had moved here in time for a spectacular autumn, then had survived the frigid winter. There hadn't much snow, but the humidity made the winter air brutally cold. With spring came rain which blanketed the land with green. Grass seemed to grow everywhere and trees stretched for the sky all over the place. It was nothing like Utah, with its stretches of dry hard earth. Here it was lush and beautiful, kept that way by rain that sometimes came in such droves that the streets were turned to rivers. She'd been told that most Are-can-sans, as they pronounced it, didn't even water their lawns in the summer time; a completely foreign practice for a native Utahn.

Each Sunday the three newcomers would drive around, immersing themselves in their new surroundings. They loved feeling like they were a part of this place.

"Let's go see Coco," Kenny suggested. Pamela had to suppress a smile. Coco was a tamed bear that lived with its owner, Larry, in a little town called Jasper, twenty miles south of Harrison. There was a large pen that faced the street where Coco was often on display for the tourists. They'd heard about him within a month of their arrival and been to see him many times.

"Is that okay with you?" Pamela asked, looking at Darla's reflection in the rear view mirror.

Darla shrugged. She liked Coco, but not with the same intensity as her brother. She preferred to find little side roads and explore them one at a time. Apparently, she was willing to cooperate this time. Pamela turned the car towards the winding forest road heading for Jasper and pulled out the hair band that held her brown hair up in a ponytail. It fell to almost the middle of her back. She shook her head and ran her fingers through her hair a few times to remove any tangles. She wished she dared to cut it and go back to the shoulder-length style she preferred. With summer coming, it would become heavier and hotter than it already was. But she had to look different than the woman she'd been, and she'd decided that longer, darker hair was a better choice than shorter, lighter hair. It was also cheaper. Every six weeks, she bought Clairol #615, burnt brunette, and for five dollars and fifty cents, turned her auburn roots to a nice muddy brown. The fantasy of getting a salon color always tempted her, but it was beyond her means. Thrift had become a ruling principle in her life.

During her marriage she'd never balanced a checkbook, reconciled a bank account, or even paid a bill. David had done all that. Now, she was an expert budgeter who could figure out the price-per-ounce of laundry detergent or green beans faster than any calculator. She did her laundry at the local laundry mat and skipped luxuries like perfume and new clothes for her or the kids. *The skills of necessity*, she mused sadly. It was amazing that she'd ever been so out of touch with what was now stark reality.

As they drove, she looked around and enjoyed the spring colors dotting the landscape. It was mid-April and the day was perfect. If every day were as gorgeous as this, every person in America would want to live in Arkansas. Well, everyone that was white, Christian, and heterosexual, anyway. She'd learned rather quickly that Arkansas held tightly to its prejudices. There was even a monument at the city government building that memorialized the Mountain Meadow Massacre which had occurred in Utah back in 1859. The wagon party that was attacked and murdered had originated just outside of Harrison. Pamela's understanding, before moving here, was that it had been an isolated situation born out of miscommunication and supposed self-defense. The monument depicted it from a very different point of view, and not a forgiving one at that. Although she didn't share the fact that she was Mormon, she'd heard many anti-Mormon sentiments anyway. There were few black people or any other ethnic group living in town and there was a thread of white supremacy that still ran through the population. In fact, Boone County, which included Harrison, was the birth place of the Ku Klux Klan. She'd been a little anxious about the details as she learned them, but despite her differing opinions, the people she'd met were very nice and kept whatever feelings they had to themselves. She did the same.

This part of town was nice, she noticed, changing the direction of her thoughts. As they got away from the city center, the houses spread out along the highway became farther and farther apart. Most homes were made of brick and were well cared for. There was a fair number of trailer parks and dilapidated neighborhoods within the city limits, but the homes outside of town, along Highway 7, were very nice.

"Mom, look!" Darla suddenly said, pointing to the right-hand side of the road. Pamela slowed, looking around quickly to see whatever it was that had caught her daughter's attention. It couldn't be a smooshed armadillo or turtle on the side of the road; they'd seen plenty of those and no longer exclaimed over their appearance. "Valley View," Darla said, pointing behind them. Pamela turned in her seat to look at the street sign a few yards behind them. "Isn't that our old street name in Salt Lake?"

"How on earth did you remember that?" Pamela asked. "But yes, we used to live on Valley View Drive."

"Let's drive down that road," Darla said excitedly as if it were some kind of link to the past.

"You said we could go see Coco!" Kenny protested.

"We always see Coco," Darla countered, no longer being quite so cooperative.

"We'll drive along here for a bit and then we'll go see Coco," Pamela decided as she turned down Valley View Court, sharing in her daughter's curiosity. They drove up the slight hill and looked at the large church on the right hand side of the road. Churches in Arkansas still surprised her. Growing up in Utah, she was used to the *other-than-Mormon* denominations having little churches. Out here all those denominations had huge, beautiful buildings. There were more religions here than she could count and their places of worship were everywhere—much like LDS churches in Utah. This church was the Assembly of God and the large, gray and white stucco building was complete with a cross on top. Farther up the road was another church, made of brown brick and quite a bit smaller than the first. She drove slowly, trying to determine whether it was Presbyterian or Lutheran. There was something different about the building, but she couldn't quite put her finger on it. The lawn was dark green and recently cut, with shrubbery and flowers along the edges of the building. But it was the steeple that suddenly caught her attention. She parted her lips and let out a slight gasp as she put her foot on the brake, stopping in the middle of the road.

An LDS church! It wasn't big and fancy like the ones she was used to, but it was well-kept and to her, it looked like a temple. She'd stopped looking for Mormon churches a long time ago, but now a pang of longing filled her chest. Oh, how she missed having the church in her life. Several times she'd been tempted to find a local congregation, but she hadn't been willing to take such a risk. Church would be an obvious place where people would watch her. She'd learned that at her first safe house. She also knew that even if she went, she couldn't tell people any of the truth; certainly not that she was a baptized, endowed member. Lying about her membership and risking being found anyway, tied her stomach in knots. The fact was that Gloria Stanton couldn't exist anymore. But then again, Pamela Bennion didn't really exist either.

What risk was there today, though? she thought rebelliously. She didn't know many people in town, certainly no Mormons that she might run into. If asked, she'd simply say she was a visitor who drove by and decided to stop in. She wouldn't be lying about that. Would one visit really be so risky? Would the slight risk be worthwhile?

She turned in her seat, smiling broadly. "How would you like to go to church?"

Darla's eyes went wide as she realized what this building was. "Really?" she said in awe as she stared at the building through new eyes. "Primary and everything?"

"I don't know," Pamela said as pulled into the parking lot. "We'll have to see."

To Darla's disappointment, Primary was over, but a young mother trying to comfort a crying baby in the hallway said Sacrament meeting would last another forty minutes. Pamela thanked her and they slipped into the back of the room. It was a small chapel with no more than fifty people sitting in the pews, but the feeling of being in the Lord's House was staggering. A young man was giving a talk about obedience and she listened intently, taking in every word as if it were manna from heaven.

————

Bryan Drewry noticed the woman slip into the back pew from where he sat on the stand. She sat her children down quietly and then leaned forward, watching the speaker with an eagerness that was almost palatable. It wasn't often that they got 'unattached visitors,' meaning visitors who didn't sit next to a ward member. And as the ward mission leader, he knew most of the inactive folks who popped in now and then. He'd never seen this woman before. The attentiveness with which she listened held his attention and he found himself watching her almost as intently as she watched the speaker. Maybe he could make an appointment to meet with her and her family.

After the first speaker finished, a few young women came to the front and sang. When they returned to their seats, it was his turn to speak. At the pulpit, he looked up from his notes, and his eyes went immediately to the stranger on the back row. She was crying, and it shocked him.

After a moment, he looked away and focused on his talk. The subject he'd been asked to speak on was sacrifice, and he'd spent the better part of his Saturday researching and writing down his thoughts on the subject. Each time he looked up from his notes, his eyes found hers. She was riveted. For a moment, he wondered if his talk was better than he thought. But the Jensen children on the front row were as rowdy as usual, and Mr. Sterling was asleep in the back; it was a normal Sunday, and just a normal talk. Except that this woman seemed to hang on his every word. He sought out Barbara, his girlfriend of almost six months, and she smiled warmly; but his eyes were drawn to the stranger again. There was just something about her.

He talked about the Atonement, about the sacred nature of personal sacrifice and finally, of our commitment to sacrifice all things as God commands. No matter how many times he made eye contact with someone else, the woman in the back always reeled his attention back. By the end of his talk, he felt almost as if they'd shared a private conversation. In the four years of his membership in the church, he'd only spoken in sacrament meeting two other times, but he'd never experienced anything like this.

"To conclude," he said when his time was up, "I'd like to read D&C 138, verse 50: 'Behold, I have seen your sacrifices, and will forgive all your sins; I have seen your sacrifices in obedience to that which I have told you.'" Bryan then ended his talk in the name of the Savior and took his seat. When he looked up again, the woman was still staring at him. He smiled at her and she smiled back, wiping at her eyes. The closing hymn was announced. Bryan located his hymn book, opened it and looked up again. She was gone. He looked quickly towards the exits, to catch a glimpse, but she had disappeared.

————

"Can we go back next week?" Darla asked as they got in the car.

"Umm, I don't know," Pamela said, still a little dazed from the experience. "I'll think about it."

"I thought we were going to do fun stuff," Kenny said as he buckled his seatbelt.

"That's Primary," Darla said. "Primary's different. You play games and sing songs with other kids. It's real fun."

"Can we go see Coco now?" Kenny whined.

"Yes," Pamela said with a nod as they pulled out of the parking lot.

When they got home a couple hours later, Pamela set up a game of Candy Land she'd bought at a garage sale for a dollar. Then she excused herself for a few minutes. She went into her bedroom and shut the door, ignoring the high-pitched squeak, which usually made her cringe, and being sure to lift the door to compensate for the loose hinge. On the top shelf of her closet was a jewelry box her father had given to her on her sixteenth birthday. It was a beautiful case made of pewter. Intricate arrangements of flowers decorated the sides and her real name, Gloria, was engraved in large swirling letters across the top. Inside the box, nestled in the soft velvet lining, were some of the reminders of her life before. She placed the box on her bed and lifted the lid.

The light scent of lavender and the memories it stirred made her smile as she removed the velvet boxes that held the few items of jewelry she still owned. Her patriarchal blessing was there, as well as the original birth certificates and social security cards for herself and her children. Finally, she reached the single piece of notebook paper. It was still crisp, and deeply creased, as she removed it reverently. Once unfolded, she stared at her own handwriting and thought back to the moment she had made the decision to run from David.

She'd received notice on a Tuesday that during David's preliminary hearing the judge hadn't heard enough evidence to bind him over for a jury trial. The criminal case was over before it even began. David's visitation privileges, suspended during the divorce proceedings, had been reestablished. On Friday, David was to take her children for three days.

The district attorney had said he'd continue to gather information, and they'd get another preliminary hearing in a few months. But until then, there was a court order demanding that David get the same visitation entitled to any other loving father. Failure to honor the order would put her in contempt of court and she'd be the one to lose rights to her children.

An incredible exhaustion had overwhelmed her that night and she prayed desperately for guidance. She'd done everything she could, and yet the court had ordered her to give her daughter to a child molester. It was wrong—the system she'd counted on for protection had let her down. She begged and pleaded with the Lord to help her find a solution that would keep her children safe. Of course, she'd been praying for their safety every day since this ordeal began, but that night, she was desperate. When she finished praying, she went to the doorway of her daughter's room and for almost half an hour she watched her daughter sleep, unaware that in a few days she'd be handed over to the man who had hurt her so badly. Finally, Gloria returned to her own bedroom. In pure submission she knelt beside the bed she'd once shared with David and poured out her heart to her Father in Heaven again. She was reminded of the story of Enos, who prayed all night and then all day for help—and eventually got it. She drew upon every promise she'd ever been given that if she knocked it would be opened unto her. She had always honored the spirit; prayer and faith were basic elements to her. Yet, she'd never challenged the Lord as she did that night. She reminded him of the blessings she'd been promised throughout her life, she reminded him of her stewardship of her children and she asked to know, without a doubt, what she should do that day, that moment. If the answer was that she should let David take her children she'd do so—as long as she knew it was what the Lord wanted her to do.

After several minutes, a feeling, sweeter and stronger than anything she'd felt before, wrapped around her like a cocoon. When she finally said Amen, she felt compelled to open her scriptures. She'd heard stories of people being led to scriptural passages in times of need, but until that night it had never happened to her. The book opened to section 138 and her eyes were immediately drawn to verse 50. The message she found in that passage began what she came to understand was a personal revelation. She had scribbled the words onto a piece of paper, folded it, and placed it in the jewelry box as she began collecting her things. The next morning she retrieved the note she'd found on her car months earlier that had given her a phone number to call if the courts failed to protect her children. She called the number from a pay phone. That afternoon, she faxed her case summary to an anonymous number along with the medical reports and divorce settlement papers. At two o'clock in the morning, her phone had rung and she was told that the organization was willing to help her. Two days later she emptied her bank accounts, loaded the kids into the car and left Gloria, Katie, and Nicholas Stanton far behind her. Kenny had been four and Darla was seven.

As the memory faded, Pamela read the words on the paper out loud. "Behold, I have seen your sacrifices, and will forgive all your sins; I have seen your sacrifices in obedience to that which I have told you." She paused for a moment. This is where the speaker at church had ended. But she continued the final lines, the most powerful lines, as far as she was concerned. "Go, therefore, and I make a way for your escape, as I accepted the offering of Abraham and his son Isaac."

Pamela took a deep breath, refolded the paper, and placed it back in the box. A sweet sensation of comfort surrounded her as she reflected on the spirit that had led her here. Abraham had been asked to do the unthinkable, to go against his strongest feelings. It was because of his willingness to obey the Lord that he had been spared—as had his son. Pamela closed her eyes. Some day she too would be spared. She didn't know when and she didn't know how, but she knew the day would come when everything would be made right. Until then, she lived by faith. Until then, her faith would be enough.

Chapter Three

"Hi there, Donny," Pamela said Monday night as she put her purse in the drawer beneath the register and tied a fresh apron around her slim waist. The trip to church had energized her and she had an unusual spring in her step. She smoothed the apron and was reminded that whereas she used to be trim because of her gym membership, she was now skinny because of a tight food budget.

"Hey," he grunted from behind the cook's counter. He grumbled something else but Pamela didn't hear him.

"What was that?" she asked as she began wiping down the counters that the day-shift waitresses hadn't bothered to clean.

Donny removed the cigarette from his mouth. "The new night cook quit today and then the food order got delayed," he explained gruffly. "I've worked all day long and now I'm down to my last two pounds of bacon. Them truckers ain't gonna like it."

Pamela frowned. A few dozen long-haulers would be stopping in before the night was over, and two pounds of bacon wasn't going to last an hour. "How about sausage?" she asked.

"I'm okay on sausage, but you know those guys—some of 'em will only eat bacon. Sausage won't keep them from throwin' a fit, and I ain't in any mood for a night of trucker tantrums."

"Hmmm," Pamela said, as she thought for a minute. "What if we create a special? Something they haven't tried, and then price it low."

"A sausage special?"

"Maybe," Pamela said with a shake of her head. "But I was thinking of something different. Something to distract them from the bacon. Something like . . . strawberry crepes or German pancakes." Donny looked at her like she'd just spoken Italian. She decided her idea needed a little explanation. "Crepes are real thin pancakes that you fill with ham and cheese or fruit and whipped cream. They're really good. German pancakes are light, fluffy pancakes that you top with fruit, too."

"You think these truckers will eat whoopin' cream?" Donny replied, clearly not impressed with her ingenuity.

Pamela lifted her chin stubbornly and turned to the nearest customer seated at the counter. The large, bearded trucker was sipping his coffee as he looked over the stained menu. "Ever had a German pancake?" she asked.

"Don't care much for Germans," he said without looking up. Donny snickered, but Pamela persisted.

"If I make one will you eat it?"

"A German?" Donny laughed out loud that time.

"No, a pancake," Pamela said with exasperation. "It comes with free coffee," she added as an afterthought.

The man shrugged. "I like pancakes."

Pamela nodded and went around to Donny's side of the counter. "Take the front," she said as she began gathering ingredients. Donny shook his head, but he complied, so she went to work. It wasn't the first time she'd run the grill since working at the diner, but she soon remembered why she preferred working the front. The cooks made an atrocious mess and she had to ignore the dried egg and splattered grease that covered almost everything.

Ten minutes later, she slid the round, puffy pancake onto a plate and topped it with the apple-orange juice sauce she'd prepared while it cooked. The canned apples were usually used as a garnish, but since there was no fresh fruit she'd had to improvise. She added a sprig of wilted parsley and took the plate out front. The big trucker was still there, sipping his coffee. He looked up at her curiously as she put the plate in front of him.

"It's on the house," she reminded him as he eyed the food with suspicion. "Just tell me what you think."

She couldn't stand waiting and watching him, so she went back to the kitchen and began working on some more of Donny's orders. When she returned to the counter, Donny was standing in front of the trucker, shaking his head in disbelief. He looked up at her. "I don't think he's eaten fruit in a year," he said, the ever present cigarette bobbing up and down as he spoke.

"It's good," the trucker said as he shoved the last forkful into his mouth.

"You want another one?" Donny asked. Pamela knew he wasn't

being nice, he wanted to be sure it was enough food.

"I'm about near to pop," the trucker said, causing Pamela to smile. "But I'll take one for the road. I'll roll it up like a taco."

"It'll cost ya four-fifty," Donny said. The trucker scowled but then nodded and said he'd pick it up after he used the john. Pamela smiled brightly as Donny turned to look at her.

"What you grinning about?" he asked in a harsh tone, although is eyes were smiling. "You just got stuck cooking all night."

At 5 a.m., Donny came to the back and Pamela showed him how to make their newest menu item. She'd already made a large batch of the topping and explained it should last him through the morning. No one was more surprised than she was to see her idea taking off so well. They'd still run out of bacon and there was plenty of attitude about that from their clientele, but the new special had either helped temper their annoyance, or at least given them something else to talk about. 'Crazy Yankee food,' they called it as they shoveled it into their mouths.

After she showed Donny how to make the pancakes he shoved a handful of bills into her hand. "You made pretty good tips," he said. Pamela smiled her thanks. In spite of the cigarettes and his penchant for foul language, she liked Donny. Actually, he was probably the best friend she had, and they weren't really friends at all.

"Hey, Pamela," Donny called from the back as she was finishing up a couple of hours later. "You've got a phone call."

"I'll get it in the office," she said as she wiped her hands on her apron and headed toward the closet they called the office. It reeked of bacon grease and stale cigarette smoke. Because she couldn't afford a home phone, and didn't received many calls anyway, Donny gave her permission to receive calls at work.

"This is Pamela," she said when she put the phone to her ear.

"I'm glad I caught you," the voice said. "It's Carla; how is everything?"

"Can't complain," Pamela said as she felt herself relax. She had a recurring nightmare of picking up the phone one day and hearing David's voice on the other end. As her contact to the underground organization that helped her to hide from the world while she awaited justice, Carla kept infrequent contact, only calling when necessary.

"Really?"

Pamela smiled. Carla knew better than anyone what this experience was like. Leave it to her to call Pamela on it. "It's lonely," she admitted. "But it's good, too. The kids love being in school and they have a few friends now, so they're more content than they've ever been."

"You did the right thing, then?" Carla asked. "Going out on your own?"

"Absolutely," Pamela agreed with a nod. "After two years of being dependent on others, it's great to be earning my own way."

"And you haven't had any problem with the IDs?" When she'd left the last safe house she'd paid two thousand dollars for fake birth certificates.

"Nope, the school took them just fine and I got my license without a hitch. It's almost scary how easy it's been."

Carla laughed. "It's tricky finding just the right outlaws to work with." Pamela laughed too, still amazed that she operated on the fringe of society like this.

"I have some good news," Carla suddenly said, getting to the real reason for her call. "There's a doctor in Florida who's been a big help on a couple of court cases back east. I got Katie an appointment."

"You're kidding," Pamela said, gripping the phone tighter.

"He's been great. So far, he's turned the tide on three of our cases; he and his partner specialize in diagnosing sexual abuse and he's very reputable. I got you an appointment next Monday if that will work?"

"Yes, of course," Pamela said as she fished around the shelving for a pencil and paper. Finally, she pulled her order pad from her apron pocket and jotted down directions to his office. "What time?" she asked when Carla finished.

"Eight thirty in the morning. The appointment's in my name and I told them to send the report to me so that I can go over it; just to make sure it's what we want. Call me if there are any problems."

"Do you have a new number?" Pamela asked. Every few months, Carla got a new cell phone number so that she'd be harder to track. Pamela hadn't talked to her since just a month after moving here, so she was sure the number had changed.

"Yeah, you ready?"

Pamela said that she was and jotted down the number beneath the address.

"Thank you," she said when Carla said good bye.

"Don't mention it," Carla said.

Pamela hung up the phone and butterflies erupted in her stomach. Two doctors in Salt Lake said the evidence was inconclusive and that the symptoms Katie showed could be attributed to something else. She hated the idea of putting Darla through the ordeal of another doctor's exam, but if this doctor could make a conclusive diagnosis it might get them another preliminary hearing. It was a long shot. She didn't fool herself about that, but long shots were all she had these days anyway.

When she'd left Salt Lake she felt sure she'd be gone a few months while the DA prepared a new hearing, then David would go to trial and she'd go home. She hadn't realized that her leaving would put everything on hold. Without new evidence they wouldn't allow another hearing. And without Katie's testimony there was no case anyway since she was the sole witness of the crime. Pamela was stuck. If she went back without reliable evidence proving the kids weren't safe with David, she'd go to jail and the kids would go to David. Trying to find that evidence and hide at the same time was almost impossible.

Since she was already thinking about home, she made a call to a number she had memorized, slipping a dollar into the "phone can" that Donny used for collecting his long-distance fees. The line rang twice.

"Hello?"

"Janice?"

There was silence for a moment. "David was here," Janice said quickly.

"What?" Pamela asked in alarm.

"Last week," Janice explained. "He wanted to know if we were in contact."

"Okay," Pamela said, getting a grip on her fear. "I'm sorry, I won't call anymore."

"Wait," Janice interjected. "There has to be some—"

"No," Pamela cut her off. "It isn't worth the risk. Thanks for all you've done." She hung up before Janice could say anything else.

The thrill of Carla's news was now replaced with dread. Janice had been Pamela's neighbor in Salt Lake. They'd served in a Primary presidency together and car-pooled their kids to swimming lessons. Janice was the person she ran to for help when Darla told her what David had done. Janice was the only person Pamela dared tell of the note left on her car months later. They had decided early on that if Pamela had to leave, she could contact Janice on a limited basis. In the two years and a half since she left, Pamela had called Janice only twice before. And now David was suspicious. Knowing he was still looking for her put her stomach into knots. She wouldn't risk getting Janice any more involved than she already was. If David knew they had been in contact . . . oh, what should she do now?

―――――

"We got something," the young investigator announced as he entered David's office. He carried a small tape recorder, placed it on the desk and pushed the *play* button. "We logged a call to Janice Fillmore this morning," he said quickly before the voices began.

"Hello?"

"Janice?"

"David was here."

"What?"

"Last week, he wanted to know if we were in contact."

"Okay, I'm sorry, I won't call anymore."

"Wait, there has to be some—"

"No, it isn't worth the risk. Thanks for all you've done."

The line went dead and the young detective pushed the *stop* button. David nodded. "I knew it," he said with satisfaction. "The way she looked at me that night . . . I knew they'd been in contact. Destroy the tape and remove the illegal bugging from her line while they're at church on Sunday. Track the number, and let me know what you find." The investigator nodded and left David to his own thoughts.

For the first year after their disappearance David had tried everything he could to find them. He'd gone on TV, been interviewed in newspapers and pleaded over and over again that they come home. He even joined a support group in order to keep sympathy levels high. Because of the public display of his case and Gloria's silence, he'd been labeled the "victim" from the beginning and he took full advantage of the opportunity. Eventually, his campaign began to change his life for the better without his kids, specifically in his law practice. He'd received free advertising, in a way, and in the year following their disappearance had become a popular defense attorney in divorce cases, specifically when there was allegations of abuse. He started getting more cases than he could handle and since, he knew all the right moves, he won almost without exception.

Six months ago, he'd worked with a father who he felt was a slam dunk. To his chagrin, however, they lost. The court system had caught up with the man's pornography addiction and it had been the guy's hardest hit. The client was sentenced to five years in prison after having his whole life picked apart and held up for the public to gape at. Until then David had never doubted that when he found Gloria, he'd be exonerated of all charges against him and she'd pay for what she did. He'd been sure that he could keep his private life private and what he chose to hide would remain hidden. This case ruined his faith. In the aftermath of the loss, his fears had grown until he realized that the only guarantee he had would be if Gloria weren't found. The case against him would stay cold until she came back. Based on that understanding, why would he want her to come back and potentially ruin everything?

His focus changed immediately and new plan was put into play that would preserve his power; his control over his own destiny. In this way he could learn from the mistakes he'd made and use the situation to his advantage. The people involved didn't know enough to put the pieces together, they thought they were helping him find her when in truth they would eventually help motivate her never to be found. So far things were going well.

———

"You must be Mrs. Bennion," the doctor said as he entered the room. Pamela smiled and shook his proffered hand. Kenny was in the small waiting room watching cartoons, whereas Darla was on her mother's lap, trying hard to look brave.

"I'm Doctor Garcia," the doctor said, directing his comments to Darla rather than Pamela. "I just need to ask you some questions and then do a brief exam. Your mom can stay with you the whole time."

Darla nodded, but her chin began to quiver. Pamela pulled her closer to her chest and smoothed her hair. "It will be okay, baby," she whispered, although she too had a lump in her throat.

A short time later, Darla was led out to the waiting room so that Pamela and the Doctor could discuss the situation. "I'd like to have her meet with a colleague of mine. I can do the physical diagnosis, but he conducts the psychological portion of the exam. He's already blocked out some time this afternoon, and my receptionist will schedule an appointment, although it might delay your departure. I'd also like him to meet with you as a separate appointment."

"Me?" she asked. "What for?"

Dr. Garcia paused. "Quite frankly, Mrs. Bennion, not every child we examine has been abused. The supposed evidence I find in the physical exam can be attributed to other things, but state of mind is much more difficult to counterfeit. By talking to the child and the parent, we can usually determine whether or not their accusations are true as well as determining possible reasons they would falsely accuse. The worst thing I could ever do as a doctor, is validate sexual abuse that never happened because it then puts every true victim under suspicion that they too are making it up."

Pamela's first inclination was to take offense to the statement, but it only took another instant for her to see the wisdom of the procedure. "I'll do whatever it takes."

"I was hoping you'd say that," he said with a smile. "The crackpots usually storm out of my office when I get to this part."

She let out a breath of relief that she hadn't expressed her offense as she nodded her understanding. "Do you believe my daughter was abused?"

"Before I answer that, let me give you a little education. When I started my practice, statistics said that one of every four girls and one of every six boys would be sexually assaulted sometime in their life; now those numbers are one of every two girls and one of every four boys." Gloria closed her eyes, sick to her stomach. "The abuse ranges from being forced to watch or hear explicit things, to touching . . . and it only gets worse. Most conclusive abuse cases are determined because there are witnesses, other victims of the abuse that substantiate the accusation, because the child contracts a sexually transmitted disease, or because an exam is done immediately after the trauma; none of that is the situation here. However, your daughter's pelvic exam showed some scarring that isn't normal in a nine-year-old girl and looks to have occurred within the time frame you explained."

"Both doctors in Salt Lake said the scarring could have been caused by an infection or even a birth defect."

"That's true, but studies done in just the last few years have shown that it's more likely caused by sexual trauma. And I would guess they didn't do a psychological evaluation in conjunction with the physical one, did they?"

"No," Pamela agreed.

"Along with the psychological symptoms, the physical symptoms are hard to refute. I'll work up my report this afternoon. After my colleague finishes, we'll send a certified statement to the district attorney in Salt Lake saying the full report is on its way. That will give them time to prepare for the full report. We'll then send the full reports to Carla. I assume that's still how you want it done?" Pamela nodded and tried to blink away her tears. Even after all this time, it was so incredibly painful to know what had happened to her little girl.

"And then what?" Pamela asked, pushing her emotion away.

"Then we wait for Carla to approve it. If she wants us to reword anything, we can do it so long as it doesn't compromise our findings. Then she'll need to order signed copies from me to send out, but she knows all that. The district attorney will decide what to do with it from there. If I need to, I'll testify. For now, I'll see that you get those appointments this afternoon. Is there anyone that needs a full report before Carla checks it out?"

Pamela thought back to her phone call to Janice. In the days following the call, she'd almost decided to leave and move again. David's visit made her nervous and was enough reason to end her phone contacts with Janice, but was it enough reason to move and uproot her children? Especially when they were just getting comfortable?

"No," she answered, shaking off the disturbing thoughts. "Just send the report on to Carla." Her voice must have betrayed her fears that this report would do no more good than the last two had done.

The doctor raised his eyebrow. "Too much hope can be painful, Mrs. Bennion. But no hope leaves us with no reason to try."

Several hours later, they began the long drive back home. The psychologist had met with Darla for over an hour. Then he'd sat down with Pamela. He asked detailed questions about her childhood and marriage, including intimate questions regarding her sex life with David. It had been extremely uncomfortable, but she forced herself to do what was necessary. Then he asked about how she learned of the abuse and what she did about it. When he exhausted his questions he smiled and expressed his sympathy for her situation.

"I have no doubt that the allegations against your husband are true. Both you and your daughter have consistent stories and have been through a lot. I hope we can help you find the justice you deserve."

Those words rang sweetly in her head as she drove. It gave Pamela chills to think of being so close to getting this over with. Both reports would go to Carla by the end of the week. Carla would take it from there and keep Pamela informed. For just an instant, Pamela wondered if it was wise to count on Carla doing everything; perhaps she should have received the report herself. But she reminded herself that Carla knew a lot more about this stuff than she did. It was important to trust her.

Chapter Four

"Have you ever been here before?" Bryan asked as he shut the door to his truck on Wednesday morning.

Charlotte slammed the passenger door and squinted up at the sign again. "Once or twice," she said with a shrug. "Never found anything worth the extra drive."

Bryan nodded and put his keys in the pocket of his Wranglers as they headed toward the door. He was dressed in his usual work-day attire which consisted of Wranglers, cowboy boots, a white western shirt and a brown felt cowboy hat. If it were cold, he'd include a sport coat, but today was much too warm to necessitate the additional warmth. "A teacher at school said it's the best breakfast she's had in ages and since I'm finally finished with early morning basketball practice, I thought maybe this would give you an incentive to hang out with your little brother."

Charlotte rolled her eyes as he opened the door to the diner and then slugged him playfully in the stomach as she passed him. He made an exaggerated grunting sound before hitting her back and removing his hat. He glanced at his watch and determined he still had plenty of time. School didn't start until 7:30 and his first period was his prep period anyway. Since Charlotte's husband worked swing shift he could do the morning routine with their three kids now and then.

"What can I get for you?" the waitress asked a few moments after they slid into the booth.

Bryan set the menu down after only glancing at it. "We've been told you have some German pancakes to die for." He looked up at the waitress and his smile faded. It was her! The woman from church. The one who had cried through his talk.

She smiled warmly and tucked a stray lock of long brown hair behind her ear, oblivious to his scrutiny. "For both of you?" she asked, looking from one to the other.

"Yep," Charlotte said, folding her menu and pushing it to the edge of the table.

"The meal comes with free coffee—would you like anything else to go with it, orange juice maybe?"

"Uh . . . no," Brian stammered, still staring. He absently ran his fingers through his hair as he watched her, hoping his "hat head" wasn't too bad this morning.

"And don't worry about the coffee," Charlotte added. "Water will be fine."

She looked at Bryan and raised her eyebrows. He paused a little too long. "Oh, uh, no coffee for me either. And water'll be good."

The waitress turned to go and Bryan hurried to find an excuse to make her stay just a few seconds longer. "Uh, well, how about a hot chocolate," he quickly added. If only he'd seen her up close that day. Even if it was her, it was obviou she didn't recognize him.

She wrote his order on a pad of paper, smiled, and headed back to the counter. Bryan watched her pull the top sheet off her order pad and clip it to the turnstile that she spun around. He hoped to get another opportunity to study her.

"I thought I was your date this morning?"

Bryan looked back at Charlotte and shook his head. "Sorry," he muttered, taking another glance in the waitress's direction.

"I don't mean to point out the obvious," Charlotte said after another pause, "but you've got a real pretty girlfriend."

"What's that supposed to mean?" Bryan asked, furrowing his brow as he faced his sister. However, he couldn't hold eye contact very long, so he started fiddling with his hat, smoothing the rim with his fingers.

After reading the Book of Mormon four years ago, Bryan had given the copy to his sister. Charlotte was three years older than Bryan, but they had always been close. He had hoped for some objectivity. She showed none of his hesitancies and beat him to the baptismal font—much to the dismay of their mother. After living in Little Rock all her life, Charlotte and her nonmember-but-supportive husband moved to Harrison for a new job shortly after her baptism. During the next year, the remaining Little Rock family members tried everything in their power to distract Bryan from the new religion in his life. However, he withstood their efforts and decided to follow her up north. He started looking for a teaching position in the area schools and was lucky enough to find a job at Harrison High school where he taught Sophomore Sciences, two periods of auto mechanics and was also the assistant basketball coach. He loved it. Getting away from the anti-Mormon sentiments of his family had been good for him, and having more time with his sister was even better. Although right now, he wished she wasn't looking at him so closely.

"She's not even blonde," Charlotte continued with a teasing grin. "I thought you only went for blondes?"

"I do," Bryan sourly. "And you're completely misreading my interest. She looks like that lady from church I told you about."

"The one who bawled through your talk?"

"She was very touched by the spirit I invited to that meeting," Bryan answered with feigned offense.

Charlotte laughed out loud. "Good thing she doesn't know you very well." She paused and shook her head before shrugging as she continued. "Don't worry about scoping out new territory, ya know I'm not a big fan of Barbara anyway."

Bryan smiled tightly and was just about to say something equally sparring when the waitress returned with his hot chocolate. Bryan took the chance to observe her a little more closely. Her long brown hair was pulled into a braid that was coming undone, and she wore no makeup. By no means was she homely, but as he had determined that first day, she wasn't particularly striking either. She had soft hazel eyes that he wished he could get a better look at, but she quickly finished serving him and began making rounds to the other tables. Bryan followed her with his eyes while Charlotte continued to smirk about the whole situation. Across the diner, Bryan watched her laugh at something some trucker said and sat up a little straighter. When she smiled, it was like her entire face illuminated. It was a phenomenal change and Bryan felt something inside him twitch. She might not be blonde, but she had a smile that lit the room like nothing he'd ever seen.

"You and Barbara are still coming for dinner on Sunday, right?" Charlotte said after a few moments. Apparently she was tired of watching Bryan watch the waitress.

"Of course," Bryan said. "I never miss a homemade meal. It will be a homemade meal, won't it? You're not going to try and pass off some frozen dinner."

"Beggars can't be choosers," Charlotte continued with a grin. For the next few minutes, they continued their banter. Despite himself, however, Bryan couldn't help but keep track of the waitress as she hurried from one thing to the next. He wished he knew if it was really the woman from church.

A bell rang from the cook's counter and he watched her retrieve their order. A few moments later, she set the plates down in front of them. "Can I get anything else for you?" she asked.

They both said no and she moved down to the next table to take their order. Bryan watched her intently as she talked with a couple of truckers. He couldn't hear what they said but suddenly the waitress's cheeks turned red, and then she smiled. Just like before her whole face lit up. She had a broad smile—almost too big for her face—that showed perfectly straight white teeth. He couldn't get over the amazing change in her features. She went from being a rather plain-looking woman, to anything but plain. It reminded him of Julia Roberts in a way.

"How's your meal?" the waitress asked several minutes later. She'd returned with another waitress. The new one had big red hair, big red lips, and chomped gum vigorously—like a cow chewing her cud. Bryan pulled his plate protectively closer to himself to avoid any foreign objects "Big Red" might inadvertently add to his meal, before swallowing and looking at his nearly empty plate.

"I'd have to say it's about the best breakfast I've had since I don't know when. Our Grandma used to make these things, smothered them with sour cream and brown sugar. For a meal like this, I might just become a regular."

"Well, ya ain't gonna be the first to be seduced by Pamela's cookin'," Big Red said with her smacking lips and a wink at his waitress.

"You made this?" he asked, looking at Pamela. How wonderful to have her name!

Her cheeks turned pink—the extra color looked good on her. "Not really, I just supplied the recipe."

"Darn thing started as a special and ended up at the top of our menu. We can't hardly keep up," Big Red added with a hand on her hip. A trucker entered the diner and headed for the counter; she winked a big false-eye-lashed eye and gave him a smile that made Bryan wince. Parents that didn't put braces on their kids should be ashamed of themselves. He wondered how anyone made it to adulthood with teeth like this woman's. Then again, at least she had teeth. There was a fair number in Arkansas who just went without.

Pamela smiled and laid their ticket on the table. "I'm about to go off shift and I wanted to introduce you to Peg; she'll take care of anything else you need."

Bryan and Charlotte nodded and the waitresses moved onto the next table. For the next two minutes, he watched his waitress carefully while Charlotte finished eating. When the waitress grabbed her purse from behind the counter, he jumped up and hurried to the register, ignoring Charlotte as she rolled her eyes. Just as he hoped, the waitress stayed long enough to ring him up. While he put the change into his pocket she said good-bye to the cook, waved at a few patrons, and went toward the door. Bryan rushed over to hold it open for her. She smiled a little nervously and nodded her thanks.

Once outside, she headed for her car.

"Hey," he called. She stopped and turned, looking even more anxious than she had before. "The tip."

"They'll save it for me," she said, shifting her weight from one foot to another while he extracted a five-dollar bill from his wallet. She looked at it but made no move to take it from him. "Your meals only came to eleven fifty," she said.

"I'm a good tipper," he replied with a smile. "Consider it a thank you for serving something without bacon grease."

She hesitated a moment, but finally smiled that great smile. "You noticed that too, huh?"

"I've a feeling you're going to be very good for business here."

"Thank you," she said, as she took the money and put it in the front pocket of her apron. "I guess I'll see you around."

"I guess you will." She glanced nervously into the restaurant and he followed her look to see that she was watching Charlotte get up from the table.

"That's my sister," he quickly said.

"Oh, I—"

"Just so you know," he said with a smile.

She nodded quickly once more and headed for her car at a quicker pace. He wondered if he'd scared her. Once inside her car, she looked at him once more and then backed out of her parking space. He watched her go.

"I'll let you buy my breakfast to pay for my silence," Charlotte said from behind him as the car disappeared. He turned to look at her and she handed him his hat she'd retrieved from the table where he'd left it.

Bryan shook his head, both at Charlotte's comment and at his own behavior. They began walking toward his vehicle. "I just wanted to know if it was her."

"Did you ask her?" Charlotte asked, leaning against the truck and looking amused.

"Uh—no," Bryan admitted. He ran his hand through his dark hair and shook his head before putting his hat back on. "But she's not blonde," he added pointedly, a half smile on his lips as he pulled the rim of the hat down enough to shade his eyes from the rising sun. "That alone should prove my intentions are completely honorable."

"And I hated black-eyed peas till I was twenty-four. Now I can't find enough recipes for using them."

"You're way off the mark," Bryan said with finality as he headed for the drivers door. He put his hand on the handle and hesitated. Barbara probably wouldn't take this as well as Charlotte had. Despite all of Barbara's good attributes, she had a fair amount of southern territorialism. "But I can trust you'll not share your suspicions?"

"With Barbara?" Charlotte asked, still smiling. She was loving this. "That cute blonde thing you've been dating for the last six months? I suppose I can keep quiet."

Bryan nodded, uncomfortable with the way Charlotte had agreed to keep it their secret.

"My lips are sealed," Charlotte said as she pulled open her door.

Bryan glanced at his watch and began moving a little faster. If he didn't hurry he'd have to explain to his students why *he* was late today. Luckily, Charlotte lived on the way back into town, so dropping her off wouldn't slow him down too much. When they pulled into her driveway, she turned to look at him. "Besides," she said with a teasing grin, "sometimes ya gotta flirt to convert."

"Wait a minute," he stammered.

Charlotte laughed and slammed the door before he could protest further.

———

"You're back," Pamela said the following Wednesday morning. She placed a mug of hot chocolate in front of him. She felt funny about being so nervous when he'd talked to her last week but she *was* glad he was alone this time. "What would you like?"

The dark-haired man looked at the mug and smiled. "You remember me," he said in a tone that told her he liked being remembered.

Pamela kept her cool. She didn't say anything about how nice it was to see him again. She didn't get many customers that didn't greet her with a "hey, Hun" and she liked his clean-cut look. "You gave me a 50 percent tip; I'm bound to remember."

"I'll keep that in mind," he said with a smile as he met her gaze. His eyes were dark and penetrating—the kind of eyes that threatened to sweep unsuspecting women off their feet. Luckily, she was not an unsuspecting woman. In fact, she was as suspecting as they came. "You don't even need to ask what I want today." He handed her the menu and gave her a crooked grin. An extremely attractive crooked grin.

"Thank you, sir," she said with a smile as she moved away.

"Bryan," he said. Pamela turned back to look at him. "My name is Bryan," he clarified.

"Well then, thank you . . . Bryan," she said and turned toward the cook's counter again. When she delivered his food he asked how her day was going.

"My days and nights are a little backwards," she answered. "But my night's been pretty good." He smiled again and she couldn't resist smiling back. Glancing at the stack of tests next to him, she took a guess as his occupation. "Teacher?" she said simply.

"Very good," he said. "High school science, mostly."

"Wow," she said appreciatively. "I thought being old and boring was a prerequisite to teaching science."

"So you think I'm virile and stimulating?"

Her face flamed and she was speechless for a moment. Had she really implied that? His eyes sparkled at her embarrassment and she closed her eyes for a moment as she tried to come up with a response that wouldn't prolong her discomfort. Snatching his empty mug, she turned away from the table. "I'll get you a refill."

As she filled the mug she shut her eyes again. One of the few men she served who didn't smell like stale cigarettes or dirty socks and she acts like some high school preppie. She managed to avoid too much conversation throughout the remainder of his meal, although that quirky grin of his continued to disarm her. His plate was almost empty when she saw him glance at his watch and pick up his pace. He must be running late. When he finished his meal and hurried for the door, he waved good-bye and she waved back. When she turned back to the counter Donny was smirking at her.

"What?" she asked.

"Oh, nothing," Donny said with his hands raised to signal a truce. "Nothin' at all." But he winked and it made her uncomfortable. On the way home, she admitted that she had been flirting with the guy. That had to stop.

"How was work?" Darla asked when Pamela entered the house.

"Same old, same old," Pamela answered as she smoothed Kenny's hair down flat in the back. He had a stubborn cowlick that refused to comply with the rest of his hair. Surely, if she continued to smooth it down every day she could retrain it. He tried to pull away but was still eating, so it proved impossible. "Only made twenty-seven dollars in tips, though," she added after a moment. "Wednesdays are always slow."

"It's Thursday," Kenny corrected her.

"For me, it's still Wednesday," she said with a smile. They went through this little game of what-day-it-is at least once a week.

"I bet I know how you could make more tips," Darla suggested after Pamela collapsed into a chair, groaning with the relief of being off her feet.

"Oh, yeah?" she asked, not really paying attention as she began removing the braid from her hair.

"Wear makeup again."

Pamela looked at her daughter in surprise as Darla hurried to explain. "Remember when you used to wear lipstick and stuff on your eyes? You were real pretty. I bet you'd get more tips if you was prettier."

"Were prettier," Pamela corrected absently. She wanted to correct the entire statement but resorted to grammar correction instead.

"Women don't need makeup to be beautiful," she finally said, addressing the concept of Darla's comment.

"I know," Darla agreed easily. "You don't need toothpaste to brush your teeth either, but it helps."

Pamela paused for a moment, then she laughed, "Where on earth did you hear that?"

Just then the bus honked and they began the daily race to get outside. Pamela watched the bus disappear and then went back inside. She went into the bathroom and finished undoing her braid. As her hair fell across her shoulders, she brushed it slowly. After a couple minutes it was full, lifted by static. With her hands, she smoothed down the wayward strands and took a long look at herself in the mirror. She looked old and tired. What used to be lines around her eyes were now wrinkles. When she'd stopped using makeup, she'd overlooked skin care, too. She was now looking all of her thirty years. Furthermore, she'd let her bangs grow out and looked like an old, brown-haired version of Marsha Brady.

On an impulse, she shuffled around in her drawer and found an old tube of lipstick. She'd gotten it at one of those sample tables at the grocery store once, and even though the color didn't fit her, it brought out some color in her cheeks. In the kitchen, she found Kenny's crayons. With the blow dryer, she heated up a still-pointed brown and then applied the warm color to the edges of her eyelids. It was a trick she'd learned back in the sixth grade before her mother would let her buy makeup. Again, it didn't look right—too thick and not the right shade. But it emphasized her eyes. She stood back and twisted her hair up on top of her head, showing off her strong cheekbones and graceful neck.

For over two years, she hadn't cared what she looked like; she was focused on her children. And in order to avoid attention, she had needed to be average, painfully so. Perhaps it was time to take a step back toward being the woman she once was. She was happy here, the kids were happy, and they were enjoying a good life in Arkansas. Surely, she could begin incorporating a few more facets of normal life. A little mascara and lipstick, infrequent trips to church, and a little less fear sounded incredibly tempting.

Chapter Five

"So what did you find?" David Stanton asked as he entered the office.

"We know where the call was made and we're working with a contact in Arkansas who will check it out."

"Working," David said insultingly. "It's been almost two weeks since that call. She's probably long gone by now."

"We don't think so," the investigator said with a shake of his head. "The call was made from a business number. What business owner lets just anybody call Utah on his dime? We think she must work there or perhaps the owner is involved with the underground network that's helping her out."

"And yet you wait two weeks," David snarled. "It's been two and a half years, you finally have her voice on tape, and you wait two weeks to do something about it?" He turned away in disgust, clenching his jaw in annoyance before he continued. "There was an article in *USA Today* that said the feds are closing in on one of those underground operations. If they beat you to her, you lose half your payment."

The investigator cleared his throat, ignoring the threat. "One of the reasons I held off on taking action was that we found out that the DA received a statement from a doctor who feels he has sufficient evidence of abuse. The DA's waiting for the full report." David froze and simply stared straight ahead, his jaw tensing again. "We're not too worried about it. She can take your daughter to all the doctors in the world, but unless she shows up to personally push the case through, it's pointless."

"None of that is your concern. I pay you to find her and tell me where she is. That's it," David finally said as he turned and placed both hands on the desk. He leaned towards the other man. "I want to get this over with once and for all."

"Yes, sir," the investigator hurried to say. "And we'll do all we can to find her before the feds do, but if this doctor's report is—"

"I didn't ask you what you thought of the doctor's report," David said.

He paused for a few moments. "I want the number of your Arkansas contact. I'll take it from here."

"That's not necessary, we—"

"Obviously it is necessary. There are already two reports that say her allegations are false. You're either with me or you're against me and I don't have time for your doubts. I'll pay you and we're done." He pulled his wallet out of his back pocket and started counting out hundreds. "Come to think of it, I'll find my own contact in Arkansas."

———

"So can I go?" Darla asked, her eyes pleading more than her words. Pamela looked at her and felt the tug on her heart. Darla had made friends with a girl from school named Jenny. Jenny had come to their house a few times and she seemed very nice, but Pamela felt uneasy about Darla going to Jenny's house.

"I don't know, Hun," she said as she tasted the spaghetti sauce and added more salt. She glanced at Kenny in the living room to be sure he wasn't listening. He was young enough that he accepted their life as normal. She didn't want him to start asking hard questions any sooner than necessary. "Remember what I told you about friends."

"But Jenny's never asked where I used to live or where my dad is. I haven't told her anything."

"But her mother will probably ask questions you can't answer."

"Then I'll say I don't know," Darla whined as if lots of kids didn't know where they used to live or where their dad was. "Please, Mommy, I want to go real bad."

Pamela looked at her little girl and sighed. This was the hardest part of living all the lies—misleading people. All her life, she'd been taught to be honest. And yet now she lived a life where none of them could tell the truth. Pamela had taught her children to lie—because they had too. How sad was that? Sometimes Darla seemed to be nine-going-on-thirty.

"If you promise me you'll be careful," she said finally. "You can't call me to come and get you if something goes wrong."

"Nothing will happen," Darla said as she jumped from her chair. "Everything will be fine."

The next day, Darla took the school bus home with Jenny. Pamela worried about it all day, but when she and Kenny picked her up at 6:00, everything was fine. Pamela met Jenny's mother and siblings; her dad wasn't home from work yet. They seemed very nice.

"Darla says you're from Detroit?" Jenny's mother said as they were heading for the door.

"Uh, yeah. We lived there for a while," Pamela said nervously. She quickened her pace so as to avoid any more questions, "Thanks again for having her."

"Anytime," Jenny's mother said.

Once they were in the car Darla began telling them all the great things they had done. Jenny had a tree house in the back yard, and a trampoline. They played Nintendo and Darla helped Jenny and her mom make chocolate cake for their dessert. They had wanted her to stay for dinner, but they had no way of contacting Pamela. Pamela ignored the wishful undertones. The fact was that phones were too expensive and calls were too easy to track. Besides she couldn't imagine not calling her mother if she had access to a phone all day long.

"What else did you tell her about us?" Pamela asked casually, when Darla stopped speaking.

"Just that you and Dad are divorced, and you're a waitress at Donny's."

A divorced waitress with two kids, Pamela thought to herself. It was incredible to fit that description. "Good," Pamela said, pushing aside the dark thoughts of herself. "Why don't we get some groceries and pick up some hamburgers for dinner."

"I don't want any pickles," Kenny said from the back seat where he was playing war with his green plastic soldiers.

"No pickles," Pamela said as they pulled into the grocery store parking lot. "I promise."

That night, she told the kids the story of Nephi and Laban. It was one of their favorites. Pamela liked to think she was doing something similar to what Nephi had done. Kidnapping her children was wrong. Lying to people about who she was, where she came from, and how she got here, was wrong, too. But the greater good was just that—greater. Nephi's actions saved generations. She just wanted to save this one.

When the kids were asleep she straightened the house, read her scriptures for a few minutes and then went into the bathroom to get ready for work. She'd washed and ironed her uniform today, so it looked as good as it ever did. After seeing the kids off that morning, she'd run to a drug store and purchased a few items. Now she removed them from a drawer in the bathroom and hoped she remembered how to put the stuff on. Ten minutes later, she stepped back and felt like a whole new woman. It amazed her what a little color and shading could do for her features. Her eyes looked larger, her cheekbones appeared sculpted and she looked five years younger. She smiled and shook her head; was she really ready for this next step? After another minute, she decided she was. She wet her hair and combed a few strands over her eyes. Carefully, she cut them, following the curve of her eyebrows. Then she curled them slightly, before pulling her hair into the customary ponytail. She'd always looked better with bangs and the transformation made her feel younger, lighter—almost normal. For at least one night she was going to do something without overanalyzing her intentions. She wanted to look like she knew how to take care of herself. What was so wrong about that?

The next morning, she returned home smiling. "Guess how much I made in tips today?"

Darla looked up from her breakfast. "Mom—you're wearing makeup," she said with a smile. "And you cut your hair."

"Guess?" Pamela repeated, ignoring her daughter's attention to details.

"A hundred dollars," Kenny offered. His eyes were wide and she knew he was seeing visions of bicycles in his head.

"Not that much," Pamela said with a wink. She pulled out a chair, grabbed a notebook and started writing down numbers. "I usually make about thirty dollars on Thursday."

"But it's Friday," Kenny said with a teasing grin. Pamela smiled and Darla rolled her eyes with big-sister annoyance.

"Last night, I made forty-two," she continued. "That's a twelve dollar increase, meaning that I increased our income by almost 25 percent."

"Because of the makeup?" Darla asked.

Pamela thought about it for a minute. "I don't know," she finally said. "Maybe the makeup and hair had a little to do with it, but I think the real difference was that I felt good about myself and my customers knew it." She looked at her children. "It's not so much the makeup as it is feeling good, but I guess the makeup helped a little."

Darla smiled. "Are you going to wear makeup again?"

"And make 25 percent more in tips? You betcha."

They both laughed just as the blasted horn honked. Pamela stood, handed out backpacks and waved good bye. *Not a bad night's work*, she thought, as she put the money in her money jar. Not bad at all.

———

Carla Godfrey removed the mail from her post office box and shut the small metal door. On her way to the car she shuffled through the pile, looking for anything interesting. She received her "public" mail, as she liked to think of it, at her home, but she had other interests that necessitated the rental of a private box on the other side of town. The letter from Dr. Garcia in Florida made her smile. She'd been waiting for this.

She placed the stack of mail on the passenger seat and pulled out of the parking lot, anxious to read the report as soon as she got home. It had already taken longer than she'd expected, and she was anxious to get things moving for Gloria. She'd make sure the report included all the necessary details, nothing that could be misconstrued, and if it all checked out, she'd then get the information to the appropriate sources. Anonymously of course. She hoped that this would be the beginning of a happy ending for Gloria and Katie Stanton. The white sedan that pulled into traffic behind her a few blocks later went unnoticed.

When she got home, she pulled into the garage and entered the house. Her children were grown, her husband had passed away several years earlier, and yet she still struggled with living alone. Now and then her own home became one of the safe houses she supervised across the country, but right now she was alone and she missed the sound of other voices.

She'd started working with the organization almost fifteen years earlier, when her daughter was in need of protection from an abusive husband. She'd been amazed to find there was so little protection and so many loopholes for the right attorney to take advantage of. After finding her way into the secret world of safe houses and false identifications, she herself had become an integral part of the system. There were no paychecks or acknowledgements to encourage her participation, just the sure knowledge that she was saving lives. When the courts ran out of options for protecting the innocent, Carla stepped in.

She placed the mail on the table and removed her sweater before pulling out a chair, locating her letter opener, and slitting open the envelope from Dr. Garcia. When she finished scanning the report, a satisfied smile lingered on her lips. This information would likely be enough to keep the children away from their father while a case was organized against him. And she had little doubt that a jury would find this report sufficient to demand a guilty verdict. They would still have to work out the criminal charges against Gloria, but if she turned herself in, things would probably go much more smoothly. Carla began planning the rest of the day, being sure to include ordering the signed copies from Dr. Garcia's office. Once she received them, she'd send them on to Gloria, the DA's office in Salt Lake, Gloria's parents, David's attorney, and anyone else she thought could use the information. By the end of the next week, Gloria could be packing in preparation to return to the life she'd left behind.

The doorbell startled her. She took just a moment to open the top drawer of the china cabinet next to the table and slip the letters through the nearly invisible slot made in the false bottom there. If she was ever caught, she felt secure that very little, if anything, would be found. It paid to be cautious and she was very cautious.

Once the report was securely hidden, she went to the door and opened it, smiling warmly at the young man standing there. "May I help you?" she asked, her voice calm and grandmotherly.

"Are you Carla Godfrey?" the young man asked.

"Yes, I am," she said, still smiling.

He lifted his hand and with the flick of his wrist opened what looked like a small leather wallet. As she read the FBI identification card, her smile faded.

———

Pamela wondered if Bryan would show up on Wednesday morning for the third week in a row, and she wasn't disappointed. Promptly at 6:15, he walked in the door with two other men she'd never met before. They all sat at his usual booth. She smiled a hello from the counter where she was buttering toast and he smiled back before engaging his friends in conversation. Her embarrassment at their exchange last week had faded in the last seven days, but whereas last time she was glad he'd come alone, today she was glad he'd brought company.

"Do you need a menu today?" she asked a minute later as she put down his hot chocolate and pulled out her order pad.

"Nope," he said, lacing his fingers together and resting his hands on the table. "This is Larry and Joe. They want German pancakes, too," he said by way of introduction. She smiled warmly. "And this is Pamela, the best waitress in Harrison." She shook her head at his summary, but couldn't help smiling. "You look very nice today," he added after a moment. Larry and Joe shared a look.

She looked away from his eyes, but couldn't help looking back to take in his features once again. A strong jaw softened the roundness of his face, while the shadow of what looked to be the potential for a thick beard added a touch of exotic appeal. He was quite handsome and the fact that his nose was a little too big for his face was the only negative feature she could see. By far his best feature were those eyes. Eyes that made her want to trust him automatically, but she was smarter than that. "Thank you," she said with a smile. "Can I get you fellas anything to drink?"

"Coffee," they both said in unison. She wrote it down and nodded. "I'll have your order in about ten minutes."

Several minutes later she served their meals, interrupting a discussion on hunting. "Do you guys teach at the school?" she asked his guests when she returned with the coffee pot. "I do," Joe said with a nod. "But Larry here spends his time at Edwards."

"The hardware store?" she asked.

Larry nodded. "I believe you've been in before," he commented. "You're living in the rental by the freight yard, right?"

"Larry knows everyone in town," Joe quickly added.

"Apparently so," she said with a touch of nervousness. She looked at Larry again. "Now that you mention Edwards, you do look familiar. I've been trying to fix hinges and faucets since I moved in. Not my forte."

"You ought to have Bryan give you a hand with that sorta thing. He loves to help damsels in distress."

Pamela glanced at Bryan briefly, embarrassed, but was surprised to see a shameless smiled on his face. "I'd be happy to help," he said boldly.

She was the one with a flushed face now. He looked at her for several seconds, his smile widening. She looked away first and decided to change the subject. "Can I get you guys anything else?"

"This will do," Bryan said with a smile. Larry and Joe nodded, still grinning about the game they were playing. She didn't have a chance to dwell on it though, since the morning rush was off to a good start.

A few minutes before seven, she clocked out, having introduced Peg to her customers and done her side work. Bryan was sliding out of his booth, still engaged in conversation with his friends, but she avoided eye contact this time. After unlocking the car door and sliding into the seat of her car, she adjusted her mirror and pulled out of the lot. When she checked her rear-view mirror a few minutes later, she saw a blue truck behind her.

She looked ahead and continued driving, making a mental list of all the things she needed to do when she woke up that afternoon. She turned left at the second stop sign and glanced in her mirror long enough to see that the truck was still behind her. She could see there was a man behind the wheel and her heart started to pound. She made another turn and the truck did the same. Her stomach sank. She was being followed!

Speeding up, she drove past her own street, and around the next corner. The truck followed and began flashing its headlights. *He found me*, she thought as she made another quick turn, thinking of the call to Janice. She should have left; she was a fool to have waited! Her mind was racing, but she tried to sort through her thoughts. The bus would be at her house any minute. She had to get to the kids before they left for school. She turned left, making a circle around her street and headed for the street after hers whose houses joined the back yards of hers and her neighbors. She pulled behind an abandoned house and ran from her car. Ducking behind a woodpile, she heard the truck drive slowly past the house. The diesel engine was loud and made her think of a lion lying in wait for its prey. Within a few seconds, the sound faded away. She ran east, toward her house, dodging sheds and clotheslines as she ran through the back yards of neighbors she'd never met and ignoring the barking of various dogs. She was grateful for leash laws and the fact that few people in Arkansas bothered to fence their yards.

Whoever was following her probably didn't know where the house was since they had been following her. She'd get the kids, grab a bag and then . . . she didn't know what she'd do then. She'd have to find a phone, and call Carla. That's it! Carla would know what to do.

Finally, she reached her yard and ran through the back door, startling the kids as they were finishing their breakfast. "Pack a bag," she said. "Quick. Someone followed me from work."

She ran to her bedroom at the end of the narrow hallway as the kids hurried to the bedroom they shared. They'd rehearsed this before; they knew just what to take and what to leave. In three minutes they would all be packed and ready to go, with nothing but the necessities. The blue suitcase Pamela had used the first time they ran was kept under her bed. She pulled it out, threw it on the bed, and began emptying drawers into it. She couldn't believe this had happened. She'd become too comfortable; she'd stayed too long! David must have tracked her through the call she'd made to Janice; that was the only explanation. This was unbelievable.

When the doorbell rang, she froze. For several seconds, she waited. There wasn't a sound in the house. Slowly, she turned and walked toward the front door, waving to the kids to stay in their room. They looked terrified, and jumped as the doorbell chimed again; their wide eyes were riveted on her, seeking instructions. Her heart was pounding so hard she could barely breathe. "Who is it," she said as she reached the front door. She could hear Darla and Kenny moving behind her. She could feel that they were as scared as she was.

"It's Bryan."

Pamela furrowed her brow. *Bryan*? "What do you want?"

"You left your purse at work and I said I'd catch you, but you were too fast. I didn't mean to frighten you." A silence hung for a few moments.

"How did you know where I lived?" she asked suspiciously after digesting the information he'd just told her.

"It's on your driver's license," he explained in an apologetic tone.

The bus honked and Pamela sighed as the fear left her. She turned to her frightened kids. "I'm sorry, guys," she said. "I guess I screwed up." They both just stood there. "Grab your backpacks, the bus is here." They still wouldn't move. "We'll talk about it after school, okay?" she said in what she hoped was a reassuring tone. "Everything's fine, now hurry." They finally went into action as she opened the door to face a very confused and anxious Bryan. "I'm sorry," she said with a shy smile as the kids passed by them both. They looked at Bryan suspiciously, but she told them to hurry again and they ran for the bus just as it honked for the second time.

"I've got to get to school," Bryan said nervously turning slightly toward the door. "Is everything okay?"

"Everything's fine," she said, searching for an explanation. "I . . . uh . . . get kind of crazy when I'm tired."

He handed her the purse. "I really didn't mean to upset you."

"I just overreacted," she explained again as she took the purse and backed away. She partially closed the door as he turned, but then he turned back.

"Can I ask you something?"

She didn't open the door any wider but nodded nervously. "Did you go to a church a few weeks ago?"

She just stared at him, unsure of how to answer. "Why?"

"I gave a talk at my church and there was woman with two children in the back that I'd never seen before," he said. "When I saw you that first time at the diner I thought maybe you were that woman, but I wasn't sure. Now I saw your kids and I just wonder if it was you."

Again she hesitated. Giving information was a bad thing. But did she really need to lie about this? Was it really that big of a risk? Besides, he was the one who had given the talk that had been such a light for her. It was hard to believe she hadn't recognized him at the diner after the impression his talk had made on her. "Yes, it was me," she said. She quickly added, "I like to visit different churches."

"If you have any questions about our faith I—"

"I don't have any questions," she interjected. At least that much was true. "You better get to work."

He hesitated a moment. "Are you sure you're all right?"

"I'll manage," she said, shutting the door. "Thanks again."

She closed the door all the way and leaned her back against it. Even though it had only been Bryan, the fear was still with her. Her body still trembled in reaction to the adrenaline rush.

A few moments passed before she left the house through the back door to retrieve her car. She felt so foolish, so frustrated, and yet she still felt anxious. Bryan must think she was crazy. With a heavy heart, she admitted that she needed to make arrangements to move when school was out for the summer. She'd stayed here too long. She'd become too comfortable and that put all of them in danger. There was still the chance that the doctor's report would make it possible for them to go home, but she didn't dare hope too much. The sheer possibility was almost too much for her. It would be better to focus on what was certain—that she needed to leave here. There were three weeks of school left—that would be enough time to plan the move. By the time the kids started school again, they'd be living a whole new life—one way or another.

Bryan returned to his truck and climbed in. "Everything okay?" Joe asked.

"Oh, yeah," Bryan said evenly. "She works nights, it made her a little nutty."

"A little," Joe said with a chuckle. "It was like some TV show."

Bryan laughed politely and glanced at the dashboard clock. They'd have to hurry to get to school in time. He wasn't sure what to make of the morning incident. She'd been so scared, so instantly sure that he was chasing her. He wondered what made her react that way. Then he smiled as his thoughts turned. She was the woman from church. They'd made a connection that day—he knew they had, and now he had the opportunity to turn that connection into something more. Maybe he could introduce her to the gospel and forever change her life for the better. He paused for a moment and questioned his motives. His interest made him uncomfortable, but he convinced himself that his motive was strictly religious. Maybe he could get her to come to church again. She seemed like a nice woman, with a good heart. He'd love to see her find the truth; he knew it would bless her life if she were willing to accept it.

"Did you like it?" Bryan asked his companion, trying to change the subject from Pamela's odd reaction.

"Breakfast?" Joe clarified. Bryan nodded. "I missed my grits," he admitted. "But it was pretty good; my girlfriend would love it."

———

"Donny's Diner," Peg said into the phone as she picked it up off the cradle and held it against her ear with her shoulder.

"Yes," said the unfamiliar female voice on the phone. "is . . . Pam Bennion . . . there?"

"Who?" Peg asked as she counted back the change to a waiting customer.

"Pam Bennion," the woman repeated slowly.

"And who's this?" she asked, waving good-bye to the trucker she'd just rung up.

"Can you just tell me if she's there?" her voice betrayed her frustration.

"Well, I suppose I can tell you since I ain't got a clue who you's talkin' 'bout," Peg said with attitude. She pulled a cigarette out of her front pocket and put it between her lips.

"No one by the name of Pam works there?"

"That's what I said," she said. "Now I gotta go, customers and all." She hung up and went to retrieve the order Donny had just put up.

"Who was that?" Donny asked.

"Someone asking if a Pam was here."

"What did you tell them?" Donny asked with unmasked concern.

"Just what you told me to say to those kind of calls, I don't know nothing." She placed the plates on a tray. "You think I want to start paying half my check to the IRS? Besides, the gal talked kinda hesitant-like, and its Pamela not Pam. Anyone who needed to talk to her would know that."

The young agent tapped her pen on the name "Pam Bennion" on her list. Earlier that day, she'd been given a list containing names of nearly a hundred people and their phone numbers. Someone in the Bureau had compiled the list from papers found in the home of Carla Godfrey.

So far she'd talked to every repair man Mrs. Godfrey had ever used. She'd also called a few neighbors, a bakery, some grandchildren and a local hairdresser. She circled the name "Pamela Bennion" on the list. This was the first name that hadn't matched the number. It likely meant nothing, but she'd mention it just in case.

Chapter Six

When the kids came home from school, Pamela sat them down and explained what had happened that morning. Kenny accepted his mother's explanations easily. When he asked if he could go next door and play, she was satisfied that his curiosity was appeased. With Darla, she discussed the reasons they should move and was surprised that Darla didn't protest too much. Looking into her daughter's eyes, she could see that she accepted this change as a part of their lives. But Pamela's heart still ached. They deserved a much better life than this.

Sometimes, she almost wished she'd get caught, just to end it all; but when she thought about the consequences, she strengthened her resolve. When she got caught, she would be arrested and the children could be returned to David. She couldn't take that chance. She needed to hide out long enough for her case against David to come together. Carla was supposed to contact her soon about the progress made by the doctor's report. In fact, Pamela had been waiting to hear from her for nearly a week. Once she heard from Carla, she'd have a better idea of what to do. Until then, she'd continue with her plans to move after school ended. She'd already begun researching a few possibilities.

The shift was especially long that night. She hadn't slept well the day before, and she felt heavy with the burden of responsibility she carried. She called Carla around 5:30 a.m. and got her voice mail. She didn't leave a message since she'd never gotten the voice mail before and wasn't sure whether it was okay to leave a message or not. She'd just try again tomorrow.

To her surprise, Bryan showed up a little after 6 a.m. It was a Thursday, not his usual morning for German pancakes, and he was alone. Yesterday's incident made her more uncomfortable than ever, but he didn't bring it up so she relaxed except for her usual caution. She still felt a connection, chemistry, or whatever, and although it continued to bother her, she couldn't seem to help it. She wondered if the closeness was because he was

LDS. Maybe she had sensed his spirit from the beginning, like Mormon karma. Then again, it could simply be because he was one of the few clean-cut, nice-looking gentlemen she interacted with in her life right now. Donny's was a low-end truck stop after all. But whatever the reasons, she knew it was inappropriate for her to feel anything toward this man, and her feelings gave her one more reason to move. But until then, she could continue to be friendly. How long would it be before she met another member of the church anyway?

"You're going to get sick of these things if they're all you eat," she chided when he ordered German pancakes, again.

"Until then, I'll go with my gut."

She smiled and wrote up his order.

"I was wondering," he asked hesitantly when she returned with his plate several minutes later, "if you had plans for Saturday?" She froze, more out of shock than fear. Was he asking her out on a date? Her spine tingled at the possibility.

She avoided his eyes and hoped not to betray her feelings in her voice when she spoke. "Saturday is a family day for us."

"Every few months, my church has a family activity," he continued, not commenting on her response. "This Saturday, we're going to float the Buffalo River. It's just for fun, no pressure or hype about it. We'd love for you and your children to come."

So much for the date possibility; not that she was tempted to accept. He was just being a good member missionary now that he knew she'd had enough interest to attend a meeting. The thought was strangely disappointing. However, the idea of a church activity was almost more than she could refuse. But of course she intended to refuse anyway. "I use my weekends to sleep off my night shifts."

He looked at her for a long time; this time she didn't look away. He seemed to know she wanted to go, and he wasn't giving up easily. "It doesn't start 'til two o'clock," he said softly. She could tell he was trying not to sound pushy, although that was exactly what he was being. "We have about thirty people signed up and we'll only be going a few miles. It's an easy float and I know your kids'll love it. I'd be happy to pick ya'll up if ya like."

"I don't think it will work out," she said, looking away so he wouldn't read the disappointment in her eyes.

He smiled and shrugged his shoulders as he pulled a piece of paper out of his shirt pocket. "This is a flier for the activity," he said as he handed it to her. "If you change your mind we'd love to have you come."

She hesitated but finally took it with a small smile. "Anything else?"

He shook his head and she went about her morning routine. When he left, she was helping a customer and Peg rang him up. It was just as well; she didn't know if she'd have been able to tell him no if he invited her again.

That afternoon, Kenny bounded into the bedroom after school and jumped on the bed. She sat up immediately and began looking around the room with quick jerky movement. "What?" she asked anxiously. "What's wrong, who's here?"

"Nobody, Mom," Kenny said with a little shake of his head that seemed to say *my mom's nuts*. "What's this?"

She blinked a few times and took the paper he was holding out to her. It was the flier Bryan had given her and she berated herself for not throwing it in the garbage when she got home. "It's nothing," she said as she swung her feet over the side of the bed and stretched her arms over her head.

"Darla said it's an invitation to a party," Kenny said, watching her with hopeful eyes. "Are we going to a party?"

"It's not a party," she said as she stood and headed for her robe hanging on the bathroom door. "It's a church activity."

"Oh, are we going to a church activity?"

She turned to look at him, and softened at the hopeful look on his face. They had so few chances to just have fun and she hated denying them this one. For the first time she noticed Darla standing in the doorway, she too looking hopefully at her mother. "Did you put him up to this?" Pamela asked with one eyebrow raised as she tightened the robe around her waist.

"Can we go?" Darla asked.

"Are you sure you want to?" Pamela asked, looking between the two of them. "We don't know anyone there."

"We don't know anyone anyway," Darla added.

Pamela chuckled and shook her head. "There will be rules."

"I don't care," Kenny said with a huge grin.

"Me neither," Darla chimed in.

Finally she put up her hands in surrender. "Okay, you talked me into it." Within moments she was besieged with two sets of arms hugging her intently. She hugged them back and hoped she wasn't making a mistake.

Saturday, she got the kids ready and spent an unusually long time choosing her own clothes. Her wardrobe was pathetic, being made up of clothes packed in Salt Lake two and a half years earlier and some Salvation Army pieces she'd picked up since then. She finally settled on some stretched-out faded jeans and a big, dark T-shirt; neither of which was very flattering. She had a few pair of shorts, but she worried about tipping anyone off on the fact that she wore garments. There were very few people who chose to wear knee-length shorts these days. Hiding her temple garments was the same reason she chose a dark shirt, rather than a lighter colored one that might show the tell-tale neckline. How weird was this? She was finally spending time with Saints and had to hide the truth that she was one of them. She curled her hair at the ends, applied her newly acquired makeup and then shook her head in the mirror. "Why do you even bother?" But she shrugged off her self-criticism. Bryan was not the main reason she was going. However, she refused to admit how many times she'd thought of him since the invitation.

Since that Sunday over a month ago, she missed the church more than ever. She missed the community of saints. She missed the Spirit. She missed being in company with people who lived the way she did and believed what she did. However, in a few weeks she would leave this place and be quickly forgotten. She would become a new woman, in a new town, possibly with a new name. She would, once again, be surrounded by strangers.

But today she had the chance to be with friends—brothers and sisters in Christ—and her heart was rejoicing. Not a soul there would know how important the experience was for her. She knew she might not get another such opportunity for a very long time, so she would treasure it as the rare gift it was.

When she entered the living room, her kids stared at her. "Mom, you look so pretty," Darla said.

"Thank you," she said with a laugh. You'd think she'd become an old hag the way her kids went on and on about a little lipstick and mascara. "Now, you guys remember the instructions?"

"Don't talk about things we're not supposed to talk about," Darla chimed.

"Right," Pamela said with a nod as she grabbed her keys. "And if anyone gets nosey or makes you uncomfortable, you tell me and we'll leave. Okay?"

"Okay," Kenny answered for them both, already standing at the door.

The flier said there would be a potluck dinner afterwards, so they had baked cookies although secretly she didn't plan to stay for the meal; it would be pushing things a little too much. While retrieving the cookies from the kitchen counter, she shooed the kids toward the door. "Let's go."

Bryan spotted them and waved as they walked across the parking lot several minutes later, unable to hide his surprise at their attendance. "I'm so glad you came!" he said excitedly as he placed a welcoming hand on her shoulder. Immediately, bursts of electricity exploded beneath his fingers. He looked at the kids and smiled, welcoming them as well. Their hesitancy reminded Pamela that they'd only met him after she ordered them to pack because someone had followed her home. Luckily, Bryan didn't seem bothered by their somber greeting, although she wondered if perhaps they'd changed their mind about being here. "Let me introduce you to some people," he said, guiding her to a group of people, some of whom were wearing the long shorts she longed for at this moment. The humidity of the day was already making her sweat.

They reached the group, and Bryan began introducing them, leaving out the Brother and Sister prefixes she was sure he normally used. She recognized his sister, from the café, and learned her name was Charlotte. She, along with everyone else in the group, was very friendly. He left the blonde to his right for last. "And this is Barbara," he said with a smile.

The petite blonde extended her hand across the small circle of people and smiled warmly. It took only half a second for Pamela to determine that Barbara was a little rich girl, much like she herself had once been. She was overdressed for a canoe trip with a diamond tennis bracelet on her wrist, half-carat studs in her ears, and she probably paid the mortgage on a salon somewhere in order to achieve the precise shade of blonde to accentuate her large eyes and sculpted features. Perfect eyebrows, perfect skin, perfect nails, and perfect hair added up to a nice chunk of change. Pamela smiled kindly, tried to hide her envy of the lifestyle she'd left behind, and shook the proffered hand. She looked from Barbara to Bryan. *Were they a couple?* she wondered. She didn't have long to wait for the answer. As soon as Barbara retracted her hand she placed it on Bryan's shoulder and leaned against him. *Yes, they were definitely a couple*, Pamela decided. She smiled even wider to cover the momentary twinge of disappointment she felt.

The fact that it bothered her at all, bothered her a lot. Bryan was a nice, good-looking single man; of course he had a girlfriend. His having a girlfriend shouldn't matter to her one bit. Yet, it bothered her a lot, and furthermore, she didn't think they fit together very well.

"So what brought you out to Arkansas?" Barbara asked, still leaning against him as if she needed him to hold her upright. Pamela suspected she had one hand in the back pocket of his swimming trunks, but she couldn't be sure and, of course, she shouldn't care.

Pamela took a few moments to consider her response. Carla had once told her to tell as much of the truth as possible. The more lies, the more likely you were to trip on them. "I needed a fresh start." There was a bit of a pause, as if they were waiting for more information. She acted as if she didn't notice.

"Well, where are you from originally?" Charlotte finally asked.

"There's not a trace of southern in your voice," Barbara added.

"Nor in my pedigree," Pamela said. She didn't like this woman and yet she had no reason not to. "I grew up in California," she lied. She'd adopted her mother's history a long time ago.

"That's a long way from here."

"Yes, it is," she answered evasively.

"Barbara's a foreigner, too," Bryan explained, giving her an affectionate glance. She smiled adoringly, loving the attention. "She's from Fred, Texas."

"What brought you here?" Pamela asked politely

"I sing back-up for a show in Branson," she explained. "We met at church."

Pamela smiled politely. Branson, Missouri, was a show town forty miles north of Harrison. It boasted more live shows every night than New York and Las Vegas combined. It was a hub for senior citizen audiences and, from what she'd heard, offered good, clean, Christian-oriented entertainment. She'd never been there.

Pamela suspected the group not only knew about what Barbara did for a living already, but had heard about it more than once, since the conversation quickly turned to discussing the details of the trip. They were heading down toward Jasper, then stopping at a campground to unload the canoes. They would then float a few miles until they reached another campground, where some trucks would meet them, load up the canoes and take them back to the church. She wanted to take her own car, but soon realized it wasn't an option. It was already arranged to load up the larger vehicles so that fewer people would need to stay behind.

As the conversation continued, she couldn't help wondering how they would react if they knew her whole story. But none of these people knew anything about her, and none of them ever would, so she stopped thinking about it. She would just enjoy the time she had with them.

She didn't have the opportunity to talk with Bryan, or Barbara, very much. They separated themselves from the group and seemed to be having a private conversation of their own, which included little giggles and pats on the shoulder now and then. Pamela wished she didn't notice at all, but she couldn't help glancing at them every few seconds. She felt a strange ache at seeing two people be so comfortable and happy together. In her heart, she wished them luck. After the tragic failure of her marriage, it was hard for her to understand the space Bryan and Barbara were in. It hurt to be so close to it somehow. It seemed to make her feel even more lonely and she placed a hand on each of her children's shoulder. She wondered if Bryan and Barbara were going to get married and then wondered why she cared so much.

Around two thirty, a half hour later than expected (Mormon standard time), they were loaded and driving. Pamela, Darla and Kenny were in the same van as Charlotte and her three children. Bryan and Barbara were driving in another vehicle, which was just as well. Charlotte's husband had had to work that day, she said, or he'd have been the first one on the river. She was very nice, comfortable to be with and they conversed about school and kids throughout the drive. Charlotte didn't press into "before Harrison" issues, but Pamela was still careful. She'd learned she could never be too careful about that.

When they arrived at the river, several canoes were already in the water. Once out of the car, Kenny and Darla followed her hesitantly; they'd never done anything like this and weren't used to being with groups of people. Bryan was helping to unload canoes from the five level racks pulled behind a few of the vans, but as soon as he spotted them, he called another man to take over his job. He wiped his hands on the front of his shorts as he approached them.

"What do we do?" Pamela asked when he reached her. She was feeling out of place, since everyone seemed to know what they were doing except her.

"Well, first we grab life jackets and paddles over there," he pointed to a large pickup, overflowing in the necessary equipment. "Then you grab a canoe," he indicated the line of canoes on the shore. People were dragging them into the water almost as quickly as they were being unloaded from the racks.

She ignored her discomfort and followed his instructions. She secured the life jackets, handed the kids their paddles, and walked toward the river. When she arrived at the canoe, she turned to Bryan, "There are only two seats."

"That's right," he said easily. "Two-man canoes. One of the kids is welcome to go with me."

"Uh," Pamela started, she hadn't anticipated not being with both kids.

"Don't worry," he said, not noticing her discomfort. "Barbara isn't into this kind of thing. She's driving one of the vans down to the landing point. I was going to take one of Charlotte's kids, but she ended up with even numbers."

"It's not that," she said uncomfortably. "I—" She was going to say something about letting one of her children float the river with a stranger, but she wasn't sure how to say it without offending him. Finally, she saw no other option. "Can you stay close to me, so I can watch him?"

"Sure," he said slowly, as if just now realizing her reticence. "If it would make you feel better."

She nodded and turned to Kenny. "Would you like to ride in Bryan's canoe?" she asked as she looked down at her son.

"Okay," he said easily enough. She met Bryan's eyes, embarrassed for not trusting him. "Thanks," she said, although her hesitation still showed in her voice.

"No problem," he said. "We'll be right alongside of you."

He was as good as his word and it became obvious that he'd done this a lot since he knew just how to be sure there was never more than thirty feet between their canoes. Shortly after getting on the river, Bryan produced a small net with which Kenny could fish for turtles. Kenny was in heaven.

However, Darla and Pamela made an "interesting" team. Pamela hadn't canoed since girls' camp twenty years ago and Darla hadn't ever paddled anything. They were slow and uncoordinated for the first while, but finally got the hang of it. Pamela was sure most of the group passed them before they even figured out how to paddle straight. But once they figured it out, Pamela became completely absorbed in the gorgeous surroundings. The river was one more example of how beautiful this area was. Dense trees lined the river, interspersed with rock walls that dripped with tiny water falls. *Utah could use a little of this moisture,* she thought.

It was supposed to be a four-hour float, and several people overturned throughout the trip. Each time they watched it happen, Darla and Pamela exchanged a frightened look. They did not want to experience this river that intimately. Bryan and Kenny stayed dry until Kenny leaned too far forward in an attempt to catch a small turtle sunning itself on a rock. He threw off their balance and the canoe rolled. Pamela watched from about ten yards behind and her first thought was panic. Her baby had just disappeared! She began paddling like a mad woman. Moments later, two heads popped out of the water alongside the overturned canoe. Kenny's eyes were like golf balls and he looked stunned. Bryan let out a hoot of laughter as he shook the water out of his hair now stuck in glossy dark curls across his forehead. Immediately, he looked for Kenny, located him, and swam the few strokes it took to close the gap between them.

"You okay?" Bryan asked, laughter still in his voice. Kenny was still a little dazed. "Kenny?"

"Are there s-snakes in here?" she heard Kenny ask while he looked around fearfully.

"Not anymore," Bryan said, pulling Kenny toward the canoe by his life vest. "Wouldn't you swim away if something fifty times your size fell out of the sky?"

"Are you guys okay?" Pamela asked breathlessly when she was within a few feet of them. Kenny nodded; he even smiled.

"We could use some help righting the canoe," Bryan said with a smile. "Jump in and give me a hand."

Pamela paused for a moment, wondering whether or not he was serious. He silenced her wonderings by starting to laugh. "Looks like you've got a pretty good handle on it," she said dryly.

He laughed again and got the canoe to shore. Bryan climbed out of the water and she inhaled deeply at the tingling sensation that whipped down to her toes. His T-shirt and swimming trunks clung to his body, as water dripped to the rocky shore. Every line of his body was accentuated in such detail that her stomach flipped. He looked like the guy in the Diet Coke commercials all those years ago. She closed her eyes quickly and turned her head. She didn't think she had the ability to notice things like that anymore and she certainly didn't want to start noticing them now. She forced herself not to look at Bryan again and instead watched her son intently. Kenny scrambled onto the bank, his face brightening as he realized what a great adventure he'd just had. Bryan emptied the water from their craft and within a minute, they were back on the river and Pamela could look at Bryan again without her wicked thoughts intruding.

"Can we do that again?" she heard Kenny beg a few minutes later.

"Sure," Bryan agreed as he paddled on one side and then the other, raising his voice to make sure Pamela could hear him. "Only this time, we'll take your mom and sister with us."

Darla turned to look at her mom in abject horror. "He's kidding," Pamela assured her. Then, raising her own voice, added. "You're kidding, aren't you, Bryan!"

He just laughed, which was not the reassurance she wanted. Within half an hour, Kenny had tipped their canoe again. This time, rather than rushing to their rescue, Pamela immediately back paddled to keep a safe distance from Bryan while he was in the water. "You're in with us next time," he sang as they hauled the boat to shore again. Kenny clapped his hands, loving the game. Pamela was sure to keep her distance while she chided her son on being a good guest. He showed no sign of having heard her.

A light rain began to fall. She didn't mind, although she knew her makeup and hair would be ruined if it went on much longer. "See, ya'll gettin' wet anyway," Bryan crooned from a few yards down river. She just gave him an irritated smile. A hundred yards farther down the river, Kenny began shaking their canoe again. "It's getting old," Bryan warned him, but Kenny didn't listen. Within seconds, the bottom of the boat was in the air again. Pamela just shook her head; she felt badly for Bryan this time. Kenny's head popped up shortly and only then did Pamela realize she'd been holding her breath.

"Where's Bryan?" Darla asked a few seconds later. Pamela began scanning the river; there was no sign of him anywhere. Is he under the boat? she thought, looking at their inverted canoe. Should she jump in and save him? Just then, she felt a shudder go through her own canoe.

"Mom!" Darla cried fearfully. A hand suddenly appeared on the edge of the canoe and in a split second she realized his threats had not been idle. The boat flipped, throwing her into the water at the precise second she opened her mouth to scream. The river water stifled her yelp as she gulped in a mouthful of the dirty water. Immediately, she pushed for the surface. She came up sputtering and spitting while looking for her daughter. She spotted Darla and swam toward her, slowed by the buoyancy of the life vest. To her relief, there was anger instead of fear in Darla's eyes when she reached her. "I can't believe he did that," Darla spat as she pushed her hair off her face.

"Me either," Pamela echoed evenly, looking around for their attacker. He was a few yards down river, smiling from ear to ear and already dragging their canoe to the shore.

"You gals okay?" Charlotte asked from her boat. She'd been hanging out behind them most of the trip; she was piloting her four-year-old son and floating the river at a leisurely pace.

"Yes, thank you," Pamela said, moving toward Bryan and her boat.

"Chivalry has died with you, hasn't it?" Charlotte hollered to her brother.

"What's that?" he called over his shoulder as he pulled the canoe onto shore.

"She said you have no manners!" Pamela echoed, causing everyone in hearing range to laugh and making her wonder if she'd been too harsh.

He just laughed with everyone else and returned to the water to get his and Kenny's boat. Pamela dragged Darla and herself to the bank and crawled out, twenty pounds heavier. The water streamed off them as they shared a disgruntled look, although the twinkle in her daughter's eye told her it hadn't been a completely negative experience. She didn't feel at all positive however; she hated wet Levis. They dumped the water out of their canoe and got back in, sure to give Kenny and Bryan a wider berth this time. There was a bend in the river twenty yards ahead and as they turned with the river, Pamela's eyes narrowed. On a stretch of sand, men were pulling out canoes, collecting life vests and directing the group toward the vans. "You knew we were almost done, didn't you?" she accused loudly toward Bryan's wet back.

He laughed and shrugged his shoulders. "We were running out of time," he said as he jumped out of his canoe, without even tipping it she noticed. In her mind, she began devising a way to reciprocate his prank, but just as an elaborate plan began to form, a blonde bombshell appeared on shore.

"There y'are," Barbara said cheerily. "People started pullin' in half an hour ago." She had her hands on her hips. Bryan immediately ran toward her. It wasn't until he was five feet in front of her that she realized his intention. "Don't you dare," she shrieked, turning and running to the vans still hidden in the trees. He followed her. A few seconds later, a shrill scream rang back to the group on shore. Pamela was helping Darla out of the boat and smiled. Apparently, Bryan had caught her. She looked up in time to catch Charlotte roll her eyes. Charlotte met her eye a moment later and offered a weak, apologetic smile. Pamela didn't push for an explanation. Instead she helped a shivering Kenny out of his life vest. The three of them began walking to the van.

"So what brought you to Harrison?" Charlotte asked, causing Pamela to turn around. The question had been asked before, but now that it was just the two of them she didn't want to be rude.

"Change, I guess," she said easily, slowing her step so that she was parallel with Charlotte. "I've never lived in this part of the country."

"And what do you think so far?"

"It's great," she said. "The kids and I love it." She felt herself steeling for the remaining questions and sure enough Charlotte began asking about the "before Harrison" life they had lived. Pamela answered short and fast, but quickly turned the conversation to Charlotte and her life. Most people loved to talk about themselves and so she acted almost overly interested in order to keep the conversation away from herself.

When they reached the last van—apparently, they were the last of the group—Barbara was nowhere to be seen, but Bryan's smile had faded considerably.

"Did the Princess stomp off in a huff?" Charlotte asked innocently when no one except she and Pamela were in hearing range. "That's so unlike her," she added with exaggerated sarcasm.

Bryan gave her a forced smile. "Just get in," he said. She acted shocked by his brusque response but the teasing grin on her face further convinced Pamela that Charlotte wasn't fond of her brother's girlfriend. For some reason, that knowledge made Pamela feel better.

They arrived at the church around six o'clock to find the pot luck dinner in full swing. Pamela had already decided not to stay, they'd had a great time but she didn't want to push it. They would take the cookies home and enjoy them at their own kitchen table. She was herding the kids toward the car when Charlotte called her name and waved her over. Pamela turned but didn't make any move to join the group.

"You've gotta stay and eat," Charlotte said, grabbing her arm.

"Oh, I don't know," Pamela said weakly.

Charlotte pulled her toward the group. "Come on."

"We're all wet," Pamela said in her final attempt to get out of it.

"We all are, that's why we're eating outside."

Pamela had no more protests so she looked at her kids and they just smiled, staring at the tables of food. "Okay," she said with a sigh of surrender. Surely it wouldn't be too dangerous to eat with these people. "I have cookies in the car."

Charlotte narrowed her eyes and shook her head. "Well, go get 'em; I'll wait for you right here."

When Pamela returned, Charlotte stayed at her side while they made up plates. Darla and Kenny were quickly invited to join the other children on blankets on the lawn while Pamela and Charlotte sat with adults at a table. Bryan and Barbara were already there, but although Barbara didn't look the least bit worse for wear, she was making a point of not speaking to Bryan. He accepted his punishment easily enough and joined with the rest of the group in recounting their river adventure. For the most part, Pamela was content to listen, absorb the experience, and enjoy the party. Despite her continued discomfort, this was the most comfortable she'd been with people in a very long time and she found herself just wanting to savor the happy experience.

A little while later, an older gentleman stood on a chair and waved everyone to silence. Pamela had to turn in her chair to see him.

"I'd like to thank everyone for coming out today," he began. "Especially those of you who are not usually part of our congregation." Pamela looked around and saw a few heads nod; that surprised her. She didn't realize there were other nonmembers in attendance. "And I'd like to share a story with all of you before you go." The audience quieted down even more as his mood got serious. "There was once a man who went to a beach to take a morning walk. On this particular beach, thousands of starfish were washed onto the shore every night. If they weren't taken back to sea with the tide they would certainly dry up and die in the afternoon sun. It was a familiar sight for this man, and he thought little of it. But this one morning, there was a boy running along the beach throwing starfish back into the ocean. As he approached the young man, he shook his head. "Boy, you're wasting your time," he said. "There are thousands of starfish on this beach. This is nature, it's inevitable, and you can't possibly make a difference."

The boy looked at him, starfish in hand, and flung it into the sea. "Sir," he said, "with all due respect, I made a difference to that one."

The man telling the story paused and looked around. "I want all of you to know that the difference you make in the lives of others is profound. A seemingly simple act is often a life-saving service for someone else. We're so grateful to those of you that made this trip possible today. The Lord loves each and every one of us. He knows our hearts and he knows our potential. He rejoices when we gather together. May God be with you 'til we meet again." He then folded his arms and bowed his head. Pamela tried to keep from sobbing as he evoked a blessing on all those in attendance. But as he finished, she couldn't hold back her tears any longer and excused herself from the table. Walking quickly, she headed for a grove of trees, away from everyone. How embarrassing to break down like this.

"Pamela."

She turned to see Bryan hurrying after her and she wiped at her eyes. "Are you okay?"

"Yes," she said in a cracking voice. "Could you keep an eye on my children for a minute?"

He looked at her with concern, but nodded. She smiled and turned again towards the trees, wrapping her arms around herself and thinking of the story. She thought of the countless times people told her she didn't have a chance; she thought of the many times she told herself the same thing. Often she'd berated herself for putting everyone through this—her parents, her children, and herself. She didn't know if she would be allowed full membership in the church when she returned to Utah. It was likely that she'd even spend time in prison for what she had done. But just like the boy and the starfish, she knew she was making a difference. Every day she kept Darla safe was making a difference. Every day that Kenny escaped his father's twisted example was making a difference. Every time someone considered "what would make her do such a thing," she was making a difference.

When trees safely surrounded her, she sank to her knees on the wet grass and bowed her head. Feeling the Spirit among these good people had taken her by surprise and it was overwhelming. She began praying, offering her sincere thanks for all she'd been given. She thanked her Father in Heaven for her children, thanked Him for their safety and thanked Him for her testimony of the gospel. She was so grateful to have come today, to be among the saints and partake of their spirits, to show her children that there were other people like them in the world and that it was okay to have fun.

Through this trial, she had discovered so much about what love is, what it isn't, and where the truly important things in life were found. She was so much stronger than she ever guessed, and at that moment she knew—without a doubt—that she was making a difference. And someday this would all be over; someday her children would understand and the Lord would be with them then, just as he was now. When her prayer was finished, she stayed there, absorbing the Spirit that surrounded her.

"Pamela," said a soft voice.

Still on her knees, she turned and looked into Bryan's face as he crouched beside her. His voice was so soft; his eyes so searching that she didn't feel anxious or uncomfortable. "You can trust me," he said as he looked at her deeply.

Pamela smiled and wished it were true. In a sense he was right, she could trust him with some things. "I used to be Mormon," she said, looking off towards the road. "And I miss it."

Bryan raised his eyebrows in surprise and paused for a moment. "There's always a way back," he finally said.

"I know," she said, rising to her feet. "I'm trying to find it."

"I can help you," he said. She didn't doubt his sincerity. She stared at him, considered his kindness and thought back to the connection she had felt with him that first day and every other time they'd been together since.

"Can you?" she asked pointedly, cocking her head to the side.

"I'm a convert to the church," Bryan explained. "I've been a member for four years, but I still remember the difference between having the Spirit in my life and not having the Spirit. I understand where you are, I can help you the rest of the way back. We all can."

It was a tempting offer, even if he didn't know what it was she really meant about finding help. But it wouldn't work to allow him to get too close, or anyone else for that matter. It would only make things more complicated. Barbara came to mind, and she was reminded of just how complicated things already were. She had to use her own strength. "It's something I have to do on my own."

There was a brief pause as he seemed to consider what she had said. "We can still help you."

"You have," she said with a sincere smile. "More than you know."

The wind blew a lock of hair across her eyes. She reached up to push it away and brushed against his hand, intent on doing the same thing. She paused for a moment before lowering her hand and allowing him to tuck the hair behind her ear. The intimacy of his touch surprised her and she met his eyes. For a moment she just stared at him. It was as if he could feel her very soul. Where had this tenderness come from? She wondered. Did he make everyone feel this way?

"I'd better get going," she finally said, stepping back a bit. "And you'd better get back to Barbara. She'll be worried."

"Will you come to church tomorrow?"

"I'm not sure," she finally admitted, putting her armor back on and creating a distance between them.

Together with Charlotte they gathered the kids. The three of them waved good-bye before Bryan and his sister turned back to help clean up the dinner. Bryan thought back to the passages of scripture that said 'and his heart rejoiced' and he felt he could truly relate to it. It had only been six months since he was called as ward mission leader. He'd helped two people prepare for baptism since then, but Pamela felt different. He'd seen something in Pamela that was glorious and it seemed as if . . . no one but he would be able to help her. *Was that possible?* He wondered. Through little things she'd said and done, he'd guessed that she had some kind of connection to the church, but to have her admit it out loud, and to express interest in coming back was wonderful. He was anxious to help her, despite her surety that she didn't need help.

"She's very nice," Charlotte said, interrupting his thoughts.

"She is, isn't she," he said with a smile. "She's been a member," he continued.

"She *is* a member."

"What?" he asked in surprise. What did she mean *she is a member?*

Charlotte opened her mouth to answer but then closed it, looking past him. "I think the Princess would like a word with you."

He turned and looked toward Barbara standing at the corner of the building. He turned back to hear Charlotte's explanation, but she was already on her way back to the group. Turning again, he walked toward Barbara, putting out his arm when he reached her. She took it like she often did when they went walking; it was very . . . Gone With the Wind. They headed back toward the tables, but Barbara tugged on his arm, steering him away from the group and he followed obediently. He wanted to talk to her about Pamela anyway. Barbara's friendship might just play an important role in this situation.

"So what were you and Pamela talking about?"

Bryan looked at her quickly, surprised by the edge in her voice. "What do you mean?"

She shrugged. "She ran off into the trees and a few minutes later you ran off after her. Everyone was watching," she said accusingly. "It makes me wonder if something's going on that I should know about."

"You have got to be kidding," Bryan said with disbelief. His earlier lightness faded quickly. "She's a potential investigator, she looked upset, and I went to see if she was all right."

"Was she?" Barbara asked as she pulled him to a stop and turned to face him. Her pretty face was critical and scrunched up, making her much less attractive. She appeared to think he'd done something inappropriate.

The look on her face convinced him this was very serious to her. He knew he'd better treat it as such. "She's a nice person, Barbara," he said in an even tone, despite the fact that he felt this whole discussion was ridiculous. He considered telling her everything he knew about Pamela's past membership, but he decided against it. Her attitude sparked a certain distrust in him. "She's investigating the church and I'm the ward mission leader."

Barbara was silent. "When I hear about you tipping her canoe over and taking her kids under your wing, it makes me wonder. And then you take off after her in front of the whole ward." She paused as if contemplating whether to say more, finally she continued. "When you look at her there's something . . . something that doesn't seem right."

Now he was getting angry. He took a deep breath, amazed that Barbara was taking it this far. "My dad left when I was two years old, Barbara. Mom really struggled to raise us. Maybe Pamela reminds me of her, maybe I see a certain similarity that makes me want to help her any way I can. If you had come down the river with us, and spent some time getting to know her, you would not be so suspicious."

For several seconds, there was silence. He could see her weighing the information, but could also see that she wasn't softening. There was nothing more he could say, or would say, to defend his honor.

Barbara put her hands on her hips and cocked her head prettily to the side. "Isn't this where you tell me how much you love me and that no one can come between us?"

Bryan clenched his jaw, his own streak of southern stubbornness kicking into high gear. "If you're telling me what you want to hear, then I guess it's already been said."

Her eyes went cold. She turned and stalked off toward the parking lot, leaving Bryan to shake his head after her. He hadn't meant to anger her that way, but he hated being manipulated into saying just the right things, in just the right way. He'd call her tomorrow, he decided, as he walked back to the tables. Maybe time would restore her reason.

After helping put down the tables Bryan caught up with Charlotte on her way to her car. "What did you mean when you said she was a member?" he asked as he ran the last few steps. She looked at him quickly.

"What did you mean when you said she *used* to be a member?" she countered

"She told me," he explained. "When I caught up to her in the trees, she was praying and said she used to be a member."

Charlotte stopped and looked at him thoughtfully. He returned her stare with a confused one of his own. "I guess I should be impressed that you didn't notice."

"Notice what?" he asked in exasperation.

"It's hard to hide a garment line in a wet T-shirt."

Chapter Seven

The next few days were wonderfully different for Pamela. She didn't go to church on Sunday. Despite how badly she wanted to, she knew she couldn't risk the attention she'd draw to herself. Maybe next week would be better. But she could still feel the spiritual rejuvenation she'd gained from that one afternoon in the company of saints and she basked in it. Things seemed clearer, the children seemed more at peace and life just seemed a little lighter for all of them. The fact that she hadn't heard from Carla didn't bother her as much as it had before. The move she was still planning once school let out for the summer didn't even seem so bad. There was a peace that she'd missed for a long time.

Tuesday afternoon, Pamela was considering whether or not to go to church the next week, a thought that had occupied a lot of her time lately, while she made dinner: tuna casserole. The ringing of the doorbell interrupted her thoughts. She looked at the clock and tried to control her anxiety. They received very few visitors and when people dropped in, it always made her nervous. It was just after five o'clock. Darla had gone to Jenny's house and Kenny was watching cartoons until it was time to pick her up at six. It was probably some Jehovah's Witnesses. "I'll get it," she called to Kenny who was already half-way to the door. To her surprise, Jenny's mother was at the door, looking both worried and irritated.

"Darla's upset," she explained as soon as Pamela opened the door. "She's in the car." Without asking Pamela to follow, she headed for the silver sedan parked on the side of the road. Pamela followed quickly, ignoring the fact that she was barefoot. Darla was in the back seat, her knees pulled up to her chest and her eyes swollen from crying. As soon as she saw her mother through the window, she started to cry again. Pamela took a deep breath and said a little prayer in her heart as she quickly opened the door and pulled Darla into her arms, although she could barely hold her. Darla cried softly and clung to her mother as if she were still a baby. Pamela soothed her and told her she would be okay. Then she looked at Jenny's mother reproachfully.

"What happened?"

"Nothing," Jenny's mother said, still wavering between sympathy and annoyance. "The girls were playing in Jenny's room and all of a sudden she came running downstairs saying Darla was crying. I went up to talk to her, and found her curled up in a corner. All she would say was that she wanted to go home. Jenny said nothing happened. You really ought to get a phone."

"That's really not the issue," Pamela finally said in clipped tones. Until she found out what had happened, it would only make things worse to freak out on this woman. However, she'd be all over her like tar and feathers if anything *had* happened.

"Is she okay?" Jenny's mom asked.

"If she isn't, you'll be the first to hear about it!" Pamela said as she headed for the door, where Kenny stood looking concerned. Just before entering the house, she heard the car drive away. She took Darla to her bedroom, laid her on the bed, and covered her up. "I'm going to finish dinner," she said, smoothing the hair off Darla's face. "When I'm done, we'll talk about it."

She needed the time to calm down and push her own fears aside. Otherwise, she knew she'd overreact. She reminded herself of the other times when Darla had misconstrued a look or been frightened when a strange man said hello. However, Pamela couldn't ignore the fact that she'd never reacted this intensely before.

When she returned to Darla several minutes later, she sat on the edge of the bed and asked Darla what had happened, steeling herself for the worst. Hesitantly at first, Darla explained that she and Jenny were playing Barbie's in Jenny's room when her big brother came home. His bedroom is next to Jenny's and they could hear him laughing with his friends. "And then they came into the room," Darla said and the fear returned to her eyes.

"What happened then?" Pamela asked with forced calmness.

"They said they wanted us to go get them a soda," Darla said reproachfully.

"And . . ." Pamela prodded.

Darla's chin started to quiver. "Jenny said no and her brother started to tickle her. Jenny kept telling him to stop, but he wouldn't. I tried to leave the room but he grabbed me." Her chin started to quiver as she continued.

"He wouldn't let me go, Mom."

"He tickled you?" Pamela asked.

Darla shook her head. "He just held my arm like this," she closed one small hand around her other arm. "He wouldn't let me out of the room."

Pamela stared at her daughter's re-creation of being restrained. "Was Jenny laughing?"

Darla paused, but eventually nodded as she put her hands down.

"Other than holding you back, did he do anything else?"

Darla again shook her head. Pamela moved so she was leaning against the headboard next to Darla. She took a breath, relieved that it hadn't been worse. "Sometimes big brothers and sisters tease the little kids in their families. It doesn't sound like he was going to hurt her and I think—"

"But he wouldn't stop, even when she told him to," Darla whispered and Pamela's chest tightened. "And he wouldn't let go of me." At this moment Pamela would have given anything to be facing her ex-husband with any kind of weapon. He had ruined Darla's whole perception of people—men especially.

"It was wrong for him to hold you back," Pamela explained. "But I don't think he meant to hurt you. He let go when he knew you were upset, didn't he?"

Darla nodded. Pamela smiled and repeated much of what she had already said, emphasizing that Darla hadn't done anything wrong she had just misunderstood. "I'm sorry this happened, but I'm proud of you for following your feelings," she finished. "I'll talk to Jenny's mom and make sure it doesn't happen again."

"I don't want to go to Jenny's house again," Darla said resolutely. "I only want her to come here."

"That's probably a good idea," Pamela agreed, making a mental note to send Jenny's mom a note apologizing for her immediate reaction and thanking her for driving Darla home. "Are you okay now?"

Darla nodded, but Pamela could see that she was still upset. Maybe "confused" was a better word. She had information overload for such a young girl, she knew too much, feared too much, and without even noticing it found implication in situations that were harmless.

"I sure do love you, sweetie," Pamela said as she stood. Bending down, she planted a kiss on her daughter's forehead, wishing there was more she could do to take the hurt away. "When you're ready to eat, come out. Okay?"

Darla nodded and Pamela left the room, still wrestling with her anger and sadness. For the first year and a half that they had been in hiding, Darla had access to psychiatric care. The last therapist felt that Darla was dealing with everything very well. Her progress was one of the deciding factors in moving out on their own. It was disappointing to realize she was still struggling. Perhaps the counseling hadn't been enough after all, and she wondered if Darla would ever overcome this. Her heart sank at the thought that even after everything she'd done, she could never change what had happened. She could never replace the innocence Darla's father had destroyed.

———

Bryan showed up at the diner the next morning; Wednesday of course. Pamela was hoping. A few days before, she had showed Donny how to make strawberry crepes and the locals had caught on to them already. Weird, since even the ever-popular Waffle House restaurants didn't offer fruit toppings, unless you consider pecans a fruit. If this kept up, Donny would have to hire another morning waitress. She'd never imagined that deep southern folk would like her recipes so much. She had barely enough time to say hello and good-bye to Bryan. When she rang him up at the cash register, however, he asked her about attending church again. She was a little irritated by the reminder that, once again, it was her interest in the church that sparked his interest in her. At the same time, she wanted to kick herself for thinking that. Why did she care?

"The kids want to," she said. "But I'm not sure I'm ready yet." The incident at Jenny's house reinforced their need to avoid outside relationships—even with Bryan. She longed to go to church again, but it just didn't seem worth the risks.

He was quiet for a moment, and she read the disappointment in his eyes before he looked away. "I don't want to sound pushy, but—"

She nodded and she retrieved his change. "I appreciate your help, but I need to do this my way."

He gave her one of his long stares and then nodded, as if he understood, although she knew he didn't. "All right," he finally said, taking his change and putting it in his pocket.

She smiled and nodded as the customer behind Bryan handed her his check. Bryan moved out of the way, looking as if he wanted to say more. Finally, he just left. She felt badly and wanted to soften the exchange, but decided it was better this way. She'd been honest and he would just need to accept that.

Darla stayed home from school. Pamela suggested it, mostly so she could spend some one-on-one time with her. They waved good bye to Kenny and then baked some brownies. Soon, Darla's countenance had brightened. Pamela told her stories from her own childhood that made her daughter laugh. They ate brownies and Spaghetti-O's for lunch before Pamela, barely conscious after working all night, laid down to sleep. Darla kept Kenny busy when he got home from school and Pamela slept until almost six. Darla seemed much better after the extra attention, so Pamela decided the yawns and heavy eyelids were worth it.

When she arrived at work just before ten, there was a woman sitting at the counter. She had shortly cropped red hair that was purposely tousled into some new age look that was unusual in this part of Arkansas. Bonnie, the evening waitress that night, introduced Pamela at each table, as was their routine, and then pointed out the counter people. Bonnie described the red-head as a "city girl" and said she'd been coming in every couple hours all day for a cup of coffee. She'd been sitting there for over an hour this time, reading the paper and smoking her cigarettes. After Bonnie left, Pamela took the coffee pot around. The woman put her hand over her cup, but looked at Pamela for moment, smiling slowly. "Can I get you anything?" Pamela asked, curious as to the woman's scrutiny.

"No, I was just leaving," the woman said as she stood, retrieved her purse and laid down a ten-dollar bill. As she walked off, Pamela called after her.

"Ma'am," she said, heading for the register. "Let me get your change."

"Don't worry about it, sweetheart," she said in a condescending tone. "I think you need it more than I do."

Pamela's smile faded as she watched the woman leave.

"Don't worry about them city folk," Donny said from behind the cook's counter. Obviously, he had overheard the woman's insult. "They wouldn't know manners if they took their Mama on a hayride."

Pamela smiled to show that it was no big deal, but the comment made her feel very small. Did she look like some country bumpkin? Or did she just look pathetic?

———

"David, are you okay?" Carrie asked after watching him from the doorway for a moment. "Mom was asking about you."

David turned from the kitchen window and smiled at the rather homely brunette he'd been dating for the last few months. They'd met when David's law firm represented the school where she worked in a real estate dispute with a neighboring business. Her shy, quiet personality had interested him immediately, and her personal circumstances had been icing on the cake. She was just the kind of woman he could start over with. Carrie was perfect for him.

"I'm fine," he said as he walked over to her. For a few moments he looked into her face, finally taking both her hands in his. "I think it's time that I speak to you and your mom." When he looked up, her eyes were wide, her mouth slightly open. He'd invited them to his condo for dinner tonight for this very reason. So far it was going exactly as he planned.

Carrie's father had passed away when she was very young so she had no siblings. Her mother had never remarried. When Carrie was seventeen, and three months pregnant, she married "under duress" as her mother put it. The marriage produced two daughters before it ended; Carrie had remained single ever since. When David's attention turned her way, she sopped it up like a sponge. She wasn't the first woman he had pursued since the divorce, but she was the perfect mix of desperation, sweetness, and naïve expectations.

Within a few minutes, David sat in a recliner across from Carrie and her mother. He found it rather amazing that they could both fit on one loveseat. Carrie was far from trim, and her mother's girth dismissed any hope that her shape would improve with time. But David had decided long ago not to let that bother him, and it didn't. He'd married for looks and pedigree once before—he wouldn't make another mistake. This time he wanted adulation and complete control.

Both women looked at him expectantly as he cleared his throat. "This is a little uncomfortable," he began with a shy smile. "But I feel it's time that I cleared up some things." They blinked almost in unison and he continued. "I'm sure that you have some questions about my previous marriage and divorce." He caught an almost guilty look pass between them and nodded his understanding. "I've been accused of horrible things, so horrible that I've avoided bringing it up before now because I wanted to make sure that you knew me well enough to know how utterly impossible the allegations against me are. It's come to the point, however, that you deserve to know the whole truth from my own lips."

He took a deep breath and clasped his hands in his lap. "This is so hard," he finally said softly. In an instant, Carrie was kneeling beside him;

he resisted the urge to laugh at the compassion in her face. She placed her hand on his knee and gave him a sympathetic smile. He gave her a grateful look, "took strength" from her support, and sat up a little taller. "Gloria and I married just before I graduated from law school," he continued, allowing a hint of wistfulness into his voice. "She was only eighteen, eight years younger than me, and we were both very idealistic. For a while, we were pretty happy. I had a good job and made enough money to indulge her extravagant tastes. She tinkered around in college for the first few years and we looked forward to our future." he explained. "But . . . well, Gloria was always a little bit unstable."

He watched Carrie's mother straighten a little and knew she wanted as much dirt on this ex-wife as she could get. He had no problem indulging her. "She was very spoiled as a child and very demanding as an adult. Nothing I did was ever enough for her. She also suffered bouts of depression, on and off, for those first few years. It was something we could control until Nicholas was born. After she had him, she really went downhill. She had to take medication and I hired a nanny to take care of the children. I did everything I could to help her," he said sadly. "But, as usual, nothing I did was enough. She would stay in bed for days at a time and often erupt into angry rages. It was horrible. I was afraid for her, but even more afraid for the children." He paused for several seconds, waiting for their discomfort to increase.

Looking up, he met their eyes. "I'm ashamed to admit that when she filed for divorce, I was relieved. I had taken care of her for so long, and it had become so very unfair to the kids. I had no doubt that I would get the children, since she was always saying that she couldn't take care of them. But I was wrong. She asked for full custody, something we both knew she couldn't handle. Right then, I knew that I had a fight on my hands, but I had no idea she would do what she did to me." His eyes filled with tears on cue and his chin even trembled. "The fact that she would accuse me of . . . of hurting my own daughter was devastating." He placed a hand on his chest and looked at Carrie; her eyes were also filled with tears. "I was shocked at first, but then I realized that she was a lot sicker than I previously thought. I had to make sure that the children didn't end up with her and her twisted thoughts. The divorce was bitter, but I hoped she would come around. I now believe that she was so mentally unstable that she truly believed I had done those things. I think she nearly convinced Katie that I did them, too." Another long pause for effect. "The case she made was ridiculous," he finally continued. "The court thought so, too. The judge didn't even send the case to trial, it was so stupid. But I had no idea that she would actually steal my children." He brought his hands to his face as if to hold back his emotion.

Carrie placed her hand on his back and rested her head on his shoulder. The room was silent. When he finally looked up, he barely hid a smile at the sympathetic looks on their faces. "It's been a horrible nightmare for me," he said. "But I've just recently realized that I can't wallow forever." The sympathy on their faces turned to expectation. He turned and looked at Carrie. "Carrie has shown me what real love is all about. And although the pain of losing my children will never go away, I feel like I'm ready to start over." He looked back at her mother, whose cheeks were already wet with tears of joy. "Carrie has reminded me of the joy God has promised everyone, even me. I know that it will still take time, that we both have things to overcome from our previous marriages, but I want to ask for your blessing." He smiled warmly at the way her mother's face lit up. "I want to know that Carrie and I have your support as we continue to learn about one another." Now he turned to look at Carrie as silent tears slid down her cheeks as well. "Your daughter is an amazing woman, the kind of woman I want to spend the rest of my life with."

Just then, a slightly chubby six-year-old ran into the room. Carrie turned to face her with an expectant look. "Mom," the child pouted. "Anne-Marie won't share the popcorn." Carrie began to stand, but David put a hand on her shoulder as he quickly came to his feet.

"I'll take care of it," he said as he took the little girl's hand and walked with her from the room. When he was gone, Carrie looked at her mother. "So what do you think?"

"He seems like a wonderful man," her mother cooed. "I can't believe how much he's gone through." Carrie nodded her agreement.

"But isn't he great," Carrie bubbled, coming to sit next to her mother once more. "Isn't he the kind of man Daddy would have wanted me to marry?"

"Of course he is," her mother replied, patting her daughter's knee. "He goes to church doesn't he?"

Carrie paused for just a minute. "Of course he does," she finally said, although she wasn't certain just how active he was. He'd explained to her how hard it was to go to church and feel people censure him there. But he said he was still trying. She believed that he was sincere, and that was enough for her.

"Then he's perfect," her mother said with a little laugh. "He'll make a wonderful father to those girls of yours."

"I know," Carrie beamed, amazed that she had ever found such a man as David. "I just know he will."

————

The encounter with the redheaded woman soured Pamela's mood for the rest of the night. When Bryan came in that morning, she was far from cheerful, although she tried to hide it as best she could. She wished he'd just go back to coming only on Wednesdays; she was much too keyed up when he was here. His friend Larry was with him again and she said good morning to both of them in what she hoped was a normal tone.

"Are you okay?" Bryan asked when she brought him his plate a while later. "You look like something's bothering you."

"I'm fine," she said flatly, avoiding his eyes. "Just tired, I guess."

"Have you ever noticed that you use being tired as your excuse for everything?" he gave her a half smile, which she didn't return. Instead she shot him a look devoid of any humor. She wasn't up to insults or banter, and really didn't care which category his comment fell into.

"If you worked nearly fifty hours a week, raised two kids alone and tried to stretch every dollar into three, being tired would be your excuse, too." She turned and marched back to the counter. She didn't have any patience today, but when she returned a little later, both men remained silent and she wanted to kick herself.

"I'm sorry," she said half-heartedly. "I'm having an off day." She smiled weakly at Larry, who smiled uncomfortably. This was only the second time he'd come; she doubted he'd come back.

"That's okay," Bryan said sincerely.

"I'll feel better tomorrow," she said as Peg breezed through the door with her trademark "Mornin' y'all." She was almost ten minutes late. "I've got to get going," she added before turning toward Peg.

She immediately turned the till over to Peg and didn't introduce the tables in hopes that she could still beat the school bus to her house. With heavy feet, she headed for her car, not paying much attention to anything going on around her.

"How's it going, Gloria?"

She froze instantly at hearing her name and looked up. Leaning against her car was the redhead from last night. The woman dropped her cigarette and twisted her black leather boot on top of the smoking stub to put it out. Pamela just stared at her, too shocked to come up with words. "Yeah, I know who you are," the woman added. "And I know what you've done."

Pamela swallowed. "Who are you?" she finally managed to say.

"It doesn't really matter, does it," she said with a half-grin. "All that matters is who sent me."

"I know who sent you," Pamela said. Only a private investigator would talk to her, and only David would hire a PI.

"You're a smart one," the woman said with a little click of her tongue. "And that's why I'm doing you a favor." Pamela narrowed her eyes, not trusting the woman. "I was supposed to find you and report your whereabouts to David," she said, her voice no longer sarcastic and demeaning. "He's anxious to get this over with."

"I'm sure he is, so what's the favor?" Pamela snapped. She was too anxious to stand around and shoot the bull; she had to get home.

"I'm giving you a head start."

"A head start?" Pamela repeated after a moment of shocked silence.

"I'll wait 'til Saturday to tell David where you are; that gives you two days to clear out; for good, this time. You ought to be able to make some distance before anyone figures you've gone."

Pamela stared at the woman for several seconds, trying to read her eyes. "Why would you do that?"

"Because I've had a chance to talk to your ex-husband," the woman said, her voice sounding sincere. "I'd do the same thing you're doing if I were you. He has no doubt he'll get the kids and you'll get nothing but jail time."

Pamela stared at her for several moments. So this woman believed her instead of David? That was a first. David had a way of charming everyone he talked to into believing, without a doubt, that he was innocent and Gloria was crazy. Why did this woman see through his lies when no one else could? It didn't make sense. The redhead moved away from the car. "You'd better hurry," she said. "I'm sure you need all the time you can get."

Pamela ran the remaining few feet to her car. She opened the door and was just about to step inside when she looked at the woman again. She knew she wasn't being told the truth, that something wasn't right, but she didn't have time to figure it out. "Thank you," she said skeptically.

"Don't mention it," the woman said, scanning the parking lot as if looking for eavesdroppers. "Now go."

Gloria got into her car and pulled out of the parking space quickly. She had to get home; she had to catch the kids before they left for school.

Chapter Eight

The redhead watched until the old Toyota was out of sight before sauntering back to her car, a crooked grin of satisfaction on her lips. Once inside the car she punched a number into her cellular phone and put it to her ear. After two rings a male voice said hello.

"She's packing her bags as we speak," she said with satisfaction.

"You're sure?"

"Why wouldn't she?" the woman countered. "She didn't take it hook, line, and sinker, but she's not going to pass up a break like this."

"Good," David said. "Did you find anything out about the federal investigation?"

"Nothing concrete, just that they've made a few arrests in *an* underground organization. There's at least a dozen of those outfits, but their success with this particular network has been centered in the south, so it's a definite possibility. I guess you're hoping she's in another one, right?"

"I didn't pay you a thousand dollars to get her out of there just to have the feds find her," David said with irritation. She rolled his eyes, alpha males were not her type. "You're still going to keep your ear to the ground for a couple more weeks, right?"

"Sure," she said as she tapped an unlit cigarette on the dashboard. "I'll let you know if anything turns up. Keep in mind that if she is involved in this organization, she'll probably be making contact today. That could get her caught."

There was silence on the other end of the phone. "I already thought of that," David agreed. "Just let me know what you hear."

"Sure will." She pushed the *end* button and lit her cigarette while she reflected on the little encounter with Gloria. She was good at what she did.

———

Pamela raced home as fast as she dared, making a plan as she went. The bus was just pulling away from the house when she got there. She sat in the car and considered her options as the bus disappeared around the next corner. Surely she would be better off taking time to do this right. They had devised a plan, when they moved here, of what to take in an emergency, but since the kids were not home she could take a little more time. There were things they couldn't live without and things they could leave behind. The kids would only make it more difficult to decide what belonged in which category.

Once the decision was made, she pulled back onto the street and headed back to the closest pay phone. She had to call Carla and get some help. They'd need new identification, and a safe house for a few weeks at least. She thought about getting her last check from Donny, but wasn't sure she had the time to ask for it.

Carla's phone rang three times and then clicked to voice mail. Pamela hesitated before hanging up. She'd try again later; she still didn't feel right about leaving a message. There was an emergency safe house in Little Rock. Carla had given her the address as her closest hiding place when she'd moved to Harrison. Pamela would go there for now. Carla would find her there and they'd make a plan.

When the kids got home, they took one look at the car stuffed full of boxes and bags and they knew. She could see it in their eyes. Kenny went next door to play with Robert for half an hour; he wasn't too concerned about the move. He made friends quickly and didn't understand the danger they were in. For him this was another adventure. Darla was the one with a pinched look. Once Kenny was gone, Pamela sat down with her daughter and explained what had happened that morning. Pamela's scare last week, and then Darla's incident at Jenny's house, had put them both on edge. She could see in her daughter's eyes that it was almost a relief to be getting away. The two of them spent a few more minutes gathering one last box of things they would take along. Most household items, like furniture and dishes, would stay here to confuse the landlord when he stopped by in a few weeks to collect the rent. It would be as if they just disappeared. With any luck, that's exactly what they would do.

Darla picked up Kenny from the neighbors while Pamela started the car. They drove to a gas station where Pamela called Carla again as the kids picked out a few dollars' worth of snacks for the trip. When the phone went to the voice mail again, she decided to leave a message; hopefully, Carla would get it in time to call the safe house and warn them of her arrival.

The kids were back in the car when she hung up the phone. Pamela complimented their choice of snack food and reminded them to fasten their seat belts. She slid into the driver's seat, took a deep breath, and turned the key. The engine made a clunking sound she'd never heard before, but it started okay and she didn't dwell on it. Another life was a few miles down the road; it was time to get started.

————

Bryan finished grading the assignments he'd collected that afternoon and organized his desk. A quick glance at the clock told him it was after 4:00 and he ought leave for home. He was meeting Barbara in Branson for dinner between her afternoon and evening shows. He still needed to stop by his house before meeting her at 6:00. He wished he was looking forward to the date but, in truth, he was in no mood to see her tonight. Pamela was weighing heavily on his mind. He was trying to figure out why she hadn't leveled with him about her membership. She was so mysterious and he was stumped. He'd tried to give her the opportunity to come to church again, he'd attempted to further build their friendship and she'd stonewalled him. It was making him crazy. Hopefully, spending some time with Barbara would take his mind off Pamela. However, it seemed unlikely.

There weren't a lot of single LDS women around; he'd considered himself very lucky to have found Barbara. They had their differences, for sure, but they also had a lot in common. They were both ambitious, hard working, and ready for family life. Barbara had put off marriage and family in order to focus on her singing. At twenty-five, she was finally accepting that she would never be a singing sensation and she was ready to settle down. Their most obvious difference was money, but Barbara was a trust fund baby and although he had yet to be convinced, she reminded him over and over again that she didn't care how much money he made so long as he didn't mind the way she spent hers. He hadn't made his peace with that yet, but he was trying, and it hadn't been enough of an issue to affect their relationship so far. There was so much to love about her, he didn't want his pride to ruin the opportunity.

Before his conversion to the church, Bryan hadn't ever focused on marriage and family. His own family was a mess, and it made him shy away from commitments. However, the gospel had changed his heart in many ways. He felt that Barbara and he could build a happy life together. She was the first woman that had ever made marriage look like an exciting venture instead of a dull existence.

Saturday, however, had made their differences more obvious than before, and he began to doubt the direction in which they were headed. But he did owe her an apology after his final words to her after the picnic. He'd called her Monday night and, although she said he was forgiven, she remained pouty. Finally, he'd asked her to dinner tonight, in hopes that her maturity would kick in and they could have a nice evening together. There was a lot to love about Barbara, but her actions this past week made him wonder what their future really was.

After straightening up his classroom, Bryan locked the door and headed for the parking lot, waving good-bye to the janitor on his way out. He threw his briefcase onto the passenger seat of his truck and smiled as the diesel engine growled to life. The truck had been his gift to himself on his last birthday. It wasn't new and he'd had to replace the transmission himself in order to be able to afford it, but he loved his truck.

He turned out of the parking lot and headed south toward Jasper. He'd bought an old house a few miles outside of town last summer. It had been a foreclosure and he'd gotten it for a great price. Since closing, he'd spent most of his weekends fixing it up, more grateful than ever for his handyman tendencies. On his way home, he turned up the radio and began tapping his thumbs on the steering wheel in rhythm to the music. He was planning the questions he'd use for his pop quiz in the morning, when a car on the shoulder of the road caught his attention. A brief glance as he passed registered no immediate recognition, but when he looked in his rear-view mirror, his foot eased up on the accelerator. The mirror bounced in time with the worn road and he couldn't make a clear identification, but the possibility was strong enough that he made a U-turn as soon as he could.

Pamela had popped the hood and stood staring at the engine. At her last safe house, she'd been given a crash course in auto mechanics. She'd learned the basics of do-it-yourself car care. Once a year, she would get a full service on her car and have all the components cleaned and filled. The oil changes and other routine care she did herself. Staring at the engine, she realized that whatever had caused the engine to seize up the way it had, was something she couldn't fix. She blew out a breath and cursed silently. *Couldn't it have waited until Little Rock?*

The roar of a diesel engine was barely noticed as she wiggled hoses.

Surely, if she looked long enough she'd figure something out. In truth, she didn't know what else to do, her mind was blank.

"I thought it might be you."

Pamela flipped her hair over one shoulder and peered up at the familiar voice. "Bryan?" she asked, the late afternoon sun silhouetting his broad shoulders. She shaded her eyes with one greasy hand to make sure she had identified him correctly.

Bryan took a step toward the car and smiled his greeting before looking into the engine. "Car trouble?"

"Uh, yeah," she said haltingly. She glanced into the car and her heart sank as the boxes and bags stuffed into every available nook made it impossible to hide the fact that they were leaving town.

"What happened?" he asked, not yet noticing the evidence of flight.

"It started losing power about a mile back and limped this far."

Bryan continued to check the engine, moving from one side to another, as he tested wires and hoses. Finally he looked up at her.

"Have you replaced your fuel filter lately?"

"The whole car got overhauled in February and it's been running fine."

He continued poking around for a few minutes. Pamela shifted from one foot to another, her anxiousness to get out of town becoming unbearable.

"I can't be sure, but it sounds like your timing belt," he said. "And unfortunately, the car's pretty much dead without it."

Pamela bit her bottom lip. "Any idea what it takes to fix it?"

"In a Ford or a Chevy, you take a few things out and put a new belt on; it takes a couple of hours. But in a Toyota," he blew out a breath and gave her a look she didn't like. "They have such compact engines that it sometimes means lifting out the whole engine to get to it. It's quite a process."

Pam stared back at the engine in despair. "I can't afford to have it fixed," she said.

"I live just a few miles down the road. Why don't I go grab my ropes, tow it home, and look it over? I've got most of the equipment to do the labor at the school," he said simply, as if lifting the entire engine would be easy. "The part's only about a hundred dollars and I can loan you the money if you need it."

"That's not what I meant," she said softly, looking down the road. If she had only made it to Little Rock. There was silence for a few moments. When Pamela turned back, Bryan was looking through the windshield of her car. Darla and Kenny stared back at him from the back seat and then at their mother. She smiled slightly and they managed to smile back. He looked back at her and she knew what was coming.

"Where are you guys going?" Something in his voice told her that it was not a flippant question and he didn't want a flippant answer. She looked at him for several seconds and decided to be honest.

"We're leaving," she said simply with a slight shrug of her shoulders as if to say it was no big deal. "At least we were."

"Why?"

She ignored his question. "We were going to Little Rock." He said nothing as she stared down the road again, thinking of her options and running a hand through her hair. Without planning to, she turned around and found herself staring at his truck.

Several moments passed before she turned back to him. She cocked her head to the side. "How much do you think I could get for this?" she nodded toward her car. He looked at her for a moment, as if trying to decide where she was headed with this question and then walked around to the driver's door. The sun reflected off the blue paint as he put his hands on the roof and looked back at her.

"Without making the repairs, maybe five hundred," he said.

She walked toward him, stopping just a few feet away and looked him boldly in the eyes. "I'll trade you the car for a ride to Little Rock."

His brow furrowed and he pulled back as if surprised. "What?"

"I need to get to Little Rock. I can't afford the time or the money to fix this. If you could—"

"Wait," he said, putting up a hand to stop her from speaking. "You want me to drive you three hours to Little Rock in exchange for your broken down car?"

She nodded, although her confidence was waning. "I have to get there. Tonight."

Again he stared at her, his brow still furrowed. "Are you in trouble?" he finally whispered.

She looked down at the ground and took a breath before she dared meet his eyes again. "I have to get out of here," she said softly, daring a glance at the two small faces still peering out of the car.

The time it took for him to answer seemed like an eternity and she said a little prayer in her heart that her trust in him would not be misplaced. Her gut told her it was an acceptable risk.

"I've got class in the morning."

"I'm not in the habit of taking help from anyone. But I have to get to Little Rock, and I can't do it alone."

Again they shared a look, a long look. "I'll have to make a few calls," he finally said, although doubt was evident in his voice.

She smiled with relief and put a hand on his arm. "Thank you, Bryan," she said sincerely. Letting go, she hurried to the car window, poked her head in and explained the change of plans to her children. They both looked at Bryan and seemed as if they wanted to argue. Instead, they each grabbed a bag and followed their mom to the truck, while Bryan pulled the cell phone from his pocket. She noticed that he hesitated a little before finally punching in a number and then he made a point to get out of hearing distance as he spoke. He didn't speak long before hanging up and then grabbed bags from the trunk without comment.

The next time she caught his eye, she smiled her thanks and he returned her smile with a slight one of his own. She knew he didn't understand how important this was, and the fact that he was still willing to help her was rather astonishing. When they finished, Pamela grabbed a roll of paper towels from under Bryan's seat and went to the car, wiping down the doors and hood. When she got in the truck Bryan asked what she was doing and she just shrugged before immediately engaging the kids in conversation. She hoped he wouldn't bring it up again.

The first hour passed with little conversation between the two adults. The questions sizzled in the air between them, but they remained unasked and unanswered. Instead, Bryan talked to the kids who were squeezed in between them. They were shy at first, but Bryan's easy-going personality got them to open up. Kenny told him all about the bike he wanted, and he talked about school as if he would be catching the bus the next morning like always. Darla wasn't as easily friendly, but smiled at his jokes and answered questions directed to her. For the most part, Pamela just listened, enjoying the fact that another adult had earned their trust, and ignoring the butterflies in her stomach. Kenny was particularly comfortable with Bryan and she assumed that having taken a few river dunks together could accomplish that.

As the sun slipped below the western horizon, Pamela smiled at her sleeping children who were illuminated by the golden light of the evening sky. The conversation had tapered off over the last twenty minutes until they had finally gone silent. Darla's head rested on her mothers' lap and Kenny leaned against Bryan's shoulder. The four of them looked much like a family, but she quickly ignored the thought. Instead, she steeled herself for the questions she felt sure were about to be asked now that little ears weren't so alert.

Sure enough, after another thirty seconds Bryan cleared his throat. "So, why the hurry to get out of town?"

Pamela looked out the passenger window and said another little prayer for guidance in knowing what to say and what not to say. "It was time for us to move on," she said in what she hoped sounded like a confident tone.

"I'm not stupid," Bryan said with a hint of exasperation, making a sweeping motion that included all her things, the children and herself. "All this is more than some casual decision to move on."

She turned to look at him. "Have you ever been married?"

He cast a brief look at her before shaking his head no. She nodded. "It wasn't pretty when my marriage fell apart and we now do whatever we can to stay out of his way."

"Did he show up?" Bryan said with cautious alarm.

"Not yet," she said. "But I learned that he knows where we are and so it was time for us to go."

For several seconds there was silence. "Whoa," Bryan finally said as if unable to come up with anything else. "That's tough."

"Yeah," she agreed as she looked out the window again. "But we'll be okay. I have some friends in Little Rock that are going to help us out for a little bit."

"You know a lot of people here for being from California."

She looked at him, but saw no suspicion in his face. "It's all about networking," she said with a smile, hoping to soften the mood.

"Saturday, you said you used to be Mormon. What did you mean?"

She took a breath as she gathered the right words. "I am Mormon," she said. "But an LDS ward is the first place my husband would look for me, so I have to be careful."

Bryan considered her answer for a few seconds before probing further. "Did you mean it when you told me you missed it?"

Pamela looked directly at him. "Yes, I did," she said, wanting to make sure he understood this part. "I've held church every Sunday; I read my scriptures and I wear my temple garments. I just couldn't actually *go* to church. I couldn't safely tell the truth and yet I just couldn't lie about my membership, either."

"But you did come," Bryan added after a moment.

Pamela smiled slightly as the feelings from that day came back. "I couldn't help it," she said. "I hadn't seen a ward house for so long; I guess you could say I had weak moment."

"Or a strong one," Bryan said, glancing at her briefly.

Pamela said nothing as she considered his comment. "Perhaps," she finally said. How different would things be now if she hadn't gone to church that day? Maybe nothing would be different, maybe everything would be. She looked at the road ahead for a minute and then announced she was going to try and get some sleep. She hadn't slept yet today so she was exhausted. Then, too, she didn't feel ready, or willing, to discuss all this just now. Bryan nodded, although she could see there were still a lot of questions he wanted to ask. Little Rock was only another hour away; she'd spend that time sleeping and then she'd thank Bryan for his help and watch him drive away. The sadness that crept into her chest surprised her, but reminded her of one more reason why she needed to leave. Bryan was a good, honest, religious man; for her that meant he was trouble.

––––––––

"Is everyone here?"

Five heads nodded yes. One man placed his hands on the computer keyboard, ready to enter the information. The young agent in charge of the emergency meeting stood, loosened the knot in his tie and cleared his throat. The statistics were fresh in his mind, but he decided to say them out loud anyway, just to make sure the team knew how serious this is.

"Last year over 150,000 kids were stolen by their parents. Most were found quickly, but we still have over 5,000 of these cases open. That's 5,000 kids who think one of their parents doesn't want them; it's becoming epidemic and now that these underground networks are getting involved it's downright scary. With their money and support a parent can literally disappear forever. We've tracked parents from Europe to Mexico, mansions to crack houses and there is only one way were going to stop them; by scaring the hell out of them. We need every person in America to know that if they let these felons hide in their homes, they'll go to jail. We need every parent to know that they will not win their battles by cheating. That's why this case is so important. Carla Godfrey is involved in the inner circle of this network and we've got her! If we do this right we could break this thing wide open and make a statement no one can ignore. We can put these custody cases back where they belong, in the courts." He took a deep breath and continued. "This was left on Carla Godfrey's voice mail not quite an hour ago," he explained. "We're hoping that the information will give us the break we need so desperately. Pay attention and get ready to brainstorm."

He pushed a button and a voice came on. Immediately, the information was keyed into a special database. *"Carla, it's Gloria. I'm taking the kids to the safe house in Little Rock. David's private investigator found me. Please get hold of the house when you get this message. I expect to be there around eight o'clock."* The tape went dead.

"Have we uncovered a safe house in Little Rock?" someone asked.

"No," the young agent said with a shake of his head. "This is the first we've heard about it and it definitely complicates things. The call came from a pay phone in Harrison, Arkansas, a two-and-a-half-hour drive from Little Rock." Simultaneously everyone looked at their watches. The caller said she expected to arrive in Little Rock at eight. It was now six-fifteen, Arkansas time.

"We don't have a lot of time, but what if we—"

"I got it," the man at the computer interrupted. Everyone stood and gathered around his computer as a face slowly downloaded onto the screen. "Her name's Gloria Stanton; she has two children, Kathryn Leigh and Nicholas Reed. She went missing October 18th, two and a half years ago and hasn't been found. Her husband's name is David."

"Okay team," the lead officer said quickly. "Let's make a plan."

Chapter Nine

"Pamela," Bryan said as he gently shook her. She sat up slowly and looked around to get her bearings. Sleep still felt deliciously thick and she wished she could remain curled up against the door just a little longer. After a few moments of blinking and stretching, she looked at him. "We're a few miles out of Little Rock," he said.

"Oh, good," she said in a still sleepy voice. "What time is it?" As soon as she asked, the glowing numbers on the console of his truck caught her eye. Eight minutes after nine. Not bad, considering the extra time it had taken them to load the truck and push the Toyota a hundred yards down a side road where they hoped it would remain well hidden until Bryan could get it to his house. Bryan had wanted to take it to his house right then, but she hadn't wanted to waste any more time, other than wiping off the fingerprints again.

"Where am I taking you?" Bryan asked as they stopped at a red light.

Pamela pulled the paper from her back pocket and handed it to him. It didn't show a name or a phone number, just an address. He read it between glances at the light. "I know about where that is," he said. "It's not too far from where I grew up, actually."

"I didn't know you were from Little Rock."

"You didn't ask," he said with a teasing smile. Then he shrugged. "My mom and brothers run a bar on the east side."

"A bar," she repeated with raised eyebrows. "I guess they aren't as religious as you."

"No," he said with an exaggerated shake of his head. "I used to tend the bar there myself."

"You were a bartender?" she said, unable to imagine him behind a counter mixing drinks.

"Before I turned twenty-one I stocked the back, cleaned up after the boozers and hustled pool; once I was legal I paid for school by tending the bar on the weekends," he answered.

"And I guess the gospel changed that?"

"You could say that," he said with a chuckle. "All my life, I've been fascinated by how things work. Cars, calculators—anything that has some kind of seemingly invisible power source. That's why I went into science, and teaching. It's fascinating to me to see kids grasp concepts that were a mystery before they enter my classroom. I love it. One day, three years into my career, I gave my speech on how great science is, how it explains the unexplainable and makes sense of so called 'modern miracles.' The next day, I found a blue book on my desk. Inside the cover, a student I barely knew had written his testimony; he ended it with the explanation that this book could answer questions that science could not. I took it home, showed it to my girlfriend," he cast a look at her. "She wasn't interested, and I wasn't either—then. But that Christmas, when she went home for the holidays, I found it again and read it." He shook his head as if remembering how amazed he had been.

"I've always had questions about God, but never bothered looking for answers. I read the book in three days; finished it on Christmas Eve and I just knew. When school started, I found the student and began asking him questions. He put me in touch with the missionaries." He stopped speaking.

"And?"

"And when they got to the law of chastity I kicked them out."

Pamela winced internally. "I guess that would be hard when you're living with someone," she commented lamely.

"Not hard," Bryan clarified. "Ridiculous." He paused and gave her another smile. "My girlfriend thought so, too." Pamela wasn't sure she wanted to hear any more, but she had to admit she was intrigued. She didn't know many converts, surely none that had such black and white lives.

"When did you call them back?"

"It took me a week to think it through before I dared pray about it," he said humbly. "And when I did, my heart and understanding changed. When I asked my girlfriend to marry me, she started packing."

"Had you been together long?" she asked, sensing the difficulty of the situation, despite his nonchalant explanation.

"Two years," he said softly. "It was very hard." They lapsed into silence for a few moments. "When the missionaries came back, they started where they'd left off. When they got to the Word of Wisdom, I kicked them out again."

She couldn't suppress a chuckle at the imagery; he hadn't had an easy time of it. "I went to my sister Charlotte's house and told her I was crazy to have investigated at all. I told her everything and expected her to agree with me and tell me to forget all about it. Instead, she asked if she could borrow my Book of Mormon. Two days later, she called me crying. She wanted the missionaries' phone number. I watched her progress for a week or so before realizing that if any part of the gospel is true, it's all true. The spirit had testified its truthfulness to me long before I learned about all the rules. I decided to have faith in the rules, too. Surely, if I could accept celibacy, I could accept sobriety." She listened intently. "I was baptized two weeks later, after exhausting those two missionaries with questions."

"I can imagine," she said. "Was Charlotte baptized at the same time?"

"A week earlier, actually. She's married to a Baptist, so I think God was a little more real to her than He was to me."

"Is her husband a member now?"

Bryan shook his head. "No, but he's a good man and supports her activity."

"So why did you move to Harrison?"

"Ray, Charlotte's husband, got a job at Duncan Manufacturing in Harrison."

"The company that makes parking meters?" she asked.

"Yeah," he answered. "He's a supervisor. I followed them up north a year or so later, to make a break from the rest of my family. They still think we're both crazy. My relationship with them will never be the same, but Charlotte and I have grown lots closer and that helps."

She smiled. "I guess you stayed active?"

"I did," he said simply. "I've always been an all-or-nothing kind of guy, and I knew the Church deserved my all."

"Wow," she commented, more impressed with him than ever. They were silent for a moment, until she gathered her courage to ask the questions weighing on her mind. "When did you and Barbara meet?"

He hesitated a minute and she watched the change in his expression. It was guarded somehow, which she found interesting. He'd just told her about his sordid past with nothing but openness. Why would he become cautious when his girlfriend's name came up? "She started with the show in Branson last year and began coming to church in Harrison. We've been dating for about six months."

"So it all worked out," she said.

He looked at her with uncertainty and she hurried to explain. "You lost the woman you loved because of the church, but now you've come full circle and love another woman. A better one."

He nodded, but didn't say much. She wanted to ask a hundred other questions, but she held them inside. It was none of her business, and hearing about Barbara made her feel a little jealous. He smiled politely and put his foot on the accelerator as the light they were stopped at turned green. "Do you mind if I stop for gas? I'm about dry."

"We could use a bathroom stop anyway," Pamela said as her children begin to stir. Kenny asked where they were and she told them. A minute later, Bryan pulled into a gas station and proceeded to fill the tank. Pamela escorted the children inside the convenience store.

It took several minutes to fill the tank and Bryan cursed the high gas price as he returned the nozzle to its cradle. He was sauntering towards the convenience store to pay, when Pamela suddenly hurried out the door, pulling her kids with her.

"We've got to go," she said frantically, putting a hand on his chest to stop him. For a moment he just stared at her. He looked at the confused kids before looking back at their mother.

"I've got to pay for the gas," he said, wondering why she was in such a panic. She hesitated, her eyes darting around the parking lot until finally nodding with obvious reluctance. Bryan stared at her and she gave him a repentant look. Bryan couldn't imagine what had upset her.

Without hesitating any longer, Pamela ushered her kids to the truck as Bryan went inside. He could hear the sound of the television mounted above the counter but didn't pay it much attention until after handing the cashier his money. With nothing better to do while waiting for his change, he glanced upwards, and his whole body froze. The photo was old enough that if he had not seen Kenny just seconds before he probably wouldn't have recognized him at all. The caption underneath the photo said the child's name was Nicholas Stanton. The background voice then explained that with the technology of photo aging he should look similar to their next photo, which immediately replaced the first one. The similarity was amazing. The screen then flashed back to the blonde newscaster, and the little square to the right of her face produced a photo that, although it too was outdated, was definitely the face of the woman with whom he had just driven into town. "If you have any information about this woman or her children, please contact this station or the Federal Bureau of Investigation. Now we'll go to Harold Bowman—"

"Sir," the cashier said, holding out her hand. "Your change."

"Oh, yes," Bryan said, taking the money slowly and stuffing it into his pocket. He looked at the cashier, who smiled back at him kindly; apparently, she hadn't been paying much attention to the broadcast. Bryan turned toward the door and walked to the truck, going over the information he had just learned. As he slid into the driver's seat he could feel her watching him, but he avoided her eyes; he had no idea how to handle this situation. He started the engine and told everyone to put on their seatbelts. The anxiety in the car was suffocating, especially when compared to the friendly atmosphere of their earlier conversation. He could literally feel Pamela's fear and apprehension. They drove a few blocks, turned right, and then Bryan pulled into a small park, deserted except for a couple of teenagers playing basketball by the light of a streetlight. It was too late for most people to bother coming to the park, but the temperature was nice. He looked down at the two frightened children crammed next to him and smiled sincerely, hoping to decrease the fear in their eyes. "Kids, I need to talk to your mom for a minute. We can all get out and you guys can play for a few minutes, or you can stay in the truck and watch us talk outside."

Both kids looked to their mother. She cleared her throat. "It's up to you," she said in a soft voice. "You'll be able to see me the whole time." She then looked up at Bryan for confirmation and he nodded without making eye contact with her. The kids decided to play, so everyone got out of the truck. The kids headed for the playground while the two adults stood in front of the truck, waiting until Darla and Kenny were out of earshot. For a few moments, neither of them said anything.

"I'm sorry, Bryan," she finally said, folding her arms across her chest and rubbing her arms. "I didn't mean to get you involved in this."

Bryan just shook his head and consciously kept his tone even. "Involved in what?" he asked. "I don't have any idea what I'm involved in."

She looked at the ground and took a deep breath before looking up to meet his eyes. "I took the kids."

"Took?"

"I—I kidnapped them."

Bryan let out a humorless laugh. "You kidnapped your kids?" She nodded. He turned away from her and ran his hands though his hair. "I can't believe this," he muttered to himself.

"I had to do it, Bryan," she quickly said. "I—"

"You lied to me," he said, with more hurt than anger. "You told me you'd had a messy divorce, you told me your husband was after you, you even lied to me about your name, your children's names—everything."

"I *did* have a messy divorce," she countered. "And my husband *is* after me. I took my children because the court was making me give them back to him. I'd never run away like this unless I had no other choice. You have to believe me."

"Believe you!" he said incredulously. "And what am I supposed to base my trust on? The fact is that you broke the law, stole your children, and lied to me about all of it." He turned away and shook his head again. "This is incredible."

"I did everything I could to protect them legally, but it wasn't enough. I couldn't keep them away from David unless I took them away from everything. It was—"

"Why?" Bryan interrupted bluntly. "Why was it so important to keep them away from their own father?"

"He raped her," Pamela spat back. The words hung in the air like a frozen lightening bolt and Bryan just stared at her in silence. Pamela took a step closer to him so that their faces were only inches apart. He was nearly a foot taller than she was, yet he could feel how powerful she was right now. "Katie's father," she whispered angrily. "The man I married in the temple was molesting my six-year-old daughter. I confronted him, I immediately filed for divorce, and I counted on justice. I took her to see doctors and lawyers, presented my case to social workers and judges. I did everything I could to ensure that my little girl would be safe. But they ordered me to give her back to him." Her eyes glowed with indignation. "The night I received the court order, I fell to my knees and pleaded with the Lord to show me what else I could do. No matter what it took, I knew that I had to protect my kids. I'd done everything *within* the law and it hadn't worked. So yes, I took them away from their father; yes, I changed their names and changed mine, too. And if I had to do this all over again I'd do it exactly as I've done it. I wouldn't change a single action I've taken."

The power of her explanation was impossible to ignore, her depth of belief in what she'd done was impressive. But he wasn't convinced. "I don't believe the Lord works that way. I believe he would find a way within the law, not outside of it," he finally said. "With enough faith, anything is possible."

"Exactly my point," she said bluntly. "I received an answer to my prayer and I followed the direction He gave me because of my faith; it isn't lack of faith that brought me here."

"And so you become a criminal, in the name of righteousness?"

"The Lord told Lehi to run away," she said. "He told Nephi to kill Laban and steal the gold plates. He commanded Moses to raise the Hebrews in rebellion against the Egyptians and he commanded Alma to allow women and children to be burned to death. Joseph was told to marry his pregnant girlfriend. The Israelites sent a young boy armed with only a slingshot to do battle with a man twice his age and several times his strength and power. Esther married a man outside her faith, lying to him about her ancestry." She paused and her nostrils flared slightly. "I am not a hero, I'm not a prophet, and I'm not trying to save a nation from destruction. But I am a mother, the only protector my children have. I am absolutely certain of the guidance that led me to make my choice, a choice that was not easy. I did what I *had* to do."

He was so confused and so angry, not so much as at what she'd done, but rather that she hadn't trusted him enough to tell him the truth from the start. And now he was involved in something that could destroy everything he'd worked so hard to build in his life. "How convenient to use scripture as justification," he said as he headed for the truck. She immediately grabbed his arm.

"Convenient?" she said with a humorless laugh. "You think I did this for kicks? I gave up everything, took my kids from every security they had in their lives. You don't think I agonized over my decision?" Her eyes were on fire and her fingers continued to dig into the flesh of his arm. "The gospel is all about truth," she said. "It's about learning to follow the spirit. The doctrine of the church teaches us what we need to know to protect ourselves from evil and give us the happiness we've been promised. My little girl needed protecting and the courts failed her; I wasn't about to do the same."

"So you turn your back on your covenants and break the law?"

"I didn't turn my back on my covenants," she nearly screamed. "I made a sacrifice, a very difficult one, in order to keep my covenants."

"Do you pay tithing?" he asked, raising one eyebrow accusingly. She looked away, her chest heaving. "Do you testify of Christ, of his Atonement, and share your belief in him? Do you consecrate your time to the building of His Kingdom? Are you honest in all things, repentant, forgiving, living as He would live? Has your nine-year-old daughter been baptized?" he stopped when she let go of his arm and wiped a single tear from her cheek.

"Some things are more important than others," she said quietly. "I've had to make some difficult choices."

"Yes, you have," he said dryly. "And your choices affect more than just you." She wrapped her arms around herself again and looked across the park, wiping at her eyes every few seconds as she watched her children play. The indignation, the defensiveness and passion that had been so intense just moments before disappeared from her countenance. Now she just looked sad, overwhelmed, and alone. When she spoke, her voice was soft and trembling. "If you'll take us to a motel, this will all be over for you."

As Bryan followed her eyes to the playground, his anger dissipated. What was he supposed to do? His mind drew a blank. "What about your friend?"

"It was a safe house," she explained quietly, still watching her children. "The network that's helped us has several homes that will give people like me protection when we need it. But since I'm on the news, I can't go to the safe house. I would put the whole network in danger if I did." She looked at a spot just over his left shoulder, unwilling to meet his eyes, and tucked her hair behind her ear. "Are you going to turn me in?" she asked. He didn't miss the fact that she wasn't arguing her position any more.

"I'll take you to a motel," he said. "And then I'm going home." He turned toward the truck. "But, no, I won't turn you in," he said as he started walking.

He drove a few miles to a Motel 6. When he pulled up in front of the office Pamela opened her door before hesitating. "I'll get you a room," he said, putting the truck into park.

"No," Pamela said quickly. "If anything happens I don't want you connected with me."

"I'm already connected." She didn't respond as he got out of the car. He entered the office and signed for a room before returning to the truck and driving to the end of the building. Without saying a word, he began unloading the truck; the children watched him anxiously and he wondered how much they understood about the life they lived. When he caught Darla's eye, she quickly looked away and his stomach tightened. It all seemed so terrible. None of this made sense. Not Pamela's situation, nor his conflicting feelings about it.

When the truck was empty, Brian bent down to the kids level and pulled a pack of gum from his pocket. It was a peace offering, and when he held it out, Kenny quickly stepped up and grabbed it. Bryan smiled and ruffled his hair. "I guess this is it," he said evenly. Both kids nodded. He risked a glance at Pamela but she looked away. He wished he could tell them he'd see them again, or that he hoped they'd enjoy their new school but he didn't know what was going to happen to them now. Finally, he just wished them luck and straightened up. Pamela met his eye for the first time since leaving the park.

"Thank you," she said sincerely. "I really appreciate this."

Bryan nodded. They held eye contact for a few moments before he finally turned and let himself out. Part of him wanted so badly to reach out to her, to tell her he believed her explanations and ask what he could do to help. But another part of him felt like stone when he looked at her. He thought he'd come to know her—he felt they had a connection, but now he knew he had been wrong. He didn't know her at all. Sliding into the seat of his truck, he headed for the freeway; he was anxious to put some distance between himself and the situation.

The on-ramp was only a few hundred yards away when he noticed the address Pamela had handed him earlier that night. He'd placed it on the dashboard and apparently she'd forgotten it. Slowly, he pulled off onto the side of the road, picked up the paper, and just stared. She'd called it a safe house; it was her connection to some kind of network and yet she hadn't been able to go there. He looked out into the darkness of the night and considered details of Pamela's situation that he hadn't thought about yet. Her face and those of her children were all over the news. She had no car, no one to help her, and he'd left her, too. What was she going to do? For several seconds, he thought about the choices he faced. To do anything more than he had already done would put him in serious legal jeopardy, but could his conscience handle doing nothing?

She'd said she was doing what was right, that she was honoring her covenants and he had ripped her apart. He still believed she was wrong, but for the first time, he asked himself what was right. Would it have been right for Pamela to let her daughter go to the man who had molested her? It was a horrid thought. Maybe if he had children, he'd see her side of it more clearly. But the only question that really mattered right now was what was right for *him* to do now? Was it right to leave her there, even if she was wrong? He groaned out loud and hit the dashboard with his fist. For what felt like the millionth time he wondered what *he* was supposed to do. How had he gotten involved in this? Why was he here at all?

A few minutes passed before he turned on his left blinker, checked his mirror and made a U-turn. He'd be careful, but he simply couldn't leave things as they were. Bryan was not a man who gave up easily and it just didn't feel right to give up on her now.

Chapter Ten

The clock in his truck showed him it was a few minutes before ten when he pulled up in front of the large brick home. The classy neighborhood surprised him, and he checked the address again before turning off the engine and heading for the front door. For some reason he'd expected a dilapidated house with unkept people who existed on the fringes of legal society. When he reached the door, he knocked rather than using the bell at this hour of the night. He waited a few minutes and then knocked again. Finally, a voice spoke to him through the thick wooden door. He leaned forward to make sure he didn't miss anything.

"Who is it?" a muted female voice asked.

"My name is Bryan Drewry; I'm a friend of Pamela Bennion."

"A friend of who?"

"I don't know her real name," he fumbled, wishing he'd rehearsed for this a little better. "It's something Stanton, she was coming here tonight but she saw herself on the news and got scared. It sounds like the FBI is after her."

There was silence for a moment. "I don't know what you're talking about," the voice finally said. "Are you with the police?"

"No," he answered quickly. "I'm a high-school science teacher from Harrison." What could be more harmless than that? He wished she'd open the door so he could speak in a normal tone. "We got into town a little bit ago and she's all over the news; I took her to a motel." Boy, he hoped this was the right house.

Again there was silence for several seconds. "Come back in half an hour. If the porch light is on, come to the door. If it's off, then I've called the police and you'd better high-tail it out of here."

The porch light flicked off and Bryan stood there for a few seconds before heading back to his truck. *What on earth am I doing?* he asked himself as he opened the door to his truck. This had to be the craziest thing he'd ever done.

To pass the time, he went to a corner fast food stand and ordered a hamburger, guiltily wondering what Pamela, or whatever her name was, had done about dinner. The kids must be starving and she certainly couldn't get them anything. While waiting for his dinner, he wandered to a community bulletin board nailed to one wall of the small building. Staring back at him was the same photo of Pamela he'd seen on TV that night. *Boy, the feds moved fast.* He read the information on the flier and then glanced around briefly before pulling it off the board and casually stuffing it into his pocket. Just then they called his number and he went to retrieve his food. He finished his burger just in time to head back to the house.

When he pulled up to the curb, his eyes lingered on the glowing yellow light above the door. This was his last chance to turn away. If he proceeded into that house he'd be very much involved. He felt as if he were standing at the edge of a cliff preparing to jump, but unsure whether or not his parachute would open. He knew he had no idea what the outcome of this decision would be. Did he really want to know? Was he willing to accept the fact that there might be no parachute at all? After a few more seconds, he turned off the truck, said a little prayer, and opened the door. At some point in her journey, Pamela had come to rely on strangers. He wondered if she had been as scared, then, as he was now.

———————

"Did you get enough to eat?" Pamela asked her children. She'd packed some apples, crackers, and peanut butter, just in case. It had become their dinner.

"I need a drink," Kenny said. She nodded, got up from the floor and filled one of the plastic cups by the sink with water.

"Mom," Darla said. "What are we going to do?"

She felt sick at not being able to answer that question. "I don't know," she said sadly. "Maybe we should go to that last shelter we were at in Detroit." She started asking herself questions she knew her kids wouldn't ask. How would they get there? What if they got caught?

Darla nodded her understanding. "I think we should say a prayer," she said. "Maybe Heavenly Father knows what we should do."

Tears came to Pamela's eyes because of her daughter's faith. "I think that's a great idea." She looked at Kenny, he nodded and they all got on their knees. Pamela took a breath. "Our dear Heavenly Father," she began, her voice already breaking. "We thank Thee for all the blessings you've given us and pray for your guidance as we face a very difficult situation . . ."

as was her habit, she laid out the details of their situation. She'd found that saying her prayers this way gave her greater clarity as to what it was she was praying for. When she finished the prayer, she looked up at her children. "What do you think?" she asked.

"I think we'll be okay," Darla said with a smile. The peace of her countenance lifted Pamela's spirits.

"Me, too," Kenny said. "And I'm tired." Pamela smiled and nodded her agreement. She didn't know what to do next, but she did feel better. She'd sleep on it, and hopefully things would be clearer by morning.

However, sleep was hard to come by. At one A.M. Pamela was still awake. She was fully clothed, lying on her side next to Darla, staring at the orange glow of the motel sign that shined through the window. The kids had fallen asleep a couple of hours ago. But she continued to go over her situation again and again, seeking an answer. There were just so many questions. Why couldn't she get hold of Carla? Why would the redhead tell her to leave and then plaster her all over the TV? Nothing made sense.

Tomorrow she'd start work on disguises. She'd start with coloring and cutting her hair, maybe the kids' hair too; then she'd find a way out of Arkansas. The shelter in Detroit seemed like their best option, but getting there would be difficult. Fear of getting caught threatened to consume her, but she pushed it out of her mind. Faith and fear could not exist together; she had to choose one and she knew that fear would get her nowhere.

A light tapping on the door startled her and she froze for a moment before silently getting out of bed. A glance at the children told her they were sound asleep. When she reached the door, she fastened the chain and pulled the door open a couple of inches. To her surprise, Bryan was standing there.

"Bryan?" she whispered, ignoring the flutter in her stomach. "What are you doing here?"

"Can you come outside and talk to us?" he asked quietly. "I don't want to wake the children."

"Us?" she repeated as her stomach sank. Had he called the cops? Just then a short, rather plump, middle-aged brunette stepped in front of Bryan.

"My name's Sharon Lewis," she whispered. "You were headed for my safe house tonight."

Pamela blinked and looked up at Bryan; he looked away as if embarrassed. She glanced at her sleeping children before closing the door, removing the chain, and pulling it open again. She shut it quietly, after making sure she had a key in her pocket, and followed them to Bryan's truck. Once they were all inside, Sharon, who sat in the middle, looked at Pamela and smiled. "I bet you're scared to death right now."

"That's an understatement," she said softly. "None of this makes sense." She cast a look at Bryan's profile and wavered between wishing he weren't here and feeling so grateful that he'd come back. After taking a breath she told them about the redhead, how she'd given Pamela a head start. She shared her feelings of confusion as to why the woman would then turn on her.

"It might not have been her at all," Sharon said when she finished. Who else could it have been? "You know how carefully we screen the parents who come to us for help. However, one slipped past us somehow. About a month ago, one of our moms was arrested. She'd been in hiding for less than six months and was dealing meth out of a safe-house basement apartment. Once in custody, she told everything she knew in order to get a plea bargain." Sharon shook her head. "Everything she knew consisted of very little, but it was enough to put the feds onto our network. They dug around and uncovered a couple of houses and few individuals here and there. We've been on alert ever since. We were all warned to stop making contact until further notice. Carla was the mom's case worker. They caught up with her last week."

If Carla had been arrested, then the feds probably had her cell phone. If the feds had her cell phone—they had access to the messages left on it. Pamela shook her head in dismay. She'd told them exactly where she was going.

Sharon continued. "You weren't contacted because only Carla knew your current name. She was supervising fifteen cases and she was the only one that kept records of their current identities and locations. Once she was out of the picture, we lost all information about her cases. So far, none of her other cases have been uncovered. Until now, anyway."

Pamela nodded, still in disbelief that this had happened. She glanced briefly at Bryan; he was listening as carefully as she was. "What happened to Carla?"

"She's out on bail because they haven't been able to get any hard evidence on her; she's a master at hiding things. However, she's being closely watched and for her protection, as well as everyone else's, she's not doing anything."

"And they haven't cracked your house?"

"The safe houses are very well protected," Sharon explained. "But I'm also not taking any chances. I changed my phone number and e-mail account. Lucky for me, I was empty when the whole thing came down. The full houses are the ones that are in real danger. It's still possible that if the right person talks, I could get pulled into this whole mess. But right now, I'm just playing it safe and hoping it blows over."

"Will it blow over?" Pamela asked.

Sharon let out a breath. "No, it won't," she said sadly. "It will take years to recover from this, and the FBI hasn't even begun to scratch the surface. Carla's done; she won't involve herself again because it would be too risky. We can only hope that their progress stops soon, so we can all breathe again. But I'm telling you things you don't need to know. What we need to deal with is your problem right now, and it's a big one. You and your children are on every news broadcast in the state; there are fliers posted all over the city; you're like a big bull's-eye right now. We've got to get you out of here."

"I don't have anywhere to go," Pamela admitted.

"Which is why I'm here," Sharon said. She looked quickly at Bryan and smiled. "Bryan and I came up with a solution."

Pamela looked at Bryan in surprise. He smiled slightly and nodded, although she could still read hesitation in his eyes. Sharon continued. "I made some calls and found a summer home in Missouri, outside of Rolla," she explained. "From what I understand, it isn't anything fancy and it needs some fixing up but it's remote and it's empty. You can stay there for a while. But if you are found, the owners will claim they have no idea who you are and they'll press charges to prove it. What do you think?"

"I . . . I think it's an answer to my prayers," she said after a thoughtful pause. "How will I get there?"

"Bryan agreed to drive you and the children there in the morning. He'll get you settled, stock the pantry, and help with any necessary fix-ups over the weekend."

Pamela's mouth was stuck in the open position. Was this for real? Sharon continued. "You'll be by yourself in the middle of the Ozarks," she explained. "It's not going to be the most comfortable or even the safest place. But I don't know of anything better." Pamela's eyes shifted to Bryan, she didn't know what to say and he looked embarrassed again.

"I already left a message at the school that I won't be there in the morning, but I've got to be back Monday. I'm going to stay at Sharon's tonight and I'll come for you in the morning." He talked fast, like he was nervous. Unbidden tears came to Pamela's eyes.

"Thank you," she said quietly. "I didn't know what I was going to do." She raised her hands to her face, overcome with emotion.

Sharon put a hand on Pamela's arm. "You are saving your children, Gloria," she said. Pamela started at the sound of her real name and looked over her hands. "We'll do whatever we can to help you do that."

————

The sun was just setting behind the trees two days later when Pamela opened the screen door and stepped onto the large porch. The door banged shut behind her and she took another step so that she stood next to Bryan. He didn't look at her, and for a moment she didn't speak. "You haven't had much to say," she finally said. Out of the corner of her eye she caught a slight nod.

"Neither have you," he said. "At least not to me." She'd expected him to leave soon after they arrived, but he'd made no indication that he was in a hurry. They'd spent the last two days cleaning and fixing things. In truth, there hadn't been much time to talk, but they both knew that neither of them had tried to make an opportunity. There were a few more seconds of silence before he spoke again. "I hate leaving you here alone."

The tenderness in his voice made her dread his leaving, too. "I'll be okay," she said. In truth, she was quite nervous about the whole situation. The closest town was nearly ten miles away, and although there were probably several cottages like this one nearby, she hadn't seen them and she wasn't going to introduce herself to the neighbors. The woods surrounding the cottage were filled with the sounds of insects and animals. The constant sounds made her skin crawl. They'd already killed a dozen spiders and Kenny had come into the house screaming "snake" twice. The situation was definitely not ideal, yet she couldn't deny that it was certainly heaven sent.

"How long have you been hiding?" he asked, finally getting to the subject they'd been to avoiding.

"Two and a half years," she answered. She'd already decided she'd keep no more secrets from him. He deserved her complete honesty, whether or not he agreed with what she'd done.

"And you plan to stay in hiding until when?"

"I don't know," she said sadly. "I really thought I was close to going home until yesterday. Carla was confident that we were very close, closer than we'd ever been."

"The doctor in Florida?"

Pamela looked at him in surprise. "How did you—"

"Sharon told me about it," he said. "She said you mentioned it when she walked you back to the motel room."

"She's going to put some thought into what to do now."

"I told her I'd help if she needs me to."

Again she looked at him, her surprise only growing. "Why are you doing this?" she asked. He'd hardly said a word to her since she told him the truth about who she was and yet he was planning to do more?

"To be honest," he said softly. "I don't know."

"You shouldn't do anything more than you've done," she said quickly. "You've already done too much."

He just stood there, looked at the trees that now completely blocked the sun. "When I read the Book of Mormon I couldn't explain why it affected me so much—it just did. I feel that way now. I don't know why I'm here; I don't know what brought our lives together. I'm not even sure what you've done is right. But my gut feeling is that I should help."

"Perhaps it's just an inflated sense of honor. The whole 'damsel in distress' syndrome."

He smiled for the first time and shook his head before looking at her. His brown eyes were so soft, enveloping in their warmth. "Perhaps," he said. "But I think it's a little more than that."

Her cheeks colored and she looked away, knowing she'd taken his comment the wrong way. When she looked back he was looking at the trees again. "I'm going to pick up some groceries before the Sabbath," he said, avoiding her gaze. "Can you make a list?"

"Oh sure," she said, grateful for the excuse to go back inside. He followed her in and waited while she wrote out a lengthy list of what she would need for the next few weeks. She was sure to be very detailed; she couldn't afford to miss anything. When she finished, she handed him the list and headed toward the stairs. "Let me get some money."

"Sharon gave me some already," he said. "She said you needed to hang onto yours."

Pamela paused and turned back to face him. "Oh," she said, slightly embarrassed by her dependency.

"She said it was from the network," Bryan continued. "Where does the money for all of this come from?"

"The safe houses cover their own expenses, utilities, mortgages; those kind of things. Everyone is a volunteer, and then they have private people that donate money, too. To get in I had to have at least five thousand dollars to cover my own costs for as long as possible. I was lucky enough to get almost twelve. I haven't had to use much of the network's money so far."

"But your ex was loaded, right?" Bryan asked. "Wasn't it hard to go from that to this?" He indicated the ten-by-ten living room full of mismatched furniture.

Pamela shrugged. "My focus was elsewhere," she said easily. "It took some time, that's for sure. But in the end it was an inconsequential element."

Bryan nodded, a look of respect on his face that gave her a sense of pride. "Well, I better go," he finally said, turning toward the door. "I won't be long."

————

It was almost two o'clock Sunday afternoon before Bryan returned home. He couldn't remember the last time he had been so tired. With a groan, he collapsed onto his bed, not even removing his shoes. His body ached from the loading and unloading, monotonous driving, cleaning, and repairs he'd done all weekend. He'd slept on a lumpy couch Friday and Saturday nights and headed home this morning. The weariness of his body, however, seemed trite when compared to the numbness of his mind.

The fact that he could do all he'd done and still not be sure it was the right thing to do was amazing. The whole situation was in absolute contrast to his value system of honesty, integrity, and faith; yet he couldn't *not* do this. It was the strangest feeling; one he couldn't really describe and dared not look at too closely.

After their conversation on the porch Saturday night, things changed. They both relaxed and he felt that Pamela trusted him more than she had before. She had told him her real history, and he finally knew who she really was. Yet he was still confused. She was a desperate mother, willing to sacrifice everything for the safety of her children, and yet he still doubted that there had been no other way. It was like a huge vicious circle without end; one question leading to another. Still, when all was said and done, it boiled down to the fact that Pamela needed someone, and he was the someone God had apparently provided for her. Thankfully, his fatigue put his complicated thoughts to rest and he finally fell into a heavy sleep.

The pounding on the door awakened him some time later and he pulled a pillow over his ears. He felt as if he had just barely fallen asleep, but a glance at the clock told him he'd had a few hours of rest. When the knocking continued, he reluctantly pulled himself out of bed and dragged himself to the door. He opened it while rubbing his eyes. A blonde fireball burst through the door and fixed him with a look that could kill.

"What is going on?" Barbara nearly screamed. Her eyes were like lasers, but Bryan was too tired to do anything more than notice.

"Barbara," he muttered, forcing a smile. "What are you doing here?"

"What am *I* doing *here?*" she repeated, her southern accent further emphasized by the passion in her voice. "You leave a message on my phone breaking our date Thursday, disappear for three days, don't even show up for church, and you want to know what *I'm* doing *here.*" She placed her well-manicured hands on her narrow hips and cocked her head to the side. "I'm here to find out what on earth is going on with you. Where have you been? What were you doing? And why didn't you call me?"

Bryan blinked, still not sure his brain was fully alert. "I had to go to Little Rock," he said as he searched for a way to answer her questions without incriminating himself any further. He'd hoped for a full night's sleep before this confrontation.

"What for?"

"Family stuff." He hated lying but saw little choice. He took a few steps toward her and placed his hands on her shoulders. It was like reaching back in time and grasping the old, wonderfully normal life he used to live. More than ever, he wanted to continue their relationship. He wanted everything about Pamela to just disappear; he wanted everything to be the way it was. He'd tell Barbara the truth, just as soon as he put the pieces together for himself. "I'm sorry, darlin'," he whispered, brushing a lock of hair off her forehead. "I didn't mean to worry you."

"Well, you did worry me," she said in a pouty tone, although her eyes had softened. "It scares me when you get so secretive. What—"

"It won't happen again," he said, pulling her to rest gently against his chest.

After a few moments Barbara pulled back and looked at him, apparently willing to accept his lack of communication. "Ya know that woman you brought to the ward party last week?" Did he ever. "She's wanted by the FBI for kidnapping those poor children."

"I saw the news," he said with a sad shake of his head. His stomach felt tight and he wished again that he'd planned for this. Barbara continued to watch him. "It's all anyone could talk about at church today. I hope the FBI doesn't ask us a bunch of questions." Did she suspect his disappearance had something to do with Pamela's?

Bryan tried to swallow the huge lump in his throat. "She just came to one activity, Barbara. How were we to know?"

"Of course, but I just knew there was something funny about her."

He looked away, hoping to hide how badly her comments were bothering him. Luckily, she changed the subject. "You look so tired," she said with a smile, her head cocked prettily to the side. She lifted a hand to his face and caressed his jaw with the back of her fingers.

"I'm exhausted," he said, placing his hands loosely on her hips. She stared dreamily into his eyes for several seconds before stepping back. "We're still going to dinner at Charlotte's tonight, right?"

"Uh, of course," he said with a forced smile to hide that he had in fact forgotten. He suddenly remembered Pamela's car. He knew he couldn't get it as he'd originally planned. If the police hadn't found it by now, they soon would. "Can I take a shower first?"

"I guess so," she said. "But hurry, my mom's calling at nine to discuss the reunion and I don't want to miss the call. Are you sure you can't get the time off to join us?"

Bryan resisted rolling his eyes. Every year, Barbara's family had a family reunion in Houston, where most of her mom's family still lived. She'd been pestering him for months to go, and he'd been telling her, for months, that it was impossible. "I've talked to everyone. I can't just miss the first week of summer school and no one can cover for me. I'm sorry." He'd apologized a hundred times already at least.

"Will you make it up to me?" she asked coyly, taking a step toward him.

"Of course I will," he said as he leaned forward to kiss her softly on the lips. She reached her arm around his neck, pulling his face to hers again. The kiss intensified, yet he had to force himself not to pull away. Of all things, Pamela popped into his mind and he wanted to scream. When Barbara finally pulled back, she looked at him oddly as if sensing his lack of interest. "Are you okay?" she asked carefully, as if not really wanting the answer.

He smiled broadly. "Of course I'm okay," he said, forcing himself to act as she expected. He winked brazenly and added, "I'm with you aren't I?" She smiled and he headed toward the bathroom as his weariness threatened to overwhelm him. He shut the door and leaned against it. He wasn't up to dealing with Barbara right now. He wondered how long of a shower he could get away with taking before raising her suspicions. Maybe the shower would beat some sense into him.

As Bryan let the water wash over him, he realized that the lie he'd told about having "family stuff" in Little Rock might easily come up at Charlotte's tonight. He groaned out loud; he hated this so much.

By the time they reached Charlotte and Ray's house that evening he thought he'd come up with a solution to the problem he'd created. Within minutes of his arrival his absence from church came up.

"What were you doing in Little Rock?" Charlotte asked in surprise. It was the moment of truth; Bryan hoped he'd be able to pull it off.

"You really want to know?" he asked. Every adult eye turned to look at him; intrigued by his response. "It started with a call from Cal."

Immediately Charlotte's eyes darkened. She lifted her hands and shook her head. "Stop," she said strongly. "I've heard enough."

"Who's Cal?" Barbara asked as Charlotte went outside to flip the chicken on the barbeque.

Ray was smiling. "Cal is their cousin," he explained. "He came to our wedding with a date. His wife showed up half an hour later and by the time the cops arrived the cake, tables and decorations were totally trashed. Charlotte has yet to forgive him."

"I don't blame her," Barbara said with a sympathetic shake of her head. "Sounds like white trash to me." She gave Bryan a disappointed look that made him look away.

It didn't come up again, but Bryan felt no satisfaction in the victory.

Chapter Eleven

"David, come in here," Carrie called from the other room. David looked up from the computer where he was catching up on some work he'd brought home to work on during the weekend. He let out a breath and pushed the chair back from the computer desk Carrie kept in the kitchen. His house had been swarming with reporters since Gloria's near-capture and they made it impossible for him to concentrate. An unfortunate accident involving a pitcher of water had befallen his own computer and completely fried his hard drive.

"Watch this," she said excitedly when he entered the room. He sat down on the arm of her couch and reached over to rub her shoulder affectionately. She smiled brightly but kept her attention on the screen.

"What is it?" he asked

"*Unsolved Mysteries,*" she said quickly.

Robert Stack was describing the early years of a difficult marriage. The forlorn husband came on, and explained that he and his wife had drifted apart, finally separating when their son was two years old. The wife then began searching for religion. Eventually, she took the son and disappeared into what the father suspected was a cult. David's stomach started to knot up when the screen flashed a photo of the boy whom the father hadn't been seen in two years. He had an idea where this was going. Carrie muted the TV and turned to face him. "I think we should call them." David was silent for a moment, deciding to play dumb.

"Why, have you seen him?"

"No," Carrie said, her eyes shining. "I think we should call the show. Maybe they would feature Gloria."

He mentally screamed in frustration, although his face showed only mild surprise. "Oh . . . I don't know," he said slowly, stalling.

"They solve something like eighty percent of their cases. We can get the whole country looking for them; they won't be able to hide anywhere."

"I don't think I can handle much more of the *local* press, so how can

I take on national attention? It's just—"

"David," Carrie said, moving closer to him on the couch and placing her hand on his knee. "This could bring your children home to you," she said sweetly, interpreting his reticence as fear of failing. "I'll be beside you the whole way. You won't have to face it alone." Her eyes softened, showing the depth of her love for him. "We were so close David; we can't give up now."

David looked down at the floor, deep in thought. How could he argue with that?

"No," he said decidedly as he stood up. "I can't do it; I can't have my life laid out on TV for the entire nation." He waited for her to say something, but when she didn't, he looked down at her. Her expression was thoughtful, and not supportively so. She looked up at him, deep questions in her eyes. "I thought you would do anything to get your children back," she said, her tone bordering on criticism.

"I . . ." he stumbled. He didn't like the doubt he saw on her face. Finally, he forced a smile; he was trapped. "I guess it's worth a try," he said. Carrie smiled, her doubts gone, and got up from the couch.

"Good," she said. "I'll call them right now." She left the room, leaving David alone. He exhaled angrily and looked at the ceiling. All he wanted was to put everything behind him. Thanks to Gloria, he was stuck in a kind of time trap and going nowhere. He wanted a normal life, with a wife and children. He wanted everyone to forget all about Gloria and her accusations. How could he do any of those things unless she disappeared completely?

———

"What happened?" David barked into the cell phone the next morning as he drove to work.

The redhead pulled the phone away from her ear and grimaced. She'd been expecting this call all weekend. Taking a deep breath, she forced herself not to return his anger. "I don't know where she went," she said evenly as she put out her current cigarette and propped her feet up on the desk. "I did everything we talked about and then the whole thing blew up. I warned you this might happen, I told you there was a chance she was involved with this network."

"Yeah," David snorted. "A slim chance." He was silent for a few moments. "I've got TV crews on my front lawn asking for a statement, my boss is wondering if I can handle my case load and my girlfriend wants me to call *Unsolved Mysteries*. This is exactly what I was trying to avoid."

"Oh, that's funny," the redhead replied with deliberate sarcasm. "I thought what you were trying to avoid was being taken back to court."

David didn't answer for a very long time, but she wasn't bothered by his anger in the least. He paid her to do a job, that didn't necessarily mean she agreed with the job she was doing. "Find out where she is," he finally said.

"She's gone," the redhead said with a frustrated shake of her head. "If she were trackable, she'd have been tracked by now; she's hiding out and you're probably safer than ever."

"The FBI is limited in ways you're not," he yelled. "I don't care what you have to do or how much it costs. Find her and take care of her once and for all."

The redhead was quiet for several seconds as she silently pushed the *record* button on her phone. She didn't use this option very often, but now and then it came in handy. If he meant what she thought he meant she'd be sure to get it on tape. She might be a shady investigator, but she wasn't any worse than that. She had lines even she wouldn't cross. "Are you asking me to have her killed?"

"No," he said quickly. "I want her out of the country. We talked about that before."

The redhead nearly laughed at herself, she'd forgotten about the overseas option. "I don't know how I'm going to pull that off since I don't know where she is."

"You'll find her," David said. "I've got a twenty thousand dollar check that's yours when she's gone for good."

"You're that desperate to keep her away from a judge?"

"Look," he said in a patronizing tone. "If I get convicted of this, I lose everything; my license, my religion, my future. Everything. I won't take that chance."

"All right," she said with a shake of her head. He'd told her all this a dozen times, but visions of spending twenty thousand dollars danced merrily in her head and her desire to argue was quickly disappearing. "I'll find her," she said with confidence; a new plan coming to mind already. "And when I do, I'll get her out of here."

———

They'd been at the cottage almost ten days before Pamela got around to scrubbing the bathroom floor. It was very old tile that she assumed was a grayish-brown color. It hadn't taken too much scrubbing to realize it was actually white. If she'd known it was this disgusting she wouldn't have put it off for so long. To think she'd let her kids walk on it for a week and a half! What she'd thought would take an hour had become a day-long project. She didn't mind too much though; it was good to have something to do. Ever since Bryan left ten days ago, she'd felt a little blue. Her mood was ridiculous—she knew that—yet reminding herself of her insanity two hundred times a day didn't seem to be helping. She felt both lonely, and overwhelmed. It was difficult to go from a life full of people, a demanding job, and activities for the kids, to a life like this. A life where they were totally and completely alone. She wondered what Bryan was doing, then pushed the thought away. Thinking of him only made the isolation more depressing.

When she heard a car outside, her heart began to race. She hurried to the front window and peered out in time to see Sharon step out of the car. With a sigh of relief, she hurried to the door, holding it open as Sharon stepped past her toward the kitchen.

"I planned to get here yesterday," Sharon said as she placed a large box on the kitchen table. "But I just couldn't get away."

"That's fine," Pamela said with a smile. Sharon had promised to check in on them. Pamela had been looking forward to it.

Sharon held out a white envelope and gave Pamela a sheepish look. "I found some information for you," she said.

"Information?" Pamela repeated.

"If I were in your shoes, I'd would want to know who I was dealing with."

Confused, Pamela took the envelope and pulled out the paper inside. She glanced over it and looked at Sharon in surprise. "A background check on Bryan?"

Sharon just smiled. Pamela scanned it more closely before nodding and folding it back up, "I'd be lying if I said I haven't wondered about his past."

"Wonder no more," Sharon said with a nod. "He's not clean as a whistle," she said as she turned her attention to the box she'd brought in, "but I don't think you have anything to worry about as long as he doesn't drink anymore."

Pamela stuffed the envelope into her pocket and helped Sharon with the box. "Four years sober I think," she said, relieved that his record was so clean. He had an underage drinking charge and a public intoxication a few years after that. It coincided with the period of his life he'd tended bar. She had absolute faith that that lifestyle was behind him.

"I've got news," Sharon said brightly a few moments later. "You're going to Jacksonville next Friday."

"What?"

"I got you an appointment with Dr. Garcia," Sharon continued.

Pamela's mouth dropped open, "You're kidding!"

Sharon was in no position to take this kind of risk. She'd already made herself vulnerable to help them out this much.

"You're so close to wrapping this up, I can feel it," she explained. "I called his office and he requested that you come in. He wants to talk to you once more and get permission to prepare multiple original reports." Sharon looked up. "I thought the trip would be worth it in the long run. I hope you agree."

Pamela's head was spinning. "I can't believe you did this," she whispered. "I . . . I can't leave yet. I must still be in the papers."

Sharon held up a little white jar in one hand and a roll of tin foil in the other, "We can take care of that today. Have you ever been a blonde?"

Bryan sat on Charlotte's patio as her children ran through the sprinklers. They laughed and screamed at one another while he stared at nothing. Spending time with his nieces and nephew each Sunday night was a highlight of his week, yet he couldn't force himself to join their fun tonight. In fact, for the last two weeks he'd struggled to take part in anything. It seemed that no matter where he was, who he was with or what he was doing, Pamela was always on his mind. At first, he told himself he was just worried about her, but he had no reason to believe she wasn't just fine. Sharon had assured him that her needs would be met, and he believed that. Still, Pamela seemed determined to hang out in his head, increasing his fears that he was, in fact, losing his grip.

Barbara, his young, gorgeous, wonderful girlfriend, was becoming impatient. He knew she wouldn't put up with his aloofness much longer and yet he wasn't sure if he cared. She was the only woman he'd ever really loved in a pure, eternal way. Yet his feelings were waning. He could feel it and he suspected she could feel it, too. He often went all day without thinking of the woman he'd been planning to marry. Instead, it was a rather plain brunette, and her two children, hiding from the law in the Missouri Ozarks, who occupied his thoughts.

As a result of his distraction, Barbara had become aloof in her own way. She didn't call as often as she used to and when they did speak she seemed wary and suspicious. He sensed, from some comments she'd made, that she wanted him to pursue her. Yet, instead of trying to prove his devotion, he was counting the days 'til she left for her family reunion in Houston. Maybe he could sort things out while she was gone. This was all just so crazy! If it were up to him, he'd forget all about Pamela. But somehow it wasn't up to him any more. Pamela was affecting every area of his life and it was making him insane. He longed for some peace of mind, yet it seemed beyond him.

"This seat taken?"

Bryan looked up to see Ray, Charlotte's husband, standing next to an empty lawn chair next to his own, with a beer in his hand. Bryan smiled. "It's your house," Bryan teased. His eyes focused on the silver can before he forced his gaze away. His mouth suddenly felt very dry. At times like this, he craved the relief of alcohol. He'd once been quick to drown his sorrows and wash away his frustrations with a can of beer, or a shot of whiskey; some times a few of each. Even if the temporary relief solved nothing, at least it was relief. He'd changed his lifestyle but still lived with an appetite that continued to hang around, raising its ugly head when he needed it the very least.

"What's got you so bound up?" Ray asked after taking a long slow sip of his beer.

"Me?" Bryan asked with feigned surprise as if nothing were out of the ordinary. "Nothing. I'm fine."

Ray laughed and shook his head. "Yeah, that explains your somber expression and lack of personality," he replied with sarcasm and took another drink. "I bet it has to do with your Little Princess."

Bryan looked across the lawn, not wanting to let Ray read his expression. Of course he would guess it was Barbara who was on his mind. "Not exactly," he muttered after a brief pause.

For nearly a minute, they sat in silence. Finally Ray cleared his throat. "So who is she?"

"Who is who?" Bryan said casually as he tried to focus on the three children squealing a few feet in front of them.

"There's a certain tortured look that a man only gets when a woman is driving him nuts," he laughed at his own joke, stopping only when he realized Bryan hadn't cracked a smile. "I'd guess it's your waitress, but that was cut short. So who's the new crush?" Bryan looked at his brother-in-law in surprise. "Charlotte told me all about her," Ray said with a wink. "About the diner, the river; and the look on your face whenever she was around."

Charlotte hadn't mentioned "a look" to Bryan, however. "Barbara and I are serious. You know that."

"And you sound so very happy about that," Ray countered sarcastically. Bryan looked at him, trying to come up with a clever response, just as Charlotte opened the sliding glass door. She pulled a patio chair up close to her husband's and sat down, a can of Sprite in her hand. Bryan remembered that she'd been big on wine coolers in her drinking days and he wondered for a moment if she ever missed the booze like he did.

"What are we talking about?" she asked, looking back and forth between the two men.

"Women," Ray said before taking a swig of his beer.

"Oh, I'm an expert on that subject. What do you want to know?"

"Bryan's having second thoughts about Barbara," Ray said easily.

"What?" Bryan sputtered. "I didn't say that."

Ray nodded his agreement. "That's true. He's just sitting here, lost in space over some woman who *isn't* Barbara."

"Wha— What are you talking about?" Bryan stammered. "I never said anything like that."

"You didn't have to."

Charlotte picked it up from there. "You have been way out of it for the last two weeks. If Ray's wrong, then what is it?" Bryan said nothing. Ray and Charlotte said nothing, waiting for him to speak. Finally, the temptation to unload proved to be too much.

"I can't get her out of my head," he said in surrender.

"Who?" Ray asked.

Charlotte was silent, thoughtful. Suddenly, she leaned forward, her brow furrowed. "Not Pamela?" she asked.

"She's in my thoughts all the time," Bryan admitted after a long painful silence.

"Well, get her out of there," Ray said, as if it were a simple thing to do. So much for wise advice. "Look, Bry," he said. "If she were still around, and not wanted by the FBI, it would be a whole new situation. But she just isn't here any more. So the best you can do is forget about her."

He made it sound so simple. But actually, he'd given Bryan an idea. "You're right," Bryan said after a few moments. He grinned at his brother-in-law. "Thanks."

"Anytime," Charlotte said with a wave, not the least bit surprised that they'd brilliantly solved his problem in twenty seconds. Bryan suddenly stood up.

"Thanks for dinner," he said, turning toward the driveway where his truck was parked.

"You're leaving already?" Charlotte asked, craning her neck around to watch him.

"I've got something to do," he said, waving once more without turning around.

"Let me know if you need to talk again," Ray called after him. He looked at his wife, and smiled. "We're a swell team, you and me," he said. She smiled and leaned forward to give him a kiss, ignoring the taste of beer on his lips. "We sure are," she said, just a hint of sadness in her voice that she knew he wouldn't catch. He got up, leaving his can next to his chair, and ran toward the kids, causing another round of squeals as he picked up their youngest and tucked him under one arm like a football. Charlotte sighed. When she said she wanted to become a Mormon, Ray said he'd support her so long as he still got to live his life the way he wanted. Sometimes the compromise was hard to honor. Yet as she often did, she reminded herself that she'd choose Ray all over again. Temple marriage or not, with the priesthood or without it, she loved him. She was thirty-four years old, which gave her another fifty years or so to convince him that they deserved to be together forever. She was determined to fight for him, no matter how long it took.

The drive home was a time for Bryan to think. Charlotte and Ray had advised him to forget all about Pamela, since she wasn't around. But she was around. And he certainly should learn why she was becoming such an important part of his life, shouldn't he? His thoughts continued in that direction as he made his way home. When he arrived, he checked his messages. "Bryan, it's me. I'll call you at eight-thirty." It was Sharon's voice; he was sure of it. Twenty minutes later, the phone rang, and he picked it up on the first ring. When he hung up a few minutes later, he let out a deep breath and smiled. Was he being handed the opportunity to put his idea to the test?

Whether the situation was heaven-sent or not, this coming weekend would be a decisive one. The first week of summer school started tomorrow and would run Monday through Wednesday for the next three weeks. Barbara was leaving Friday morning; by then, he'd already be on his way to Jacksonville. When Barbara came back, he would be prepared to either tell her everything he'd been hiding, or admit that his feelings for her had changed. Either way, this weekend would be a turning point for both of them—an important one.

Chapter Twelve

Pamela stood in front of the full-sized mirror that hung on the back of the bathroom door. Her once long brown hair now ended just below her shoulders, with the ends flipped out. Her face was framed by gradual layers that emphasized her cheekbones. The layers were also Marilyn Monroe blonde. Sharon had done a good job of giving Pamela a whole new look. So much so, that it was hard to believe it was her own reflection staring at her. After the make over, Sharon had returned to Little Rock. She'd be back today, Thursday, to stay with the kids while Bryan and Pamela went to Jacksonville. Pamela had tried to persuade Sharon she could go by herself, but Sharon wouldn't hear of it. Someone else needed to buy food, get motel rooms, and do everything else so that Pamela could remain "invisible."

"Mama, you look so pretty." Pamela turned to see Darla standing in the doorway. She looked her mother up and down and then nodded her approval. Today was the first time Pamela had done her hair and worn makeup since the transformation. "You look like a movie star."

Pamela smiled and gave her daughter a hug. "Thank you," she said. "Now are you sure you're okay with the arrangements?"

Darla nodded with confidence. "I like Sharon," she said.

Pamela stared at her daughter for a few more seconds. Thank goodness the kids were comfortable with all this. Pamela wouldn't have left if they had raised the slightest protest.

"Yahoo!" Kenny shouted from downstairs, causing both of them to look towards the stairs. They looked back at one another and smiled; Bryan must have arrived. A jolt of energy traveled from her head to her toes as they bounded down the stairs to see him.

"You're blonde," Bryan said in a tone of shock when she reached the front porch. Both kids were already outside welcoming him.

His response caught her off guard and she stopped short. Absently she lifted a hand and touched her hair. "It's not natural," she said foolishly. He could certainly tell it wasn't natural. He continued staring at her as if he'd never seen her before. His blatant admiration made her blush.

"I like it," Bryan said. A few more seconds passed during which time her cheeks turned from pink to red and his smile grew until he finally shook his head and turned his attention to the kids. They were obviously happy to see him, although Kenny was the most open about it. "I brought presents." He glanced at Pamela again, as if unable not to, but she avoided his gaze. There was a look in his eyes that made her pulse quicken.

Both kids eyes went wide at the mention of gifts. Kenny immediately asked what his present was. Darla looked at her mom for permission to accept Bryan's offering. Pamela smiled uncomfortably, but nodded that it was okay.

"You want to see?" Bryan said in a questioning tone, as if he didn't know the answer.

"Yes! Yes!" Kenny shouted, jumping up and down.

Bryan turned to Darla. "Do you want to see?"

She nodded shyly, but her eyes were aglow and Pamela knew she was just as excited as her brother. Bryan then looked up at Pamela. "And how about your mom? Is it okay with her?"

Way to put me on the spot, she thought to herself. Kenny immediately ran to her and pulled her hand, dragging her down the porch steps. The whole ten seconds of suspense were apparently too long for him. Pamela chuckled and gestured for Bryan to go ahead as she held Kenny back for a moment. Bryan led them to the back of the truck. He began rubbing his chin with his thumb and forefinger. "Now are y'all sure you want to see this?"

Both kids' heads nodded up and down furiously—even Darla had lost her reticence. "Okay," he said with a wink. He pulled up on the tailgate handle and let it fall open. For several seconds, there was total silence.

"Bikes," Kenny breathed, his voice reverently hushed with awe. He took a step closer and then looked up at Bryan. "These are for us?"

"Yep," he said. Kenny immediately began scurrying into the back of the truck. Bryan climbed up with him and helped him stand up the more masculine of the two bikes.

"Mom, look at this," Kenny said, running his hand across the handlebars.

"Wow," Pamela said with a smile. "That's the coolest bike I've ever seen."

"Do you know how to ride it?" Bryan asked as he lifted the bike and lowered it to the ground. Kenny scampered after it like a mouse chasing cheese.

"Yeah," he said, his eyes still focused on the bike as if it might disappear any moment. "I rode Troy's bike all the time."

As soon as the bike was down, Kenny jumped on it and began pedaling, making circles on the gravel drive. "Mom, can I ride it in the woods?"

"Yeah," she said hesitantly. "Just stay on the paths close to the house."

"And don't forget this," Bryan said as he tossed him a black helmet with flames painted on both sides. In five seconds, he'd disappeared into the trees. Darla was still speechless and Bryan smiled as he presented her bike, a red five-speed with white lettering. Once it was on the ground, she walked up to it and placed her hand gently on the seat. "This is really for me?" she asked.

"All yours," he said. "Can you ride?"

She looked up at him with offense. "I'm nine," she reminded him.

"Of course," he said apologetically. "Sorry." He tossed another helmet to her and she strapped it on like a pro before climbing on the bike.

"Can I ride in the woods?" she asked her mother.

"Yeah," Pamela agreed. "Just be careful." She promised that she would be and took off after her brother. Bryan climbed out of the bed of the truck and put the tailgate back up. "I hope you don't mind," he said after a moment.

"It's a lot of money," Pamela answered. She'd hidden it from the kids, but she was a little uncomfortable.

"All Kenny could talk about the last time I was here was that he wanted a bike; they have an auction at the freight yard every weekend and I picked them up for fifteen bucks apiece. I've been worried about you guys being bored and came up with a way to make things a little better. I'm only trying to help."

She nodded, and gave him a grateful smile. "Thank you," she said. "I just feel like we're taking so much from you. I've already complicated your life so much; you don't need to do more."

"Don't worry about it," he said in an easy tone. "I'm a big boy and a meticulous saver—I'm all right."

There was a long silence as she thought of all the questions she wanted to ask him. Some more important than others. "Have you told Barbara?" she just blurted it out and then didn't want to hear the answer. Bryan looked at the ground and then leaned against the truck.

"No," he said simply, looking up at her. "She's not ready yet." *Yet?* Pamela repeated in her mind. Bryan continued, "She's out of town 'til next week. I plan to tell her everything when she gets back."

"I don't want to ruin what you two have going," she continued.

"I've got something for you too," he said, ignoring her comment and changing the subject. He walked around to the passenger seat, opened the door and pulled out a plain cardboard box. "Open it," he said as he handed it to her.

She decided to follow his lead and leave the subject of Barbara alone for the moment as she accepted the box. Pulling back the flaps, she grinned. "*Ensigns*," she said as she extracted one of the thin magazines. For several seconds she just stared at them.

"They're the ones published since December of the year you left," he said. "I keep them, but rarely reread them once I'm done. I thought maybe you'd like them."

"Oh, Bryan," she said softly as she thumbed through the treasure trove. "You have no idea how much I've missed these."

"If I had no idea, then I wouldn't have brought them," he answered playfully. She just shook her head and returned the magazine she held to the box.

"Thank you," she said sincerely. They shared a look until he looked away and changed the subject again.

"Sharon's not here yet?"

"No," Pamela answered. "But I'm sure she'll be here soon. Want to come inside while I make lunch?"

"You're not making Yankee food, are ya?"

Pamela laughed. "Yankee food?"

"Yeah. Stuff with tuna fish or that has low-fat in the title."

"How about a German pancake?"

Bryan raised his eyebrows. "Now *that* sounds good," he said following her up the steps. "I haven't had one in weeks."

She declined his offer to help, so he sat at the table while she worked. "There was an article in the paper about you," he said after a few minutes. Her hands slowed for a moment, but she didn't comment. "It was titled 'Who Is Gloria Stanton?'" he added.

"And let me guess what it said," she responded, just a hint of defensiveness in her voice. "That I'm a vindictive woman willing to emotionally harm my children for the sake of getting vengeance on an innocent man."

"Not quite," Bryan said, although she was close. "It talked about the court case in Utah that was discontinued. Your attorney says he'll be trying again once you return. It did tell about underground organizations that hide parents like you, though." He gave her a chance to speak but she didn't take it, she just continued what she was doing. "It said that most parents take their children for revenge when they don't receive the custody rights they wanted in a divorce. It said a lot of children are abused or harmed in some additional way after they're taken away, and that they often struggle with their new life, new identities, etc."

"How many were abused before they left?" Her back was toward him and she shrugged before continuing. "There are no easy explanations, Bryan. For what it's worth, I had to fax Darla's medical reports and the court documents before the organization agreed to help me. I've spent nearly two years in training and Darla spent that time in therapy. This whole thing is about helping my kids, not hurting them." Pamela washed her hands, turned, pulled a dish towel out of the drawer next to the sink and proceeded to dry her hands as she leaned back against the cupboards. "I'm sure there are instances where a child is put into another abusive situation after they leave, because other organizations aren't as thorough as this one is. I don't know. But my kids are safer here, despite all the hardships. I assume the article didn't make me into some hero?"

"No," Bryan answered.

"Good," she said, turning back to the sink.

"Good?" Bryan repeated with a chuckle, assuming she was kidding. She turned to look at him again and his smile fell. She was serious.

"Taking my children was the last resort—the absolute-no-other-choice thing to do. It isn't something to take lightly. Every time I read an article that applauds what I've done, I feel sick inside. I wonder how many vengeful parents read it and think 'what a great idea!'" Pamela looked away. "I'm here because I have to be," she said. "What the papers don't say is that as soon as I get caught my kids will be fair game for David. They will have one parent under suspicion of abuse and one parent accused of felony kidnapping."

"Have you ever wondered if you only made things worse by leaving?"

"The reason I left was because sexual abuse is hard to prove. When you're married to an attorney, it becomes even harder. I needed time to—"

Bryan lifted his eyebrows. "He's a lawyer?" he interrupted; the article hadn't mentioned that.

"Real estate mostly," she answered. "But he is a shrewd attorney and he has a lot to lose if everyone finds out what he did. He also knows which loopholes to look for, and all the tricks. I couldn't keep up with him. I just believed that the truth would be discovered and it would all go away, but he launched a campaign against me. The doctors couldn't find 100 percent conclusive evidence, and he denied it vehemently to every journalist and news camera he could find. When Darla took the stand during the hearing, she broke into tears and said she forgot what to say. It was a mess." She looked back at Bryan and he could see the anger in her eyes. "I had . . . complications when Kenny was born." She paused for a moment and then hurried on. "Afterwards I took antidepressants and David hired a nanny to help out for a few months. I stayed on the medication for a year—boy, did David had a heyday with that.

"As soon as I filed for divorce, he pushed it through as if it had been his idea. As soon as the divorce was final he filed a new custody suit in which he attacked me from every angle he could imagine. He found experts to go on record stating that there is no such thing as postpartum depression, and that I had a chemical imbalance which made me an unfit custodial parent. He started a petition for full custody on the grounds of my inabilities and false allegations." She let out a dry chuckle and shook her head as she threw the dishtowel on the counter. "It was such a nightmare. And then I was court-ordered to give him private visitation. I was left with only one way to protect my kids and that was to get them out of his reach."

"And this new doctor," he said. "The one we're going to see can change all that?"

"I hope so," she said. The sound of a car caught their attention. They shared a look and Bryan wished Sharon had been a few minutes later. There was so much he still needed to know. He liked that they were able to discuss this without the anger she felt during their first argument in the park. It was much nicer this way. He was looking forward to the drive to Jacksonville more than ever.

Peg laughed at some friendly comment from the trucker she was serving and winked before heading back to the counter. Peg's third marriage was ending and she was seriously considering finding herself a long-haul truck driver to fill the husband bill for her fourth time around. She couldn't imagine a better husband than one who was gone three weeks out of every month. The bell above the door jingled and she turned, plates in hand, from the cooks counter. "Well, if it isn't Frank Farley," she said with another wink. "Haven't seen ya round much lately."

Frank smiled nervously and looked around. He was a quiet man. Not too smart, very shy and pretty much a loner. His hands were deep in his pockets as he looked around the diner. "Donny here?" he asked almost too softly for her to hear.

"Sure is," she said as she walked past him. "Just let me serve up this order and I'll take you back. He's doing bills."

A few minutes after showing Frank to the back, Peg casually returned to the office and leaned toward the door. There was barely room enough for two people to stand inside the office and she knew when Donny shut the door, that whatever was being said was worth being overheard. Donny didn't believe in upgrading things like paper thin doors because that wouldn't increase his profit margin. For several minutes she listened intently, completely oblivious to neglected customers a few yards away. When she heard Frank say he needed to get going, she hurried back to the counter and started making rounds with the coffee pot as if she'd been busy the whole time.

It was nearly five o'clock when she returned home to an empty house. Husband number three had moved out a few weeks earlier. She headed immediately to the phone, pulled a small white card out from within the pages of her address book and dialed the number. The FBI had been asking for information for weeks, but they never offered to pay for it.

"This is Peg, from Donny's Diner," she said with a smile. "You still got that hundred bucks to give away?"

"Of course I do," the woman said. Peg listened to papers being shuffled around. "Go ahead."

"You bring me the money first." Peg demanded.

As soon as she had paid off the waitress and had the information recorded, the redhead called David's cell phone. "We got something good," she said as soon as he answered. "Apparently Gloria's car broke down on her way out of town. It was found a couple of days after she left on a side road off the highway. They found her prints inside, but the outside was clean. The cops asked everybody for information. Someone had to have helped her get away, but no one offered anything. However, I've just learned that someone *did* see her. The guy went to her old boss today to ask what he should do. Apparently he was poaching or something when he saw her and a man pushing her car off the road. They didn't see him. He's afraid that if he goes to the cops, he'll get in trouble for hunting out of season. At the same time, he doesn't want to get her caught either, since he's a friend of her old boss. The boss told him to keep his mouth shut and not stir things up."

"So where is she?" David demanded.

The redhead grimaced, was it impossible for him to show some gratitude. "Well I'm not sure, but some tall, dark-haired guy in a blue, full-sized truck drove off with her and the kids. Peg said there was a guy who used to come in and see Gloria who fits the description. His name is Bryan Drewry."

"So where is she?" David asked again, this time his voice was very flat.

"I'm going to find the guy tomorrow. I'm sure he'll take a payoff for—"

"Call me when you've made some real progress," he snapped. "None of this garbage interests me." The phone clicked off and she gritted her teeth. If he didn't pay her so well she'd never put up with his attitude. Why on earth did Gloria ever marry this jerk?

Theresa Carson braced the laundry basket against her hip and walked slowly up the stairs. The kids were asleep and her husband was on his way home from working swing shift at a medical equipment factory. She placed the laundry basket on the floor and turned on the TV. With three children, two of them still in diapers, and a part time job as a dental assistant she didn't get many opportunities to watch programs of her choice. With the remote control, she surfed the channels until hearing the familiar theme music to the show *Unsolved Mysteries*. She paused for a moment, surfed a little longer, and finally accepted that there wasn't anything else of interest. She settled on the floor and began sorting socks as Robert Stack's throaty voice began laying out the background facts of the next segment.

She had finished folding the whites and was half-way through the darks when a familiar voice made her freeze. For several moments, she stared at the nightgown she was in the process of folding. Then, slowly, she lifted her head. He was older than she remembered, but of course he would be. It had been almost twenty years. She listened to his plea for help and had to close her eyes to keep her composure from crumbling.

She remembered the day, all those years ago, when her mother had confronted him about her accusations like it had been yesterday. He'd been seventeen years old, almost a man. She was only nine and still very much a child. They'd called the police, but despite her detailed account of what he'd done, everyone believed that *he* was telling the truth. By the end, even she was almost convinced that her experience had been harmless and she'd misinterpreted his behavior. Her mother seemed relieved to believe it had never happened and they'd never talked about it again.

However, she'd come to learn that not only was the incident far from harmless, it had changed the girl she'd been. It had taken nearly ten years of therapy but she was finally feeling like a normal person, living a normal life. She'd married a good man who knew what had happened and was willing to wade through the difficulties it often caused in their relationship. Seeing David on TV now, explaining how desperately he missed his children reminded her of something her therapist had once explained to her. "Child molesters aren't always aware of what they've done," she'd said. "We tend to expect them to be monstrous demons, intent on destroying lives. But they're usually much different. They aren't always conscious of the opportunities they create to act upon children. Once it happens, they often try to deny it to themselves, downplay it or justify it in one way or another. They don't think of themselves as molesters or abusers, and because it's a child they often don't think what they do is even harmful." It had been a difficult concept for Theresa to accept, but watching him there, and remembering his vehement denials of what he'd done to her, made it all come together.

"What are you watching?"

She turned quickly at the sound of her husband's voice and smiled. "Oh, nothing," she said, changing the channel. He kissed her on the cheek on his way to take a shower and she stared at the commercial for shampoo. Things had been going so well, she wasn't sure she was capable of allowing this pain back into her life again. She thought of the photo they'd showed of his daughter, the one his ex-wife had kidnapped because of unconfirmed accusations of abuse. She ached for that little girl. Thank goodness her mother had taken her away. At least she was safe now.

Chapter Thirteen

"How does this one look?" Bryan asked. Pamela surveyed the small gas station, her eyes stopping at the outside restroom door.

"Perfect." They'd been looking for a station where she could change her clothes in the bathroom without going inside. Bryan pulled up just a few feet away from the door marked "Gals" and she climbed out of the truck. "I'll be right back."

A few minutes later she opened the truck door and climbed back in, smoothing the skirt of the black suit when she was seated. Bryan whistled, but said nothing.

"Sharon brought it up today," Pamela said as she took off the black pumps and wiggled her toes. She'd always hated wearing heels. "She was afraid she'd bought it too big, but I think it fits real nice."

"Real nice," Bryan agreed. She looked up and met his eyes, but only briefly. The unmasked approval in his eyes made her stomach flip.

"We'd better get going," she said as she slipped the fake wedding ring on her finger to complete the disguise; Sharon had thought of everything, down to claiming a pretend marital status. "I can't be late." They had left the cottage at three o'clock in the afternoon the previous day and stopped in Birmingham, Alabama, around ten o'clock. They'd gotten separate rooms and slept until eight before hitting the road again. They entered Jacksonville with thirty minutes to find the doctor's office. They found it ten minutes early and she thanked him again before climbing out of the truck. "You know this thing wasn't designed for women in skirts," she commented when she reached the ground.

"Oh, I don't know about that," he said with a wink. "I'll meet you right here."

It took a few seconds for Pamela to compose herself outside the office, but finally she lifted her chin and walked confidently inside. She'd gone over the plan in detail all week long and it was now committed to memory. She was nervous anyway; she hoped with all her heart that this meeting would be the beginning of the end of this ordeal.

Bryan was waiting in the parking lot when she stepped out of the front doors almost an hour later. When she climbed into the passenger seat she grinned triumphantly and slapped a stack of papers on the seat between them.

"You got it?" Bryan asked.

"They made me all the originals I'll ever need. He even had his partner there so I wouldn't have to make a separate appointment," she replied. "It couldn't have gone any smoother." She let out a breath, energized by her success, as they pulled into traffic. They drove a few more blocks before she spoke again. "I'm starving. Can we stop and eat?"

"I know of this little place in Stockton, Alabama," he said. "If we hurry we can make it before they close tonight and get a *real* meal."

"Do you think it's safe for me to go out in public?"

"I think you'll be fine; you look a lot different than that picture that's circulating, and we can get some drive thru to hold us over."

"Can we stop somewhere so I can change?"

"No."

"No?" she repeated.

"I like the dress," he said easily without meeting her eyes. A pink flush crept up her cheeks and she leaned back against the seat, unable to hide a smile at his compliment. If he wanted her to stay in the dress a little longer, she'd stay in the dress.

They grabbed a hamburger at McDonald's before following Highway 10 across northern Florida. It was nine-thirty when they pulled up to the restaurant. Lambert's Café reminded her of Cracker Barrel Restaurants. It had a large, covered porch along the front of the wooden building that protected a collection of rocking chairs from the elements. "I think I'm overdressed."

"You look fabulous," Bryan said as he parked the truck. She reached for the door handle. "Don't touch that," he said sternly. She pulled her hand away and watched as he walked around the truck and opened the door for her. He stretched out a hand, which she reached for slowly. The few moments of contact while he helped her down from the truck warmed her whole body and she couldn't take her eyes off him.

Inside, the walls were covered with old advertisements for Coke, cigarettes and movies. There were loud friendly voices and the aroma of home-cooked food was heavenly. A hostess showed them to a table. Pamela was just sliding into her chair when an object whizzed through the air above them, causing her to duck and sit down faster. Whatever it was, bounced off the table behind them, causing the room of people to burst into laughter. She looked around in order to see what was happening. A large black man seated two tables away had his hands up in the air, cupped as if he were going to catch a football. Suddenly, another object shot over her head. She ducked again, although this time there was plenty of clearance. The man hooted as he caught the projectile. She turned to question Bryan; this was unlike any restaurant she'd ever heard of.

"Lambert's Café," he proclaimed. "Home of the Thrown Roll."

She looked up as another roll soared across the room and into the hands of an elderly man who then punched his fist into the air to celebrate his catch.

"Rolls?" she asked.

Bryan nodded, then lifted his hands. A young man standing beside a wheeled cart some ten yards away nodded, pulled a roll out of a pan on the cart and tossed it into Bryan's hands. "You want one?" he asked after dropping his prize onto his plate.

She laughed. "Sure."

He lifted his hands again. This time, the roll was too high and it hit the woman sitting behind him in the head. She just laughed along with everyone else. Bryan raised his hands again. This time he caught it and handed it to Pamela. "This is one of my favorite restaurants," he said as he broke open his roll. A waitress offered him Sorghum Molasses from a can, but he shook his head no. Pamela shook her head, too. If a good Southern boy didn't like it, she wasn't going to try it either. "They have one in Ozark," he continued.

"Ozark, Arkansas?" she asked. Ozark was located about an hour and half south west of Harrison.

Bryan shook his head. "Ozark, Missouri, it's just outside of Springfield."

The waitress took their order; Pamela ordered the catfish just as Bryan did. While they waited for their meals, several servers came around with large pots of side dishes such as fried potatoes, cole slaw, giblets in gravy, and fried okra. She skipped the giblets but tried everything else as she continued to watch dozens of rolls sail through the air. The restaurant was entertaining, the food was great, and the company was excellent. The more time she spent with Bryan, the more she wanted to spend; her feelings scared her but her heart felt light. She'd have to make a clean break from him soon.

This couldn't continue. A roll whizzed through the air from behind her and hit Bryan in the forehead, interrupting her thoughts. He quickly picked it up off the table and threw it back at the roll-thrower, laughing. Her stomach flipped as a warm sensation traveled through her whole body. He had a great smile. She looked at her plate and focused on her food again. How on earth was she supposed to make a clean break when just being near him made her feel so good?

————

They stopped for the night at a motel in Stockton and Bryan rented two rooms. Pamela spent the first half hour staring at the common wall between their rooms. She imagined she could hear him breathing and finally forced herself to roll over and close her eyes. This fantasy was getting out of hand. *He has a girlfriend, for heaven's sake,* she told herself. And she had little doubt he was already asleep.

Bryan, however, lay in his own bed with his hands behind his head as he stared at the ceiling. Shadows danced on the plaster above him, but what he saw was Gloria in that dress. The shape of her calves when she wore those shoes and the way her hair shone in the sunlight was enough to send him to the shower. Again. When he'd pulled up and seen her blonde hair, his mouth had gone dry, and his feelings hadn't been tempered since then. Until today he'd always seen her dressed for work or in oversized clothing. The suit Sharon had brought for her to wear was downright wicked; at least it made him feel wicked. It was disconcerting for her to be on the other side of that wall. So close, he thought, and yet so very far away.

Saturday morning they stopped at a few car dealerships en route to Missouri. They went out of their way to avoid Arkansas as they did so. So far, Sharon and Bryan had kept her from needing to go to town. But she was anxious about having no transportation and would feel more secure if she had a car. In Springfield, just as she thought she'd never find a dependable car in her price range, she hit pay dirt and bought a 1991 Honda Civic for two thousand dollars. Bryan was now free to go on home to Harrison, but he insisted on following her to the cottage. To make sure the car wasn't a lemon, he said. As she drove, she couldn't help glancing in the rear-view mirror several times a minute. Each time she did so, her stomach fluttered. Each time she felt the increasingly familiar flutter, she rolled her eyes and berated herself.

When the two vehicles pulled up at the cottage on Saturday afternoon, the door flew open and both kids bounced down the steps. Sharon caught the door before it banged shut and watched the reunion. "How'd everything go?" Darla asked as Pamela bent down to catch her daughter in a hug.

"Perfect," Pamela said. She glanced up to see Bryan holding Kenny while Kenny told him how much fun they'd had on their bikes. It was such a heart warming scene that the ache in her heart increased ten-fold. She had to turn away. Holding Darla's hand, they went up the steps. "How were things here?" she asked, choosing to focus on her daughter instead of on Bryan.

Sharon smiled toward Darla. "You've got a couple of great kids."

Pamela looked down at her daughter and gave her a little shoulder squeeze. "I do, don't I."

"Did you get the reports?" Sharon asked anxiously. Pamela held up the papers triumphantly. A wide grin spread across Sharon's face as she held the screen door open. "Then let's get to work," she said. Casting a look at Bryan she added, "Will you keep the kids busy out here?" Neither of them needed to hear what the report said.

"Of course," Bryan said. Darla went back down the steps. He looked at the kids and rubbed his hands together. "Do we work on that fort or pull some weeds?"

Sharon and Pamela shared a knowing look while the kids begged to work on the fort they'd been building behind the cottage. Once inside, the women went to the table. There was silence for almost ten minutes while Sharon reviewed the report. When she finished, she looked up and smiled. "I think you're on your way home."

Tears sprang immediately to Pamela's eyes. The wave of warmth threatened to overwhelm her completely. After a moment she managed to speak. "Really?"

Sharon nodded and returned the paper she'd been reviewing to the stack of others on the table. "Carla was right about Dr. Garcia, he's very thorough and specific. I don't think you can get a better assessment than this."

"Wow," Pamela breathed, looking at the table top in disbelief. "Going home . . . it sounds so unreal."

"You need to mail these to the district attorney's office in Salt Lake, your personal attorney, David's attorney, and probably your parents. Wait a week and then call your lawyer and take his advice."

"I can't believe I'm almost finished with this," Pamela said, still shaking her head.

"Don't get too excited. You're just beginning the hardest leg," Sharon said sympathetically. "You'll be arrested, the kids will be taken away, and you'll have the fight of your life on your hands."

"But you think I've got a case?"

"I don't think it could be any better," she said carefully. "On the other hand, you know better than anyone that there are no guarantees when a judge and jury get involved. If you don't think you're ready, then hold off for a few days, or even weeks if you want. The reports aren't going to go anywhere, but once you're in Utah, there'll be nowhere left to run."

Pamela looked out the window and let out a breath. "I'm tempted to stay in hiding forever," she admitted quietly, looking up into the face of the other woman. "Is that crazy?"

"You know your kids are safe here," Sharon said with an understanding nod. "That's a powerful reason to stay put. If you decide to stay, I'll help you any way I can, but this could be your chance for freedom. Freedom you deserve." She smiled sadly, feeling the gravity of Pamela's decision. They sat in silence for another minute. Finally Sharon stood. "I hate to rush out, but I've got to get going," she said.

"Of course," Pamela said, getting to her feet. She gave Sharon a long hug. "Thank you so much," she said quietly. "You've been such a blessing."

"Now don't go blaming Him," Sharon said with a laugh. "I'm just doing what's right." The two women paused for a few moments before Sharon spoke again. "I'll keep an eye on the papers. If I don't hear anything I'll check in with you in July. If you need me you can call my cell phone but—"

"I won't call unless I absolutely need to."

"Good luck," Sharon said as she picked up her bag from where it sat beside the door. "You're in my prayers."

Bryan and the kids left their fort-building to tell her good bye. Bryan told the two of them to return to their project, and he'd join them in a few minutes, before turning to face Pamela. "So what did she think?"

"She thinks I'm ready to go home."

"What do *you* think?" Bryan asked after a slight pause, during which she wished she could read his thoughts.

"I think it's a big decision," she said, kicking at a small rock as they slowly walked toward the fort hidden in the trees behind the cottage. "This is probably my last chance. If it doesn't work . . ." Her voice trailed off and they remained silent. "I need to take some time to think it through." Out of the corner of her eye, she saw him nod. "What do *you* think I should do?"

"I think you need to follow your heart," Bryan said. She looked up at him and their eyes locked for several seconds until she looked away.

"It wasn't so long ago that you didn't believe in what my heart told me to do," she said. He turned to look at her and she continued. "I followed my heart in the beginning. Are you sure you'd advise me to do it again?" Bryan looked away thoughtfully.

When he looked back, his expression was soft. "I think you need to follow your heart . . . again."

She couldn't help but smile at knowing that his feelings had changed. His mouth turned up at the corners and she marveled that he was here at all. The kids called for Bryan to hurry. He rolled his eyes, smiled and quickly disappeared in the trees. Her heart was doing all kinds of weird things these last few days. She hoped she could still it.

Pamela had expected Bryan to leave soon, but just as during his first visit, he didn't seem to be in any hurry to go. They played softball in the backyard and then he showed the kids how to catch fireflies in a jar to make a nightlight. Bryan was like a new toy for them and they couldn't get enough of him—Pamela included. Even Darla was at ease with him. She still kept a little distance and didn't initiate contact, but she laughed and teased in a way that convinced Pamela that she trusted Bryan. That alone made Bryan very dear to her. He was the first man in a long time who didn't bring fear to her daughter's eyes.

When Pamela announced it was time for bed, the kids groaned and protested at a pitch that surprised her. When she threatened to ground them from their bikes the next day, they quickly stopped protesting.

After finally tucking them in, Pamela came down the stairs to find the small living room empty. A creak in the direction the front porch told her Bryan was enjoying the summer night. Bryan sat in one of the wicker chairs with his feet propped up on the railing. He craned his neck to smile at her when the screen door squeaked open. "It's a beautiful evening," he said, looking back at the scene in front of them. The three-quarter moon was behind the cottage, but cast a silvery sheen on the trees that protected the little haven. Pamela took the other chair, propped her feet up on the railing too, and enjoyed the night sounds of crickets and cicadas.

For several minutes they sat there, together but separate, enjoying the fragility of the peaceful night. "Thanks for all you've done," Pamela finally said. "I really appreciate it."

"My pleasure," he said with a smile. The depth of his voice was softer than usual; soothing. "Thank you for good company and a wonderful dinner. What was that stuff called?"

"Alfredo," she said with a laugh. It seemed absurd that he didn't know about Fettuccini Alfredo. "I'm glad you liked it, although it's definitely Yankee food."

"I liked it anyway," he said with a chuckle. They lapsed into another silence until he stood, surprising her. "I'd like to leave this with you," he said. He stepped toward her and pulled a small black item out of a pouch on his belt. She recognized it right away. He handed it to her but she didn't take it. Her eyes traveled, somewhat slower than she intended, up his body before resting on his face.

"I can't take your phone," she said.

"You need something up here to—"

She shook her head and retucked her hair behind her ears. "Phones are traceable, even cell phones. If this somehow got traced back to you as the owner, you'd be in big trouble."

"I realize you can't call just anyone," he explained. "But you might need to call your doctor's office, or your attorney. And I'd like to know when you decide about going back."

She continued to stare at him, but said nothing. He smiled his crooked grin and pressed the phone into her hand. "I've got to get going," he said.

"Right now?" she said, standing up to join him.

"I've got meetings in the morning," he said. "and Barbara's expecting me to call her in Houston before church."

Barbara again. Why was it that Pamela found it so easy to forget about that woman? "Of course," she said, hoping her disappointment wasn't obvious. "When does she get back?" She hoped he didn't notice the sting in her voice.

Bryan looked at her for a few minutes, as if considering her response. "Barbara and I are pretty serious," he said, not bothering to answer her question.

"Good," Pamela said, now avoiding his eyes. She had no desire to talk about Barbara and looked out at the trees as if fascinated by them. The last thing she wanted right now was to have a conversation about Barbara. Actually though, maybe that's exactly what she needed. This little fantasy of hers needed to put to rest and Barbara was probably the fastest means to that end.

"We've talked about getting married. I think I could spend my whole life with her," Bryan continued as if she hadn't spoken. She could feel that he was still staring at her.

"Congratulations." Her tone was flatter than she intended and she wished he'd look away from her face so she could wince just a little.

"There's just one problem."

Where was he going with all this? In two steps he was beside her. He put his hands on her waist and turned her to face him. She didn't pull away, but her body stiffened as little bolts of electricity prickled in her chest. Her reaction didn't dissuade him and he brought a hand to her cheek. With one finger, he slowly traced her jaw line. She nearly stopped breathing and her heart began to race. All she could do was stare. "Barbara isn't the woman I think of day and night."

The words hung like perfume in the air between them and Pamela continued to stare, her lips slightly parted and her eyes wide. Did he really say what she just heard from his lips?

When he leaned into her she automatically pulled back, leaving a space between them. He'd just told her he was practically engaged. Yet it seemed like a silly reason not to give in to her feelings for him. His eyes were soft; enveloping, and she sensed he was thinking the same thing. Sharing a kiss would be wrong and yet it was obvious that neither of them cared. He leaned in a little farther and this time she did the same. Thoughts of felony kidnapping, Barbara, everything but the two of them, evaporated. Right or wrong was of no consequence, especially since this felt so right. Their lips met, just barely, and for a moment they didn't move. A line had been crossed and they were not turning back. Then his hand moved into her hair and she turned her head slightly, to a better position that he quickly took advantage of. Every worry in her life melted away as she gave in to the euphoric feeling of being joined with this man in the wonder of a first kiss. She slid a hand around his neck, pulling him closer as she savored the roughness of his face against her mouth, the smell of his cologne and the slightly salty taste on his lips. The pulsing in her veins increased and the air around them became thick and hot.

The intensity grew to a point where this felt as normal and as natural as anything else she'd ever done, until he stopped it sharply. He pulled away with a look of shock on his face. She wondered if he was surprised by the chemistry passing between them or by his ability to end it. They just stared at one another, unable to speak for several seconds as their breathing returned to normal and the air ceased to sizzle. She wanted nothing more than to pull his mouth to hers once again, but she restrained herself. "I'll be back Thursday," he whispered, slowly tracing her jaw once more, then her neck, her collarbone. She moaned internally and ached for more.

The passion lingering in his eyes gave him a vulnerable look when he smiled. "We'll have things to talk about." She nodded slowly. For a few more moments they remained this way, his arms loosely at her waist, her hands resting on his shoulders. The look in his eyes told her he was just as fearful of the power they'd created as she was. Finally he leaned in, kissing her softly on the mouth one last time. Not another word was said as he released her, went to the truck, and started the engine. But no words were necessary right now. They'd shared volumes within just a few moments. She truly felt there was nothing left to say.

As the door shut behind her and the sound of Bryan's truck disappeared down the lane, Pamela couldn't help but smile to herself. She lifted a hand to her lips and relived the moment of being in his arms, with his mouth pressed against hers. What a sensation it was! Had she ever before felt that kind of passion in a single kiss? It was an easy question to answer. She'd never experienced anything like this.

She climbed the stairs, still reliving the moment and was startled to find Kenny watching her from where he lay in her bed when she entered the room. Smiling at her son, she laid on her stomach and bunched up a pillow to prop herself up. The daze had yet to fade completely.

"You're supposed to be asleep," she said, tapping him lightly on the nose. Kenny smiled mischievously. "Darla's a sleepyhead," he said flopping onto his back. One skinny leg was tangled in the bedding while the other lay on top of the covers. The T-shirt he'd worn to bed was huge and his hair was tousled, which made him look younger than he really was. His arms were out from his sides taking up almost half the full-sized bed. He turned his head and looked at his mom once more. There was a twinkle in his eyes. "Are you and Bryan getting married?"

Married. The word echoed in her head. Married, like a normal person, living a normal life? The question took her off guard and forced her to take an objective look at what was really happening between herself and Bryan. The cloud she'd been floating on disappeared and she felt as if she were falling back to earth. Back to reality. Several seconds passed before she attempted to answer him. When she spoke, the words felt heavy on her tongue.

"No, buddy," she said softly. For an instant her consciousness protested. There was a chance, a slim possibility, that everything would work out somehow. He obviously cared for her, and she knew she was on the fast track to falling in love with him. But she was a realist, not a romantic. This flirtation may have distracted her from the truth, but it had changed nothing. To be with her meant that he would have to give up everything. Much more than he could realize. She was a fool to have let her fantasy get so out of hand. "Bryan and I are not going to get married." Trusting a man again, feeling protected and loved, had until recently seemed an impossibility to her. And yet with Bryan it had been so easy. If she didn't know better, she'd have thought it was meant to be. But she did know better, and there was no future for them. Her heart began to ache as the realization solidified in her mind.

"But I saw you guys kissing," Kenny said after a moment. Pamela's eye's left the ceiling where they had come to rest and returned to the confused eyes of her son.

She knew that now she was supposed to give some inspired explanation, but no words came to mind. Kenny looked confused and a little irritated, and Pamela didn't blame him. She was confused and irritated, too. With no other options coming to mind, she changed the subject completely. "How about a chocolate sundae?"

Kenny watched her for a moment, as if trying to find another way to get a better answer. Finally, he just got out of bed. "Okay," he said, his tone rather flat for a six-year-old about to have ice cream at ten o'clock at night.

Once Kenny was back in bed, Pamela fully faced the situation. At another time, in another place, their attraction could have been a starting point for something glorious. But here and now made it impossible. She sat down heavily at the small kitchen table and stared out into the moonlit night. Taking a deep breath, she looked at the reports still sitting on the kitchen table. With Bryan filling her thoughts she'd forgotten the reports; her ticket home. Going home—the thing she'd been longing for these past two and half years and had nearly forgotten about today. It was time to fully analyze the situation, find an answer and make a decision. She got on her knees, turning to face the chair she'd just been sitting on and asked her Father in Heaven for help. When she finished, her face was wet with tears and her heart was still heavy. She retrieved her pewter jewelry box, removed its contents and read the scripture that had guided her before. When she finished reading, she knew what she needed to do. God had prepared her escape once; now it was time for her to return and finish the fight. She'd mail the reports on Monday, then she'd prepare to leave for home. As for Bryan, she knew what she *wanted* to do; she also knew what she *should* do. She felt sure she knew what was best for everyone.

It was gut-wrenching to turn her back on him. But she knew the big picture of the situation they faced and he only knew bits and pieces. In the back of her mind, she flirted with the possibility that when all this was over they'd get another chance. But she knew it wouldn't happen. For all his goodness, Bryan wanted a normal life, with kids of his own and she couldn't give him either of those things. Not ever. Within a week she and the children would be on their way to Salt Lake, to begin a new chapter in their lives. Bryan would stay here, where he would move on without her toward the future he deserved.

Chapter Fourteen

Bryan arrived home around midnight. He parked in the driveway and entered through the back door. The house was dark and stifling with the heat and humidity trapped inside for the last three days. He threw his keys on the table and sat on a kitchen chair to pull off his boots.

"Where have you been?"

His head snapped up and he looked around quickly until making out a shadowy form sitting on his sofa. His heart was thumping wildly but began to calm as he identified the voice and the shadow. "Barbara?" he asked carefully.

His eyes had adjusted to the darkness enough to see her lift a hand towards the lamp next to the sofa. A click sounded and light filled the room. He had to squint for a moment, but when his eyes focused Barbara was staring at him. "Where have you been?" she repeated, her voice as dry and flat as it had been the first time she'd asked the question just moments before.

Bryan swallowed. This was not the way he wanted this to happen. He'd planned to organize his thoughts while she remained in Houston. He had hoped that by then he'd have found the right way to tell her that things between them weren't working out. Once again she hadn't given him the chance to plan the confrontation.

"Can't you answer a simple question!?" she suddenly shrieked, making him jump because of the instant intensity. She didn't wait for him to answer before continuing at a fever pitch. "I drove home today because I felt we had some things to work out. And since you'd said you had household projects to do this weekend, I thought it would be a good opportunity to talk about whatever has happened to us in the last few weeks. Imagine my surprise when you weren't here. I waited and waited, assuming you were running some errands. After a few hours I started looking around." She calmed down slightly and her voice became less shrill, but her anger was still intense. He watched guiltily as she picked up a stack of papers laying next to her on the couch. He had not yet noticed them and it took him a moment to recognize them as various receipts he'd collected on his recent trips to Missouri. When he left, they'd all been tucked away in a drawer of his desk awaiting his bank statement at the end of the month. "I found these," she said, her anger dissipating to a point where pain was the most obvious emotion in her voice. Her voice trembled as she continued, "What's going on?"

Bryan swallowed again. "Barbara," he began softly, his heart sinking. "I'm so sorry."

"About what?"

He remained silent, unsure of how to explain what had occupied his mind and time and . . . heart lately. She nodded as if she understood already and extracted a white, full-sized paper from the stack of gas and restaurant receipts. He recognized it right away and his stomach sank another foot. She smoothed the paper on her leg and held it up so he could see Gloria's picture on the Wanted flier that he'd taken from the burger stand in Little Rock all those weeks ago. "You know where she is, don't you?" she said, tears coming to her eyes. "You've been seeing her, haven't you?"

An oppressive silence hung in the air, but she wasn't going to rescue him from answering her questions this time. She waited as her tears overflowed. He hung his head, feeling terrible for hurting the woman he'd once loved; still loved in a way. "Yes," he finally admitted. He looked up and met her eyes with a wretched expression of his own. "I ran into her as she was leaving town. Her car had broken down and she asked me to drive her to Little Rock." Barbara stood and turned away from him, wrapping her arms around her waist as if to shield herself from this. Bryan stared at her back and continued. "When we got there, she was all over the news. She had nowhere to go, no one to trust."

"Except you," Barbara said, still turned away.

"I couldn't just leave her there."

"Sure you could," she said angrily as she turned to face him again. "She made the choices that put her there. It wasn't your problem."

"Her husband abused her daughter Barbara; she was only trying to protect—"

"Says she," Barbara spat. "I can't believe you would keep this from me for so long. Do you expect me to just smile, accept your explanations, and pretend everything is fine between us?"

"Not really," Bryan said after a moment.

Barbara turned her head quickly to look at him. "What?" she said.

"I didn't want it to happen this way," he explained. "I had hoped—"

"Are you in love with her?" Barbara interrupted, turning slowly toward him. Bryan opened his mouth to say no, but something entirely different came out.

"I don't know."

Barbara's face crumpled and she closed her eyes. When she opened them again, tears streamed down her face. "I never want to see you again," she whispered walking toward the door. Bryan stood and grabbed her arm as she passed him.

"Don't leave like this," he pleaded. "Let me tell you what happened, why I didn't tell you."

"Go to hell," Barbara said between clenched teeth. "And take your little whore with you." Bryan pulled back, scorched by her words. "I thought you were a changed man, Bryan; I thought your wild days were over, but you were just waiting for an opportunity, weren't you!"

"No," he said forcefully. "It isn't anything like that. It was circumstance that—"

She pulled her arm out of his grasp. "I never want to see you again," she repeated as she rushed for the door.

Bryan pushed his fingers through his hair. She didn't deserve this. And yet he couldn't see any other way. He dropped his head and closed his eyes as the door slammed, causing the whole house to shudder. Knowing he was responsible for her heartache was excruciating. *Please help her understand,* he prayed silently. *And while you're at it send a little understanding my way, too. I'd love to know why life has suddenly become so complicated.*

————

Kenny was already outside riding his bike when she went upstairs to check on her daughter Sunday morning. Darla was curled up on her bed. "Are you okay?" Pamela asked as she sat on the edge of the bed. Darla opened her eyes, but only for a moment. "I'm tired," she finally whispered.

"Sounds like someone's getting sick," Pamela said placing her hand on Darla's forehead. She didn't have a fever; that was good. Darla pulled the covers up to her chin. "Get some sleep," Pamela said, only mildly concerned. It was probably just a cold. "I'll check on you later." As she returned down the stairs, Kenny came running through the door.

"There's a white car out front," he said fearfully. Pamela hurried to the window, and sure enough the front end of a white car was barely visible, poking out from the trees that lined the drive. Instantly, she shut the blinds and took a deep breath as she wondered what she should do. She parted the curtains and looked again, but the car was gone, leaving her relieved but still anxious. Maybe it was just someone lost on a side road. But she couldn't help expecting the worst. *Who could have found us here?* she wondered. And what could she do about it?

When it was time for church, Darla was still asleep and Pamela sat on the edge of her bed, watching her with deep concern. In just a few hours, Darla's illness had gotten far worse. She placed the back of her hand against Darla's forehead and the warmth there told her that her daughter now had a fever.

In the kitchen, she retrieved her box of treatments—herbs and medicines she'd learned about in one of the shelters so as to cut down on trips to doctors. A few minutes later she awakened Darla enough to get her to drink the tea she'd prepared and take a few pills to control the infection that was somewhere in her body. Darla was barely able to wake herself, and as Pamela laid her softly back down she said a little prayer that she'd feel better before the end of the day. Pamela had been making new plans, but if something were seriously wrong with Darla, those plans would change again.

The improvement she prayed for didn't happen. At two o'clock she helped Darla into the bathroom, gave her a cool bath and helped her eat some soup. Darla went back to bed right afterward. Throughout the afternoon, Pamela continued to make her drink water, gave her another tepid bath and took her outside once the evening air cooled. But Darla's fever wasn't affected, causing Pamela's motherly instincts to prickle. She did all she knew to do and finally laid Darla in her own bed so she could watch her through the night. If she didn't see some improvement by morning she'd have some serious decisions to make.

Kenny had been riding his bike most of the afternoon and after reluctantly taking a bath, he climbed into his own bed. Pamela told him the story of Esther, a personal favorite of hers, and kissed him good night. "Is Darla going to be okay?" he asked as he pulled the sheet up beneath his chin.

"Sure she will," Pamela said with a forced smile. "Now get some sleep."

The peace she'd tried to convey wasn't as strong as she wished. She sat in one of the wicker chairs on the front porch and listened to the night sounds rise up around her as she considered her options.

"The kids asleep?"

The sound of another human voice brought her to her feet. Whipping her head from side to side, she looked for person she'd heard and was just beginning to doubt herself when the redhead from the diner, all those weeks ago, emerged from the trees. Pamela remained frozen as she watched the other woman approach. "I didn't mean to startle you," the woman said. Pamela just watched her, every muscle in her body tense. The redhead looked at the cottage. "Did you and your boyfriend have a nice weekend?"

"What are you doing here?" Pamela asked evenly, trying hard to keep her fear and shock to herself.

"What are *you* doing here?" the woman countered. "When we met last, I felt sure you'd get out of here for good. Do you have any idea how easy it was to follow Mr. Drewry up here? Now that he's gone, and the kids are in bed, I can finally talk to you." She sounded irritated. The woman continued, "You can't keep doing this."

"I'm doing the only thing I can do," Pamela countered.

The woman stopped her approach a few feet shy of the porch steps. "You and I both know that there is only one way left for you to truly protect these kids," she said. "You've been all over the news for weeks, they even had a spot on *Unsolved Mysteries* the other night; your days are numbered. You've got to get out of the States."

Pamela just stared at her and wondered again what this woman was trying to do. She considered telling her she was planning to go home, but something told her to keep that to herself. "And you've waited around all weekend to help me again?" The sarcasm in her voice was unmistakable.

"You're used to not trusting people," the woman replied as if she alone were worthy of that trust. "And I don't blame you, but you've got to believe me. If I can find you, the feds are only a day or two behind; just like last time. You've got to get out of here."

"Out of the country?" Pamela asked in disbelief. She watched the redheaded woman intently, waiting for some clue as to the real motivation behind all this.

"I know someone who can help you." *Isn't that ironic*, Pamela thought to herself. This woman wasn't only interested in seeing her "safe," she was willing to wait until Bryan was gone to approach her. On top of that, she wanted to help her actually leave the country. "I can get you into Canada," she continued. "And from there it won't be hard to get you to England. I can have everything in place by tomorrow night."

Pamela didn't answer, but her skin crawled. She walked to the edge of the porch and forced an interested look on her face. "I don't have much money."

"How much do you have?"

"Two hundred dollars," Pamela answered after a few moments.

"I'll make up the difference, if you can give it to me now." Pamela nodded and went into the house, trusting her instincts which told her to cooperate. International hiding required thousands of dollars. If it wasn't money this woman was after, there was another motivation behind this. But what was it? From her remaining funds, she pulled out two one-hundred-dollar bills, leaving herself with only six hundred dollars more to make the trip to Utah, which she still planned to do. It was crazy to give so much of her money away, but something continued to prod her to follow through. David had hired this woman. What had he hired her to do?

She returned to the porch and extended the money toward the other woman. Just as the redhead was about to take it from her, she pulled it back. "Are you sure about this?" Pamela asked with feigned concern. "This is all I've got."

"I promise," the redhead said with assurance that sounded much too sincere to be real. "Be ready to go tomorrow night." Pamela nodded, as the woman turned back to the trees from where she'd come.

Pamela waited a few more seconds before she quietly descended the porch stairs. With slow, careful steps she followed the other woman, remaining in the trees to the left of the road. She ignored all the warnings she'd been given about going into the woods at night and tried to remain as quiet as possible. Cigarette smoke became thick in the air and Pamela had little trouble following its odor. About two hundred yards from the house, she saw the outline of a vehicle parked on the edge of the driveway. She crouched behind a tree and listened to the door open and then close. Something small and rodent-like squealed before running between her legs and she had to fight down a scream. The redhead flicked on the interior light, allowing Pamela to watch as she picked up her cell phone and dialed a number. Although she couldn't hear the conversation, she had little doubt whom she had called. Soon, headlights turned on and the car backed down the lane. The vehicle disappeared before Pamela finally stood, quickly left the trees and used the driveway to make her way back to the cottage.

It took a few minutes for her to put the pieces together, but when the realization hit her, she stopped walking. All she could do was stare ahead as she understood the answers to all the little questions buzzing around her head. The heat of anger flowed up her spine, making her neck and face tingle as she realized that David was trying to keep her from coming home. She closed her eyes slowly and took a deep breath. When she looked up again, she felt confident once more. Everything made sense now. David knew where she was; the redhead would be returning tomorrow to sneak them across the Canadian border. If David wanted her in hiding, then it was definitely time to come out. She would not leave the country; of course she'd never expected that she would.

To complicate things even further, when she reached the cottage Darla's fever was up to 102. As she sat on the edge of the bed, a new plan began forming in her mind. It wasn't the option she'd have chosen just an hour ago, but in light of what she knew now, it seemed to be the only real choice she had.

She looked around the small bedroom and sighed. She'd enjoyed her time here and knew she'd never come back. But there was work to do now and she couldn't afford to waste it being mournful. Time was of the essence.

The next morning, Pamela loaded the last of the boxes into the car. She'd spent most of the night putting the cabin back to rights before getting a few hours of sleep. The car held the only evidence of their stay and soon even that would be drastically reduced. The passenger seat held garbage, mostly food that they didn't need now. There was another box of food in the backseat that she would drop off at the food bank in Rolla, Missouri. Everything else was coming with them, at least in a sense. The car would be seized by the feds, they'd go through everything, take any evidence, and then give the rest back; it could be weeks before she'd see it again. But most of their property would eventually be returned.

It was only six a.m., so after checking on Darla again and finding no improvement, she returned to the kitchen table with a box of stationery. It was another one of her past-life treasures, something she hadn't used since leaving home. While packing, she had set it aside for later, which was now.

Large gold letters gracefully spelled out *Gloria* across the top of the heavy paper. It had been a Christmas gift from her parents the Christmas before she left. She'd used it for thank you notes, birthday greetings, and basic correspondence with her friends in the few months that followed, but hadn't used it since. Now she would use it to say good-bye to Bryan.

It took nearly half an hour to pen the words she knew were necessary. Finding a nice way to say it proved to be impossible, so she finally just said it. She told him that she was going home and that their worlds would be very different then. She thanked him for his help and asked him not to contact her. It would make the legal aspects of her situation too difficult. The wording was choppy and without the emotion she felt, but she knew it was better this way. Of course he would be surprised, but she tried to convince herself that he would understand. She wished *she* understood.

Once the envelope was sealed and addressed, she placed it in her purse with the reports she'd be mailing at the first post office she saw. She then placed her purse by the front door and took a final look around the cottage. When she'd left Utah she was sure she was doing the right thing, despite how difficult it would be. The very fact that her current feelings were so similar didn't ease her fear of what lay ahead, but it brought her some peace.

Nearly an hour later Pamela picked up the smooth, cold, plastic handset of the payphone and put it to her ear. The kids and all their belongings were in the car parked a few feet away. It was hard not to think of how similar this moment was to the moment she'd stood at a pay phone in Boulder, Colorado, and started this whole experience. But it wasn't Carla she'd be calling this time.

She pressed the zero button on the phone, and when the operator answered she said she wanted to make a collect call. When asked who was placing the call she cleared her throat, "Gloria," she said. The names Pamela, Darla, and Kenny were now resigned to the category of costumes they had used to hide in for more than two and a half years. From this moment on, she was Gloria, mother of Katie and Nicholas. She was again a daughter and a sister, with a heritage to claim and a cause to fight for. Her end of the line went quiet for a time and then a cautious voice that she could never forget spoke.

"Gloria," her mother said softly. "Is it really you?"

Unbiddenly, tears filled her eyes; she had missed her family so much.

All the longing, all the fear and regret she'd experienced since leaving overwhelmed her, and she could barely speak. Her mother repeated the question, "Is it really you?"

"It's me, Mom," she managed to say, her chin trembling and tears rolling down her cheeks. "I'm coming home."

There was silence for a moment until Gloria was able to contain her emotions enough to speak. "Can you and Daddy come to Missouri?"

"Missouri," her mother breathed, as if relishing the very knowledge of her daughter's whereabouts.

"Darla's sick," she explained. "I'm taking her to the ER at Phelps Regional Medical Center in Rolla, Missouri. I'll need you guys to stay with her and Nicholas."

Her mother was silent and Gloria was sure she understood the implication of her request. Gloria would be arrested, leaving the children alone. "I'll catch the first flight I can."

"Thanks, Mom," she said softly. "I've missed you so much."

There was too much to say over the phone, so Gloria said good bye and hung up. She went to the passenger door, retrieved the items that were going in the garbage and headed for the dumpster a few feet from the phone booth. Bryan's cell phone laid on top of the box and she tried not to look at it. She'd never even used it, and now she was throwing it away. She wanted him with her so badly it hurt. She wanted to hear his voice, collapse in his arms, and be told that everything would be okay. When she reached the dumpster she hesitated, but after a moment tossed the box over the edge. She refused to hope that she would ever see him again. She'd already mailed the letter and the reports. That decision all but assured that he was no longer a part of her life.

The clock hanging over the Emergency Room desk said 8:56. There were a few scattered people in the foyer, but it was relatively quiet. Katie was much too big for Gloria to carry, but whatever illness had overcome her body had left her with too little strength to walk. Besides, Gloria didn't mind. She ached to hold her daughter close, if only for a little while longer. She tried to forget the imminent separation that lay ahead of them, but it seemed to hover around her like a thick vapor, slowing her steps and causing her to rethink her decision. Nicholas had been quiet since she explained that they were going back to their old home in Utah and that he was going to see his grandparents and that people would be calling him by a name he didn't even remember. He walked next to her and looked around anxiously. He had little idea of how much their lives were about to change, but it was clear that he sensed her anxiety.

She hoisted Katie up a little higher onto her shoulder and approached the front desk. A black woman was keying information into the computer and looked up at her. "Can I help you?" she asked in a thick southern accent.

"My daughter's sick," Gloria said. "She's had a fever for twenty-four hours that isn't responding to any medication, she's lethargic and weak and this morning when I got her up, she couldn't put her chin to her chest, which I've heard is a sign of meningitis."

"All right," the woman said. "Let's get her into a room and then we'll get her information."

A few minutes later Gloria sat at another desk, in front of another woman, and watched her daughter lying on the narrow white bed not too far away. A young intern was taking her vital signs; Darla barely responded to him as he spoke, poked and prodded.

"Do you have insurance?" the woman asked, her hands poised above her keyboard ready to type. Gloria knew that as soon as the information entered the computer, it would only be a matter of time. A year or so ago she'd seen a news broadcast showing the state of the art computer system of a modern Emergency Room. The computers were networked to check all admits against a criminal database. When a match was found, the information was sent to the local police. Gloria wondered how long it would take. Her eyes filled with tears and her voice shook when she spoke again.

"I believe she's covered through her father, but I'm unsure of his current plan. We haven't had to use it for a while." She pulled a white plastic card out of her pocket and handed it to the other woman. "This is what he had last I knew, but I'll sign for self-payment as well."

The woman looked over the card, far from pleased. "Well, we'll see what happens." She said as she began typing. "And what's your name?"

No words came. The woman raised her eyebrows. "Gloria Stanton."

She had imagined a look of surprise on the woman's face, and gasps of shock from people sitting near enough to hear. But no one responded. The questioning was soon finished and she pulled Nicholas onto her lap for comfort as fear began to overcome her. Maybe she wasn't up to this, but it was too late now and she knew it. What would they do with the children? What would they do with her?

She was directed to take a seat and wait; she tried to protest, but the woman was unbending. Gloria would not be allowed into the treatment area. Reluctantly, she took a seat that faced the door and held Nicholas even closer. For what seemed like only a few minutes, she held him, rocking gently and talking about all the fun things they'd done together. He didn't understand why it was important, but he caught the spirit and soon they were both giggling and whispering as if they hadn't a care in the world. Between shared memories, she kept a vigilant eye on her daughter. The short distance that separated them felt like miles, but she refused to give into the grief that was already settling in her heart. She'd done the right thing. Despite how frightened she was, despite how painful it was; she'd done what was best for all of them.

The doctor finally approached and told her that Katie was being treated for dehydration while they ran some tests. She'd be okay, he said, and Gloria smiled with relief. That was all that really mattered, she reminded herself. All she ever wanted was for her kids to be okay.

Not long after being updated on Katie's condition, the automatic doors opened and she watched them intently as she had each time someone else entered the ER. Tears came to her eyes as two police officers, a man and a woman, followed by two other people, whom she assumed were social workers, entered the room. Her heart sank and the full reality of what faced her became nearly suffocating. Her chin began to tremble and her chest became tight. "I love you so much," she whispered in her son's ear as the officers scanned the room and focused on her. "Grandma's going to be here soon," she said quickly as they began walking towards her. "And I'm going to be okay."

Nicholas looked up at her, alarmed by her sudden fear and instant tears. "What's the matter, Mom?" he asked anxiously just as the officer reached them.

"Gloria Stanton?" the woman asked. Gloria just stared at her, they both knew who she was. A pair of arms reached over and pulled Nicholas from her. She instinctively pulled him back. An indescribable panic consumed her and she held him possessively.

"Wait," she said loudly, holding on as tight as she could. "I need to explain this to him."

The male officer immediately interceded, grabbing Gloria's wrists, while the woman officer pulled Nicholas from her arms. He screamed out in fear and it set off every maternal instinct she had. "He doesn't understand," she yelled as she twisted out of the officer's grip and headed towards her son. In only moments, she was thrown to the floor, her head cracking against the tile. The officer placed a knee in her back and told her she was under arrest. "But he doesn't understand," Gloria repeated through her tears. Her head was pounding. She twisted her neck around to get a glimpse of her son but he had already disappeared around the corner. She heard him calling for her frantically and she struggled once more with all the strength she could muster. If she could just see him for a minute, explain what was happening so he wouldn't be so scared. But the knee in her back pressed down harder, as the officer started shouting about resisting arrest and full restraints. "I love you," she finally shouted at the top of her lungs before having her head pushed to the floor. She began to cry as she went limp and let the officer snap on handcuffs and pull her to her feet. She'd known it would be hard, but not this gut-wrenching.

A camera confronted her as she was stood up, and she tried to look away. Did the cops have to call the camera crews? Her heart stung and her chest ached from her racking sobs. She tried to get a glimpse of Katie—one last look. But the officer grabbed the back of her neck and pushed her toward the door. Tears ran down her cheeks as Gloria was shoved into the back of the patrol car.

She didn't bother sitting up after landing on the smelly upholstery. Instead, she turned her face into the back of the seat and cried like a baby. All she'd ever wanted to do was protect her children. That's all she ever wanted. Did it really have to end this way?

Chapter Fifteen

"This is David Stanton," he said into the phone. He was in his office, finishing up for the day. Tonight he and Carrie were going to her mother's for dinner. The courting was going well and he had little doubt that they'd be married within a couple of months. They'd talked about it some, but hadn't set a date yet. The sooner the better, as far as he was concerned. He was tired of living alone.

"Mr. Stanton," the unfamiliar voice said. "I'm Agent Larring with the FBI."

"Hello," David said without concern. This wasn't the first time he'd been contacted by the feds. In fact, he'd received nearly a dozen calls since the *Unsolved Mysteries* segment had aired almost two weeks ago. He'd protested as much as he reasonably could about doing the show, but it was ultimately no longer in his control. Carrie insisted they needed to do all they could to find the kids and he finally agreed. Since then, he'd held his breath each time they got a call with a possible tip. So far, he'd been lucky. His fear of Gloria being found was waning and he was regaining his confidence that this whole thing was almost over. "What can I help you with?" he asked.

"Actually, I have good news." David straightened. "Gloria was arrested this morning." The blood drained out of his face and he closed his eyes, cursing silently. "Katie is ill and your ex-wife took her to a hospital." He paused, waiting for his congratulations. "Mr. Stanton?" the agent asked after a few seconds. "Are you there?"

"Yeah," David said shortly. "I'm here."

"Aren't you pleased?" the agent prodded. "Your kids are coming home."

"That's great. Uh, thanks for calling, but I've got to go." He hung up the phone and slammed his fist on the desk. Now what was he going to do? A few minutes later, the phone rang again. He picked it up and identified himself. "Hi, darlin'," he said with forced feeling once he realized it was Carrie.

"Isn't it great," Carrie said breathlessly. "Oh, I can't wait to meet your kids. This is perfect."

"Yeah," he replied. "Just perfect."

Less than an hour later, his cell phone rang. He picked it up slowly, looked at the caller ID and clenched his jaw as he pushed the *talk* button. "Hello," he said calmly.

"I wanted to call before I head out so you'd know what's up."

David took a deep breath. So his southern PI had decided to update him—how nice. "What's that supposed to mean?"

"Well," she said, obviously very pleased with herself. "I found her!"

"Really?" he asked dryly. Was this some kind of joke? He had hired her because she was unethical. Too bad she was also an idiot.

"She's staying at some cottage in the Ozarks, but not for long. I'm meeting her there tonight with a guy that's going to take her and the kids to Canada. From there she'll head to England where, with any luck, she'll never bother you again."

"That sounds like a great plan," he said sarcastically. "Except that she's in a Missouri jail."

There was a long pause. "What?"

"Don't you bother to watch the news?" he shouted angrily. "She was arrested this morning."

"That's crazy," the PI countered. "I talked to her last night; how—"

"She took Katie to a hospital and they picked her up. Thanks to you she'll be extradited by the end of the week."

"Thanks to me!"

"If you had done the job you were supposed to do, she'd have been in Europe already. You totally botched this job and now my butt's on the line all over again."

"Hey, wait a minute. This is not my fault."

"Well, I'm holding you responsible. I'm sending you a money order for two thousand dollars to cover your expenses—"

"You owe me almost twice that," she cut in. "I could tell the FBI a thing or two."

David was silent for a moment; when he spoke it was in a hiss. "You make the slightest move against me and I'll destroy you. If you know what's good for you, you'll forget you ever met me." He pressed the *end* button and slammed the phone onto the desk, swearing under his breath. It was time to plan a new strategy. One that would work.

———

Monday afternoon, Bryan walked briskly to his truck, whistling the theme from the movie *Titanic*. How the tune got into his head was a mystery, but he'd been replaying it in his mind all day long. He tossed his briefcase onto the passenger seat, turned the key and headed towards home. There were a lot of things he needed to do before heading back to Missouri on Thursday and he was anxious to get started on them. For some reason, he had extra energy lately that was begging for an outlet.

Sunday night, he'd had a chance to discuss his situation with Charlotte. It had been incredibly helpful. She'd ended their conversation with the advice to pray and then follow his heart. He'd done just that and felt lighter than he had in weeks. He still felt badly about all that had happened with Barbara, but he had no doubt that it was better for both of them this way. He'd never been more excited about his future. A future he felt sure Pamela would be a big part of.

The *Titanic* tune returned to his head and he rolled his eyes. There had to be some way to get rid of it. A familiar country song came on the radio but he started punching buttons in search of something with a stronger beat. He settled on some song he'd never heard before and tapped his thumbs on the steering wheel. He began thinking of what he would say to Pamela on Thursday. A chill ran down his back just thinking of her. He couldn't wait to see her again. The song ended after a minute or so and the station began all its babble about traffic before giving a news update.

If the broadcaster hadn't used her name at the first, he probably wouldn't have paid any attention to the report. As it was, the whole world seemed to slow down as the words sank in. "Gloria Stanton, mother of two and a fugitive facing two charges of felony kidnapping in Utah, was arrested after a brief struggle at a Missouri hospital this morning. Both children have been taken into protective custody and she awaits extradition to Utah where she'll be prosecuted for her crimes . . ." The horn of another car blared him back to reality soon enough to get him back in his own lane, but his whole body felt numb.

An hour later, he watched what had happened on the five o'clock news. A lump formed in his throat as he watched her being forced into the police car, sobbing. He listened as the newscaster explained she had brought her daughter to the hospital for treatment and had given her real name for the records. The news moved on to other things but he just sat there, staring blankly at the television. She was gone. She must have known she'd get caught if she went to a hospital, and yet she hadn't even called him. Before they'd even had a chance—it was over.

The next day, he received her letter in the mail. It was brief and it was cold. She didn't want to see him again and she said that they would both be better off if he went on with his life. It was signed Gloria, and it was as if she really were a stranger to him. Again. She'd already done this once when she tried to run from Harrison without telling him. He could hardly imagine facing this again. Pamela didn't exist anymore, and this Gloria was new and strange. He thought he knew her; he thought they had been building a relationship of trust. How could he have been so wrong? As he refolded the letter, an intense feeling of betrayal filled his chest. He crumpled the paper in his hand, threw it at the wall and swore.

————

Gloria was led to a white room with a large thick window that separated the inmates from their visitors. She'd seen such visiting rooms on TV before, but now realized that film could never simulate how lonely and heart-breaking it was to be on her side of the glass. Sitting on the other side of the window was her mother. Her mother had been in her early forties when Gloria had been born, but until today she'd never thought of her mother as old. Two and half years had aged her mother a great deal. Her eyes filled with tears. Quickly, she pulled out the chair, sat down, and picked up the phone.

"How are you?" her mother asked right away, her eyes searching Gloria's face as if looking for clues.

"I'm okay," Gloria said without feeling. She'd never felt so close to hell in her life, but saying that would only cause her mom greater worry. "How are the kids? Have you seen them?"

"I've been able to see Katie every day," she answered with a sad smile. "She's doing quite well and is responding to treatment."

"It was meningitis, then?"

"Yes," her mother responded. "Bacterial meningitis and it's easily treated since you caught it early. She'll be out in a few more days."

"And Kenny—I mean Nicholas?"

Her mother's face fell. "I can't get in to see him," she answered slowly. "He's in a foster home."

Gloria closed her eyes and willed herself not to scream. When she opened them again, her mother's face was etched with a reflection of her own pain. "Can you talk to him or anything?"

"I've talked to the social worker and she says he's doing fine. They're ready to send him to Utah, but apparently your lawyer's kicking up a lot of dust over returning the kids to David."

Good. "Is David here?"

"Yes," her mother said hesitantly. "He and his girlfriend are camped at the hospital. I think he's been able to see Nicholas as well, but they've told him he won't be taking the kids for a while."

"Thank goodness," Gloria breathed. She knew he would come here, and she'd steeled herself to hear it. The girlfriend was a surprise, though. One she had no energy to think about right now.

"Your lawyer is petitioning for me to get temporary custody of the children, and so far he's optimistic. But it will be a few more days. How much longer will you be here?"

"I waived an extradition hearing and agreed to go back tomorrow," she said sadly. "I don't know what's more important, having you here or there. Are you sure you're up to taking the kids if you get custody?"

Her mother raised an eyebrow. "Don't start judging me by my laugh lines. I still swim five days a week and I'd be a tennis pro if I were forty years younger. I want them more than you know. And Sissy's flying out here tonight to be with Katie," she said, speaking of her younger sister and Gloria's favorite aunt. "She wanted to do something and if she's here, I can be in Utah waiting for you or Nicholas to join me."

Gloria was quiet for a moment. It seemed so unfair that she couldn't be with her children. Yet, everything had happened just as she expected. "Where's Dad?" she asked after a moment. She hadn't seen him yet but knew that he must be here somewhere. Her mother's face fell but she didn't answer. Gloria's heart began to race as her mother looked down. "Mom, where is he?"

When her mother's eyes met hers, they were full of tears. Gloria's stomach began to burn. "He died in March, honey," her mother said, barely able to speak the words. Gloria's lips parted and she could feel the blood drain from her face. She brought a hand to her trembling lips and closed her eyes as the phone slipped down to rest on her shoulder. It couldn't be true. Her father couldn't have died without her somehow knowing.

"Stanton, your time's up," said a voice behind her and she quickly moved the phone back to her ear. She looked at her mother again.

"I'm sorry, Mom," she said in strangled tones. She couldn't believe what she'd just heard. She felt numb as a thousand questions and apologies swirled in her head.

Her mother's mouth moved but the phone was taken away as the guard hung it up. "Time to go back, Stanton," the guard said. Gloria stood and followed the guard dumbly, staring at her mother until she was blocked from her view. She watched her plain white shoes as she walked the long corridor and then sat silently on her bed for what seemed like hours. She'd missed her own father's funeral. She didn't even know how he died. Being so much younger than the other kids she and her Dad had always spent a lot of time together. He was semi-retired for most of her life and they would often go fishing together. Every summer the three of them, Gloria, Mom, and Dad, traveled all over the States visiting family members and finding fishing spots. They'd always had a special bond and yet now he was gone—just like that. Her children were saved and her father was dead, without her telling him how much she loved him, how much she missed him and how grateful she was to be his daughter. She brought her hands to her face and began to sob. If this was the depths of despair, she wouldn't wish it on anyone.

———

Bryan was in the process of correcting summer school assignments Wednesday afternoon, when there was a knock on his door. The door was open, so he looked up to see who was requesting entrance. The two men were strangers to him.

"Can I help you?" Bryan asked, tapping his red pen on the desk. The two men began walking forward simultaneously. Bryan took a breath as they held up FBI badges. He placed the pen on the desk and leaned back in his chair. Before joining the church he'd lived a far from perfect life, but because of it he knew how to handle law enforcement.

"We'd like to ask you some questions about Gloria Stanton."

"Who?" he asked with feigned confusion.

"Gloria Stanton," the man repeated. "We have reason to believe you assisted her in evading capture."

"Gloria Stanton," Bryan mussed. "Can't say as I know anyone by that name."

"How about Pamela Bennion?"

"I do know Pamela Bennion; she used to work at Donny's Café."

"Pamela Bennion is Gloria Stanton," the officer informed him, still trying to gauge whether Bryan was playing a game or was truly ignorant.

"But she was captured, wasn't she?"

Their eyes lit up. "We're talking about the attempted capture before that."

"The capture before she was captured?" Bryan quizzed. He leaned forward, resting his arms on the desk. "I'm not following you."

"Did you drive Gloria Stanton out of town on May 21st?"

"Yes."

The men looked surprised at his quick and honest answer. "We're looking for information about the organization that assisted her in kidnapping her children."

"I don't know anything about any organization."

"We know they assisted in her evading capture."

"The capture before she was captured?"

"We aren't here to play games," the larger of the two men said angrily.

"Me, neither," Bryan said humbly. "But I can't help you."

"You're facing charges of aiding and abetting a fugitive."

"That is no longer a fugitive."

"But was when you assisted her."

Bryan put up his hands in surrender. "Ask her about the organization then, if you've arrested her. Like I said, I drove her out of town to a motel in Little Rock; check the Motel 6 off of Highway 41. I put the room in my name. Incidentally I thought I was doing her a favor and didn't know she was running from the law." That was mostly true.

They remained silent as he stood. "We need a full statement."

"I just gave you a full statement," Bryan said boldly. "And unless you're prepared to arrest me, which I doubt, you should probably go."

"We'll probably be back," one of them said as they headed for the door. "So you might want to think real hard about working with us on this."

Bryan just smiled. Once they were gone he sat back down, raised his hands to his face and let out a breath. He'd had two of the most miserable days of his life. He'd spent every moment reviewing his interactions with Gloria and trying to come up with a solution. He'd come up with nothing. Now he had the FBI on his tail. He wondered how much they knew, if they were on Sharon's tail and how serious his involvement really was.

————

"This is all he had to say?" Agent Larring said into the phone as he read the faxed notes sent by the agents in Harrison.

"That's it," the younger agent of the two said on the other end of the line. "And we checked out his story, he did register a room at the motel in Little Rock and we can't find any information beyond that. I can't seem to find anyone willing to verify when he returned from that trip or anything else for that matter. You know how these small town folks are—they don't like us getting involved."

Larking nodded thoughtfully and let out a breath. "We received an update on Mrs. Stanton's case this morning and the higher ups want us to back off."

"What?"

"They've received a new doctor's report and they want us to hold off on our investigation until it's validated." Larring crumpled up the paper and threw it toward the trash can. It hit the rim and bounced onto the floor. "I was hoping you guys would get something I could use to convince them to continue, but since we didn't, we best pull it in. We'll wait to see what the Utah Court decides to do and go from there."

"But we've worked so hard on this!"

"I know, but I guess they don't want us spending so much time and money until they're convinced she had no right to take those kids in the first place. If they prove the abuse happened, it'll get really ugly for us if we're still trying to get evidence against her."

————

A week following her arrest, Gloria found herself in a Utah court. She'd arrived in Salt Lake on Friday night, but the arraignment hearing couldn't take place until Monday morning. The bright orange jumpsuit issued by the prison system made her feel like a neon sign. The courtroom was full, and she tried not to show her embarrassment as she was led to stand before the judge. She'd been raised in privilege, the daughter of a well-known doctor and upstanding citizen, yet she was a criminal. She'd never felt so small. David's family sat bunched together on the left side of the room, although she didn't see him among them. Her family was on the right and reporters armed with notebooks and tape recorders filled all the other seats. She'd spent hours with her lawyer, a few brief minutes with her mother, and now she was here, like some kind of circus freak awaiting her opportunity to entertain the crowd.

The judge finished reading the papers in front of him and cleared his throat. "This is an arraignment to determine in what direction this case goes. Gloria Stanton," he said, looking at her for the first time. "You are charged with second-degree felony kidnapping, child endangerment, and violation of a custody order. How do you plead?"

Such a simple question, she thought to herself. She was guilty of the kidnapping and the custody violation, but she was *not* guilty of endangering her children. To plead guilty to any of it, however, would move things too quickly and she needed time. She was left with little choice. "Not guilty," she said boldly, ignoring the whispers behind her.

"All right," he said with a nod that indicated he'd expected that response. "What provisions does the state suggest?"

An attorney representing the state stepped forward. "Because Mrs. Stanton is an obvious flight risk and has connections that can keep her hidden, the state asks for no bail and no visitation with her children."

A gasp rose from her family's side of the courtroom as her attorney spoke up. "Mrs. Stanton was acting in behalf of her children's safety, they are—"

"This is a hearing, not a trial," the judge interrupted. "State your suggestions and leave it at that."

"We ask for twenty thousand dollars bond to be issued for her release and that she be allowed supervised visitation." Gloria waited for him to expand on why it was imperative for her to see her kids, but he said nothing more and she cursed him silently.

The judge hesitated, then announced his decision. "Fifty thousand dollars bail, no visitation."

He stood and left the room as the people behind her began moving about. Gloria just stood there. Frozen. She couldn't see her kids! Her mind began to spin. She felt like screaming as the guard led her back to the holding cell in the courthouse. Her attorney had warned her this could happen, but she hadn't really considered it. Did no one care about what was best for her children? How were they supposed to deal with this situation without her?

Chapter Sixteen

Once in the holding cell, she sat on the narrow bed and waited for Robert Bryson, her attorney. He had already explained the options she had when they met this morning and she was anxious to move ahead. Being denied visitation was a painful blow, but it only further strengthened her resolve. She would fight with every ounce of power she had, and this time she wouldn't run away.

A few minutes after leaving the courthouse, they pulled into traffic and her attorney headed for the freeway. "So where are you staying?" he asked.

"At my mom's," she replied with a smile. "I guess we'll know tomorrow if I can stay there." Robert had been working fervently on the custody issue and they had a custody hearing with a family court judge in the morning. The meeting would determine whether David or her mother got custody. David's mother had also petitioned, but because she had a list of health problems the judge would probably not choose her.

"Are you nervous about the judge's decision?"

"The judge would be a fool not to give custody to my mom; although after my judiciary experiences this far, that isn't saying much."

"Hey," her attorney cut in. "I happen to be a part of the system you're deriding here."

She looked at him and smiled apologetically. "Sorry," she said sincerely. "I know it's partly my fault that things turned out as they did." When Robert didn't respond, she continued. "I was so protective of my privacy and wanted to be so fair last time that I didn't stand up for the truth the way I should have."

"If David had been as concerned about fairness it wouldn't have been an issue."

"True," she agreed. "But he started his public relations game as soon as he could and I let him play it. I was so sure that the bad guy would lose," she shook her head in disbelief. "This time I'm willing to do whatever it takes."

"If you don't mind my saying so, you behaved like a scared little kid during the first trial. You've changed a lot since then."

"I've 'grown up' a lot," she clarified. "And I've learned to trust my own instincts. I feel that things will work out okay this time, so long as I do things the right way." She paused for a moment. "Will we be able to get a preliminary hearing against him before I go to trial?"

"I think so," Robert said. "I've already met with the district attorney. He's bound by certain protocol, but he's intrigued with the full spectrum of this case. If David's guilt can be proved, your actions get some validation. He said he'll do everything in his power to get David's case heard as soon as possible."

"Well, that gives me something to pray for then," she said with a light smile that contrasted the perpetual heaviness in her chest. She knew that if she were somehow convicted before David, he'd be much more likely to get the kids. That thought filled her with an inexpressible fear. It boiled down to getting him before he got her. She was determined to see that it happened in that order.

Her mom met her at the door when Robert dropped her off and embraced her in a warm, welcoming hug. In all their interactions they hadn't had the opportunity to touch and Gloria fairly melted at the sensation of being held by her mother once again. Finally her mother, Virginia, pulled back. "How'd everything go?" she asked, leaving her hands on Gloria's shoulders as if hesitant to break their physical connection.

"Good," Gloria said simply, ignoring the heartache because she couldn't see her kids, yet refusing to give in to the self pity.

Virginia smiled and held open the door. "I fixed us some lunch," she said as she headed back to the kitchen. "It's almost done."

Gloria remained just inside the door and looked around. This was the home she'd been raised in and yet she felt like a stranger here. The furniture hadn't changed, although some knickknacks were unfamiliar. The curtains were new, she noticed. Growing up here, she'd never realized how luxurious it was. The money spent on furniture alone would have paid a year's rent for them in Arkansas; it seemed incredible that she could have lived two such totally different lives as she had. Her eyes came to rest on the wall where her mother displayed family photos. There were several more frames than there had been when she left. For several minutes, she looked from one photo to the next. Because she was so much younger than her brothers and sisters, many of her nieces and nephews were in her same phase of life. Since she left, there had been three weddings, two mission farewells, and three high-school graduations of her nieces and nephews. She'd also missed the births of five new great-grandchildren for her parents. *I've missed so much*, she thought sadly. In the center of the photos was the last formal family photograph taken before she'd left.

Her parents sat in the middle with the six children, along with spouses, surrounding them while the grandchildren filled in every other available space. Her divorce had been in the works at the time, so David wasn't there. In the photo her smile looked heavy as her hand rested on Katie's shoulder, while four-year-old Nicholas sat on his grandfather's lap. She had to close her eyes for a moment as grief overcame her. When she opened her eyes, she focused on her father's face. At any moment, she expected him to come through the doorway and announce how good it was to have her back home. It was so hard to accept that he was really gone, that he wasn't in the house somewhere.

"I had the services video-taped for you," her mother said from behind her.

Gloria sniffled and wiped at her eyes, still staring at the image of her father. "What happened?" she finally asked.

Her mother remained silent for awhile. "He was diagnosed with colon cancer the year after you left," she said softly. "We did everything we could, but . . . " her voice trailed off.

"Was he very sick?" Gloria asked.

"Yes," Virginia answered softly. "It really was a relief when he didn't have to suffer any more."

"It breaks my heart to have missed being here," Gloria said, her voice cracking with emotion.

"You get to remember your father as he was, strong and powerful. The rest of us watched him waste away. By the end, he was on so much medication he didn't even know who I was."

Gloria shook her head. It sounded so impossible. Her father had always been such a powerful man, such a source of strength. To imagine him wasting away . . . was unthinkable. She turned to look at her mother. "I should have been here," Gloria said sadly. At this moment, she'd give anything to see him one last time. "If I'd known—"

"If you'd known, you'd have stayed where you were and been even more miserable," her mother said firmly. "I made Janice promise me she wouldn't tell you if you called. You were doing what had to be done. He knew that and he wouldn't want you to doubt your decision."

Gloria looked at the floor. "It just seems so unfair, doesn't it?" She looked at her mother's sympathetic face. "If leaving was the right thing to have done, shouldn't it have worked out better than this? Shouldn't our family be together again? Shouldn't I have my children in my arms and my father by my side?"

Virginia placed her hands on Gloria's arms. "This is not a punishment for you, Gloria," she said. "It's just the way things are. You were very special to your father. He loved you very much and you know that he wouldn't want you to grieve so much that you lose sight of the full picture. You followed your heart; he knew that."

Gloria nodded, as her moment of doubt passed. "Wouldn't it have been great if none of this had happened?" she attempted a lighthearted smile.

"But it did," her mother said, smiling her understanding. "And it's almost over."

That night, Gloria lay in the guest room bed looking up at the ceiling. Earlier, she'd been able to talk to her children on the phone and it had both lifted and depressed her. Nicholas was now in shelter care in Utah. He seemed to be doing all right now that the state had gone through the contents of her car and returned his bike. But Katie was still in the hospital in Arkansas. She'd cried on the phone and told her mother to come and get her. Gloria had tried to explain, but her aunt Sissy finally took the phone away. She explained that Katie would be released tomorrow, and that she was doing well. Gloria had said good bye while Katie cried pitifully in the background.

Now Gloria lay alone, trying to revive her faith, once again. With every passing hour, the doubts grew until everything was blurred and fuzzy. Nothing seemed to make sense anymore.

Her mind wandered to Bryan and, not for the first time, her heart began to ache in another way. Try as she might to rid her thoughts of him, he remained in the back of her mind all the time. She found herself hoping he would call, or show up on the courthouse steps. Yet, at the same time, she knew his presence would only bring further complications. Sometimes she found herself fantasizing that having him here would bring her peace, as it had at the cottage each time he visited. Maybe she'd been wrong to tell him to stay away. But now was the time to fight for her children. She was in no position to entertain thoughts of a man.

With a sigh, she rolled onto her side and stared at the barely illuminated window. Her questions were in vain anyway. It was a week ago today that she'd been arrested; Bryan knew what had happened by now. Despite all the difficulties between them, she wanted him. She wanted to feel his arms around her, protective and strong. She wanted to feel his fingers caress her face once again. She wanted to feel the warmth of his breath on her cheek. But it was time she resigned herself to her situation. She'd brought him nothing but trouble and she'd told him to leave her alone. What possible reason would he have to make any further contact?

———

Tuesday morning, Gloria sat next to her attorney in the courtroom and stared straight ahead. The lilac suit she wore was much more comfortable than the orange jumpsuit she'd worn the day before and she was grateful that the room wasn't as full as it had been for her arraignment. Today, her mom and older sister sat behind her, and she was grateful for their support. There were the expected amount of reporters as well.

She heard David enter the courtroom and continued to look straight ahead. Katie had told her the night before that he'd finally left for Salt Lake. He'd had to come back for the custody hearing. She couldn't help glancing quickly in his direction and seeing the rather plain looking dark-haired woman holding his hand. *So that's the girlfriend*, she thought sadly as she faced forward again. With any luck, this woman would figure out what he really was before their relationship went much further. David came through the gate that separated the on-lookers from the trial participants and began talking to his attorney. Just hearing his voice filled her with tension. She could actually feel him look at her and it made her cringe. This was the man she had married?

She'd once kneeled across the alter from him and stared at their infinite reflections in the huge mirrors; she hated being in the same room with him now. The thought that they had ever shared a life made her feel ill. From his table, he laughed and she could feel her anger boiling. His arrogance was hard to ignore and it made her limitations, and all the other things working against her, seem that much bigger. He really believed he'd get custody of the kids and the mocking voices in her head asked her, "why not?" She closed her eyes and said another prayer, to add to the hundreds she'd already offered. She knew the truth, God knew the truth; David knew the truth too, if he'd dare to face it. *Please*, she prayed, *let truth prevail this time.*

When the judge entered, she took a deep breath and stood, as did everyone else in the courtroom. When he sat, the room followed suit. "Because of the sensitive nature of this case I have taken an inordinate amount of time to review the information presented. Nicholas Stanton is in another room of the courthouse and I've been told that Katie Stanton is available by phone. They will only address this court if I feel it is absolutely necessary." He paused and took a long look at each parent. "Mr. Bryson, you may begin."

Gloria took a deep breath as Robert stood up. In very calm, confident tones, he stated their case and all the reasons the children were better off with their maternal grandmother. He brought up the preliminary hearing against David, which, he had just learned, was scheduled in just two weeks. He explained what evidence would be presented at that hearing and why, after all they had been through, the children deserved to be safe.

As soon as Robert finished, David's attorney stood and presented his side. His accusations were much more inflammatory, so much so that the judge reminded him there was no jury to perform for. That gave her hope. David's attorney went on and on for nearly ten minutes, repeating his key points several times. When he finally sat down, Gloria looked at the judge, hoping to read his expression. The judge was silent for some time and his expression was guarded.

"Thank you," he said. He then looked at David. "Mr. Stanton," he began. "What will you do if I award Mrs. Olsen custody?"

David stood and she turned to look at him for the first time. He gave her a quick glance and then looked at the judge, confidence radiating from his face. "With all due respect, your honor, I would appeal that decision immediately. I have been denied my children for almost three years. They have been fed lies about me. I deserve a chance to be their father again. I have suffered a great deal, as have they, by being denied a relationship with me. I will fight as long as I have to in order to see justice done." He sat down with an air of cocky satisfaction. Gloria watched the judge, but he remained expressionless.

"Mrs. Stanton," he said, looking at her. "What will you do if I award custody to Mr. Stanton?"

Gloria stood slowly and faced the judge. "My ex-husband is correct in saying that my children have been denied many things. On the other hand, they *have* had safety and love since I left. Although I do not expect to be rewarded for my actions, I would hope that what I have done shows this court how truly precious I believe those things are. If their father gets custody, I pray that, this time, he will give them safety and love. At the same time, I am confident that his criminal trial will prove that he can't provide either element. I believe that if you award him custody, it will be very temporary; I only hope the harm he may inflict will be the same."

She sat down and the courtroom was silent except for the sound of reporters tapping away on the computers and scribbling down notes. Robert squeezed her arm and smiled. "I'll be back in a few minutes," the judge said, surprising everyone. It felt like hours passed before he returned. The audience stood again and sat again. Then everyone waited.

"I've spoken to your children," he began. "I'm surprised that Nicholas seems unaware of the exact reasons for your flight." He looked at Gloria and she was unsure whether he was praising her or condemning her. "His feelings toward his father are vague, but not hateful. Katie, however, seems to have a real fear of her father. Whether that fear is earned, or planted, remains to be determined." He cast a look at David before continuing. "Mrs. Stanton raised the issue of safety, and sadly I believe that these children are not safe with either of their parents. One is facing charges of kidnapping and the other is accused of abuse which led to the kidnapping. I had hoped, Mr. Stanton, that when you addressed this court you would have expressed concern for your children's welfare. However, I heard only your own welfare mentioned." Gloria glanced at David and smiled at the way his jaw hardened. His scare approach hadn't worked; her confidence level rose considerably. The judge continued. "Therefore, I award custody to Mrs. Olsen, their maternal grandmother with whom they both feel comfortable. Mrs. Stanton is to have no visitation rights but is allowed daily phone calls. Mr. Stanton is allowed supervised visitation for two hours a week until this court is asked to rule again on custody."

"Your Honor," David said as he jumped to his feet. "This is completely unfair. I'm being punished for a crime that has not and will not be proven. I object to—"

"I don't care what you object to, Mr. Stanton," the judge interrupted. "This is my court and my decision. It stands as I presented it with the stipulation that Mrs. Olsen follows my ruling to the letter. If there is even a hint of her not adhering to the regulations I have outlined, namely that Mrs. Stanton gets no visitation and only limited phone contact, these children will go to a foster home."

David came to his feet again. "Surely I am better qualified than foster parents!" he shouted. His face was red and his eyes were livid. Gloria risked another small smile to herself. He'd lost his cool and it made him look like an idiot.

"I'm not convinced of that," the judge said. "I'll wait for a jury to decide. If Mrs. Olsen will go to my clerk's office we'll take care of the details." He rapped his hammer and left the room.

Gloria spun around and hugged her mother tightly, "Thank you so much, Mom."

She released her mother and glanced at David, narrowing her eyes at the look he was giving her. Even as she watched, he began cooling down. His cocky disposition returned as he left the court room. She knew his outburst was a good sign for her; it showed he was losing his confidence. He would never have reacted so strongly otherwise. As she watched him open the doors to leave, Gloria saw something startling. Without explanation, she began pushing her way out of the courtroom. Her mother called to her but Gloria kept going. When she reached the hallway she looked around, but whatever, or whoever she thought she'd seen was gone. She looked up and down the hall again, her heart racing. It was ridiculous; the chances were so slim. But, she could swear she'd seen Bryan.

"Gloria," her mother said, finally catching up to her. "What's wrong?"

"Nothing," she said, missing him more than ever. She continued to scan the crowds. "I thought I saw someone."

Gloria watched her mother go into the clerk's office a few minutes later and wondered how close she was to her son. He had to be nearby and the temptation to try and see him, even for a moment, was very strong. She waited a few more seconds, but finally headed toward the elevator. It wouldn't look good if she were found waiting to see him and she knew it wasn't worth the risk. Besides, her sister was waiting for her downstairs. Now that the children would be staying at her mother's house, Gloria would have to find a new place to stay. Her sister Louann had offered a room; reluctantly Gloria had accepted. Louann was the sister closest to Gloria's age and had been the baby in the family for a long time when

Gloria came along. She'd always been more of a mother than a sister to Gloria and was rather difficult for Gloria to get along with. It was kind of her to offer and Gloria was very grateful, but she wasn't looking forward to her constant company. If Gloria had another offer she'd jump at it. But Louann was her only sibling in Salt Lake and so Gloria was determined to make the best of it. She only hoped Louann would cooperate, too.

———

"So what are you going to do now?" Carrie asked David as the elevator doors opened on the main floor.

"I'm going to fight it just like I said I would," he said coldly.

"How?"

"Any way I can." He opened the front door for her. Once outside Carrie stopped.

"Oh, no! I left my purse in the courtroom," she said in frustration, turning back toward the door. David shook his head and kept walking. "Aren't you going to come with me to get it?" she asked.

David turned and fixed her with an irritated glare. "I'm not the one who left it on the bench," he said in a condescending tone. "I've got to get back to work."

Carrie stared at him in surprise. He'd never snapped at her like that. "O—Okay," she said meekly as he continued down the courthouse steps. "Call me later?" she called after him.

David just waved at her and continued on his way. Carrie watched him for a few more seconds before turning away. She automatically started thinking of ways she could show him she was sorry for upsetting him. How stupid of her to leave her purse behind. He was under so much pressure; she needed to be more careful so she didn't add to his stress. She raced to the elevator, thinking that if she hurried maybe she could catch up with him in the parking lot and apologize. At the elevator, she pushed the *up* button and tapped her foot as she waited.

The elevator dinged, indicating its arrival and she waited as the doors opened. Once open, however, she just stood there gaping at David's ex-wife. Gloria stared back for several seconds before stepping out of the elevator. When she was parallel with Carrie, she stopped and turned her head toward her.

"My daughter's telling the truth," she said. "He isn't what he seems to be." Gloria continued walking while Carrie just stood there. The elevator doors began to close before Carrie pushed the up button again and, this time, stepped inside. She wished she had a quicker tongue, yet even now, she couldn't think of an appropriate response. Her stomach felt tight and she squirmed a little as Gloria's words replayed in her mind. For just an instant, a voice in her head asked her what she would do if it were true. "It's not true," she said out loud, silencing the voice. "David could never do such a thing."

Chapter Seventeen

Bryan had hurried out of the courthouse as soon as he saw Gloria look at him. Now he sat in his rental car wondering for the hundredth time why he was here. The letter she'd sent him had said they had no future. Yet, he'd begged and pleaded with every other teacher until he finally found one that would take over his summer-school for a couple of days so he could fly to Utah; still he was without a clear plan of what he would do when he got there. The principal was not happy about the situation, especially since it hadn't been that long ago that Bryan had called in the first time he'd helped Gloria get to Little Rock. Bryan knew he was on thin ice, yet he'd done it all because he suspected that Gloria wasn't all that comfortable with the letter she had sent. He'd been saving up for new flooring throughout his house, but that project would wait since he'd had to use the money to make this trip.

He watched for her to come along the sidewalk and let out a breath when she appeared. She looked wonderful. Her hair was done in some kind of up-do that showed off her face and the suit she wore was tailored perfectly. This was not Pamela Bennion, the waitress at Donny's Diner. This was Gloria Olsen Stanton, a woman he didn't know very well. Just seeing her made his heart pump faster. His reaction served to frustrate him even more.

Bryan watched in the rear-view mirror as Gloria slowed and began walking behind the other woman, whom he assumed was one of her older sisters because they looked so much alike. She passed within thirty feet of his car and never looked his way. Even without seeing her face, he could tell that she was near her breaking point. He'd arrived in Salt Lake in time to see an update of the trial on the evening news last night. It was still odd to realize that Pamela was Gloria and that Gloria was on TV. It hadn't taken much effort to learn the court time this morning and he'd been trying to decide what to do ever since. Maybe he'd just follow her to wherever she was staying. Then when he was ready, and when they were alone, he'd approach her. Whatever came after that was anyone's guess. It would be great if they could just discuss things honestly, and go from there; but that seemed a little too easy. He was beginning to think nothing that involved Gloria, Pamela, whoever she was, was ever going to be easy.

He waited until she got into the car with the other woman before turning the key in his own ignition. Tapping his fingers on the steering wheel, he waited for another car to pass him so he could back out.

Suddenly, something banged on the window next to his face. He nearly jumped out of his skin before turning quickly to see what was going on. His pounding heart gave way to a broad smile. Putting the car into park, he opened the door, stepped out and bent down, enfolding Kenny . . . Nicholas in his arms. Nicholas clung to him for a long time before pulling back, his eyes sparkling. "When did you come?" Nicholas asked.

"Last night," Bryan said with a smile. "Who are you with?" Nicholas turned and pointed toward the steps where a frazzled older woman hurried toward them. Bryan looked at the boy with censure. "Did you run away?"

Nicholas gave a guilty smile and nodded. "I was trying to find my mom," he admitted sadly. Then his eyes lit up, "And I found you instead."

Bryan brushed the boy's hair off his forehead, his chest tight as he imagined what this last week must have been like for him. He stood up, took Nicholas by the hand and began moving toward the woman he assumed was Pamela's mother. When he reached her, he stretched his other hand out in greeting. Regarding him with extreme suspicion, she kept her hands at her side. He cleared his throat and kept his hand out. "I'm a friend of your daughter," he said warmly. "I'm sorry to frighten you." Her eyebrows pinched together and he sensed that Gloria had not told her mother about him. Why was he not surprised? "My name is Bryan Drewry, from Harrison, Arkansas."

She remained unmoved by his introduction. In supplication, he nodded to Nicholas, urging him to step in and help him out. He seemed to understand. "He's nice, Grandma," he said with a smile. Looking up at his Grandma he added, "He helped us a lot. He gave me my bike!"

Grandma looked at him again, her expression was softer, but still guarded. She finally took his hand and gave him a strong but brief handshake. "I'm Virginia Olsen," she said.

"Nice to meet you," Bryan answered. "I met Gloria when she snuck into the sacrament meeting where I was speaking," he added in hopes of winning her approval.

"You're Mormon?" she asked.

"Going on four years now," he answered with a smile. Virginia nodded, still skeptical as she processed the information.

"Why don't we go get something to eat?" she finally said after another awkward, thoughtful pause, giving Bryan the impression that she was saving her judgment for later.

"That would be wonderful," he said gratefully. She nodded, pointed up the street and told him to meet them at Sizzler; Nicholas would ride with her. When he arrived at the restaurant, it was apparent that Nicholas had presented a good case for him. She was smiling and relaxed, and over all-you-can-eat shrimp he explained everything he knew. She listened intently, leading him to believe that Gloria hadn't yet filled her in on much of anything that happened during her time in hiding. Once she warmed up to him, Virginia couldn't stop asking questions and he answered all of them as best he could. When Nicholas went to get himself some ice cream, she asked him the questions she didn't want to say in front of the child.

"What's the real deal between you and my daughter?"

"To be honest," he said easily, not at all undone by her curiosity, "I don't really know. She sent me a letter telling me to leave her alone." Virginia lost a bit of her softness. He hurried to explain. "But I don't think she meant it." Virginia didn't seem convinced. "You know Gloria," he said, assuming that some things about Gloria hadn't changed. "I believe she told me to leave her alone in order to protect me from what she didn't think I should have to deal with. But there's a chemistry between us that's . . . well . . . powerful. I'm not sure I want to push it into the past just yet."

"Chemistry?" Virginia repeated, skeptical again.

"In the few months that I've known her, she's lied to me, misled me, yelled and screamed at me, gotten me involved with the FBI, cost me a girlfriend, may have cost me my job—and yet I can't sleep at night because I miss her so much. Since she's entered my life I've never been so confused. But I've never been at such peace, either. When I'm not with her, she's all I can think about; when I'm with her it's like the rest of the world disappears. I can't explain it and I don't know what to do about it. I tried to honor her request, and stay away. But here I am, ready to do something, without a clue of what that something is. That's what I mean by chemistry."

Virginia took a long sip of her drink before meeting his eyes again. "Would you give me a few minutes alone with my grandson," she said.

Bryan nodded and stood, wondering what else she needed to know that she hadn't already asked.

"I'll be outside," he said. Nicholas was just approaching the table.

"You're not leaving, are you?" Nicholas asked, panic in his voice.

"I'll just be outside," he said. "Your grandma wants to talk to you alone for a minute."

"Promise you won't leave," he added, his eyes pleading. Bryan could have kissed him. Nicholas was fighting a good battle without even knowing it.

He drew an imaginary X across his chest. "I promise."

They joined him after a few minutes or so. Virginia seemed more comfortable now. "Nicholas would like to show you Grandma's house," she said. "And I would like to hear more."

They spent the remainder of the afternoon together in Virginia's back yard. When he learned about Gloria's father his heart sank. "She must have been devastated," he said.

"She talked about him?" Virginia said, a hint of pleading in her voice. It was the first time she'd dropped her regal demeanor and he saw what a painful few years she'd had.

"She told me about their fishing trips, how he taught her to dance by waltzing with her after dinner while you washed dishes. I was looking forward to meeting him."

Virginia's eyes filled with tears and she smiled weakly. "She was his little girl," she whispered. "I told her it was better this way, that he knew it was best, too. But it broke his heart not to see her and the kids." She looked across the sprawling yard and sighed. "Maybe he's in a better position to help her now," she added. "In those last few months he kept saying that he'd be sure to get assigned as her guardian angel once he passed over."

Bryan smiled sadly. "She missed you both very much and appreciated your support," he said, hoping that would help her feel better.

Virginia shook herself out of the trancelike state and looked at him again. "When do you plan to see her?"

Bryan blew out a breath and clasped his hands on the table. "That," he said, "is a very good question."

———

Theresa went into the small room and took her usual seat in the chair across from her therapist, Joann Arlington. Joann didn't bother with any small talk. She simply handed Theresa a newspaper article. Theresa read it and then looked up; her eyes were fearful. Dr. Arlington just stared back.

"She's going home?" Theresa said, looking again at the little girl's photo on the newsprint in her hand. It was the same picture they'd used on *Unsolved Mysteries.*

"When you told me about the show, I decided to ask a colleague of mine in Utah to let me know if anything came of the broadcast. She sent this to me."

Theresa dropped the article into her lap. Strange as it was, since seeing David on TV, she'd felt better than she had in a long time. In her mind, he was always so big, and menacing; but on TV he was just an ordinary man. It had made her realize that he couldn't hurt her any more. She was a grown woman, not a child and he had no power over her unless she gave it to him. But now, his daughter was going home to him and the girl's mother was going to trial for trying to save her in the first place. That changed many things. She looked up at her therapist with frantic eyes. "What should I do?"

Dr. Arlington reverted to the usual psychiatrist technique of turning everything into a question. "What do you think you should do?" They discussed the issue for several minutes. Theresa shared her fears, her reticence, to make her own abuse known. Then Dr. Arlington asked a difficult question. A question that would haunt Theresa for many nights. "What do you think that little girl would want you to do?"

————

"So what did you do while you were in Arkansas?" Louann asked after dinner that evening. Louann was the sibling closest to Gloria, but still twelve years older. She had always been more of a mother than a sister and Gloria sensed that Louann was not supportive of her baby sister's decision all those years ago. Gloria hoped it wasn't true, she hoped that her family understood her motives, but with each passing hour the tension seemed to be building and Gloria doubted she had much sympathy from Louann.

"Well," Gloria began, as they did the dishes together while Louann's teenage children helped her husband in the yard. "I worked as a waitress."

"A waitress?" Louann laughed. "You?"

"It was a good job," Gloria defended even though she knew Louann had no concept of the lifestyle Gloria had lived. Louann's husband owned a successful family business and had always provided her with the same privilege they'd been raised with. "I worked at night and spent the days with the kids."

"You left the kids alone at night?"

"I had to work," she said easily. "I wouldn't have left them unless I'd had to."

Louann shook her head in disapproval. "When did you go blonde?"

"A few weeks ago," she said, risking a glance at Louann's mousy brown hair. "My picture was all over the papers but I had to get the doctor's report. So I became a blonde for the occasion."

"This is the doctor who's supposed to change everything?"

Gloria took a breath and willed herself to ignore the bitterness. "Yep."

"If you ask me, everyone would have been better off if you'd stuck it out the first time instead of running away to Ar-K-saws."

"Everyone but Katie," Gloria said bluntly as her anger flared. "And I didn't run away; I escaped. You may be my big sister, but you obviously don't understand everything that happened."

Louann's mouth opened. Gloria kept doing the dishes as if she weren't boiling inside.

"I don't understand?" Louann repeated. "Have you ever thought for a minute what your actions have done to us? We've been followed and investigated for almost three years. Our phones have been tapped, our mail seized, we've had reporters in our front yard. You single-handedly turned a respectable family into a side show. When Daddy died, the papers said he died of a broken heart because of you. Every one of us has suffered for you, so don't tell me I don't know anything about it. I've lived it—"

"What you've lived," Gloria interjected, "is one very small part of this experience. I know it's been hard and I'm sorry for that. If there had been any other way to protect my kids, I'd have done it, but they are my main responsibility and my main concern. You're an adult; you can handle the effects of my choice. But they needed protection and that's what I gave them."

"You protected them," Louann snorted, her eyes flaring, "by living in poverty and lying about who you are. So much for obeying the laws of the land; for having faith in God and teaching your children honesty and integrity."

Gloria took a deep cleansing breath and turned to look strongly at her older sister. "David didn't just hurt Katie's feelings or go overboard on discipline, Louann. He raped my daughter." Louann started looking around the room in shock at hearing the R-word. "There aren't enough hugs or shrugs in the world to make it go away. If you can't see into my heart and see my true motivation, then that's your problem, not mine. I'm not going to defend myself to you over and over again. I don't have the energy or interest in doing that."

"I will not be talked to like this in my own house!"

"Fine. I'll leave." Clearly, Gloria's confidence was dumbfounding her older sister.

"You—You're not taking my car!" Louann stammered as if she'd found something over which she had control.

"Nope," Gloria said easily. "I'm not. Something else I learned in Arkansas was to take care of myself. I appreciate the help you've offered me, but I don't really need it." She headed out of the room. "Thanks for dinner."

Her heart was thumping wildly as she grabbed her suitcase from the upstairs bedroom where she'd planned to stay. As she walked back down the steps, her anger began to dissipate and self-pity began. Did everyone feel like Louann? Bryan had thought the same way at one time, and likely felt that way now. Had she been branded a fool for protecting her kids? Tears came to her eyes as an incredible loneliness engulfed her. Since returning to Utah she'd kept her composure, but she was becoming overwhelmed. She'd lost her kids; she was on the front page of every newspaper labeled as a kidnapper; and now she'd told off her sister, definitely losing her support. Hot tears ran down her cheeks as she turned onto the sidewalk, unsure of where she was going.

"Gloria!"

She didn't turn around, but instead stepped up her pace. More than one reporter had come to the door of Louann's home today. She was in no mood to listen to, much less answer, any more prying.

"Gloria!" the voice called again. She gritted her teeth and called over her shoulder, "No comment." She started walking faster, wishing she'd changed out of the pantsuit and dress shoes she'd worn all day. She'd love a pair of rollerblades and shorts right about now. The summer heat was already making her sweat

"Pamela!"

She froze for a moment and then spun around. Bryan stood a few yards away. She just stared. *He came!* she thought to herself. He actually came! He looked concerned and a bit unsure of what to do next. She wasn't sure what to do either. Seeing him now seemed to dissolve the last layer of her composure. Her chin began to tremble and she brought a hand to her mouth as fresh tears came to her eyes. She'd been aching for him, and now that he was just ten feet away she didn't know what to do.

"If you want me to leave," he explained, keeping his expression unreadable, "just tell me to my face this time."

She just stared, never had she imagined the moment like this. In fantasy she'd pictured herself flying into his arms to begin a new and glorious life together. But in reality, neither of them could forget all the hardships they'd been through, all the lies she'd told, the letter she'd sent.

Bryan's expression hardened throughout her silence. "Just say it, Gloria," he said dryly. "Tell me to leave and you'll never see me again."

Never see him again! For some reason those words were like daggers. He was standing in front of her, one final time. She was being given one last chance. "*Please* don't go," she whispered.

"What?" he asked, leaning forward.

"Don't go," she said in a normal tone, her voice shaking with emotion.

"I can't quite hear you." She looked into his eyes as a half smile played on his lips. "I need to be sure I know exactly what you're saying."

He might be teasing, but he was also completely serious. "I am so . . . ," her voice shook and she took a breath before continuing, "so sorry," she whispered. "I thought I was doing the right thing; giving you a way out. But . . ." Her voice faded away; she didn't know how to explain.

"But?" he prodded.

"But I feel like . . . I feel like I left my heart in Harrison, Arkansas, with a beautiful man I treated very badly."

"And if you had the chance to change things with this *beautiful* man, what would you do?"

"I would stand right in front of him," she said taking a few steps forward so that they were only inches apart. "I would look him in the eye and promise never to lie or mislead him again. I would thank him for not giving up on me and tell him that he awakened feelings in me I've never felt before."

"What kind of things?"

"Trust, peace, joy, and—"

"Passion?"

She laughed despite herself and shook her head. "I'm not sure about that." He wrapped his arms around her and lowered his head until their lips touched. She returned his kiss, wrapping her arms tightly around his neck, pulling him closer. A few moments later, she pulled back and smiled. "I take it back," she said softly. For a moment she just stared into his eyes, relishing the feeling of being in his arms. "Why did you come?"

He leaned back and rolled his eyes. "Have we made *no* progress here?" he asked in exasperation.

She kept her grip tight around his neck. "I'm serious," she said. "I've given you little encouragement."

"That alone should tell us both something," he replied. "I dare say we're involved in something bigger then both of us."

"I didn't mean a word of that letter," she said.

He stroked her hair and kissed her lightly on the forehead. "Somehow I knew you didn't."

––––––––

"You look lovely tonight," David said when Carrie opened the front door. Carrie smoothed the front of her silvery skirt and smiled self-consciously. She'd borrowed the dress from her mother and it was a few sizes too big, but she couldn't seem to fit into her own things anymore so it had to do. David's compliment surprised her. Gray wasn't her color and the style was not very becoming. However, she was glad to see that his mood had improved since the courthouse scene that morning and she thanked him for the compliment. He smiled and walked her to the car where he opened the passenger door for her.

When he'd called and asked her to dinner, she'd readily accepted, eager to put the courtroom ugliness behind them. She'd been single for almost four years now, and had only dated a few times since her divorce; actually she'd only had a few dates since her marriage. Her husband had not been the type to dote on his wife. He preferred to hang out with the guys, while she stayed home with their children. Eventually, he met a girl on his guys-nights-out and the divorce papers came a few months after that. She looked over at David and smiled. David was so different from her first husband. No amount of legal trouble, accusations or innuendos could dispel the high regard she had for him. He was far too fine a gentleman to have done any of the things his ex-wife accused him of doing.

Now and then, she'd feel a twinge of doubt, but she was quick to stomp it out. She had to have faith in him. David Stanton was the man she loved, the blessing she'd been praying for. He could give her everything she'd never had and always longed for. Once all this trouble was over, everything would be perfect.

David took her to The Mikado restaurant in downtown Salt Lake. She'd heard great things about it, but she'd never dined there. They had a wonderful dinner and talked about the current cases he was working on. During a lull in the conversation, she asked how his kids were doing and he answered quickly that they were doing fine but moved right onto the next topic of conversation. It was strange, how reticent he was to talk about his children, but she supposed that it must still be a painful topic for him.

When dinner was finished, they walked up 100 South to the Crossroads Plaza mall. "I want to show you something," he said, pausing in front of the mall entrance. He pulled her hand toward the doors and smiled broadly. "It will only take a minute."

She smiled back and followed him into the mall, feeling a little overdressed. He passed the first set of elevators. At the second set, he pushed the button. "Where are we going?" she asked.

"You'll see." The elevator came and they took it as high as it would go. "This is the only elevator that comes up here," he said. The doors opened and she followed him onto the asphalt covered roof of the mall. Smiling kindly, she looked around. There were air conditioning units, and some other equipment. There didn't seem to be anything worth coming up here to see. He pulled her by the hand again and led her to the north side of the roof. There was a short wall that prevented them from stepping off the edge.

When she looked ahead, her mouth opened slightly and she just stared. From where they stood, they had an amazing view of Temple Square. The sun had just set, and the magnificent granite edifice was gently lit by the sun's last few golden rays. The fountains glistened in the fading light and the summer flowers added the perfect amount of color to the scene. For nearly a minute, she enjoyed the details of the picture before her. She had yet to go into the temple for her own endowments. She'd been preparing to go for the last year, yet she'd never felt such a hunger for it as she did just lately. If the outside were as beautiful as this, what was it like inside? She longed to find out.

Finally she turned to face David, to see if he shared in her awe. But what she saw took her amazement to another level. He was watching her closely and smiled as her eyes went wide. She seemed transfixed by the diamond ring he held out to her. Her mouth moved, but no words would come out.

"Carrie," he said softly. "Will you marry me?"

Her eyes left the ring and focused on his face, but still no words would come. She should be feeling ecstatic, on top of the world even, but she wasn't. In fact, she felt strangely numb. David's expression began to fade and she tried to make sense of this. "I thought we were going to wait 'til the custody was arranged."

"We can still wait," he said easily. "If you want."

She didn't know what to say, or how to feel. She hesitated for several seconds as she tried to make sense of this. "I—I'm just surprised."

He pulled her close to him with one arm, still holding the ring in front of her. Rather than enjoying the closeness, she felt oddly uncomfortable. "But it's a good surprise, right?"

"Of course," she said nervously. "I—I just don't know what to say."

"Say yes," he replied. "I know it's sooner than we planned, but I want to share my life with you. I can't wait to make you my wife, and I realized that I don't *have* to wait any longer. We've been through so much all ready, and now I'm ready to get on with things. It just feels right. Doesn't it?"

She nodded, still dazed and confused. "With everything they've been saying in the papers," she said after a few moments of thoughtful silence. "What will they think of this?"

"Who cares what they think?" David said, oblivious to her discomfort. "This stuff with Gloria is going to be over before we know it. I'm tired of living in limbo. This is my chance to start again."

"Okay," she said slowly. "But let's wait to tell anyone, just so the media doesn't make it an issue. I don't think I can handle our marriage being criticized in the papers."

His expression faltered for a moment but then he was instantly happy again. "If that's what you want," he said with a shrug as if it made no difference to him. "But don't let my silence make you think this isn't the happiest day of my life." He kissed her on the cheek and added, "I can't wait to start a new chapter of my life, with three beautiful girls beside me."

Carrie had a hard time falling asleep, feeling guilty about her thoughts. On the way home, David had talked about the wedding. He wanted something small, but beautiful; simple, yet elegant. He thought a month should be sufficient time for them to get everything arranged, and he'd pay for everything of course. He agreed to meet with his bishop this week, and she would meet with hers so that they could go through the temple. She nodded and answered questions when specifically asked, but David didn't seem to notice how strangely quiet she was. From the moment he'd asked until now, she'd been plagued with one question. *Why am I not happy about this?*

At first, she told herself that she was just in shock. Even though she was looking forward to marrying David, she just hadn't expected it so soon. But still, shouldn't she be excited? She sighed into the darkness and finally admitted to what really bothered her. David had said, "I want to share *my* life with *you; I* want to make *you my* wife." He'd said, "*I* don't have to wait; *I'm* tired of living in limbo; it's *my* chance to start again." It was the happiest day of *his* life and he couldn't wait to start a new chapter of *his* life.

Was it her imagination that he was only concerned about himself? Was she over-analyzing his comments and being unfair in thinking he was being selfish about it? But wasn't it *their* life, *their* chance to be happy, *their* future he was proposing they begin? And his final comment about having three beautiful girls by his side brought Gloria's words to mind again. Why did his comment make her so uneasy? What was it in the tone he'd used, that made her feel so suddenly protective of her daughters?

———

"Ron," Janice called from upstairs. "Get the phone." She went back to washing her face with an irritated shake of her head. You'd think a grown man would realize he ought to answer the phone himself by the fourth ring. She finished her evening routine and went downstairs.

"Who was on the phone?"

Ron looked up from the kitchen table where he was paying some bills. "It's a surprise."

Janice had already passed him on her way to the sink, where a few dishes were waiting to be put into the dishwasher. She stopped and walked backwards until she could see his face. "A surprise?"

"Yeah," Ron said with a wink, returning to his work. "They're coming over."

"It's almost ten o'clock," she said. "Who is it?"

"I'm not telling."

She came behind him and put her arms on his shoulder, bringing her mouth down to his ear. "I have ways of making you talk," she whispered seductively.

"I'm not saying a word," he answered. "Although I'll be a willing subject of whatever methods of convincing you might employ."

She slapped his chest playfully and stood up straight. "When are these 'surprise' visitors supposed to be here?"

"In a few minutes."

Five minutes later the doorbell rang and Ron hurried to the door on the first ring. Not wanting to seem overly anxious, Janice put the last pan into the dishwasher and started the cycle before going into the living room to greet their guests.

"Gloria!" she squealed. After a momentary freeze, she ran to her friend and hugged her tightly. When she pulled back, she looked Gloria over. "I've been tracking you in the papers," she said. "How are you?"

Gloria wiped at her eyes. "I'm doing all right. It's so good to see you."

Both women just stared at each other, as if unsure the reunion was for real. Finally, Gloria shook herself into action and turned toward Bryan who was standing by the door. "Bryan, this is my best friend, Janice, and her husband, Ron. And this is Bryan," she went back to him and took his hand. Janice and Ron both raised their eyebrows.

"Nice to meet you, Bryan," Ron said, stepping over to shake Bryan's hand. Janice followed, although she shot a look at Gloria that revealed she had a lot of questions to ask later.

"Come and sit down," Janice said, leading them toward the couches.

"Actually," Bryan said. "I'd love to stay but I'm still on Arkansas time and I'm nearly dead on my feet."

Janice looked a little confused. Ron hurried to explain. "Gloria has asked if she can stay with us for a few days, until her apartment is ready."

"Of course," Janice said happily. "The couch bed downstairs is all we have to offer, but you're welcome to it for as long as you like."

"Thanks," Gloria said. "Bryan was kind enough to drop me off."

"Are you sure you can't stay?" Janice asked; she was itching to become well acquainted with him.

"Thanks anyway," he said, opening the door. "Another time?"

They said their good byes and Gloria walked him to his car. Janice peeked out the window in time to see the tail end of a good-night kiss. "They're kissing!" she said over her shoulder.

"And you're spying," Ron answered. Gloria pulled out of the

embrace and headed up the walk. Janice hurried away from the window and smiled innocently as Gloria came back in.

"He seems nice," she said sweetly.

Gloria laughed, "You're about to explode with curiosity aren't you?"

Janice put a hand to her chest and opened her mouth as if shocked. "Yes, she is!" Ron answered.

Janice smiled again as she sat down and patted the spot next to her on the couch. "We have a lot to talk about," she said. Gloria accepted the invitation.

"As much as I like girl talk," Ron said as he leaned down to give his wife a good-night kiss, "I think I'll just get the short version from Janice later."

They both told him good night, then the women looked at each other. Finally, Gloria started to laugh. It felt so good to be among friends again. Bryan and Janice were rays of sunshine fighting their way through a very gray sky. The feeling of acceptance she felt right now was euphoric. "I don't know where to start," she finally said.

"At the beginning," Janice answered. "I've thought about you every day, so fill me in on what I missed."

It was after two a.m. when Janice finally slipped into bed. She snuggled up to Ron, waking him. "How'd it go?" he asked groggily.

"She's different, Ron," Janice started. "She's still kind and sweet like she always was, but she's stronger. Solid. Real."

"I'm not surprised," Ron said. "Can you imagine what it must have been like to do what she did?"

"She didn't even fill her own gas tank before; now she changes her own oil," Janice said in awe. "She worked as a waitress at some po-dunk diner and she knows how to buy fake IDs. Her mom saved the money from the sale of her house and she's already bought herself a car and found an apartment she can move into next week, she's so on top of things."

Ron chuckled. "She was always such a pampered darling."

"Not anymore," Janice said proudly. "She's taken a huge dose of reality the last few years and she's grown up a lot. There's going to be another preliminary hearing in two weeks."

"Does she think it'll make it to trial this time?"

"She's pretty confident," Janice replied. "But I can tell she's worried. I don't know what she'll do if she loses those kids."

Chapter Eighteen

"Hey, baby," Gloria said into the phone the next morning, Wednesday.

"Hi, Mom!" Nicholas said excitedly. "Where are you?"

"I'm staying with a friend," she answered. "Are you all right?"

"I'm at Grandma's house. She made me a cake last night and let me watch TV till nine o'clock."

"Really," Gloria said with feigned disbelief. "She must love you."

"Yep," he agreed. "Did you see Bryan?" he asked excitedly.

Gloria couldn't help but smile. "Yes, I did."

"Good," Nicholas said. He paused for a moment. "Where's Darla?"

"You mean Katie?"

"Yeah, Katie."

"I think she'll be coming to Grandma's today. She was supposed to get out of the hospital this morning." They had kept her longer than necessary in order to be sure she was well enough to not only travel, but to deal with the whole new life awaiting her.

"When are you coming over?"

"Oh, baby," she said sadly. "It might be a while. But I'm thinking of you all the time and Grandma's going to take good care of you until you can live with me again."

"Grandma said you might go to jail 'cause you wouldn't let us live with my dad."

"She's right," Gloria said carefully. "But we're getting it all taken care of."

"And my dad bought me my own Playstation and three games!"

Gloria was speechless for a moment. "That's real nice," she finally said, hiding her irritation about David having access to her children when she did nothing. She attempted to change the subject. "Are you doing anything special today?"

"Yeah," Nicholas said with excitement. "Grandma's going to take me to a zoo with elephants and zebras and even giraffes. Then my dad's coming over to play video games with me. Do you think I'll win?"

Gloria hung up the phone a few minutes later and stared out the window of Janice's kitchen. "Everything okay?" Janice asked from where she was feeding her nine-month-old daughter Gerber peaches.

"Besides the fact that my mom's raising my kids, that my daughter's been in the hospital for a week and David gets visitation and I don't; everything is fine." She looked at her friend and smiled to soften the frustration in her voice. "It will all work out," she said, looking out the window again. Was it wise of her to have kept her son so uninformed about his father? She had always felt that it was important not to let her hatred spill over to him, but now she wondered if she had simply set him up to be more confused, and easily fooled.

———————

David pulled into work and smiled slightly at the sight of the man standing next to the building. Most reporters would have given up by now, especially since David had ignored every one he had encountered so far. However, this man's patience was about to pay off.

"Mr. Stanton," the reporter said quickly as David approached the door. "How you feel about losing custody of your kids?" He held a small cassette player and David made sure he was standing close enough for it to pick up his voice before he answered.

"How do you think I feel?" he said with contrition. "And I didn't *lose* custody; it was taken from me, just like it was almost three years ago when my ex-wife kidnapped them."

The reporter's eyes shone like he'd won the lottery. "What do you plan to do next?"

"As a matter of fact, I'm meeting with the judge tomorrow afternoon. I feel confident that he'll give me the custody I deserve. Besides, I'm getting married soon and I'm sure the judge will see that my kids are better off with two loving parents."

"Who's the lucky bride?"

"Carrie Gunderson; we've been dating for some time and have decided to tie the knot."

"When?"

"As soon as possible."

"What are your feelings on the preliminary hearing that's coming up next week?" the reporter asked.

"No comment." David's eyes went cold and he continued on his way. Couldn't he have focused on the wedding info a little longer? Oh well, he thought to himself, he had little doubt it would make the papers anyway.

———

Bryan showed up around ten o'clock. Janice's four-year-old son Steven opened the door. "I'll be right up," Gloria yelled from the basement. Janice stepped into the living room and invited Bryan to sit down. By the time Gloria came upstairs, Bryan was just finishing telling the details of the time Gloria thought he was chasing her home from work.

"You ran through people's back yards?" Janice asked as Gloria appeared.

"Thanks for sharing, Bry," she said, giving him a dirty look. "And yes, I ran through back yards, hid behind a woodpile—the whole bit. It was very . . . James Bond. Arkansas style."

Janice laughed and got off the couch. "So where are you two kids off to today?"

"Bryan flies home around nine o'clock," Gloria said. "I've got a meeting with the prosecutor now, and then Bryan's going to visit the kids if he has time."

"What are you doing with the DA?"

"We're putting our heads together today in hopes to build as strong a case against David as possible."

———

"How can this not be enough?" Gloria asked Wednesday afternoon, trying hard not to take out her frustrations on the state prosecutor assigned to the case. Ironically, she played a very small part in the case against David. Even Katie was only considered a witness to David's supposed crimes. Mr. Staling had been the prosecutor on the first attempt; she felt lucky to have him for the second round.

"It's probably enough to get an indictment," he clarified. "But I'm not convinced it will be enough for a trial."

Gloria let out a breath. "I really thought this doctor's report would be sufficient."

The prosecutor was shaking his head. "You forget that they also have two other doctors, from the first attempt, who found inconclusive evidence." To further explain, Mr. Staling moved two pens on his desk so that they laid side by side but didn't touch. Pointing to one pen he said, "It's as if this is Katie's statement and the claims that support it." He pointed to the other pen. "This is David's vehement denial that it never happened." He picked up a paper clip and laid it across the top of the pens. "Substantiating testimony or evidence is the bridge that joins the two."

"I don't know what else we can get."

"To start, I suggest we hire an investigator. Maybe someone heard David say something incriminating, or we can find some evidence of other 'hobbies' that are characteristic of a child molester. Then we need to . . ."

Almost an hour later, Gloria shut the door behind her. Bryan stood from where he was waiting in the hallway. "How did it go?" he asked.

She shrugged. "We're going to hire an investigator and check out his computers." She looked at him sweetly and tipped her head to the side and pushed the frustrations away. "I wish you didn't have to go back so soon."

He pulled her into an embrace. "Me, too. But I'll be back," he added. Pulling away he glanced at his watch. "I'd like to go see the kids before I go, though. What time will Katie arrive?"

"Around one," Gloria said, trying to ignore her envy. Everyone could see her children but herself; it seemed very unfair. However, she looked forward to hearing about his visit. "Why don't we grab some lunch, then you can drop me off at Janice's on the way."

Bryan arrived at Virginia's around two and stayed for hours. A little after five, Virginia called to him that he should go. She'd told him already that David was coming at 5:30. She'd had the option of having an intermediary take the kids to the child welfare office for the visits, but she decided she could stand his presence in exchange for keeping an eye on him. Bryan had been playing 'Life' with the kids outside on the patio; they'd played three times and he was torn between relief at ending the marathon game and irritation that his visit was being cut short. The kids complained about his departure at a flattering level. He pulled Nicholas into his arms for a hug and then put him down. He looked over at Katie and smiled. She was feeling quite well and had seemed happy to see him. Feeling brave, he sat down in front of her.

"Katie," he said in a serious tone. "I don't ever want you to think that I don't want to give you a hug. But because you're a girl and I'm a boy, you have to ask first so that I know it's okay. Does that make sense?"

She gave him a half smile and nodded like he'd told her a great joke.

He put out his hand. "Would you rather shake my hand?" She nodded, although he sensed that she was a little embarrassed by her own reluctance. She put out her hand and he shook it.

"Thank you very much," he said. As he stood, he tapped her on the nose. He took just a moment to say good bye to Virginia before letting himself out the front door. Skipping down the steps, he didn't realize he had company until he nearly reached his rental car. The spring in his step disappeared as he recognized David Stanton from the myriad of photographs he'd seen on the news and in the papers.

"You're the boyfriend, right?" David said arrogantly. He was leaning against the door of his Mercedes as if modeling the car.

"And you're the ex-husband who hired an investigator to keep your own kids away from the court system," Bryan countered without hesitation. He continued toward his car, enjoying the flash of anger he'd seen in David's eyes. He reached his car and opened the door before making eye contact with Gloria's former husband again. "I'd say nice to meet you, but that would be a little much, don't you think?"

David kept his face calm. "She's really sucked you in, hasn't she?"

Bryan just smiled, as if conversing with this man were no big deal. "Do I threaten you?" The flash of anger he saw this time was a little more intense. He shrugged. "I can understand that," he continued, loving the way he was disarming the other man. "If I were a man like you, I'd be threatened by a guy like me, who has no problem being the dad to your kids that you could only dream of being." He smiled and began to get into the car.

"You have no idea what you're getting into, do you?" David continued, shaking his head as if disappointed although his eyes showed his anger clearly. He took a step away from his car and Bryan wondered if it would be appropriate to beat him to a pulp in Virginia's driveway.

Bryan knew he should leave, but he felt he had the upper hand in this little spar and he was enjoying it. "Actually, I think I've got a pretty good handle on it," he replied. "If either of us is in for a shock, my guess would be that the surprise will be yours. You've got that hearing coming up, right?"

David ignored the comment, but his confidence was slipping even further. "You'll never make her happy on a school teacher's salary," he said. "She'll clean you out."

Bryan laughed out loud and crossed his arms over the top of the rental car. "You obviously don't know her well. And you surely don't have a clue how's she lived without you. I wouldn't worry about it." He was growing tired of the game and began getting into the car again.

"Poor and childless; what a way to live your life."

"Childless," Bryan chuckled as he shook his head. "You really think *you'll* get custody. You are crazy."

David was silent for a moment as his eyes brightened. "She hasn't told you," he finally said with a cocky grin as he crossed he arms over his chest once more. "Gloria's had all the kids she'll ever have. Are you sure *my* kids every other weekend will ever make up for never having kids of your own?"

Chapter Nineteen

Gloria got up from the couch and parted the curtains to see if the car she'd heard was Bryan's. She smiled and went to the front door. It was after six; she'd expected him home a long time ago. Janice and her family had gone bowling and she'd been waiting for him to return so they could have a little more time together before his flight home.

He seemed to be walking slower than usual and she wondered why. Perhaps he was just reluctant to return to Arkansas. As he approached, however, she sensed it was something more. "Did the visit go okay?" she asked when he stopped a good four feet in front of her. He looked up at her, his expression guarded.

"Can you have kids?" he asked bluntly.

She stared at him for a moment and felt like she'd just been hit with a frying pan. Her heart sank and she looked at the porch steps at her feet as she tried to think of how to answer him. Bryan made a sound in his throat and she looked up, his eyes reflecting her torture. The pain and disappointment in his face made her chest tighten. "In all the conversations we've had," he said in a restrained voice. "In all the times we've talked, you never thought that perhaps this topic would be an important one to discuss?"

She swallowed and tears came to her eyes as she searched for an explanation. "I'm sorry," she said lamely. "I was going to tell you."

"When?" he said evenly. "When did you plan to tell me?"

"I . . . I don't know," she said, watching him closely for some sign of softening.

"Did you have your tubes tied or what?"

"No," she said quickly. "Nothing like that. I'd have never done such a thing on purpose." He looked down at the ground and she tried to explain, already praying he'd be able to accept this. "When I was eight months pregnant with Nicholas I was involved in a car accident. I was turning left when another car ran the light and hit me. I was hysterical about the baby and they finally had to sedate me in the ambulance. When I woke up two days later, I learned that my uterus had been ruptured in the accident. They were able to take Nicholas by Cesarean section, but they had also preformed an emergency hysterectomy." A tear ran down her cheek and she wiped it away. He continued to stare at the ground. "That's why I had such a hard time after his birth. That's why I went on medication and hired a nanny. I couldn't deal with it. I'd always wanted a lot of kids and suddenly that dream was ripped away from me."

Bryan looked up at her and she realized that she'd likely just expressed his own feelings at this moment. "Are there any more surprises?" he said. "It seems like every time I turn around there is one more mountain for me to climb with the understanding that it's the last one. You told me just yesterday that you'd never lie or mislead me again."

"I didn't lie to you," she said softly, her voice shaking. "I wasn't keeping it from you, we . . . just hadn't gotten to it yet. I'm so sorry, Bryan."

When he spoke again there was just a trace of anger in his voice and it felt like a knife in her heart. "So is this it? Is there *anything* else I should know about you? *Anything* you haven't gotten around to telling me?"

Her chest shuddered and she shook her head. For the first time since he'd pulled up, she saw his face soften; she saw tears in his eyes as well. "I love you, Gloria," he said. "But I need some time to work this one out." He turned to the car, got in and drove away. By the time he turned the corner, she was sobbing.

He landed in Kansas City, Missouri, around midnight and picked up his truck for the two-hour drive back to Harrison. About half an hour out of town, he pulled over on the side of the road. He closed his eyes and rested his forehead on the steering wheel as the full weight of the decision he faced descended upon him. Gloria had brightened his future with hopes of making a family with her. Was the dream worth pursuing if he couldn't have it all? Were his feelings for her strong enough to warrant the sacrifice? *Oh, Gloria*, he thought to himself sadly. Why does everything they wanted to share have to be so hard?

As he lifted his head a few minutes later an idea came to him. He'd come back today because, since it was the last week of summer school, there were additional classes Thursday and Friday. When he'd begged his fellow teachers for help covering his classes this week, he'd only been able to get Tuesday and Wednesday taken care of. The St. Louis temple was only few hours away. If he turned around now and caught the 7 a.m. session he could be back . . . no, he couldn't be back in time for Thursday's summer school classes. But maybe he could make some calls, grovel if he had to and find a sub for just one more day. It would only further complicate his job security, but if it could help him make sense of all of this it would be worth it. He thought about it for a few more seconds before putting on his blinker. He needed peace, clarity and some guidance. He prayed that he'd be able to make arrangements for his students. But he wasn't going to deny himself the opportunity to get some help. He needed all the help he could get.

———

Carrie sat at the small desk pointing out the large red letters on the letter board to a less than interested eight-year-old. It had been four years since Carrie had begun working with disabled children, but she didn't feel the burnout she'd been warned about since the day she began. It wasn't easy to teach basic skills over and over again to children who couldn't comprehend much of what she taught, but she liked to think she was one of the few with the gift to see their spirits. Their spirits were glorious, and so she returned to the school every morning with a smile on her face. Today she was working with Jeff, a boy with cerebral palsy, who'd been coming to the school since he was three.

"Carrie, can I have a minute?"

Carrie looked up to see her supervisor, Lisa, standing in the doorway. "Sure," she said as she pushed herself out of the chair. She told Jeff she'd be right back, but he just looked out the window. Once in the hallway, she smiled at Lisa, waiting to learn what this was all about.

"Have you read today's paper?" Lisa inquired.

"No," Carrie said slowly as Lisa handed her the newspaper. Lisa pointed to a small article and Carrie's heart sank. "David Stanton To Wed Again." How did the papers find this out? She quickly read the first few lines, then looked up with slight embarrassment. The article had included her name as well as the fact that she had two young daughters. "I had no idea this would be in the papers."

Lisa cleared her throat and spoke. "Carrie, what you do in your personal life is your business," she said. "But the board has discussed the situation and I agreed to tell you where we stand on this issue."

"Where you stand?" Carrie repeated, uncharacteristic defensiveness flavoring her tone.

"If you go through with this marriage, you need to understand that Mr. Stanton will not be welcome in the school."

"He hasn't even gone to trial on the charges," Carrie said. How could people judge him so quickly?

"It doesn't matter," Lisa said, her voice betraying her sympathy for the situation. "We are entrusted with the well being of these children and we can't allow or afford the appearance of anything inappropriate. I realize you have made a different choice, but the school will not take the risk of exposing these children to Mr. Stanton."

"He's innocent. In fact, he was awarded custody just this morning."

"He's accused by his own children," Lisa countered. "And he will not be permitted here."

"That isn't fair."

"But it's the decision we have made. You're welcome to take it to whatever legal level you want, but we remain firm in our decision. The safety of your children is your concern. These kids are in our care and we won't take any chances."

The two women stared at each other for a few moments. "I want a meeting with the board," Carrie said angrily.

"I figured you would so I scheduled you one Monday; they're prepared to hear your side, but I doubt that they'll change their mind. I'm sorry."

Lisa turned and walked away, leaving Carrie to stare after her. Finally, Carrie returned to the small classroom. Jeff was humming a tuneless melody while she sat heavily in her chair, joining him in a blank stare out the window. The indignation she felt at the board's decision made her angry—something that rarely happened. The fact that Lisa would accuse her of not taking her own children's safety seriously, further infuriated her. Yet, it reminded her of her own concerns which had been steadily growing. Carrie loved her daughters; she would never put them in a situation she believed was unsafe. If the charges against David were true, she would know; she would feel it. She felt sure she'd be able to tell. These were the kind of things David must have meant when he said he'd stand accused forever. Even if he were found innocent, there would be people who always wondered. She would not be one of them.

An hour or so later, Carrie took a break and called David's office. His receptionist forwarded the call to him.

"Did you see the paper?" she asked.

"What about it?" David asked while shuffling through a file.

"There's an article about us."

"Us?"

"About our getting married," Carrie said. She sighed heavily. "I didn't want them to know." There was a waver in her voice that showed her emotion.

David smiled to himself. "I'm so sorry, darling," he said apologetically. "What did the article say?"

"It mentioned me and the girls. It talked about the preliminary hearing coming up and how much stronger the prosecution feels their case is this time around. It was . . . critical of the woman who would marry you." David took a deep breath. He'd read the article and he wasn't happy with it. It hadn't given the portrayal he had hoped for. Since it was printed so close to the custody hearing, he felt sure it would focus on how unfair the judge's decision was to keep his children away from him. "How did they find out anyway?" she continued. "I only told my mother. You didn't tell anyone, did you?"

"Of course not," he said, sounding offended that she would even suggest it.

She sniffed on her end of the line. "I just want our marriage to be beautiful, a celebration. I can't stand all this criticism. It's not fair."

"It will be okay," David soothed, tapping his pencil in annoyance. "But, ya know, as long as everyone knows maybe we should go ahead with the wedding now that everyone knows. We'll show them just how wrong they are."

––––––

It was after two o'clock Thursday afternoon when Bryan pulled up to his house in Harrison. Other than the two hours of sleep he'd caught in the parking lot before the temple opened, he had yet to sleep and was beginning to feel deep fatigue. The temple had energized his spirit, reminded him of things he definitely needed to understand; but it hadn't done a lot for his physical well-being. He parked behind his house and was fumbling to find his key when he saw the fluorescent green piece of note paper stuck in the door jam. He pulled it out and furrowed his brow.

Call me 543-567-9876

He turned it over in search of some identification of the note's source, but it was blank. He found his key, unlocked the door, and went inside. Although he was tempted to ignore the note until after he got some sleep, he picked up his phone and punched in the number. It was picked up on the second ring.

"This is Bryan Drewry. I had a note on my door to call this number."

"How's your girlfriend doing?" the woman on the other end of the phone asked slowly. He said nothing. "Don't get nervous, I'm not with the police," she added.

"Then who are you?"

"It's who I've been working for that should be of interest to you."

"Really," Bryan said blandly; he did not have the energy to play this game.

"I really can't figure out why Gloria ever married him; he really is a creep."

Bryan straightened. "David?"

"The very one," she said triumphantly. "I think I have something of interest for you."

"I can't see how you could," he said, remembering the accounts he'd heard of David's red-haired Arkansanian PI. "Gloria's no longer in need of international transportation."

"Just listen to this, okay?" There was click on the line.

"Are you asking me to have her killed?"

"No, I want her out of the country; we talked about that before."

"I don't know how I'm going to pull that off."

"You'll find a way. I've got twenty thousand dollars that's yours when she's gone."

"You're that desperate to keep her away from a judge?"

"Look, if I get convicted of this I lose everything, my license, my family, my religion, my future; everything. I won't take that chance."

"All right. I'll find her. And when I do I'll get her out of here."

"Interesting, huh?" the woman's voice said.

"Definitely interesting," he commented as he speculated on its worth at a trial. "You're offering it to me, I assume?"

"For a price," she replied.

"How much?"

"He shorted me two thousand dollars, I'm looking to break even."

"I can give you five hundred," Bryan offered.

"No way."

"We both know it's not concrete evidence, and unless it was made with his permission it's not admissible in court."

She paused for a moment. "I thought you were a science teacher."

"Whose favorite TV show is *Law & Order*. Five hundred. Take it or leave it."

"Fifteen hundred," she countered.

"Eight."

"Twelve."

"A thousand even; I can't go higher. Ask my bank."

"Cash?"

"When I can get to my bank."

"I'll meet you at your house at eight o'clock tomorrow morning."

At five after eight Friday morning, there was a knock on the back door. Bryan had been waiting.

"Ya know what I hate about Yankee women?" the redhead said, cocking her head to the side. "They always go for the best-looking southern men we've got."

He smiled politely and held up a bank envelope. "Did you bring it?"

She pulled a manila envelope out of her purse with a smile. They traded envelopes, she counted the money and he popped the tape into his own mini-recorder to verify its contents. She finished counting and dropped the envelope into her purse.

"It's been nice doing business with you," she said. "If you need me for anything else, you can call me at that same number." She winked flirtatiously, but he just smiled as he shut the door. Holding the tape recorder in his hand, he stared at it and smiled. It might not be admissible in court, but it could be very valuable when played to the right audience. He glanced at the clock and hurriedly hid it in the suitcase on his bed before heading for school. He had a meeting with the principal before class and he didn't want to be late.

———

Friday morning, Gloria laid on her back staring at the ceiling of Janice and Ron's family room. She'd heard the kids get up over an hour ago. They'd already run out the door to catch the bus for school. She'd gotten up both mornings to help Janice with the hectic routine, but today she'd just listened to the hurried movements and strained parental proddings. She stretched her arms above her head, hitting the back of the couch, before letting them flop to the mattress. Where was Bryan? she wondered. She hadn't heard from him since he left Wednesday night which was only two days ago, but an increasingly loud voice in her mind told her he wasn't coming back again.

In the few short months he'd known her, she'd ruined his engagement, brought the police to his door, affected his relationships within his church, lured him away from his home and now wanted him to quit his job to move to a new state and support her in her hour of need and finally to give up on having children. Her stomach burned with a feeling she couldn't quite describe. She wanted him to come back so badly, yet the realization that it would be unfair for him was always on her mind. Perhaps if she'd told him sooner . . . or later; but the what if's were useless. It was all in his hands; it was his decision. Her eyes filled with tears as she faced the possibility of never seeing him again and she wished she'd shared her feelings more forcefully. She was in love with him; she ached for him and longed for him in a way that was completely foreign to her. Would those feelings go away by themselves, with time as the only relief? Or would they always flicker within her, rising up at times throughout her life to remind her of what could have been, what would have been if only she'd had more to give.

"Gloria?"

She turned her face in the direction of the basement door. "Yes?" she answered, her voice wavering in such a way that Janice would suspect she was sleepy rather than crying.

"Telephone."

She threw back the covers and grabbed her robe off the armrest of the couch. "I'll be right up." Was it Bryan? she wondered, cinching the robe and running up the stairs. *Oh, please let it be Bryan.*

Less than a minute later, she returned the phone to its cradle, staring numbly at the countertop. Janice watched her with concern. "What?" she asked after a few moments.

"David's getting the kids," she said in a shocked whisper. Janice gasped but didn't have time to answer. "He met with the judge yesterday and got a court order giving him temporary custody until after his preliminary hearing."

"But how could he do that!"

Gloria covered her mouth with her hand as her body began to shake. Janice was at her side in an instant. "It's going to be okay," she said in a soothing voice. "We'll call your lawyer, he'll—"

"That *was* my lawyer," she said as she dropped her hand from her face.

Suddenly she began looking around wildly. "Where are my keys?"

"Uh, . . ."

"He's picking them up this morning. I've got to get to them first."

Janice watched as Gloria ran for the basement stairs. When she returned less than a minute later, keys in hand, Janice followed her to the door. "What do you mean you have to get to them first?" Her tone was distrustful and Gloria could feel Janice's suspicions. She avoided meeting her eyes and pulled open the door without speaking. She was on the bottom step before Janice caught up with her and grabbed her arm. "Gloria," she said. Gloria met her eyes and lifted her chin defiantly. "Please don't do this," Janice said, her voice wavering. "Not again."

Gloria shook her arm away and ran for her car, her robe billowing behind her. The engine started and she pulled away from the curb without looking back.

A few minutes later, she screeched into her mother's driveway. When she burst through the front door she began calling for her children. The house was eerily quiet. "Katie," she yelled, looking into the kitchen before running up the stairs that led to the second floor. "Nicholas!" Her mother, standing in the hallway, brought her up short. Virginia's tear streaked face was evidence enough, but Gloria ran past her to the bedrooms, still calling out their names.

"They're gone," her mother said when Gloria finally stopped in the middle of the final guest-room. The *Toy Story* motif told her that Nicholas had stayed here, but there was no evidence of him now. The first sob rose in her chest, but she tried to hold it back. They couldn't be gone. David couldn't have them!

"They showed up almost an hour ago," her mother said, her voice breaking. "He had a court order and two police officers."

The room began to spin as the full impact of what had happened rushed upon her like the current of a river. She fell to her knees and soon felt her mother's arms around her. But she didn't want comfort. Shaking off her mothers arms, she balled her fists. "He can't have them!" she screamed, causing her mother to shrink back for a moment. Gloria dropped her face into her hands, but she wasn't crying—she was planning. Virginia tried again to comfort and calm her daughter, but Gloria shook it off and sprang to her feet. "He can't have them," she repeated strongly, her eyes furious. She turned from the room and ran for the stairs.

"Gloria," he mother called after her. The door slammed a few moments later and Virginia began to cry.

When Janice heard the car pull up that afternoon, she hurried to the front door. Gloria was dressed in clothes Janice had never seen. Before her first escape, Gloria had been quite a shopper. From the bags piled in the back of the car it seemed she'd reverted to old methods of stress relief.

"Where have you been?" Janice asked. "It's almost three o'clock."

"I'm going to stay with my mom for awhile," Gloria said in an overly calm tone.

Janice furrowed her brow but couldn't think of anything to say. Gloria turned to face her and smiled. She took both Janice's hands in her own. "Thank you so much for letting me stay here, for supporting me in all of this. I don't know what I'd have done without you."

"So what happened?" Janice asked, distrustful of the veiled expression on Gloria's face.

"My mom's expecting me," she said, avoiding the subject. She gave Janice's hands a slight squeeze before letting go and heading to the basement. Five minutes later she returned with her bags. Janice was waiting for her.

"Shall I just have Bryan call you at your mom's?" she asked.

Gloria looked at the ground. "I don't think Bryan's involved any more."

"What?"

"He found out about the hysterectomy just before he left on Wednesday," Gloria said evenly, as if it were no big deal.

"You hadn't told him?"

"I hadn't planned to keep it from him, but it's rather tricky to work into a conversation," Gloria said with the first sign of sorrow Janice had seen. Their eyes met and Janice saw the pain and heartbreak Gloria felt. "He'd already given up so much for me; I can't expect him to give up even more."

"It's only been two days," Janice explained hopefully. "He's probably just busy."

Gloria nodded and forced a smile that was supposed to show her understanding. "I agree," she said. "He's busy trying to salvage the life he had in Arkansas. It's okay; I understand."

"Gloria, you're—"

"Thanks again," she said pulling the door open.

Janice reached out and took Gloria's hand, squeezing it slightly as tears came to her eyes. "Why do I feel like I'm not going to see you again?"

Gloria paused and let out a breath before opening the door and pulling out of Janice's grip. "Say good bye to Ron and the kids for me."

———

Bryan stopped at Charlotte's house on his way out of town Friday night. The school had been disappointed about his leaving, but the principal gave him a letter of strong recommendation to take to Utah and he sensed they were a little relieved since he'd been so complex lately. They did however ask him to finish the last day of summer school, which he did before going home and completely packing up his house.

Charlotte was in the kitchen fixing dinner when he entered and tossed his house keys onto the counter. "I appreciate you helping with the house," Bryan said. The items he planned to keep were in the U-haul he was pulling back to Utah with him.

"And Ray appreciates the pool table," she said looking up at him.

Bryan smiled. It was a painful trade, but a fair one. Charlotte had agreed to clean up the place, get rid of the stuff he left and keep up the yard until it sold, in exchange for the pool table he received from his mom when he graduated from college. It used to be in the bar, and it had needed new felt, but it was a thoughtful gift; he loved pool.

"So when will we see you again?" Charlotte asked as she slid a cake into the oven and washed her hands. He knew she was sad to see him go, but was supportive of his decision.

"I don't know," Bryan replied. "Soon, I hope."

Charlotte was silent for a moment as he looked into the family room to see what the kids were watching on TV. "Barbara's been telling people you were sleeping with her."

Bryan snapped his head to look at her. "What?"

Charlotte shrugged. "Hell hath no fury like a woman scorned. Sister Jensen called me this afternoon and asked if it were true."

Bryan shook his head sadly. "I had hoped Barbara would take it a little better than that."

"I think you underestimate the power you have over women," Charlotte said with a forced tease in her voice. "How'd it go with the bishop last night?"

"Good," Bryan answered. "He asked me about Gloria and I told him everything. He agreed that I have to trust the spirit, which I can only do if I'm worthy of it. I'm glad I went; he eased my mind a great deal. Then he renewed my temple recommend, which was about to expire. I'll be stopping by the stake president's house on my way out of town to get it finished."

Charlotte nodded. "And did you think about what we talked about?" Last night, Bryan had stopped by before meeting with the bishop. Ray and Charlotte had spent nearly an hour discussing the situation in which Bryan found himself. They had let him talk openly about the situation and finally told him it was a hard decision that he had to make on his own.

"I love her," Bryan said, with great tenderness in his voice. "I'm disappointed, but having any family at all is a rather new desire for me and she has great kids. I haven't lived a perfect life and maybe that gives me a better perspective on her imperfections."

Charlotte furrowed her brow. "Don't sell yourself short because of past transgressions. You don't deserve anything less than anyone else does, Bry."

"That's not what I meant," Bryan said quickly. "It's just that I know Gloria will have to make peace with the man I once was. The least I can do is not punish us both for something she can't do anything about."

Charlotte nodded her understanding. "And it's something you can live with?"

"Gloria is something I can't live without; kids of my own doesn't tip the scales against her." He paused and looked at his sister. "If Ray's only shortfall was that he couldn't have kids, would that have changed your decision to marry him?"

"Good point," Charlotte agreed. She started pulling plates and cups out of the cupboard while she talked. "Since my baptism I've struggled with the differences between Ray's and my own values, you know that." She looked up and caught his eye, he nodded his agreement; it had been a topic of conversation many times. "It's been really hard for me to make peace with those differences, but I've realized something in the process. Life doesn't always give us a perfect pitch to sing in tune with," she said. "But if we're willing to listen closely enough, we usually find a part, all our own, to sing. A part that, when sung in harmony with the people we love, makes a beautiful song."

He stood and pulled his big sister into a hug. "You can sing in my choir any time."

She slapped his arm playfully, but said nothing and allowed the embrace to linger. They hadn't been raised in an affectionate family, but they were learning.

"I'm going to miss you guys; you've been a great blessing to me," he continued when he finally let her pull away.

"Just make sure to invite us to the wedding."

Chapter Twenty

Nicholas came into the kitchen of David's luxury condo Saturday morning. "Hey there, buddy," David said as he slid a plate of breakfast onto the table. Katie had yet to say a word to her father, but Nicholas at least exchanged pleasantries. "Where's your sister?"

"She says she's not coming," Nicholas said easily. "She doesn't like you."

David clenched his teeth. "She just doesn't know me; neither of you do, thanks to your mom. Once we have a little more time together we'll be a happy family again."

Nicholas didn't comment, but he did eat his breakfast. Once he finished, David sent him up to get his sister. A few minutes later, Nicholas returned. "She says she doesn't want to look at you."

David looked up the stairs, his eyes showing his anger and his jaw clenched. "We either go to your grandmother Stantons' house all together or you stay home with me all day," he yelled. Nicholas flinched at the power in his voice. Then they waited. Katie came down the stairs in a couple of minutes and, without a word, went out to the car and sat in the back seat. David didn't even try to talk to her. They spent most of the day at his mothers house; Katie didn't say a word the entire time. She just needed time, he told himself as he drove to Carrie's house that afternoon. Once she got used to him, she would be fine.

Carrie pulled up in front of her three-bedroom condo and turned off the car's engine. The school she worked at had a carnival today and then she'd had to stay and clean up once it was finished. It had been a long day, especially since she was now aware of their feelings about David.

The smell of something Italian in nature surprised her when she entered the front door. She paused momentarily; now and then, her mother would come over with dinner, but she usually brought Kentucky Fried Chicken. "Hello?" she called out as she placed her purse and keys on the entry table. She looked out the still-open door and smiled when she saw David's Mercedes on the other side of the street.

"You're home," a voice called from the kitchen.

She smiled as she recognized it as David's voice. She hadn't talked to him since he picked up his kids the day before, but he knew where she hid the key to the house so she wasn't alarmed. In fact she was relieved to have him here; she'd thought of nothing but him all day today. When she entered the kitchen, she smiled even wider. David had donned an apron that she wore about once a year, and he had a wooden spoon in hand. "I'm making spaghetti," he announced, as the spoon went into a pot on the stove.

"I didn't know you cooked," she said as she came to receive a greeting kiss. Maybe she should write an article for the paper that mentioned all the wonderful things he did for her.

"I heat up," he answered. "And it's about ready, so if you and the girls want to sit down." He turned toward the family room, "Katie, Nicholas, dinner's ready."

Carrie smiled sweetly as Nicholas scampered into the room with her daughters. "He looks so much like you," Carrie said, her heart swelling. David had his kids!

"Katie isn't hungry," Nicholas said as they sat down. David let out a breath and looked at Carrie sadly.

"She still won't talk to me," he said with sorrow and irritation. "Gloria totally poisoned her."

"Can I try?"

David shrugged and began dishing up dinner. "Maybe she'll talk to you."

Carrie entered the family room nervously. Disney's movie *Beauty and the Beast* was on the TV. She scanned the room until her eyes settled on the little girl snuggled into the corner of the couch. "You must be Katie," she said as she sat on the other end of the couch. From her experience with special-needs children she knew it was important not to invade a child's space. "I'm Carrie." Katie said nothing. "Your dad made dinner."

"He's not my dad," Katie said evenly.

"I know you've had a hard time, but—"

"Go away," she said, snuggling closer to the couch. "I don't want to talk to you."

"Now, now, I think—"

"Go away!" she shouted, her eyes filling with tears although she still stared straight ahead. "Just go away!"

Carrie was startled and finally stood up, unsure of what to do next. "Don't you want dinner?"

Katie kept staring at the TV. Finally Carrie left, unsettled by the encounter. The children were chattering and David was dishing up another plate.

"I'd love to stay, but I've got visiting teaching appointments we couldn't make for any time but tonight. I've got just enough time to change my clothes and grab some Pop-Tarts for the girls and me."

David looked back at the dinner bubbling away on the stove. His lips were pursed and she was instantly contrite.

"I'm sorry," Carrie soothed, rubbing his arm to try and soften the expression on his face. "We can eat when we get home, though."

"Why don't the girls stay with me?" he said, brightening. "They'll have a chance to meet my kids and I won't have wasted my efforts." Carrie hesitated as she glanced at her daughters sitting at the table. The image of Katie in the other room flashed into her mind and an odd feeling settled in her chest. David's expression turned forlorn. "Don't you trust me?" he whispered.

"Of course I trust you," she replied quickly. "But they've never stayed with you before."

"Then don't you think it's about time," he said with an understanding smile. "If we're going to get married, they're going to have to get used to having me around."

The statement didn't fill her with excitement. In fact, she felt a twinge of reticence.

"You *don't* trust me," David said bluntly, his face hard again. He put the spoon down on the counter and began untying the apron. "I can't believe that you, of all people, would—"

"I do trust you," Carrie interrupted. More than anything, even with her hesitations, she wanted this man in her life. He was her ticket to a whole new life. She wasn't going to let anything stop them. "I do," she repeated. He just looked at her for a moment, his expression sad. She leaned in and kissed him once more. "I'd better get going," she said with a smile as she pulled back. "I'll be home around nine."

Throughout the visits she couldn't seem to get her mind off David being with her girls. She thought of the encounter with Lisa at work, earlier that week, and then Katie flashed into her mind again. During the visit with the last sister, she finally asked herself if she *did* know David well enough to trust him. She preferred to have absolute faith in David, to believe him without question. And she still did. Mostly.

As soon as they finished, she returned home. The house was silent when she opened the door and it felt a little eerie. Slowly she entered, listening and watching for a sign of anyone.

"You're home early."

She spun towards the stairs and placed a hand on her ample chest. "You scared me," she said as she tried to catch her breath.

"The girls just went to bed," he said as he descended the last few steps.

"That's great," she said with a smile. "I almost never get them to bed on time."

"They watched a movie, had some popcorn and we read a few books. It was a breeze. Katie and Nicholas are in the living room."

"Thanks," she said with a grateful sigh. Bedtime was such a frustration on days like this. "I've got my monthly updates to do, and now I'll have the time to do them before Sunday." She paused for a moment, "Unless you want to stay and watch another movie or something."

"No," he said. "I took yesterday off so I could get the kids settled and registered in school. I've got a lot of work to do before Monday."

He came and gave her a good bye kiss before shepherding his kids out the front door. Katie met her eyes for the first time, and Carrie was struck by the sadness she saw there. She expected anger and hatred, not sorrow and fear.

Once he drove away, she went into the kitchen, where her computer was. To her surprise, it was already on. "That's odd," she whispered to herself as she sat heavily in the chair. David hadn't mentioned the girls playing any computer games tonight. She glanced at the clock. With all David had told her they'd done, they wouldn't have had time to play a computer game. She shook her head in an attempt to clear it; she was getting sidetracked. The updates needed to get done, she reminded herself. That's what was important.

———

Theresa had a hard time falling asleep Saturday night. She tossed and turned, for what seemed to be hours, before finally falling into a fitful sleep. Of course her husband, Rich, slept like a log. The dream she finally had was one of those where you know it's a dream from the beginning.

She was walking down a sidewalk as if it were a normal day, holding the hand of her oldest daughter, Cleo, who would be five years old next month. Ahead of them, on the same sidewalk and going in the same direction as they were walking, was a man holding the hand of another little girl. The girl in front of them looked over her shoulder and Theresa recognized her as David Stanton's daughter. The man holding her hand then looked back at her and she realized that the man was David. Immediately, she turned around and hurried the other way. She wanted to be as far away from David Stanton as possible. She looked down at her daughter, to explain why they had turned around, and found David's little girl at her side instead of Cleo. She looked back at David, only to see *her* daughter, holding his hand, being led down the sidewalk, away from her. "Cleo," she screamed as she turned and ran towards her. "Cleo!"

"Honey, what's the matter?" Her eyes flew open and she stared at the dark ceiling above her. Rich was propped up on his elbow beside her, a look of concern on his face.

"What's wrong," Rich repeated placing his hand on her shoulder.

"Cleo," she whispered, still stunned by the intensity of the dream.

"Cleo's asleep." Her chest heaved as she told herself it was just a dream and willed her heart to return to a normal rhythm.

"You're freaking me out, Theresa."

"Rich," she whispered as tears came to her eyes. She groped around in the darkness until she had hold of his hand, while tears continued streaming down her cheeks. The message of the dream was very clear. She had an opportunity to make a difference in the life of a little girl if she would only tell her story to the right person. She couldn't stay on the fence any longer. She turned her head and looked at his face, barely illuminated by the streetlight outside their bedroom window. Rich knew about the abuse of course, but she hadn't told him all the new information she'd been gathering. A sob rose in her chest as she spoke, "There's something I need to tell you."

———————

Bryan pulled up to Janice's house late Sunday night. He'd left Harrison Friday evening, but stopped in Little Rock to visit his family and stay over for the night. They all agreed he was crazy, but they'd thought that ever since his baptism and he was used to it. He didn't leave Little Rock until the next morning and he'd been driving hard ever since. If there hadn't been lights on, he'd have gone straight to a motel and come over in the morning. But the large living room window glowed in the darkness and his heart rate increased just thinking about Gloria being only a few feet away. He climbed the steps and knocked on the door, rehearsing in his mind what he planned to say to Gloria. Janice answered the door, looking confused to see him.

"Bryan?"

"Hey, Janice," he said with a smile. "Is Gloria here?"

"No," she said slowly. "She's at her mom's house."

"Her mom's?" he asked, his brows going up in surprise. "Was she given visitation?"

Janice hesitated a moment. "David got the kids back."

Bryan felt like a wrecking ball had hit him in the chest. He was speechless. Janice continued, "He talked a judge into giving him custody until the preliminary hearing; he knows so many loopholes."

Bryan let out a groan. "Oh, Gloria," he lamented. "I should have been here."

"Bryan," Janice began, then paused as if reluctant to continue. "She didn't think you were coming back."

"What?" his head snapped up to meet her eyes again. This was going from bad to worse.

"When you didn't call, she just assumed that you had changed your mind about her."

Bryan looked at the sky and willed himself to calm down. "Why is it she always assumes the worst?"

"She didn't always do that," Janice offered. "It's hard for her to trust anything anymore. She told me what happened the night you left. I don't know if it matters, but I know she was planning to tell you about the hysterectomy. She wasn't trying to hide anything from you."

Bryan nodded. "I think you're right and I know I didn't handle it well, but there's just been so much happening. I should have called." Janice said nothing, but he knew that she agreed; he should have called. "May I use your phone?" Bryan asked after a thoughtful pause. "I think she and I need to discuss some things."

Janice nodded and invited him in. He said hello to Ron, who was watching the news and followed Janice into the kitchen. Janice gave him the number and he dialed it. When he hung up the phone a minute later, Janice had a moment of déjà vu. His expression was similar to the one

Gloria had a few days earlier when her worst fears had been confirmed.

Bryan met her eyes. "She stayed at her mom's Friday night and then said she was coming back here."

They were both silent for a few moments. Janice stared at the floor while Bryan stared at the phone he'd just hung up. "Do you think she got into the apartment earlier than expected?" she asked.

Bryan shook his head and met her eyes again. "Do you?"

———

"I'm not sure how long we'll be," Rich told his mother around noon on Monday. Theresa was saying good bye to the kids in the backyard while he reviewed eating schedules and movie preferences.

"Take as long as you need," his mom said with a smile. "Theresa doesn't let me tend half as much as I'd like to. Anyway, I'm happy to have them."

"You might not be thinking that three days from now," Rich chuckled. She slapped his arm playfully. "We're hoping to get to Salt Lake tonight. I'll call you when we get settled."

"And you'll tell me what this is all about when you get back?" she asked curiously.

He held up two fingers, "Scouts honor." Fifteen minutes later, with Theresa at his side, they pulled onto the freeway. Rich glanced at his wife's nervous face and reached over to take her hand. "You're doing the right thing, sweetie."

She smiled weakly, but continued to look out the window. A sign just outside of Las Vegas, where they lived, said "Salt Lake City 408 miles." She let out a breath as the first road construction signs appeared on the side of the road. They hadn't factored construction into their time table; it was going to be a long drive.

Chapter Twenty-one

"We can only stay for an hour," Carrie called as the kids began piling out of the car. Three *okays* echoed back to her. Katie said nothing as she followed the kids to the playground. It was Monday afternoon; the time she always took her girls to the park. She'd offered to pick up Katie and Nicholas from David's mom, who was watching them during the days while he worked, and take them along too. David agreed that it would be a good idea since he still had some work to catch up on. Flat Iron Mesa Park was located in east Sandy, a suburb south of Salt Lake, and although it wasn't particularly close to her house in Draper, it was Carrie's favorite. It had two playground areas, one near the street, and the other up a small hill. An asphalt walking path rolled up and down the small hills and weaved around for almost two miles. The kids could play while she walked. She tried to come here once or twice a week and thought it would be good for Katie and Nicholas to get outside for a little while.

Katie scampered to the playground with the others, but after a few minutes she sat on the bench and just watched. Carrie's girls were nice, but they were so little. They still played pretend and Katie was way too grown up for that. She watched Carrie move farther and farther away down the walking path and wondered if she was really going to marry David.

"How are you, Darla?"

It took a few seconds to realize she'd been called Darla. She quickly turned to look at the woman who had approached her. The woman was big, like Carrie, and had long black hair. She wore sunglasses, lots of makeup, and a baseball cap turned backwards. Katie squinted just as the woman removed the glasses. Her mouth opened. "Mom?"

"Shhh," Gloria said. "I don't want anyone to know it's me."

Katie nodded and looked around to see if anyone had heard them. The kids were still playing, but Carrie had just appeared over the rise of a hill. She was coming toward them.

"When she passes by you," Gloria explained quickly, "go that way."

She pointed to the part of the path that disappeared to her right. "On the right side of the fence, there's a little path that goes down the hill. I'll meet you and Nicholas at the bottom."

Carrie was only a hundred yards away now so Gloria casually stood up and walked to the path. She hoped the pillows looked realistic. The wig and thick makeup was making her itch like crazy. She'd been watching the kids since Friday, after buying a different car, emptying out the account her mother had saved for her, and finding some new identities. She had hoped for an opportunity during the weekend, but it hadn't happened. Now, she'd gotten lucky. It just so happened that Carrie chose a park Gloria was quite familiar with. She used to jog the very path Carrie liked so much. On the north end of the park was a thinner path, off the main walking trail, that wound down the hill to a neighborhood. That's where she'd parked her car after watching Carrie pull into the parking lot. That's where they would make their escape.

It felt like she'd waited forever, but finally two little bodies appeared over the horizon. Her heart soared and as soon as they were hidden by the rise of the hill she called for them to run. In a few seconds, she was holding her children for the first time in weeks. Tears ran down her face and she wished she didn't have all the padding. She wanted to hold them forever, soak up their closeness, but she knew she didn't have time. Carrie would soon realize they were gone. She had one chance, and this was it.

"Mom," Nicholas said in awe. "You look weird."

She laughed but brushed off his comment. "We have to hurry," she said, taking them both by the hand and leading them to the footpath. They hurried down the hill, being careful not to trip on any loose stones. When they reached the bottom, she looked up and froze.

"Don't do this," Bryan said. He was standing near her car, his arms folded and his expression intent.

"I have to," she said, lifting her chin. "I can't leave them with him just because he can play the system. I've fought too hard and for too long to let them go now."

"Then I'm going with you," he said with a nod.

Gloria opened her mouth to protest. He stepped forward and put a finger on her heavily lipsticked lips. "I'm going with you."

———

"This is David," he said when he picked up the phone. Carrie began screaming, frantically trying to tell him what had happened. "I didn't know what to do," she sobbed. "I—"

"Just calm down," David said, his mind kicking into overdrive as he processed the information. "Did you call the police?"

"No, I—I called you."

David nodded with relief. "Go to my house," he instructed. "I'll call the police and meet you there as soon as I can."

"But—"

"You're too upset to think clearly," he broke in. "Just do as I say, I'll see you soon."

"Okay," she cried. He hung up the phone and leaned back in his chair. After a few minutes, his secretary knocked on the door.

"Is everything okay?" she asked when she entered. "Carrie sounded really upset."

"Everything's fine," he said blandly. "Is my four-thirty appointment here?"

"Shall I send him in?" the secretary asked hesitantly.

David nodded and leaned forward, organizing the contracts he would be reviewing. "Why don't you take off early today," he said easily. "Forward all calls directly to my office before you go."

"But—"

"And," he began pulling out his checkbook, seemingly ignorant of her concern. "I think you're due for a bonus."

She stood there, looking confused, as he wrote out a check and handed it to her. Her eyes went wide and she looked up at him. "I really appreciate all your hard work; why don't you celebrate by going shopping for a while." A wide smile spread across her face and she thanked him profusely before showing in his client. He looked at the clock. How long would it take for Gloria to disappear?

His appointments kept him busy until almost seven o'clock. As soon as David walked through the door, Carrie came running. "Where have you been?" she screeched.

"I've been trying to figure out what to do," he answered calmly.

"Did you call the police?"

"Come and sit down," he said. "Let's talk about this."

He looked into her frantic eyes once they were seated on the couch. "I've been thinking this through and I'm worried about what this will do to you if the police find out you were watching the children for me." Carrie's eyes went wide. "I've had custody for only four days, I let you watch the kids and they're kidnapped! The press will have a heyday. There will be more articles in the paper, TV crews—the works."

Carrie stared at her hands in her lap, with a look of complete shock on her face. "I'm so sorry, David," she whimpered. "I was walking while they played. I do it all the time."

David pulled her to his chest and rubbed her back. "I know," he said soothingly. "I'm sorry too, I should have told you what is necessary when you take responsibility in situations like this. But now we have to face what's happened and I don't want to make things any harder on you than they already are."

"I deserve anything I get," she said. "This is all my fault."

David pushed her away so that he could look into her eyes. "I have a plan that will spare us both." Carrie looked hesitant, but she was listening. "I'll call the police in the morning and tell them that Gloria took the kids during the night. I'll say I forgot to set the alarm system and I doubt they'll question it much. Then I won't get in trouble for letting you take the kids and you won't get in trouble for not watching them closely."

"But . . . it's not true."

"Did Gloria take the kids?" David asked in a patronizing tone.

"I think it was her, but—"

"Of course it was her," David interrupted forcefully. "She kidnapped them again, that's what is important. If we call the cops now, we'll both be put through the wringer for letting this happen. The papers will be all over it and it could permanently affect my custody rights. I can't bear to lose my children, Carrie; please cooperate with me. They've been lost to me for so long already."

Her chin began to quiver. "But she could be states away by tomorrow morning."

"The police will catch her within hours. She's a felon, she's jumped bail, and police across the whole country will be alerted. The organization she's been with can't help her—they're under intense investigation themselves. She'll be caught and she'll be punished. We don't deserve to be punished any more than we already have been. Don't you see that?"

"But the girls; they know what happened."

"I'll tell the girls I picked my kids up and took them home. They'll believe anything we believe—we'll help them. And Gloria, come on; who in their right mind will believe her?"

She was silent for a few moments. "It doesn't feel right," she finally whispered.

"Does it feel right for me to lose my kids forever, to have your name all over the papers saying you're neglectful and stupid?"

"No," she said in surrender. "I don't think I could handle that."

David patted her shoulder. "Then we agree," he started to stand. "I'll go explain to the girls that I picked my kids up when they weren't watching. Tonight, I'll take a sleeping pill to explain why I didn't wake up and I'll call the police first thing in the morning."

Carrie nodded slowly. He left the room with a sigh of relief. The hardest part would be sticking to their story. David would just have to keep Carrie as far away from the police as possible. By the time the authorities were brought in, Gloria would be long gone. He knew how determined Gloria was to hide, and she knew better than ever that when it came to playing the legal system he would always win.

———

"I'm hungry," Nicholas whined from the back seat.

"I know," Gloria said. "We're almost to Scipio. We'll get something to eat there."

By silent agreement, Bryan and Gloria had said very little during the trek thus far. Bryan had already left his U-haul at Janice and Ron's house. His truck was in a park-and-ride lot just outside of Salt Lake. He had simply grabbed his duffel bag from the front seat and climbed into the passenger seat of her car. He chatted with the kids until they fell asleep. Gloria was still dressed in her costume.

"What's your plan?" Bryan asked after several miles of silence.

"I'd like to get to Grand Junction tonight. I know of a shelter there. I'll go talk to them, see if they can help me."

He remained silent for a while. "What if he goes to trial? Will you go back?"

"Not unless he's convicted," she answered. "The charges against me will be worse when I return; I'm guaranteed a prison sentence. I'll only go back if there's no chance that he'll get any visitation."

"You're willing to hide forever?"

"Twelve years," she replied as she moved into the fast lane to pass a semi. "When Nicholas is eighteen I'll have no reason to hide anymore."

Again Bryan fell silent, carefully considering his next statement. "Do you feel this is the right thing to do?" he asked. "Do you feel like you felt the first time?"

It was Gloria's turn to be silent. "I can't let him have them, Bryan," she said with deep sorrow, reminding him of how much she was giving up once again. He knew this wasn't an easy choice for her. However, he didn't feel it was the right one for her to make. He sensed that she felt the same way.

"Do you already have new identification?"

"Yes," she said. "I'll need to get some for you if you plan to stay with us."

"Is it that easy to get?"

She shrugged as if it were a simple task. "The right people and enough money can buy just about anything."

He wondered how many Mormon housewives knew how to find ID peddlers. If nothing else, Gloria was definitely unique. "I have a suggestion," he said. She didn't comment, so he continued. "Let's stop for the night in Scipio, get some motel rooms and really think this out."

"I've already thought this out; I don't see any other option."

"You thought it out before I joined you here," he added. "Let's put our heads together and see if we can't come up with another option." She didn't comment. He continued to stare at her. "Please?"

They stopped in Scipio. Still in her increasingly uncomfortable disguise, Gloria got two adjoining rooms in her new name, Kelly Munson. Once settled in one of the rooms, she unpadded herself, dumping pillows of various sizes on the floor before removing the 3X clothes she'd picked up at Deseret Industries. It felt good to be back to size eight. She took a quick shower while Bryan ordered pizza, much to her children's delight. They ate dinner and then she set up a pay-per-view movie for the kids. She watched the first ten minutes with them, painfully aware of Bryan's waiting for her. Finally, she excused herself and made the long, slow walk of ten feet into the other room. Bryan was lying on the bed, with his hands behind his head, looking at the ceiling. Seeing him sprawled out on the bed like that made her stomach tingle, but she tried to ignore it.

"There's still time for you to go back," she said, breaking the silence as she leaned her shoulder against the doorjamb. "No one would know."

Bryan propped himself up on his elbows and looked at her before sitting up and patting the bed next to him. Reluctantly, she accepted the invitation. As soon as she sat down he put out his hand. "Give me your foot."

"What?"

"Your foot; I'm going to give you a massage."

She hesitated and he grabbed her foot and pulled it out from under her, causing her to fall backward. She caught herself with her arms and tried to pull her foot away. "You don't have to massage my feet."

"I want to make sure you can't go anywhere," he said as he began pressing his thumb into the ball of her foot. She was glad she'd just showered and could feel the tension drain from her whole body.

For a few minutes there was silence, and then he looked at her as if he hadn't seen her in years and wanted to absorb every detail. "Why are you so determined to get rid of me?"

"I'm not trying to get rid of you," she said softly, looking down at the southwestern pattern of the bedspread in order to avoid eye contact.

"Since the first time I saw you, you've been running away from me. You're just sure I can't love you enough to take the necessary risks and make the changes I have to make in order to have you in my life. Why?"

She met his eye and wanted to look away again, but she couldn't. The warmth in his eyes was magnetic. "I don't want you to be hurt," she said after a few moments. "I don't want to ruin your life."

He nodded his understanding and motioned that he wanted her other foot. She didn't fight him this time, but he didn't start right away. Instead he leaned forward and waited until she was looking at him again, her foot still in his lap. "I'm going to tell you something and I want you to listen very carefully. I love you, Gloria. I wish we didn't have all the complications. I wish we had met a long time ago and that we could have a big family together and live a wonderful, joyful life." Tears rose in her eyes. "But back then I was a bar tender and you were looking for a sugar daddy. It wouldn't have worked *then,* but it *can* work now.

"I believe we can still have a wonderful, joyful life together. I know what it means to join you in your life, and I'm willing to do it. But you have to let me in. I can't . . . I won't keep chasing you. If you're determined to push me out of your life, you will eventually succeed. But if you love me, and if you believe that I love you, then just let me in." Her tears overflowed and he could see that the words from his heart were exactly what she needed to hear. For perhaps the first time ever, the walls she'd built so carefully came down. For perhaps the first time ever, he felt they shared the same understanding. *She trusted him* and he knew that this would be one of those moments in life that he would never forget.

She watched him for several seconds as if reading his thoughts perfectly then she pulled her foot back, got on her knees and wrapped her arms around his neck. He followed her lead and for nearly a minute they just held one another. When she finally pulled back, she smiled. "I love you, Bryan," she said, tracing the line of his jaw with her finger. "Thank you for not giving up on me."

A smile stretched across his face and he wove his hands into her hair. "Now that's more like it."

––––––

"How about stopping to sleep in Scipio?" Rich asked as they approached an exit sign. Theresa had been dozing, off and on, and awoke enough to respond.

"Sounds good to me," she said sleepily. Rich nodded and took the exit, pulling into the Super 8 motel, possibly the only motel in town. The road construction had been a nightmare and the three-hundred-mile trip thus far had taken almost twice as long as they had expected. It was almost ten when he entered the motel office.

"Smoking or non?" the manager asked.

"Nonsmoking, please," Ron answered as he filled out the form that asked for their vehicle information.

"The only nonsmoking room I've got left is that one on the end." He pointed out the window and Rich followed his direction. "There's a family in the two rooms up from it, though; I've got a smoking room without neighbors."

"This is fine," Rich said as he took the key.

"We're at the end there," Rich said to Theresa as he got into the car. "Is that okay with you?"

"After six hours of driving anything sounds good to me."

"Great, we'll sleep in a little, grab some breakfast in the morning, and head into Salt Lake. Do you think we should call in the morning, to let them know were coming?"

"If we warn them, it means I can't chicken out."

Rich gave her a humored look. "I just got three days off work, we left the kids overnight with my mother, and we drove three hundred miles; you crossed the 'chicken-out' line a long time ago."

––––––

Bryan slept in one of their motel rooms Monday night, while Gloria and her children shared the other room. There was just enough room for the three of them in one of the queen-sized beds, yet they both stayed closer to her than they needed to. She didn't mind. To be with her children again was a sweet experience, even if she didn't get much sleep. When the sun came up, she gave up trying to sleep and quietly slipped out of the bed. When she entered Bryan's room, he was already up and dressed, sitting at the small table reading the newspaper.

"I picked this up across the street. You're not in it," he said as she approached the table.

"What?" she stood behind him and scanned the paper. "The press has been like ants on a sandwich for this story. How could it not be in here?"

Bryan shrugged. "I don't know; but it's weird, isn't it?"

"Very," she agreed, scanning the first few pages while Bryan watched her.

"So why don't you fill me in on what's happened since I left Salt Lake?"

She explained the court order David had obtained which awarded him immediate custody until after the hearing. "Can you fight it?" Bryan asked.

"My lawyer tried, but he got stonewalled. We've filed an appeal but the preliminary hearing will happen first. I don't know how David pulls his tricks, but I wish I had a few of them."

"And how are the preparations for the hearing coming along?"

"So-so," she explained, holding up her hand and tilting it back and forth. "The PI I hired looked up everyone I could think of that might know something. Most of them shut him out completely. He did find one old girlfriend who found David's *Penthouse Magazine* collection when she helped him move. That's something, but it's pretty weak. If we had a stronger case, and I felt sure he'd be convicted, I'd have stuck it out and prayed like crazy that it would be okay, but he attacks at every turn and the evidence we've found isn't very strong."

"But the old girlfriend, that does show a tendency," Bryan prodded.

"It was thirteen years ago."

Bryan was quiet for awhile. "Did they search his house for anything?"

"They couldn't get a warrant for that. Besides, he's way too smart to get caught. I was married to him for nine years and never knew what he was into until . . . but they did get a warrant for his computers. The one at his house had crashed a while ago; they couldn't get anything off it. The one at work was clean."

Bryan shook his head thoughtfully and was about to speak when a sleepy-eyed child caught his attention from the doorway. "Hey there, kiddo."

"Hi," Nicholas said in a sleepy voice as he walked to his mother. She grunted as she lifted him onto her lap.

"Did you sleep well?" she asked, smoothing the ever-persistent cowlick.

"Can we go get my Play Station?" he asked with pleading eyes. Gloria shared a quick look at Bryan.

"No, we can't," she said. "I'm sorry."

"Then can you buy me a new one?"

"I don't have money for that right now, buddy," she said. "Maybe—"

"Pleeeeeaaase?" he begged.

"Actually," Bryan interrupted, grabbing the well used list of amenities from the nightstand. "I think you can rent one from the front desk."

"All right!!" He jumped off Gloria's lap and ran to Bryan, grabbing at the list despite the fact that he probably couldn't read it. "I'm so good at *Spiderman* I beat Dad every time."

Gloria forced a polite smile and ignored the pang of jealously as he continued. "And at Carrie's house, Anne-Marie showed me how to play the Reader Rabbit game and I was better at it than she was and she plays it all the time. This one time—"

"Reader Rabbit's a computer game, isn't it?" Gloria asked as a little light bulb went on in her head.

"Yeah," Nicholas answered, dropping the list to explain. He continued bragging for a few minutes. " . . . and Anne-Marie kept trying to show me how to play it and I already knew how." He laughed at the memory.

"Did your dad ever play computer games with you?" Bryan asked blandly, although he gave Gloria a look that told her he was thinking the same thing she was.

"No," Nicholas said with disappointment. "Anne-Marie was going to show me nickjr.com but Dad said he had work to do on the computer."

"Did you see what he was working on?"

"He made us watch a movie, and told us not to interrupt," he said, then his eyes widened. "And he promised me I could have a turn but then he put Anne-Marie and Jackie to bed and wouldn't let me play." He folded his arms with a humph as if trying to figure out how he could still get his turn. However, he recovered quickly and climbed up on Gloria's lap again before pressing his forehead against her own, staring her down. "Can we please get that Play Station, please, please, please, please?"

Gloria started laughing and began tickling him, causing him to squirm and wiggle until she had him on the floor, laughing so hard tears came out of his eyes. "Why don't you get dressed," Bryan said after another minute or so. "And then we'll go get that Play Station from the front desk."

Nicholas disappeared in an instant, leaving the adults alone to discuss this new piece of information.

"You have to go back," Bryan said, moving his chair closer to hers so they could talk without being overheard.

"What?" she said with absolute shock.

"Well, one of us has to. We need to get to Carrie—"

"She's engaged to him!"

"I think she's caught in a spider's web she doesn't understand and doesn't want to see yet. We can appeal to her motherly instincts; play her the tape. She's the best chance we've got."

Gloria was shaking her head and she put up her hands to stop him. "Wait," she said, furrowing her brow as she looked at him again. "Back up. What tape?"

———

Within half an hour, Bryan was showered and ready to go. They had decided that Bryan would be better for this job than she would. Gloria walked him to the door. She ran her hands over his chest as if smoothing his shirt, but in actuality she wanted the excuse to touch him. She was nervous about his leaving, about staying in the motel without transportation, and about limited communication options since she'd thrown his cell phone in a dumpster. However, they both agreed that they couldn't just sit back and wait to let things happen. That would be playing David's way. If they had learned anything, it was that playing his way made him the winner. "You'll call me tonight?" she asked.

He leaned into her and gave her a quick kiss on the lips. "I'll call as soon as anything of importance happens."

"I'll be waiting," she said as he pulled the door open. He moved as if about to step outside, but then hesitated. Shutting the door, he turned to look at her, his eyes soft and his expression tender.

"There was something we need to discuss before I go," he began. She looked at him curiously. "There's something between us that's very powerful, do you agree with that?"

"Yes," she said slowly, wondering what he was getting at.

"Good," he said with a quick nod. "My plans got put on the back burner yesterday, but you need to know that I've decided to move to Salt Lake."

Her mouth fell open, but he didn't allow her to speak. "You need to be with your family, and I want to be near you."

"Bryan, I—"

He put two fingers over her lips to stop her from interrupting. "I'm a big boy and I'm well aware of what this decision means for me. I'm taking care of my end of it and I feel strongly that this is the direction I should go. However, I'm also aware of the pressure it implies for us; mostly for you. I don't want you to think that I expect more than you can give me." She frowned, but he didn't remove his fingers from her lips. "I've had the opportunity to focus a lot of energy on planning my future. I've had the luxury of making my own choices in all of this. You haven't. You've been assaulted by one thing and then another and haven't had the chance to decide what you want from tomorrow, much less from next month, next year or ten years from now.

"I love you, Gloria and I'm ready to commit my life to you and your children. But you have some big issues you need to tackle and I don't want you to minimize them on my account. If we reach a point where you're ready to share your life with me, then tell me and we'll go from there. Until then just know that I'm here of my own free will and choice and just being a part of your life is enough for me." He looked into her eyes for a few moments before removing his fingers from her lips and giving her one more kiss. "I'll call you tonight."

She smiled and he opened the door again. "Bryan," she said just before the door closed. He opened it a few more inches and looked at her expectantly. "Thank you," she said softly. His expression was neutral for a moment, before a soft smile spread across his face.

"You're welcome."

Chapter Twenty-Two

Around 9:00 a.m. Tuesday morning, Gloria donned her wig, glasses, and hat long enough to run across the street and pick up some take-out food for breakfast. She didn't bother with the pillows, hoping that her outing was brief enough that they wouldn't be necessary. The return trip was quite a bit longer as she tried to hold two paper sacks filled with styrofoam boxes while balancing three cups of orange juice—with lids, of course.

The first of their two rooms was the second one from the end and she was almost there when the door of the end room opened. The man was talking to someone inside as he backed out of the door. She quickened her pace in order to pass the door before he exited fully, but she wasn't fast enough. In fact, she was directly behind him when he turned around. His arm knocked into her shoulder.

"Oh, I'm so sorry," he said, reaching out in an attempt to save the teetering cups. His attempt to help only made things worse and they both fumbled the cups as they toppled from her arms. The lids had been sufficient to contain the juice as she walked, but proved to be incompetent for total inversion. Within seconds, the cups rolled empty on the ground, while her face and wig dripped with juice. The man didn't escape unscathed, but ignored his wet and sticky shirt front as he continued to apologize.

"It's okay," she said tightly, taking another step toward her door, anxious to just get away from him.

"Here, let me help you," he said as he tried to take the now dripping bags from her hands.

"No, I'm fine," she said, keeping hold of the bags. A woman came to the door he'd just exited. She had short brown hair and glasses. She pulled the sides of her bathrobe together and stepped outside.

"What happened?" she asked, looking at the mess and at her husband grabbing at the bags in Gloria's hands.

"Nothing," Gloria said strongly, pulling the bags to her chest again. "It's fine." She glanced anxiously at the door to her room and tried to keep her voice quiet. Any second now, her curious children would open the door to see what was happening and she wanted to avoid that situation like the plague. She continued toward the door, but the man wasn't giving up easily and continued to offer his help.

"Mom, what's going on?"

She whipped her head toward the door, her eyes wide as she pulled the bags to her chest one final time, pulling them out of the man's grip.

"Go back inside Ni . . . Kenny," she said pointedly. He just stood there looking confused. She turned her attention back to the man. "Thank you, but I'm fine," she said as she took another step toward her door. She glanced at the woman in time to see her look in Nicholas's direction. Gloria took another step just as she heard the sharp intake of breath from the other woman. Following the other woman's intent stare, her own gaze rested on the face of Katie, innocently investigating the commotion. Everyone went silent, apparently only the two women realizing the significance of the situation. When Gloria looked back at the woman, their eyes met.

"You're David's ex-wife," she breathed, her eyes wide with disbelief behind her glasses.

Gloria just stood there, not sure what to say. The man seemed to suddenly understand the situation too, as his eyes widened. He turned to the dark-haired woman, but pointed at Katie, "This is her?" he asked.

"Kids," Gloria suddenly said as her shock passed and her instinct kicked back into gear. "Get inside, Now!" They obeyed immediately and disappeared behind the faded red door which closed with a resounding slam.

"I'm right, aren't I?" the woman said, taking a step towards Gloria.

Gloria was completely speechless as she tried to make sense of the woman's odd comments. How did she recognize Katie so easily if their disappearance hadn't been reported in the morning papers? She didn't answer as she headed for the door to her room once more. Her brain was buzzing. She had no car, no way to get hold of Bryan; she was trapped. Gloria was one step shy of her door when the woman caught her arm. "I . . . I used to know David."

Gloria frowned in confusion. "We're on our way to Salt Lake," the other woman explained quickly. "I just talked to a detective there. I'm meeting him in a few hours."

"What?" Gloria asked, thoroughly confused.

"I have information that will help the case against him."

Once introductions were made, Rich and Gloria entered their separate rooms in order to take showers, while the kids ate their breakfast. Then Rich played Play Station games with the kids in one room, while Theresa and Gloria sat at the small table in the other. The door between the rooms remained open as the two women discussed their connection to one another—dark as it was.

When Theresa finished recounting what David had done, Gloria was sick to her stomach.

"When I saw that *Unsolved Mysteries* segment about you," Theresa said, nervously fidgeting with the phone book on the table, "I was so impressed at what you'd done."

Gloria shook her head, not wanting to hear it.

Theresa continued before Gloria had the chance to interrupt. "My mom didn't believe me, let alone try and save me from it."

"I didn't save Katie from anything," Gloria said sadly. "I may have spared her some, but I can't make what happened go away and in the process of getting her away from David I fear I may have created even more problems."

Theresa was silent for several seconds. "I've been in counseling for over ten years, but do you know what the root of my struggle is?"

Gloria shook her head.

"Loneliness," Theresa replied. "When it happened I felt so horribly alone because I just knew I couldn't tell anyone. Then I finally told and I felt even more alone because no one believed me. As a teenager I just felt different, set apart from everyone else, especially other girls. So I started seeking any kind of connection I could find, which thanks to David I knew more about than I should have. But it never worked. I knew they were just using me and that I was looking for something they couldn't give me.

"By the time I met Rich I already gone through treatment for Chlamydia and was basically living my life as a prostitute, going from one man to another looking for what wasn't there. Rich was the first man I ever dated that wouldn't sleep with me. I still don't know why he married me, but I'm so glad he did." She cocked her head to the side and smiled although her eyes were still sad. "I truly think that if someone had believed in me I wouldn't have made the decisions I did. Your daughter will have things to work through, there's no doubt about that, but she has you and you fought for her, loved her and did everything you could to help her; she knows she's not alone and that's priceless."

The silence in the room hung for nearly a minute before Gloria finally spoke. "Thank you," she choked. "I really needed to hear that."

Theresa was silent for a moment. "So what's your plan?" she asked, changing the subject. "Are you just going to wait here until Bryan can drive all the way back to get you?"

"Get me?" Gloria laughed. "I'm not convinced that . . ." she trailed off and looked up at Theresa with a different expression. Even if Bryan found what they thought he'd find, she'd already decided not to go back until she was assured that David's custody had been revoked. Finding Theresa gave them another nail for his coffin. "If Bryan finds something on that computer, hands over the tape, and you give your statement to the police, they might be able to arrest David—"

"Today," Theresa finished for her. There was another silence as both women considered the possibilities. Finally, Theresa leaned forward. "Why don't you come with us to Salt Lake? Bryan can meet us and we can give the detective everything we've got at one time."

"The computer might be clean," Gloria reminded her. "And I'll be arrested if I go back." But within her chest a bubbling sensation began to spread warmth throughout her body. She recognized the feeling and knew what it was trying to tell her. "But . . . you know what? David has been able to dispute everything that's come against him. Your being here is a surprise attack, and so is the tape. Maybe . . ." she smiled in anticipation. "Maybe this is exactly what he needs."

———

Carrie stared out the kitchen window, listening to her daughters play in the back yard. David had called the police that morning just as they planned. He'd called her just an hour or so ago from his cell phone to update her. The officers had descended on his house immediately, searching for clues that didn't exist. They hadn't come to speak to her yet, but her stomach burned in anticipation of having to lie to the police. Her part was easy; all she had to say was she didn't know anything. David had told her to take her daughters to her mother's house and go to work as usual, but she couldn't do it. She'd been awake all night and called in sick.

This was wrong, she knew it; but what could she do about it? If she didn't cooperate, she'd lose David. Yet in the last hour, she'd wondered if she wanted to share her life with a man who could lie so easily and so well. He'd said that he could get her daughters to believe anything; she wondered if he saw her in the same way.

The doorbell rang, startling her out of her thoughtful trance. She peeled herself off the couch and walked slowly to the front door. *Please don't be the police*, she thought. She wasn't ready to do this yet.

The tall, dark man on the doorstep was a stranger to her, deepening her fears.

"Carrie Gunderson?" he asked with just a touch of a southern accent.

"Yes?" she answered, cautiously.

Bryan hesitated and then spoke quickly. "My name is Bryan; I'm a friend of Gloria. I heard about the kidnapping on the radio this morning, but you and I both know she didn't take them during the night." He paused long enough to see the fear rise in her face. "We need to talk."

"I—I don't know what you're talking about," she said quickly, pushing the door shut.

He grabbed the door to prevent her from shutting it. "You already know he's a liar and I can prove to you he's much worse than that. Do you really want to go on pretending he's innocent when he's not?"

She closed her eyes as if wishing she could refute what he'd said but knowing she couldn't. Finally she looked up at him, a tormented expression on her face. "What kind of proof?"

Brian pulled a small tape recorder out of his pocket. "This is a recording of a phone call between David and a private investigator he hired in Arkansas." He pushed *play* and watched her face as she listened to David's instruction to get Gloria and his children out of the country. When the tape ended, she had tears in her eyes.

She seemed ready to cry as she let go of the door and turned toward the living room. Bryan let himself in and closed the door before following her. Once seated on the couch, he explained that they thought maybe David had used Carrie's computer and that it might hold some evidence. When he finished talking, she met his eye for the first time since he'd entered her home. "He uses my computer," she agreed. "But not very often and . . . I can't imagine that he would—"

"Can I see it? It will take me only five minutes to find out if what I need is there."

She nodded and led him to the kitchen. He sat down, turned the computer on, and went to work. "Was Saturday the last time he used it?" he asked.

"Saturday?" she asked in surprise, shaking her head. "I . . ." she stopped as if reviewing the night, then she let out a breath as if it held the last of her doubts. "That's the last time he was here."

Bryan nodded and checked the internet history as soon as the computer was on line. Bryan knew how to do some of this from having to do it at school, but just in case, he'd printed out instructions from the motel computer in the motel lobby before he'd left that morning. The history showed nothing, which only increased Bryan's confidence that there was something here that could help them. No online history only confirmed that someone had erased it. Carrie paced behind him, looking at the screen every few seconds. Bryan swore he could hear her silent prayer that he was wrong. He began clicking on files and folders in order to dig deeper into the hard drive. When he got where he wanted to go, he clicked on the caption that said *search*. He hesitated, trying to determine what would be the best keyword to enter. The computer would then list all the titles that included that word. After several seconds he typed *girls,* then he hit *enter.*

For a few moments the screen was blank and he held his breath, noticing that Carrie had stopped pacing and was watching the screen just as intently, yet, for very different reasons. Then suddenly titles began filling the screen. A number in the lower corner kept track of how many titles had been found: 20, 32, 49, 86, 124, 165, 201. Bryan's heart seemed to stop. This was what he'd hoped to find, but he still recoiled at the disgust of it. The screen finally stopped at 398 cookies stored in Carrie's hard drive with the word *girls* in the title. At a glance it was obvious that there was nothing innocent about any of them.

"What is this?" she asked almost fearfully.

"It's a list of 'cookies,'" Bryan explained as he began scrolling down the long list, his stomach churning at the degrading, lurid titles. "A 'cookie' is a kind of electrical tag attached to your hard drive. It allows web sites to recognize you as a returning guest. They're loaded automatically; you never know they're there unless you check."

Carrie read title after title, her face falling with every line she read. "Look at the times," she said, pointing to the right-hand column that showed the date and time each 'cookie' had initially been downloaded. She was quiet for almost a minute as she made mental calculations. "He's used it during the day . . . when I was at work, since May."

She lifted her hand to her mouth and began to cry softly. "My girls," she whimpered, turning towards the sound of their laughter in the back yard. "Oh, I can't believe this."

Bryan stood, wishing he could comfort her, but not sure how to do so. "Can I make a phone call?" he asked.

She nodded, still staring out the window.

Bryan pulled the phone number of the motel out of his pocket and punched in the number. "Can I have room 34, please," he asked the girl who answered the phone. He heard the back door open and watched as Carrie went outside, calling to her daughters, saying that she needed to talk to them. The heartbreak in her voice was thick and he realized that David's cruelty had no bounds. To keep his teaching certificate valid, he was often required to attend workshops of various topics. One of these conferences were about sexual harassment and abuse, he'd been told that the average pedophile has 117 victims during their lifetime. The statistic had never seemed so horrible as it did now.

"Uh, just a minute," the woman on the phone said. When she returned she said, "The occupants of room 34 checked out a few hours ago, but they left a forwarding phone number."

Bryan was silent and felt his jaw tense. Had she left again? "Can I get that number?" he finally asked evenly.

"Sure. Have you got a pen?"

As soon as he hung up he called the new number, bracing himself for the worst possible scenario. A man answered the phone. "Hello?"

"I'm looking for Gloria," he said with forced calmness.

"I'll get her," the man said.

"Bryan?" Gloria's voice asked a moment later.

"What's going on?"

"You'll never guess who we met . . ." She went on to explain all that had happened that morning.

"I was able to change Theresa's appointment with a detective to an appointment with the district attorney," she paused. "I agreed to turn myself in if he would video tape her statement today and let my children go to my mother's instead of going back to David."

"Gloria," Bryan breathed, his heart sinking. "Do you understand what you're doing?"

"I told myself once that I wouldn't run away again, but as soon as I got scared I did just that. You and Theresa reminded me that I don't have to fight this battle alone. My attorney will be there too; with any luck, I'll get a little mercy since I've been gone less than twenty-four hours. How did it go with Carrie?"

Bryan looked up to watch Carrie with her daughters in the back yard. "The good news is we got what we needed; her computer is full of kiddieporn and he didn't call the police until this morning. The bad news is that David broke another heart . . . or three."

Gloria was silent for several seconds. "Can you meet us at the DA's office? We'll be there at one o'clock; that's forty-five minutes from now."

"I'll be there."

———

David paced back and forth in his study. The police had been in his condo all day. They set up a command post in his dining room where they relayed information back and forth between detectives, FBI, and police headquarters. His job was to play the role of distraught father. It was imperative that he play it well. So far, everything had gone perfectly. Carrie had agreed to his plan and Gloria had a sixteen-hour head start before the police even knew she was gone. He had no doubt that she would disappear as completely as she had before. This time she wouldn't come back. After a few weeks of searching for Gloria, his life would be back to normal.

He looked at the clock; four twenty-two. He wondered how long they were going to stay. An investigator entered the house and called an immediate huddle with the other officers. They all looked at him briefly when the investigator stopped talking. Then they returned to their individual tasks. The lead detective approached him.

"The district attorney would like you to go to his office," he said.

David frowned. "What for? Did they find her?"

The investigator shrugged. "I don't know; they just want you to go down."

"Well, all right," David replied. He wanted to be accommodating.

It took him a few minutes to get ready. The investigator watched from the window as David walked toward his car. "Okay, guys," he said. "Clean it up; we're done here."

David climbed into his car and pulled out of the driveway. He couldn't pinpoint what it was, but something didn't feel right. His cell

230 — *Josi S. Kilpack*

phone caught his eye and he decided to give Carrie a call, just to be sure things were okay in that arena. He doubted the cops would have bothered her yet, but just in case he wanted to make sure she knew that he was paying attention. The phone rang five times before going to her voice mail. He pushed the *end* button and tapped his phone on the steering wheel as he considered why she wouldn't answer his call. He knew she was home since he'd talked to her this morning. A minute later he tried again, and once more it went to her voice mail. When he stopped at the next light he considered his options and then put on his blinker. Carrie was his only wild card and he felt it was worth his while to make sure everything was okay.

Carrie put a movie in for the kids downstairs before going up to the main level and turning on the shower in the bathroom. She still felt numb. How did this happen? She'd been so sure that David was innocent, but then again, had she really? Didn't she have those nagging little doubts? Didn't she wonder about him now and then? She shook her head at her own stupidity and felt the tears fall from her eyes. Rather than look at those doubts as possibilities, she'd chosen to discount them completely simply because she hated being alone so much.

She'd spent her whole life wanting what she couldn't have, a father, brothers and sisters, and then a husband. Her first marriage had started difficult and ended even worse and now that same desperation had put her here. How could she be so stupid?

She'd talked to her girls and they said David hadn't done anything but she wasn't convinced and had an appointment for them to meet with a representative of the Division of Family Services in the morning. If David would hurt his own daughter, his own flesh and blood, what would stop him from taking an opportunity with her daughters as well? The only hope she had was that they had rarely spent time with him when she wasn't right there.

The doorbell rang and she groaned. What now? First it had been Bryan, and then a police officer had come and taken away her computer tower. She didn't want to see anyone and sat on the edge of the tub to remove her socks, choosing to ignore the visitor. She'd already taken the phone off the hook an hour or so earlier. She just needed some peace right now. She threw her socks in the corner and started unbuttoning her pajama top.

"Carrie!!" she jumped and her heart began to race as someone pounded on the bathroom door. "Are you in there!!"

It was David! She started looking frantically around the room, as if looking for escape, although that was ridiculous. Her heart was racing as she tried to think of what she should do. When they picked up the computer they'd said he was being called to the DA's office. She'd never imagined he'd show up here!

"Carrie," David screamed again, the doorknob twisted and she backed up as the door opened; she hadn't bothered to lock it. He just stared at her as she cowered against the shower door.

"What do you want?" she asked fearfully, he just continued to stare as if reading her mind to find out what she'd done.

"Your computer's gone; where is it?" he asked.

Her eyes went wide as she saw the anger in his face, but she couldn't speak.

He took a step towards her, stopping just inches from her face and leaning in. His teeth were clenched and his eyes looked wild. She'd never been so scared. When he spoke, his words were slow, careful and menacing. "Where is your computer?"

She couldn't think of any explanation and started to whimper in fear. In a flash his hand swung at her, catching her left temple and throwing her against the bathtub. She slammed against the porcelain and screamed before sliding to the floor. David was in her face immediately and she covered her ears as he began screaming at her. "Where is it? Who took it?" She just shook her head and sobbed. Finally he straightened. "You are so pathetic," he spat at her, kicking her with his foot. "You have no idea what you've done. I could have given you everything you ever wanted."

"At what price," she said softly through her tears.

"What?!"

She looked up at him with red swollen eyes. "At what price?" she repeated in a louder voice. "Would I have had to give you my daughters? That's a price I wouldn't pay."

He was silent, but furious as she stared at her. "You just don't understand how deeply I loved her," he said with forced calmness. "No one does." He then turned from the room and left. She heard the door slam and hurried to check on her girls. They were watching TV, oblivious to all that had happened. She stared at them for a minute as she rubbed where David had hit her. A few moments later she picked up the phone.

Gloria sat in a small office in the courthouse with Bryan, Theresa and Rich. They had dropped the children off at her mother's house on their way to the DA's office. The four of them had talked about very little since being told that David was on his way over. When the door opened, they all looked up expectantly. The DA stood in the doorway.

"We just got a call," he said quickly. "David showed up at Carrie Gunderson's house."

"What happened?" Bryan asked.

"He smacked her around and left. He was asking where the computer was."

They all stood there stock still for a few seconds. Then Gloria ran for the door.

"Gloria!" Bryan called after her, following her immediately.

"He'll go for the kids," she called over her shoulder. Bryan turned to look a the group briefly.

"Send someone to Mrs. Olsen's house," he said to the DA before running after her.

"Can I have just one more?" Nicholas asked, putting on his best begging face.

Virginia laughed and shook her head. "How can I say no?" she said, "But I swear this is your last one." Nicholas nodded his agreement as he grabbed a cookie off the cooling rack and headed for the back yard. Virginia turned to look at Katie standing on a short stool in front of the sink. "You don't have to do the dishes right now," she said sweetly.

Katie looked up at her and smiled as she tucked her hair behind her ears and shrugged. "I like to help," she said.

Virginia walked over to her and gave her a hug from behind. "I'm so glad you're back," she whispered. "I missed you so much."

Katie giggled and pulled away. Virginia watched her for a few more seconds and then turned back to the counter.

"David!!" she exclaimed, taking a step backwards. "What are you doing here!!" Behind her she heard Katie whip around as well. Then there was silence.

"I came to get what's mine," he said angrily. He looked at Katie before continuing, "And if you know what's good for you, you'll do it the easy way."

In a flash Katie took off. She was out of the kitchen before David even started after her. Virginia looked around, saw the pan of cookies on the counter still hot from the oven, grabbed it and flung it at David. He screamed as the hot pan seared his neck, before swiping at her. She didn't have Katie's speed and he caught her shoulder, sending her to the ground. When she looked up he was almost out of the kitchen. She tried to stand, but could feel that the fall had rendered her physically incapable of doing anything more.

Katie ran as fast as she could into the backyard, screaming for Nicholas. He was jumping on the trampoline, but stopped when she erupted through the back door. "Come on," she yelled, sprinting toward the back fence.

"What are you doing?" Nicholas asked.

She reached the tramp, jumped toward him and grabbed his leg before pulling him towards the side. "Just come on," she screamed as he plopped to the ground.

"Katie, Nick! Stop right there!!" They both looked up at David, just coming out the back door, before looking at one another again. With an agreeing look they both took off toward the fence, knowing David was coming hard after them. Nicholas scrambled up the fence and launched himself over and into the adjoining yard. He looked up fearfully toward Katie as she made it to the top. She hoisted one foot over just as David reached her. David grabbed her leg and pulled her roughly off the fence. She screamed bloody murder and kicked and fought for all she was worth. Nicholas was frozen for a moment, then he looked at the house behind him and ran for help.

Katie fell to the ground and tried to run again, but David had the upper hand this time and she was easy to restrain.

"Let her go!!" Gloria yelled from the back door.

David looked up. "Give me one good reason," he spat. He pinned Katie's arms behind her back and held her against his chest, like a shield, covering her mouth. "How does it feel to have your own children ripped away from you?"

"Let her go," Gloria repeated. She'd now been joined by two police officers. He kept looking around to see if there were more, but so far he could only see the three of them.

"Maybe I'll disappear this time," he said, as he inched toward the gate in the side of the fence that led into a neighbors yard. "Then you'll know what it feels like to wonder where they are and who they're with."

"Mr. Stanton," one of the officers said. "You're in enough trouble as it is, let her go."

"Trouble," David said in a mussing voice. "You don't know the first thing about trouble. You want to make a point, fine, I can understand that. Maybe I crossed a line, but I love my kids!! And to let you punish me for it means my whole life goes to shreds. Do you know how long I worked to get where I am? I started with nothing. Everything I have I built myself and you want to destroy it." The officers started moving toward them and he pulled Katie's arms higher up her back making her squeak from behind his hand. They stopped.

Gloria swallowed a lump in her throat and tried to keep back the tears. David's hand almost completely covered Katie's face, leaving only her frantic eyes and disheveled hair visible. "Okay," Gloria said, putting out her hands. "What do you want?"

"I want my life back!!" he screamed shaking his head like an animal. "I want things back the way they were." Just then Katie's eyes fluttered closed and her body went limp.

"Katie," Gloria called frantically. She stepped forward, but he yelled at her to stop, just as Gloria saw Bryan's head rise above the fence directly behind David and Katie. Gloria purposely didn't look at Bryan, not wanting to tip David off. Without Katie supporting her own weight David had to try and hold her up while keeping an eye on everyone else. David looked around as if unsure what to do next, but finally he took his hand off of Katie's mouth in order to pick her up. Bryan continued to rise on the opposite side of the fence.

Then in an instant Katie opened her eyes and in one twisting motion managed to knee David in the jaw, kick him in the forehead and get out of his hold while emitting an ear splitting scream that startled everyone. David grunted in surprise and she hit the ground hard, but sprang up and ran for her mom at the precise moment Bryan launched himself over the fence. He grabbed David by the throat as he landed, throwing David to the ground. David was stunned, but before he had a chance to figure out what had just happened, let alone react to it, Bryan quickly pulled his fist back and hit him hard. Katie reached her mother and they both ran into the house, not wanting her to see anything else, although they both heard Bryan hit David at least once more and the two officers seemed to be in no hurry to put an end to it.

Within ten minutes the street was teeming with police cars and ambulances. David had been cuffed and was on his way to jail. Virginia was still being assessed by paramedics in the kitchen. Nicholas had been found and numerous officers streamed in and out of the house. Gloria was on the couch in the living room with a child on either side, while Bryan paced between the doorway and the window, still trying to calm down. Now and then he'd rub his swollen knuckles, but not without a satisfied grin on his face.

"Is Grandma going to be okay?" Katie asked. It had taken her a few minutes to even be able to talk and she was just now starting to come out of the shock.

"They think her shoulder's broken," Gloria said. "But she's a warrior. She'll probably stay in the hospital tonight but I think she'll be okay."

"What's a warrior?" Nicholas asked, leaning against his mom's shoulder for comfort, something he rarely did.

"It's like a soldier, only cooler," Bryan explained.

Nicholas nodded. "Am I a warrior?"

"You bet," Gloria answered. She looked up at Bryan and smiled. "We all are."

"I've got one question though," she continued, looking at Katie beside her. "Where did you get the idea to pretend to pass out?"

Katie shrugged, "I don't know. It just kinda came in my head."

"It was brilliant," Bryan said, coming to sit next to them.

Nicholas's eyes were wide. "Maybe it was the Holy Ghost."

"No it wasn't," Katie immediately countered, shaking her head as if to say "kids." "The Holy Ghost doesn't do stuff like that!"

"I wouldn't be so sure," Bryan said. "God moves in mysterious ways."

Gloria nodded and met Bryan's eyes over Katie's head. "Does he ever."

Theresa and Rich had followed officers to the house, but stayed outside while Gloria, Bryan and the kids gave their statements to the detective. But now they appeared in the doorway and asked how everyone was doing. Despite Bryan's bruised hand and Katie's scratches from being pulled from the fence, they were fine.

"I hope you don't feel like you wasted a trip," Gloria said to Theresa. "I thought your testimony would be the deciding information, but it didn't quite work out that way."

"I couldn't be more satisfied with the way things turned out," she said. "Just admitting to what he did to me and then seeing him get what he deserved, freed me in a way I never imagined." She looked at Katie. "He can only hurt me to the extent that I let him."

Gloria felt something click within her and she smiled widely as she realized just how true that was. She looked at her daughter on one side, her son on the other and then at Bryan, marveling at his presence in her life. Where would she be if he had given up on her? She thought back to the first time she saw him. The words of his talk echoed back to her. He'd spoken about sacrifice, about trusting in the Lord and following the spirit. More than any time in her life, she was grateful for the gospel, for the perspective it gave her. There was so much to be grateful for, she couldn't comprehend it all. At the top of her list, was that she was finally home— safe and sound. She could finally put the past where it belonged; behind her, and focus on the future. She finally felt the peace she'd been longing for.

Wednesday morning, Gloria and her lawyer met with the judge in his chambers. It was a closed discussion. Bryan and the children, along with Janice, waited in the hallway. Virginia had only torn a ligament in her shoulder, thankfully, but she was very sore and had stayed home today. She said she was resting next to the phone and expected a call the moment a decision was made.

Those waiting in the hall stood when the doors opened almost an hour after the meeting had begun. Gloria's expression was guarded, but Bryan saw a sparkle in her eyes that brought a relieved smile to his lips. "Five years suspended, and three years' probation. I also have to give two hundred hours of community service and pay a three-thousand-dollar fine."

"Are you going to jail?" Katie asked, her eyes wide.

"No," she said as the tears finally came to her eyes. She looked at Janice, without words to express her gratitude for all the support and friendship she'd given and then she looked at Bryan. He was standing behind her children, a hand on each of their shoulders, and she had to choke down a sob as she finally said the words she'd been longing to say for a very long time. "We're finally free—we get to go home."

Epilogue

Bryan opened the apartment door without knocking; he practically lived here anyway. Of course he owned his own one bedroom apartment on the opposite end of the apartment complex, but all he did was sleep there, much to his disappointment. He preferred to be with Gloria and the kids than be by himself. Lucky for him they seemed to prefer it, too.

Gloria looked up from the table when he entered and smiled as he came and kissed her hello. She'd remained a blonde, something he liked very much, but the heaviness in her face had slowly disappeared over the last seven months and he still marveled at how truly beautiful she was, especially when she smiled. "How'd it go?" she asked as he turned toward the fridge in hopes of finding some dinner waiting for him. It was almost nine o'clock and he knew the kids had been in bed for at least half an hour.

"Parent-teacher conferences," he said, shaking his head and pulling open the refrigerator door. "I don't know which is worse, getting called on by Arkansas parents, or having to meet with all the Utah parents, whether their kid's getting an *A* or an *F*." He smiled at the plate sitting on the top shelf of the fridge covered in plastic wrap and pulled it out.

"That's Utah for you," Gloria commented. "They're into their kids."

Are they ever, he thought to himself. Katie and Nicholas were prime examples. He couldn't keep up with the different activities the kids were involved in. Katie took gymnastics and piano in addition to weekly counseling and Achievement days—all of which were helping her become a kid again. Nicholas was formally enrolled in Jr. Jazz basketball but spent every other free minute rollerblading with his friends, riding his bike, or playing the computer. It was enough to make Bryan's head spin.

After Gloria's community service hours had been fulfilled, she'd found a job with the Child Abuse Prevention Coalition. The job was only part time, but she sometimes had speaking engagements in the evenings, meaning Bryan did a lot of the chauffeuring, not that he minded so much. She'd also been seeing a counselor of her own, and although she felt better about life in general, the subject of marriage was something she rarely brought up. He'd been true to his word about letting her set the pace, but he was getting tired of waiting.

A couple of minutes later Bryan sat across the table from her with a hot plate of dinner consisting of meatloaf, scalloped potatoes, green beans, and a roll. "What'cha doin?" he asked, looking at the notebook and phone book laying open in front of her.

"Planning," she said easily.

"Planning what?" he asked as he took a bite of meatloaf.

"What are you doing a week from Saturday?"

"You're my secretary," he said. "Why don't you tell me."

"I was thinking of having a luncheon."

"A luncheon?" Bryan asked, cutting himself another bite with the edge of his fork. "Sounds kinda formal."

"I thought informal would be better."

"An informal luncheon," he summarized, watching her now in hopes of figuring out where this was all headed. "What for?"

"Our family and friends."

He took another bite and swallowed before replying. "You mean *your* family and Ron and Janice, don't you?"

"Charlotte thought they could work it out to come and Mom said she'd pay for their airfare as part of the bridal costs. Would the rest of your family come if we offered a similar invitation?"

Bryan paused, the fork halfway to his mouth as understanding suddenly dawned on him. She smiled broadly and reached across the table to place her hand over his. Her eyes were sparkling and she couldn't keep the excitement out of her voice when she spoke. "I met with the stake president tonight and since I've done everything I'm supposed to do for six months, he renewed my recommend."

Bryan lowered his fork to the table, still reeling from the surprise. "And this luncheon is—"

"A wedding luncheon," she interrupted, giving his hand a little squeeze. She then pulled her hand away and went back to the notes she'd been making. "The only time the temple had available was at 6:40 in the morning," she made a face before continuing. "But that means we can do all the pictures and things in time for an early luncheon, say around 11:00?" She looked up at him again.

"Is this your idea of a marriage proposal?"

"Are you going to eat your roll?" She looked at his roll and back at his face. She was having a great time, but he was still a little confused. She raised her eyebrows and looked at the roll again. He picked it up, noticing it was already cut and slowly opened it to reveal a simple gold wedding band. He was glad he'd taken the roll off the plate before heating the rest of the meal in the microwave. He looked up at her and she reached across the table again, taking his free hand. He was sure his expression showed his continued confusion.

"Sitting across from you in Lambert's Café was probably the first moment I realized that I was falling in love with you."

"I thought the kiss on the porch was much more romantic," he said after a brief pause. Somehow this wasn't how he'd imagined it.

"It wasn't romantic," she said, leaning forward. "That's just it, it was ordinary, simple; the kind of thing a couple would do all of their life without thinking twice about it. But to me it was spectacular. I was dressed up, I looked beautiful, if I do say so myself, and I was sitting across from a man who had made incredible sacrifices to make sure my family and I were okay. At that time I had programmed myself not to think about the future. It was too big, too unknown. I lived day to day, but that day was different. I felt free somehow, and it was all because of you. You have blessed my life so much," her voice began to tremble as her emotions overcame her. "And I hope that you'll agree to spend forever with me."

Bryan put the roll down, covered her hands with his and looked at her strongly. "Are you sure you're ready?"

"Yes," she said boldly.

"Are you sure the kids are ready?"

"Yes," she answered just as strongly. "We talked about it and they can't wait."

Bryan dropped his head and let out a breath he felt he'd been holding for seven long months. When he looked up, her expression had fallen as if she wasn't sure how to interpret his response. He stood up, pulling her to her feet as well and leaned across the table, taking her face in his hands. He kissed her then, a long drawn out kiss that he felt well communicated his feelings on the subject of marriage. When he pulled back he smiled, "I thought you'd *never* ask."

Author's Notes

The U.S. Department of Justice's Office of Juvenile Justice and Delinquency Prevention has completed two studies concerning abducted children. The second of these studies, known as NISMART 2, released its findings in October of 2002. According to this study there were 203,900 children abducted by family members in 1999; four times the amount abducted by non-family members. Of these, there are 5,600 cases still open. It is estimated that about 10 percent of these cases are assisted by underground organizations, the most well known being Children of the Underground supported by Faye Yager who has faced criminal charges because of her involvement. There is little available information on these networks because of their secretive nature. Most of the details included in this story are from my own supposition as well as movies on the subject.

Contrary to the situation portrayed in this story, statistics report that the strong majority of these kidnappings are not committed for the purpose of protecting the children, but rather for spite, as the last resort for a parent dissatisfied with the custodial stipulations afforded them. It is in no way my desire to encourage a decision of such magnitude, only to challenge each of us to search our own hearts, strengthen our own testimonies and ask ourselves that if the impossible were asked of us, could we do it. This specific circumstance of this story is an example meant to represent the various trials of faith each of us will face, in one way or another, and remind us of how essential it is to have a testimony that affords us the opportunity to receive our own revelation and hear the promptings when they come.

According to the National Clearinghouse on Child Abuse and Neglect, over 800,000 new cases of child abuse are reported in the United States every year; 16 percent of those are sexual abuse and 87 percent of that abuse is at the hands of a family member. Between 1986 and 1993 reports of sexual abuse rose 87 percent. It is supposed that today 1 of 2 girls and 1 of 4 boys will be sexually assaulted before they reach the age of 18 and there are currently over 60 million survivors of sexual abuse in the United States today (www.yesican.org).

The number one reason believed to be responsible for the increase in these numbers is the availability of pornography. It used to be that to fulfill the indulgence of pornography you had to go out of your way to procure it. Now it's available through the click of the remote control or the computer mouse every minute of every day.

Pornography is addicting and just as an alcoholic needs more alcohol, and a drug user needs more drugs over time, a pornography addict craves more as their addiction grows. There is help available for those involved in pornography that can make it possible for them to overcome their problems, but because so many people don't see the full spectrum of porn abuse, many do not seek opportunities to overcome it. The continued indulgence creates a disassociation to the people depicted and in time visual stimulation is often not enough. Up to 80 percent of porn addicts admit to acting on fantasies portrayed in the images they indulge in, and 99 percent of all prison inmates accused of violent crime admit to have indulged in pornography at some time in their lives, often in excessive levels. Child pornography is the fastest growing sub-culture of the porn industry and continues to grow out of the belief that since children don't understand what is being done to them, they are not damaged. This could not be further from the truth.

As the moral value of television, movies and music declines and the availability of pornography increases, it isn't much of a stretch to assume the aforementioned statistics will become more frightening. The number one prevention against sexual abuse, and pornography addiction, is informed and involved parents, but sadly, even the best parenting is by no means a guarantee.

Beyond prevention there is treatment through counseling agencies, family love and support and, perhaps the most important aspect of all, a very real testimony in Jesus Christ, the One that suffered so that we could withstand our own suffering. To victims of abuse that can often sound like a trite and yet overwhelming solution, since at the very core of abuse is the attack of innocence, trust and faith. Yet, we have been promised that we will not be tried beyond what we are capable to overcome IF we allow Christ to help us shoulder the burdens we bear.

For additional information consult the following:

Parental Kidnapping

www.missingkids.com
National Center for Missing and Exploited Children

members.aol.com/underwatch
Faye Yager's Underground Watch group

Sexual Abuse

www.yesican.org
International Child Abuse Network

www.calib.com/nccanch/
The National Clearinghouse on Child Abuse and Neglect

Anti-pornography

www.enough.org
Enough is Enough Anti-Pornography

www.contentwatch.com
Content Watch-filters, audits and cleanup options

About the Author

Josi S. Kilpack is the third of nine children born to Walt and Marle Schofield. Born and raised in Salt Lake City, she graduated from Olympus High School and attended Salt Lake Community College. She now lives in Willard, Utah, with her husband Lee and their four children Breanna, Madison, Christopher, and Kylee Jo. Her love of writing evolved from her love of reading and her desire to pursue the trials of living in our times from the LDS point of view.

Outside of her writing, Josi enjoys scrapbooking, traveling, cooking, and of course reading, but spends most of her time cleaning, changing diapers, doing laundry, chauffeuring children, checking homework and the other 1001 daily tasks associated with being a stay-at-home mom. She currently serves as the Visiting Teaching Supervisor and Activities Chairman in her ward and supports her husband in his church and business responsibilities.

Josi's first novel, *Earning Eternity,* was published by Cedar Fort in 2000. She enjoys hearing from her readers and can be contacted via e-mail at kilpack@favorites.com or by mail at PO Box 483, Willard, Utah 84340.